The only tangible benefit Dare Landis has of finally claiming the title of Marquis of Raynsforth will be that the current marquis has finally gone to the Devil where he belongs. Until then, Lord Landis will continue to enjoy life on his own terms…as a heartless rake who's beholden to no one.

Nivea Horsham knows there's more to Dare than he reveals to the world. She's loved him since her older brother brought his ridiculously handsome friend home from school all those years ago. But getting him to notice her has proven to be an impossible endeavor.

Is it possible for Nivea to shatter Dare's carefully crafted facade and show him how to love?

Books by Alleigh Burrows

Dare to Love

Published by Kensington Publishing Corporation

Dare to Love

Alleigh Burrows

LYRICAL PRESS
Kensington Publishing Corp.
www.kensingtonbooks.com

Lyrical Press books are published by
Kensington Publishing Corp. 119 West 40th Street New York, NY 10018

All Kensington titles, imprints, and distributed lines are available at special
quantity discounts for bulk purchases for sales promotion, premiums, fund-
raising, and educational or institutional use.

Special book excerpts or customized printings can also be created to fit
specific needs. For details, write or phone the office of the Kensington
Special Sales Manager:
Kensington Publishing Corp.
119 West 40th Street
New York, NY 10018
Attn. Special Sales Department. Phone: 1-800-221-2647.

First Electronic Edition: December 2014
eISBN-13: 978-1-61650-578-3
eISBN-10: 1-61650-578-8

First Print Edition: December 2014
ISBN-13: 978-1-61650-593-6
ISBN-10: 1-61650-593-1

Printed in the United States of America

This book is dedicated to my family. To my mom for introducing me to romance novels. To my dad for inspiring me with his creative writing skills. And most importantly, to my husband for tolerating both of these inexplicably "odd" habits, even when they came at the expense of family time. I couldn't have written this without your unflagging love and support.

Since my kids never really believed I'd get published, they'll have to wait until the next book to get recognized. Don't worry, I still love you.

"My Lord"

I know
that he's entered the room
without even seeing
his form.
How? I do not know.

Perhaps a change in the air,
a jolt to my heart,
or a skittering up my skin.
But I am certain, when I look over,
he will be there.

Tall and proud, aloof and cool,
hair sleek, lip curled,
heads will turn.
How can they not
when he arrives?

I pray tonight he will see
Me. And know
he is mine.
My lord.
Then he dances by
without a glance,
and I am lost.

Nivea Horsham

Chapter 1

Adair Landis braced himself on the bed as he gulped in a lungful of air. The scent of perfume and passion spurred him on, and with a few satisfying thrusts, he collapsed onto the quivering body of an obliging, young widow.

That had been a pleasant treat.

He lay there motionless for a minute or two until his heart rate settled, and then he rose from the bed. It was time to go.

He fumbled across the darkened room to find his shirt thrown over the nearby chair, and drew it over his head. Through the cloth, he heard his partner's muffled sigh. "Oh, Adair, you were wonderful. I never dreamed it could be like that."

Of course she hadn't. But she'd been hoping. Dropping hints for several weeks, as a matter of fact. It wasn't until today that he'd decided to accommodate her.

"I'm glad you were pleased."

She hummed her agreement. Then, in a tentative tone asked, "Can you untie me now?"

Dare sat on the chair, thrust his feet into his breeches and yanked them in place. Once he was covered, he answered, "Certainly, darling."

With a satisfied stretch, he strode to the large, four poster bed, leaned over and untied the black silk ribbons from her wrists. "Thank you for indulging me in my little fantasy. I hope you found it to be as scintillating as I did," he said, offering a vague kiss in the direction of her forehead. Then he crossed to a brocade chair, grabbed his boots, and tugged them on.

The woman's voice quavered as she sat up, rubbing her wrists. "Oh, Adair, are you leaving so soon?"

He nodded, turning his attention toward his cravat. With a few efficient folds, he'd tied it into a complicated knot with a skill most valets would envy.

"But when will you come back? Will I see you again upon your return?"

He spared her a brief glance as he pulled on his coat. "No, Victoria, I shan't be back. But thank you for the delightful diversion."

"But, Adair? I thought—I thought—" she sputtered.

"You thought wrong." With that, he pulled open the door and strode out. At the sound of her indignant shrieks, Dare smiled. Victoria was his sister's best friend. A well-bred, gently reared woman from a good family. His sister would be furious not only that he'd bedded her, but jilted her as well. Sometimes, life could be surprisingly sweet.

Content, he headed out onto the street, climbed into his carriage, and settled into the soft velvet seat. Reaching into his waistcoat, he withdrew a jeweled snuffbox and took a pinch.

That dalliance should hold him for a few days—at least until he arrived at the Horsham's summer estate. No doubt there would be a few women there to entertain him. William's sisters were no great catch, but they were sure to have an attractive friend or two he could trifle with.

The only downside was he had to make the tiresome journey with William's sister, Nivea. Why he had agreed to convey Nivea to her family's house in Durham was a mystery. One minute, he was congratulating his best friend on the engagement of his younger sister, and the next, he was trapped into escorting the elder sister to the wedding. While riding in a carriage with a young lady for a few days did not normally fill him with dread, this trip could prove the exception. As round as she was plain, it was no wonder Nivea was still on the shelf at her age.

While most men would not even consider allowing Dare to ride unescorted with their unmarried sister, William had no cause to worry. After all, Dare did have standards.

Chapter 2

Unaware of the scornful musings of her escort, Nivea continued to fuss with her appearance. Knowing she would be spending the next several days in the presence of Adair Landis, the future Marquess of Raynsforth, she had been making special preparations.

Nivea had developed a *tendré* for her brother's friend when she was a young girl, and now, almost fifteen years later, she still felt no other man could compare. When she'd been informed she would be spending several days with him, she and her stepmother set out to finally make Dare notice.

Since her mother had died when she was a child, Nivea had never benefited from a woman's guidance. Most of her upbringing had been dominated by her father and brother. Much as she loved them, she could hardly expect them to help her navigate the challenges of *ton* fashion. In fact, the very thought made her laugh.

Fortunately, her father had remarried a few years ago and her stepmother, Amelia, was happy to help give Nivea some much needed polish.

To prepare for this trip, Nivea's hair had been styled by Monsieur Parardee, and she had been treating her skin with a myriad of creams to give it a soft, glowing appearance. Although she was larger than was fashionable, Nivea had packed her most attractive and slimming gowns for the trip.

Today's creation was a mossy shade of green. The bodice was embroidered with flowers, with a light dusting of petals cascading down the full skirt. As she perched a matching hat on her soft, brown curls, she stared at her reflection in amazement. She would have to thank Amelia once again for all her advice and support.

At the sound of a knock on her front door, Nivea's heart skipped a beat.

He's here. Taking one last look in the mirror for reassurance, Nivea left her bedroom and floated downstairs. Entering the hallway, she stopped with a sigh. There was only a coachman standing in the front hall.

Of course, Dare wouldn't come in, personally. How silly of me.

She pasted a smile on her face and nodded at the coachman. Before she could move, one of their footmen entered, having carried her bags to the awaiting carriage. "Goodbye, Miss Horsham. Have a lovely trip. Be sure to give Miss Caroline our best wishes."

"Thank you, Hartley, I will."

She followed the coachman out and accepted his hand as he helped her into the carriage. It was a beautiful vehicle, lacquered black, embossed with gold, and pulled by a team of four perfectly matched Friesians. Dare Landis would accept no less.

Settling into her seat, Nivea turned to her escort with a wide smile, prepared to offer enthusiastic appreciation for the ride. The greeting froze on her lips as Dare flicked the briefest glance in her direction.

"Good day," he drawled, before returning his gaze to the carriage window.

"Good day." A blush flared up her cheeks. All this time preparing and he couldn't be bothered to look at me? That was disappointing.

Still, not one to pass up an opportunity, Nivea took advantage of his inattentiveness to stare at him, uninterrupted. He was captivating as usual, his rich, dark hair combed back, framing his face to perfection. His jaw was firm and strong, his mouth drawn in an ever-present sneer, but his lips were so full they made women sigh. Ever the rakehell, he wore a tasteful and exquisitely tailored outfit—a blood-red jacket stretched across broad shoulders, and tan breeches molded his muscular legs. Finishing the look, his black boots were polished, spotless.

Only after a minute of relentless attention, did Dare turn his head in her direction. "Yes?"

Embarrassed, she managed to choke out a few words. "How long are you planning to stay with us at Vincent Hall?"

He raised an arrogant eyebrow and shrugged. "Until the entertainment grows dull."

"With that attitude, I'm surprised you are going at all."

"William is one of my oldest friends," he responded, unperturbed. "I think I can manage a week or two in the country for his benefit." Then he turned back toward the window, coolly dismissing her.

Feeling more than a little silly to have gotten her hopes up, Nivea slumped into her seat. The worst part about the exchange was she remembered a time when they used to be more comfortable in each other's company. When they were younger, he didn't seem to mind if she tagged along. She couldn't understand why, once he'd reached maturity, he'd become so distant.

Determined to make the best of it, Nivea turned toward the window, watching the view change from elegant homes of the nobility, to shops bustling with customers, and finally the rolling hills of the countryside. During that time, there was nary a word spoken. Nivea wished she had the presence of her maid, but Emma had escorted Caroline to Durham in preparation of her wedding. Although traveling without a chaperone should have raised some eyebrows, Nivea knew she was so firmly on the shelf, no one gave it a second thought.

It was hours before they reached their first stop. Bunch of Grapes was a popular inn for travelers, boasting a large dining area. Despite the crowd, Dare acquired a small table away from the main traffic of the room. After the briefest inquiry into her preference, he ordered a light meal for her and a bottle of wine for himself.

His brooding good looks flustered the young serving maid, but she managed to stumble through the order. It was always that way around him. Dare could charm women senseless without the slightest effort.

While waiting for the meal, Dare spent his time glancing around the room, beguiling all the other women with his appreciative smirk. Nivea's frustration grew. Why was it he chose to bed every other woman in London, but could not spend three days in her presence and manage to be cordial? She was able to make friends with almost everyone else she met—neighbors, tenants, and peers in the *ton*—but not the one man who made her world complete. Naturally, she hadn't expected him to fall in love with her, but he could at least bestow an admiring look her way. He rarely missed an opportunity to eye up a female. Unless that female was her, apparently.

Once the food was on the table, Nivea picked at the roast chicken. After a few bites, without even the courtesy of a conversation about the weather, she decided she'd had enough. "Lord Landis, you have known my brother for over a decade. We have traveled in the same circles since I came out more than five years ago, and we spent virtually every holiday together since you were boy. You used to be quite pleasant, or at least civil to me, and yet in the last few hours, you have barely spared me a glance. If we are going to make this trip together, I have to insist you have the courtesy of at least addressing me."

There. She'd done it. Her heart was hammering in her chest, from both anger and nerves, but she had stood up for herself and it felt wonderful. Until she braved a glance at him.

He was glaring at her as though he were the one who had been insulted. She suppressed a shiver as his eyes raked over her, a haughty sneer pasted on his lips. He opened his mouth to speak and then froze. She saw confusion flash in his eyes, like he'd made an odd discovery. Then it was gone. Through it all, he didn't say a word.

Now she was fuming. "Are you just going to sit there and stare at me with your mouth ajar?"

Appearing to regain his senses, he answered in his usual, bored intonation. "I apologize, milady. I have been pondering how your family would react if I arrived at Vincent Hall without you. Is it worth the aggravation I would open myself up to? Since I think not, you will be happy to know we can continue on together as soon as you are ready."

She slammed down her fork and stood up. "Let us go now then. The sooner this trip is over, the better."

"As you wish." He held out his arm, but she sailed out in front of him and climbed into the carriage.

The ride continued for a few more hours in relative silence. Dare had ordered the coachman to drive quickly, and he had taken the command to heart. The pace was so rapid Nivea's bones were clattering. She decided the best course of action was to take a nap. It took a bit of effort, but she finally drifted off.

The shadows were growing long when the carriage gave a sudden jolt, throwing her from her seat. "Ack," she screamed, snatching in vain for the cushion across the way.

The carriage tipped drunkenly to one side before slamming to a stop.

"Damn it to hell, what was that?" shouted Dare. He climbed upward, swung open the door, and leapt to the road with the grace of a cat. Nivea followed, but was considerably clumsier in her descent as she lowered herself from the elevated frame.

"What in the bloody blazes happened, Weldon!" Dare yelled, smacking his hand on the offending vehicle. Then, regaining his manners, he turned to her. "My apologies for the language. Are you all right, Miss Horsham?"

"Yes, thank you. Just a little shaken." She would have appreciated a more thorough inquiry on his part, perhaps even a comforting arm around her shoulder, but instead he returned his attention to the carriage.

The wheel had gotten caught in a rut and snapped. They were fortunate it hadn't flipped over entirely.

The coachman was bent over the axel, clucking with dismay. Straightening, he turned to Dare. "Milord, I beg your forgiveness. I thought it was nothing but a dark patch in the road. I didn't realize we'd hit a ditch."

Dare waved him off. "It can't be helped. I know you didn't do it on purpose. Are the horses all right?"

"Yes, milord." The coachman bobbed his head. "They be fine. But we're stuck here well and good until we can procure a new wheel. Then we'll have to return to Norwalk to check for other structural issues."

Dare stood rigid, glaring at the coach, saying nothing. He paced from one end to the other, bent at the waist to examine the axel again, and still nothing.

With her heart pounding in her throat, Nivea waited. When no response was forthcoming, she squeaked out, "Well, what are we to do now?"

He cocked his head, as though surprised by her question. "We will have to return to town."

Oh god, no. How could he even think that? "But it's miles away."

"Yes."

"But...we'll be well behind. We may miss the wedding!"

He shrugged. "That is a distinct possibility."

"It's my sister's wedding! I can't *not* be there. There must be something we can do." She tried not to sound like a hysterical female, but feared she failed miserably. The thought of missing Caro's wedding was unfathomable. Dare would have to come up with a better solution.

He returned his attention to the carriage, apparently considering their options. It didn't take him long. "Weldon! Unhitch two of the horses. Miss Horsham and I will take them and ride on. You wait here with the carriage. Someone should be along soon to offer aid. Then you can get the necessary repairs and meet us with the luggage at the next stop."

"Yes, milord," Weldon nodded.

Dare took a step toward the carriage, but drew to a sudden stop when he noticed Nivea's expression. No doubt she was staring at him as if he'd sprouted a third head. "No, that will not work."

"And why, pray tell, would that not work?" he asked, without sparing her another glance.

"I do not ride," she answered simply.

Ignoring her, he reached for the buckle on the first horse. "Come now, I'm sure you prefer a carriage, but it is not an option at this time. If we want to make the wedding, we will have to ride the horses."

"I hate horses."

That stopped him.

He turned to give her his full attention. "You're a Horsham," he said, as if it explained everything. In fact, it did, to anyone in the *ton*. The Horshams owned some of the finest horses in England. They hosted the best hunts, won the most races, and rarely finished a conversation without an equine reference.

Nivea sighed. "That is true. It has been rather inconvenient in my family to not share their passion."

"Not sharing their passion, I could understand. But you said you hate horses," he repeated with bafflement. She almost laughed at his confusion, but this was a serious matter, and she had to make him understand.

"I suppose it's not the horses themselves I hate. But given my size, riding them always seemed rather mean." She dreaded bringing attention to her weight, but she had never been comfortable balancing herself on a beast with such spindly legs. She knew it was irrational, but there it was. She did not ride.

"Come now," he said, waving toward the black beasts, "they are powerful enough to pull a sizable wagon with no trouble. We'll be fine."

"No! We will not be fine! I have no intention of riding that thing anywhere." Nivea crossed her arms across her bosom and glared at him.

Her response didn't impress him in the slightest. Reaching into the rear of the carriage Dare pulled out his bags. "As you wish. I will offer your apologies to your family." He motioned to Weldon who transferred his possessions into a pair of saddlebags and slung them over the horse's back.

She couldn't believe her eyes. "You cannot be serious. You are just going to leave me here…unescorted?"

"My coachman is quite respectable. I'm certain he will ensure you are protected. Isn't that right, Weldon?"

"Yes, milord," the man snapped to attention.

Nivea was dumbfounded. He must know he was putting her in an impossible situation. Either she could go back to town, escorted only by a coachman, for an uncertain length of time and risk missing her sister's wedding, or she could continue the trip, riding a horse. Good God, there wasn't even a saddle! She would kill herself for certain.

"Well, I'm off. Are you coming or not?" Dare asked. Unconcerned by her predicament, he swung himself up on the enormous horse's back and grabbed the makeshift reins. He didn't even require the assistance of a groom. That feat of athleticism helped Nivea to make up her mind. Even atop a coach horse, Dare was a breathtaking sight.

She could not pass up the chance to be with him, no matter how distressing the circumstances. "I'm coming," she huffed and turned to search through her bags.

"Only grab your necessities, please. The rest will catch up with us sooner or later. In fact, you will be better suited to pack more serviceable attire. This trip may be a bit dusty."

Naturally. Knowing she'd be riding with Dare for three or four days, she'd packed her most attractive outfits, and now she was being asked to stuff them into a sack. With a sigh, she dug through to find her most comfortable clothes. She changed into a pair of serviceable boots and handed her bag to the coachman.

Using the coach as a stepladder, Weldon helped hoist her up onto the horse. She settled on its back and trotted over to Dare, about as comfortable as a fish riding a crocodile.

The first few miles were exhausting. Nivea used all her strength to stay upright. The constant rocking of the horse made her slightly sea sick, and the jolting rattled her. Dare seemed perfectly at ease on his massive mount, riding it like a thoroughbred. He would turn back every so often to make sure she was still in attendance, but did not offer any encouragement.

After what seemed like an eternity, they arrived at a small hamlet and Dare slowed his horse. "I had hoped to be farther along today, but in light of our difficulties, I suggest we stop here. I will endeavor to find a place for us to stay tonight."

She could do no more than nod in response.

Thank God, this nightmare was almost over. She hoped she could survive until tomorrow.

Chapter 3

Dare took one look at Nivea's grateful expression and felt a pang of remorse. He should be more solicitous of her. True, she was not his most shapely companion, but she was much less disagreeable than most, barely voicing a word of complaint.

It wasn't her fault he was so ill tempered. It was *his* blasted carriage that had broken, after all. And now he was forced to ride through the countryside on a coach horse, looking like a farmhand. Dear God, how his family would laugh if they saw him. Their ridicule would be endless.

Thinking of his family brought on a familiar surge of anger. Unwilling to give in to such a relentless emotion, he slowed down and returned his attention to his companion trailing behind.

"Don't worry, it won't be much farther." He offered her an encouraging smile.

Her response was a tired shrug.

Fortunately, the second building they came upon had a small, faded sign out front, declaring itself a respectable establishment for travelers. As they turned up the entrance, a young man emerged from the stable.

Dare said under his breath, "It would be best if we pose as brother and sister, to avoid any impropriety. The rest of our story is innocent enough."

Nivea nodded, her eyes fixed on the approaching stable hand.

"Good day, sir," the young man said with a tug to his forelock, "are you anxious for a bit of rest tonight?"

"Yes. Do you have rooms available?"

"Oh, yes, milord. Mr. Ludlow will be more'n pleased to find a room for you and your…"

"Sister." Landis finished for him.

"Sister. Yes, milord."

Dare sprung from his horse, wincing as he landed. The large nag was by no means as comfortable as his usual mount. He handed off the reins and strode over to Nivea to help her down.

Keeping her eyes averted, she mumbled, "Why don't you go inside. I'll join you in a moment."

In no mood for games, he reached up his arms and gestured irritably for her to dismount.

Still she didn't move. Instead, she said, "Perhaps you could ask for some assistance. Or I could climb down onto that block over there."

Dare couldn't wait to get inside to wash off the dust from the road. It coated his face and hair—even his teeth were gritty. This was no time for arguments. "Come, it will be fine. Let's get inside where we can rest."

"I don't think I can."

Now she was being ridiculous. "Nonsense. Throw your leg over and slide down. I'll catch you."

* * * *

As much as she wanted to get down from the dreadful beast, Nivea hated to appear ungainly in front of him. But what choice did she have? If she continued to fuss, it would irritate him.

So, rucking up her skirts as best she could without exposing her entire thigh, she took a deep breath, heaved her leg over the horse, and plummeted down into his arms. He staggered a bit, but managed to guide her to her feet without incident.

As always, the touch of his hands sent a pleasant shock through her. But it only lasted until her feet hit the ground and her knees buckled. She'd never felt so sore in all her life. She hoped she could make it inside without collapsing.

Mr. Ludlow was waiting at the front door and snapped to attention as they approached. It was obvious that years of service had taught him to recognize Quality even if their mounts were not the usual snuff. "Milord, welcome to our establishment. Will you be dining with us this evening or do you and your lady require a room?"

"My sister and I will require two rooms. You may bring us both a hot bath and set up a meal in a private sitting room. If you can have everything accomplished in the next three quarters of an hour, there will be an extra shilling for you."

"Yes, milord! Please make yourself comfortable in our parlor while I see to your rooms."

He led them to a tidy little area off the front hall. Dare surveyed the accommodations before stretching out his long frame on the damask sofa. Nivea sank into a sturdy chair by the door, grateful for the steady surface.

She smiled at the sound of footsteps racing up and down the stairs. It was obvious that Mr. Ludlow was intent on meeting their needs as soon as possible.

The door opened and an older woman approached with a tray of glasses.

"'Ere is some sherry for you and your lady, sir. Sure to clear out the dust from the road." She placed the tray on the table and left with a nervous curtsey. Dare eyed the glasses warily. Picking one up, he held it up to the light. Finding it to his standards, he took a small sip and handed the other glass to Nivea.

Reaching out to accept the glass, she did her best to hide a grimace of pain. Uncertain how it would go down, she took a small, cautious sip. There was a slight burn, but after a few swallows, her jabbing pain mellowed to a dull throbbing.

"Better?" Dare asked.

"I'm sure I'll be fine," she said, not at all confident. Every bone, muscle, and sinew in her body ached. She wasn't sure she could even get out of the chair once their rooms were ready. In fact, she would have been happy to fall asleep right there, perhaps never waking up again.

"It was a bit of a bumpy ride. I assure you, we will be more comfortable tomorrow."

Nivea managed a nod, before setting down her empty glass and closing her eyes.

After what seemed like a cruelly short period of time, Mr. Ludlow reappeared and announced their rooms were ready. Dare helped her from the chair—for all appearances, acting as a solicitous brother, but in reality, he had to exert a hearty tug to get her upright. While the tingle from his touch was still there, it dimmed to a faint flicker as he helped guide her up the interminable amount of stairs and into her room. She let out a sigh of relief when the door closed. A young miss was already in attendance, and Nivea was immensely grateful as she helped her remove her travel clothes and eased her into the soothing bath.

If she had ever doubted her aversion for riding, today solidified it. How could anyone enjoy being bounced around on such an ungainly beast? Every inch of her felt bumped and bruised. Thank goodness, she would never have to go through that again.

The water was starting to get cold when there was a knock on the door.

"Supper is ready, miss," the maid called out. "I will help you get dressed so you can join his lordship."

Nivea was too tired to eat, but spending time in Dare's presence was tempting enough to drag her from the bath. She let the maid help her into her least rumpled gown and then headed across the hall.

Dare was standing by the window with his snuffbox in hand. Even without a valet, he looked impeccable. It was so unfair.

She gingerly took her place at the table, her posterior so sore, she wasn't certain she could sit through the meal. It was evident that Dare was not experiencing a similar sensation. Without offering a word of conversation, he sat across from her, his posture erect, his movements precise, as formal as he would at Court. This time, Nivea was too tired to care.

She picked at the roast turkey and forced down a few potatoes, before giving in to exhaustion. Laying her fork aside, she asked, "May I assume we will wait here for the carriage tomorrow?"

"I am afraid not."

What? "But I thought you said we would be more comfortable."

"Yes, we will. Mr. Ludlow has acquired two passable horses for us... with saddles. It will ease our ride considerably. The carriage will no doubt catch up with us by mid-day, but it would not be prudent to wait."

The news sapped the last of Nivea's energy. "Please excuse me. I would like to retire now," she mumbled.

"Yes, of course." Dare stood and walked her to the door. "We will leave at eight o'clock, so don't dawdle getting ready." He bowed as she passed through the doorway, missing her blazing glare of contempt.

Chapter 4

Dare neglected to tell Nivea that he had been given the option of a carriage, but turned it down for the freedom of riding on a well-bred horse. He had forgotten how pleasant it was riding unrestricted through the countryside. While Nivea wasn't the trial he had expected, he preferred not being cooped up inside with her.

Aware she was uncomfortable, he stopped more often than he would have needed. No point in abusing the girl too much, since all she wanted was to see her sister's wedding. A noble sentiment, considering her sister was five years younger than she, and her with no hint of a marriage prospect.

His sisters had all been married by the end of their first season. Not hard to do considering they were all reasonably attractive, well-mannered, and dowried. And, of course, their father wouldn't have had it any other way. Whether they were happy or not, was not an issue. They had done their duty and continued to do so, breeding a son or two as expected.

No doubt, they had all assumed Dare would have done the same by now too, but marriage was something he was determined to avoid at all costs, at least for the next dozen years or so. Narrowly missing the parson's trap with Constance Abbington had convinced him of that. And raising children was a nightmare he refused to contemplate. At some point, he would have to produce heirs, but once they arrived, they could stay buried in the country with their mother.

It was disheartening how many of his friends had already succumbed to marriage. Then again, they had never had the opportunity to enjoy the unmarried state as he did.

William Horsham, his closest friend, had little talent with women. He had a heart of gold and Dare loved him like a brother, but the man was no conversationalist. How his wife managed to pry any communication from him that did not involve horses, he could not fathom.

Then there was Joseph Duxbury. Charming and witty, he could be counted on to liven up any room. If only the man had an ounce of fashion sense. He had prided himself on being a dandy, but in truth was an overdone peacock. Fortunately, his wife had managed to tone down his abominable choice of colors, or at some point Dare's eyes would have jumped out of their sockets and gone running down the street in agony.

Thomas Godwin, who was no means a friend, leg-shackled himself to Abby Abbington. He shuddered to think how she could bear to look upon his scarred visage day upon day. If Dare had married Constance, he would have been forced to associate with her brother-in-law on far too many occasions.

It still stung to know Constance had tossed him over for a crippled soldier, but fortunately, her foolishness freed him up to continue his rakish lifestyle.

And he enjoyed that lifestyle at every turn. After all, a man with his looks, wealth, and title had no trouble attracting women. His pool of prospects was expansive, helped in no small measure that he made no distinction when it came to class or social status. Kitchen help or countess, it did not matter as long as they were attractive and willing. And with the slightest effort on his part, they were always willing.

There was one category of women he excluded from his conquests. He had learned not to be too pleasant to debutantes and their ilk. Not only was their innocence bland and unappealing, but showing them interest led to dangerous situations. He'd almost been trapped by several young ladies who, dazzled by the allure of becoming a marchioness, were willing to risk their reputations with a known rake. Yes, he'd made a few foolish missteps in the past, but now he knew better.

That was why he exerted such little effort entertaining Nivea. A woman of her age? Ho, no, he was not stupid enough to risk building up her hopes.

She should be content he agreed to accompany her this week, instead of haranguing him like a fishwife. He couldn't imagine what had gotten into her during their stop at Bunch of Grapes. She was usually such a biddable thing.

That's why he had intended to issue her a proper set down, skewering her with his most insulting expression. She needed to understand her role—travel companion, nothing more.

But when he had given her his full attention, he'd made an unexpected discovery.

She was no beauty, that much was certain, but she wasn't as plain as he remembered. Her outfit of dark green was quite stylish. The sunlight that had been streaming through the window had transformed her mousy brown hair to a golden chestnut. It had curled around her face, highlighting the soft pink tint of her cheeks. But it was her eyes that had caught his attention. Flashing with anger, they had sparkled a sapphire blue.

He had been surprised by the fire he'd spotted lurking behind her benign facade, and it had caused him a moment of speechlessness. A rare occurrence indeed. Fortunately, he had been able to recover and regain the upper hand by threatening the one thing women couldn't abide— being abandoned by a man.

Now that he'd set her straight, she wouldn't use such a tone with him again, of that he was certain. Content, he gave his horse a sharp tap of his boots.

* * * *

Nivea was horrified when Dare disappeared around the bend. Too tired and sore to even consider catching up to him, she let her horse plod along. That she was so undesirable he couldn't even stay within shouting distance was just too much. It was not as though she wasn't aware of it every second of the trip.

Her overwhelming frustration was more painful than the ride itself. She had planned so hard for this. She had suffered through dress fittings, had her hair yanked and tugged into fashionable coiffures designed to dazzle, and had even rehearsed engaging small talk in a desperate attempt to secure his affection.

As always, she wondered why she should be so steadfast in her desire for a man so completely out of her reach. But she only had to remember that day fifteen years ago when he first appeared at her house.

Her brother had invited him to stay with them during summer break from Harrow School. Having missed her brother tremendously while he was gone, she had jumped up from her desk when she heard him arrive and raced down the hall. She had halted at the top of the stairs and watched as William strode in, his face wreathed in smiles.

Switching her gaze to the boy next to him, her heart had stopped. Never had she seen a boy so beautiful. She had known it was not a word you were supposed to associate with the male gender, but no other description would fit. He had been tall, towering over her brother by about six inches. Where William was softly rounded, this boy had the lean form of a man. His dark hair had caught the rays of the sun coming through the windows and gave it the look of a sleek cat. His face was firm and strong, with full lips, a straight nose and the most striking black eyes she had ever seen.

She had frozen on the stairs, unable to descend. She hadn't been a shy girl, but she certainly hadn't been worldly enough to converse with this vision of manliness. She'd hurried back to the classroom, hoping by dinnertime she'd be composed enough to utter a coherent thought. Unfortunately, in the hours, days, and years to follow, that had never happened.

Instead, she had spent countless afternoons sitting near them, watching them play. Dare had been rather remote even then, but it made him all the more intriguing, like a hero in her penny-dreadful novels.

On a few fortunate occasions, William had invited her to join them. The boys had pretended to be knights, battling to free her from a hunter's cabin in the forest. Dare had obviously enjoyed the swordplay much more than the rescuing, but inevitably, he'd break through the door and carry her to safety. Once outside, he had twirled her around, crowing in triumph. It had always made her feel so special, like a princess saved by a hero.

Then came the fateful day when he become her real-life hero, rescuing William from nearly drowning in the lake. That was the summer she had lost her heart to him completely.

Yet now, as adults, he barely acknowledged her existence.

She had hoped things would change when her father married Amelia Abbington. Once Amelia had heard Nivea had feelings for the elusive Lord Landis, she had been eager to play matchmaker. An odd twist, considering it was her own daughter who had nearly married Dare several years ago. But then Constance shocked the *ton* by marrying an old beau, and Nivea was once again free to dream.

When her sister's wedding was announced, Lady Horsham saw it as the perfect opportunity for Nivea to catch Dare's eye. She'd swept Nivea under her wing and transformed her into, if not a swan, at least a fairly attractive duck. She convinced the family to retire to their country home to prepare, leaving Nivea in London. It had only taken a brief conversation with William, suggesting that Dare would be an ideal escort to bring her home, and the plan had been set in motion.

"Voila! It is foolproof," her stepmother had declared. "He is certain to fall for you by the time you reach Durham."

Nivea had her doubts, but had been caught up in her enthusiasm. Then Dare's fool carriage had broken down. And she had to ride a cursed horse for hour after painful hour. Her clothes were dusty and her hair bedraggled and her mood soured. She was so miserable, she could barely look Dare in the eye, let alone draw him into meaningful conversation. It was so unfair! The only thing that kept her going was the knowledge that she would be home soon, back with her family who loved her.

Chapter 5

"Nivea, may I have a word with you?"

At the sound of tapping, Nivea jerked out of a sound sleep and yanked the covers up under her chin.

They had arrived at the small posting house just after dusk. Once again posing as brother and sister, they acquired adjoining rooms. Nivea had managed to stumble through supper before falling asleep on the bed before the maid had even left the room. If it weren't for the sun streaming through the window, she would have guessed she'd been resting for an hour or so.

Another rap. "Nivea, are you awake?" Dare whispered through the door.

'Ummm, yes?" she squeaked, terrified he would come in and see her disheveled from sleep.

"I need to speak with you. Please make yourself presentable and join me in the sitting room."

Apparently, their appalling mode of travel was not having a negative effect on Dare. He was up and ready to go. She listened to his boots stride away before swinging her feet from the bed. She flinched as her throbbing muscles reacted to the sudden movement. Slowly rising, she staggered to the dresser to drag a brush through her hair and throw on the clothes that had been laid out the night before. After a few tugs, her cobalt-striped dress fell into place.

She then flopped on the bed and leaned over to tie her boots. And stopped.

Hmm, that was interesting. She could easily reach her feet without forcing the breath out of her lungs.

She sat up, then bent down again. And giggled.

Standing up, she wiggled. Yes, there was definitely a little more room around her waist. She pulled on a blue Spencer that matched her gown and buttoned it under her breasts. Even that was easier, causing less strain on the buttonhole. How marvelous!

Granted, she still felt like she'd been mauled by a bear, but it appeared all the exercise was doing her some good. Maybe all this horse riding wasn't so bad.

Oh, good lord. Surely, after twenty-five years of living with the most nutty of all equestrians, she wasn't going to become a horse fan simply because she dropped a pound or two. No doubt her exhaustion over the past few days had just curtailed her appetite. She'd practically landed facedown into her stew last night, after all.

Whatever the cause, she was grateful for the change. Giving a satisfied glance in the mirror, she danced across the hallway. Dare was seated at the table, set with a hearty breakfast. He stood when she entered, but he did not look directly at her. She plopped down into the chair and stared at him.

He indicated toward the food. "Please, have some of the breakfast cakes. They are quite tasty."

"No, thank you," she answered. She knew she was being silly, but couldn't suppress a flash of irritation that he hadn't noticed her slight physical change. Crossing her hands in her lap, she stilled. He'd said he needed to speak with her and she had a sneaking suspicion it would not be good news.

Her misgiving grew when he took a bite and smiled at her. "Are you certain? I charmed the servant girl into providing us strawberry jam for the rolls. It will give you strength for today's ride."

He was being quite solicitous. Talking to her, smiling, requesting tasty treats. What was he up to?

His eyes skimmed her face and then darted down to his plate. Yes, he was nervous about something.

At last, after clearing his throat, he started. "I received word last night. While I had anticipated that my carriage would catch up with us today, it is not to be. My coachmen sent word that, when the wheel broke, it damaged the entire structure and requires extensive repairs. He has arranged for another carriage, but fears it will not arrive for another day."

"So, what you are trying to say is…"

"We have to ride again today." This time, he didn't drop his gaze. But the muscle in his jaw flexed, betraying a flicker of anxiety. Dare was never anxious. It must be a good sign that he cared about her reaction. Perhaps another day on horseback with him wouldn't be so bad. And if it helped her slim down a teensy bit more before the wedding…

The wedding! How could she have forgotten? "Do you think…is there a chance we will arrive at Vincent Hall today?"

He nodded. "If we get on the road soon and keep a good pace, yes, I think we can arrive by late afternoon. Then you will have a full day to recover before Caroline's wedding. Or we can send word to your father and have him send a Horsham carriage, but it is sure to add time to the trip."

No. She didn't want to wait. As much as she had been looking forward to being in Dare's company, she wanted to get home. "I suppose I can ride one more day. Let me break my fast and then we can proceed."

Picking up a roll, she took a hearty bite. Oh, it was fresh and sweet. Two more bites and it was gone, so she reached for another. The movement shot pain down her arm. She let out a slight groan and Dare winced.

"I *am* sorry, you know. If my coachman had been more observant, you wouldn't be in such discomfort." His expression was so remorseful, she couldn't let him suffer. True, he could have been a more gracious escort, but their current difficulties were not his fault.

She patted his hand resting on the tabletop. "I accept your apology."

Their eyes met and she smiled. How could she not, gazing at such a handsome figure. The morning sun shadowed his cheeks, emphasizing the strong planes of his face and deepening his eyes to obsidian. She saw his lip begin to curl in a rakish grin. Then his eyes widened, his features hardened, and he thrust back his chair.

"I will get the horses readied while you finish your meal. Please meet me in the yard when you are done."

In a blink, he was gone, and she was left with a head of questions and not a single answer.

* * * *

They were on the road within a half hour. Their mounts were lively, and even Nivea could tell they were of higher quality. No doubt living near Horsham land raised the class of horseflesh.

Now that she had been forced to ride for a few days, Nivea admitted it really wasn't so bad. Certain she would not slip from the horse into an enormous lump in the road, she was able to take delight in the life around her. She smelled the flowers and freshly cut hay. She merrily greeted the wide range of humanity they encountered along the way—farmers off to market, children playing in their fields, and travelers heading for parts unknown. And best of all, she was now able to tie her boots without suffocating.

To celebrate, she began composing a poem in her head. She had no talent for watercolors, but she'd always found poems to be a beautiful way to express her feelings. Not that she followed the normal convention—there were no couplets, no iambic pentameter. Very little structure at all. She preferred stringing words together that bubbled up from inside. Scanning the horizon for inspiration, she began with an ode to nature.

Birds soar overhead
on a gentle breeze,
looping, swirling, without care.

Gliding through the soft blue sky,
over the lush green leaves
of the forest below.

Through the trees,
flowers burst a show of colors,
enhancing the beauty of the day.

That was certainly not one of her best efforts. Maybe she should consider a new subject. Pondering a moment, she settled on a subject who'd figured prominently in most of her writings.

Who would have thought
I would appear
at Vincent Hall
astride a horse?

Who would have believed
as the sun warms my skin,
and the ride thins my waist
that I would find cheer
astride a horse?

Who would have guessed
that despite all my work,
the man whom I love
would remain so remote
astride his horse?

Why would I think, dream,
believe, guess, or pray
that a man such as he
would...

Hmmm, would what? Fall madly in love? No. Be enthralled by my form? Not likely. Drop to his knee and pledge undying devotion? Ugh, that was too much to hope for.

Fall in love would do for now. Especially since no one else would ever hear it. With a contented nod, she continued her verse.

* * * *

Dare was bored. Bored, bored, bored. There was nothing to look at except trees and sky and the nodding of his horse's head as it meandered down the road. Clop, clop, clop, bored, bored, bored.

Lord, how he hated the country.

There was always something in London to keep him entertained, to keep his thoughts at bay. But not here. Surely Nivea could exert *some* energy to entertain him, instead of bobbing along, smiling to herself. Ignoring him.

"Women are here for a man's pleasure," his father had always said. *"Their happiness should be solely dependent upon making you happy."* While he did not see eye to eye with the marquess on most things—hell, on scarcely anything—Dare had always been partial to that sentiment.

He spotted a large oak tree up ahead, split in half long ago by a bolt of lightning. *Oh, yes,* this would make things interesting.

He pulled his horse alongside Nivea's. "We'll stop here for a brief meal."

Startled by his sudden pronouncement, Nivea jerked, causing her horse to dance.

He flashed her an innocent smile as she got her mare under control. It served her right. If she had been paying attention to him, it wouldn't have happened.

"Where do you propose we eat? There's nothing around for miles."

"*Au contraire,* I know a charming little spot, just up ahead."

As they passed the charred oak, he turned his horse down a narrow trail. The trees were overgrown, but the path was still distinguishable. It wasn't long before the brush gave way to a clearing. Sunlight filtered through the trees, giving the spot a magical appearance. A grassy area sloped down to a babbling stream, dotted with moss-covered rocks. Tiny white, yellow, and pink flowers bloomed riotously along the banks. In the center of the clearing stood two large L-shaped stones, with a third flat rock between them, forming a table and chairs.

He had stumbled across the path once when staying with William, and since then, had taken advantage of this inspired location with a number of young ladies. Surely, a brief flirtation with Nivea couldn't hurt.

Pulling his horse to a stop in the sundrenched center of the field, he announced, "The innkeeper packed us a lunch. There is bread, cheese, and a jug of cider in my saddlebag. Why don't you lay out the meal while I take care of the horses?"

He handed her the bag and led their mounts to the stream for a drink. Tethering them to a stump, he returned to the field to watch Nivea arrange the food on the stone table. Now, the game would begin.

As she sliced off a sliver of cheese, he removed his gloves and ran his hands through his hair before refastening it back into a neat queue. Women loved his hair—said the sunlight turned it inky blue. And once they had touched it, they couldn't keep their hands off, saying it was silky as a cat's. It was sure to draw her attention.

Nivea did not seem to notice.

Once she finished with the cheese, she did look up, but her attention was on the surroundings, her eyes full of wonder. "How did you know about this place?"

Warming up to his plan, he flashed her a wolfish grin and eased himself onto the boulder facing hers. With measured stealth, he reached for the cheese and removed it, while oh-so-gently caressing her palm. "There are few places in England where I have not discovered a convenient backdrop to attract a woman's fancy."

As expected, her eyes grew wide. Content he now had her interest, he slowly brought the cheese to his lips. Then he closed his eyes and waited for her to speak.

It took her a few moments longer than most women. In fact, it was such an unusually long lull, he almost peeked from under his eyelashes to see what she was about.

Finally it came.

"This spot is truly wonderful. Eager as I am to get home, I could remain here for hours. Thank you."

That was it. She was silent again.

Now, he did have to open his eyes. Most women would take this opportunity to prattle on, hoping to dazzle him with their wit or entice him with their list of virtues. Little response or even interest was required on his part.

But that did not seem to be her strategy.

So, he smiled in acknowledgement and waited for her to continue.

But no, that was all. This woman remained stubbornly silent.

It was maddening. It appeared she had forgotten he was even there.

How was such a thing possible? Women always paid him attention. The slightest nod of his head, or smile in their direction, ensured a blush from a virgin, or an appreciative gleam in the eye of an experienced woman.

But not this blasted woman. She leaned over, broke off a bit of bread, and then took a sip of cider. Ate a slice of cheese, smiled at him for a for a brief moment, and returned her gaze to the riverbank.

Really, what was she about? Yes, the area was beautiful, but it was supposed to be an attractive backdrop to set the mood. And because he was so thoughtful, the attention would be focused back on him—*thank you very much.*

He narrowed his eyes to stare at her while puzzling on his next step.

There she sat, with the sun shining on her hair and the blue of her gown enhancing the azure color of her eyes. As she leaned forward he could see the full, soft curve of her breasts straining against the fabric of her gown. In fact, if he tilted his head just so, he could see down the gap in her dress and into the valley of delicate white flesh. It was quite alluring.

A little shiver of desire prickled through him.

What the devil? This was just plain, plump Nivea. There was nothing desirous about her. But that wasn't true. Just this morning, after he'd apologized, her eyes grew soft, her smile sweet. Then she touched his hand and there'd been a spark. Heat. Like the intimate warmth of a lover's touch.

No, that couldn't be right. Nivea didn't make him burn.

Peeking at her from under his lashes, he once again eyed up her lush curves, her breasts rising up with each breath. Taunting him. Then her tongue darted out to lick a drop of cider from her red lips and *whoosh,* fire flashed to his groin. Try as he might, he could not tear his eyes away from her.

Damnation, what was going on? He had no business eyeing up his friend's sister. His oldest friend's unmarried, unfashionable, untouched sister. His code of conduct was fairly flexible, but that rule was unbreakable.

He ripped a bit of bread off with his teeth, desperate to regain control. Of course, Nivea chose that moment to hold a conversation. "I did not expect to enjoy myself this trip. At least once the carriage broke. But I will admit, it has not been as much of a nightmare as I feared."

"Hmph," he answered, his mouth full.

"Can I tell you what the best part will be?" she said, leaning forward in a slight whisper.

He was not so far gone that he couldn't guess the answer—telling all her friends about the romantic lunch she shared with the rakish, rogue, Lord Landis. No doubt embellished with tales of soft words of love and gentle caresses.

He didn't answer, in part because he was valiantly trying to look anywhere but at the enticing bosom still straining toward him.

Fortunately, she did not notice and continued. "The best part will be riding up to my house and seeing the total disbelief on my family's face when they see me on a horse."

"What?" he gasped, choking down his food. "Why would that matter?"

"Well, I have never quite fit in with my family and their passion for horses. When my father sees me arriving astride a beautiful mare, like a queen on procession, he will likely burst with pride."

"Surely, you don't believe you can gain your father's admiration through such a simple act."

"Oh, it is no small thing. He loves me for who I am, but he has never understood me. He will crow about this for days."

"Do not get your hopes up. A father's affection is not so easily won… if there is any at all."

Nivea brushed off his warning and continued weaving her fantasy. "Of course I have his affection. We are family. We are loved despite our differences."

This time, Dare did not suppress the snort of contempt. He knew better than anyone the lack of constancy in any relationship, especially within a family. "Please do not bore me with such drivel."

"Adair Landis, you have been a constant guest of our family for years. How can you even question it?"

"If his love depends on your ability to ride a horse, how can you even consider it?"

She paused a moment, her fingers twisting a stray lock of hair, before she replied, "I am sure you are aware, I am the only one in the family not immersed in equine pursuits. I have never shown any interest or inclination to the subject. I have no doubt, if I had trifled with our footman and foisted a house load of bastards upon him, my father would be more understanding than my lack of interest in horses."

With that, Dare barked out a laugh. "I'm certain that is not the case."

She smiled, but it did not reach her eyes. "Perhaps not, but I know my lack of interest has been a disappointment. William and Caroline are much more similar to him. They love to ride horses and play games, while I prefer to sit and observe. Still, while he understands them better, I know he loves me just as much."

Dare could only shrug in response. She was obviously delusional regarding familial love. True, her family was more accommodating than most, but he'd always thought it was a bit of an act.

He had just raised the cider to his lips when she made the most absurd statement of all.

"Once you have children of your own, you will understand."

Dare almost choked on his drink, "What!"

Her brows shot up in surprise. "I am certain there is no greater experience than having children. Watching them grow, helping them learn, supporting their interests. I hope someday I am fortunate enough to have a family."

Remembering his own upbringing, he could not begin to fathom her logic. The thought of having a family be supportive or even desirable was ludicrous. Painful and humiliating, certainly, but supportive? Never.

Determined to set her straight, he wiped the cider from his lips. "Trust me. You are in the ideal position right now. No responsibilities, no worries, and at your age, few expectations."

"I'm in an ideal position?"

He couldn't understand why she looked so shocked. "Yes. Society will accept you whether you wed or not. I, of course, must get married and have children. As a peer with a title, it appears to be my sole duty in life. I can win or lose a fortune, commit virtually any crime without repercussions, and spout out as much nonsense as I deem necessary in the House of Lords. But dying without issue is the greatest sin."

Satisfied he'd made his point, he withdrew his jeweled snuffbox from his pocket, took a pinch, and snapped it shut.

Nivea gave him a tight smile. "And yet you have done neither, married nor had children.

He tipped his head with an ironic twist of his lips. "Too true. Nor do I plan to for a good long time. I rarely do what is expected."

"Why is that?" Nivea cocked her head.

The conversation had suddenly taken far too personal a turn. He had no intention of explaining himself to her, or anyone for that matter. Without a word, he drew to his feet, brushed the crumbs off his clothes, and strode toward the horses. This misadventure had gone on long enough.

Chapter 6

Nivea had mixed emotions as they arrived at the outskirts of Horsham property. Much as she loved returning home, she had not managed to win Dare over. Despite her best efforts, he was still treating her like a bother. As they plodded through the woods leading up to Vincent Hall, they hadn't exchanged more than ten words since their picnic.

But when they finally turned up the road to her house, she couldn't suppress the joy that bubbled up inside her. Vincent Hall was a large, comfortable house, nestled in a side of a hill. The stone structure glowed orange in the afternoon sun, and the windows glinted yellow, like eyes of a contented cat. Beyond the house, she could see the lake, and past it, the forest where they had roamed as children. She sighed with pleasure, reminded yet again how much she preferred her home to the bustle of London.

As they approached the entrance to the house, the Earl of Cheltenham came flying out the door. As usual, his jacket was rumpled, his face flushed, and his brown hair curling willy-nilly around his collar.

He grabbed at her horse's bridle. "What is this?" he exclaimed, his grin stretching from ear to ear.

"What do you mean, Popa? We are here for Caroline's wedding. Surely, you were expecting us," Nivea answered, keeping her voice as nonchalant as possible.

"Yes, but in a carriage, for goodness sake. Whatever possessed you to arrive on horseback?"

She couldn't help smiling as he stared at her in wonder. "Ah, yes. Well, our carriage broke. In order to arrive on time, we had to ride."

Without hesitation, the earl tugged her from the horse and gave her a solid hug. He was as surprised as she'd hoped and it brightened her mood. Then he turned his attention to her mount. Giving it a quick appraisal, he patted its neck fondly. "Nice piece of horseflesh. I will have to learn of its bloodline. I'd wager it's got a bit of Daltrey's Devilment in it," he murmured to no one in particular.

Well used to her father's obsession, Nivea took no notice. Her attention was diverted by Dare as he leapt from his horse and handed it off to a groom. Despite his aloof behavior, her heart still raced seeing him stride over, all long legs and strong shoulders.

He gave her father a curt bow. "Lord Horsham, I confess we had a bit of a mishap, but I deliver you your daughter, unscathed."

The earl turned toward her escort, his face a mixture of bafflement and joy. "Lord Landis, sir, I must say I have never been more surprised in all my life." He clapped Dare on the shoulder and might have pulled him into a hug if Dare hadn't stepped out of his reach. Too delighted by the afternoon's turn of events, her father took no notice. "I don't know how you did it, but I have to thank you for accomplishing a miracle. Bringing my Nivvy along on horseback…this is like unexpected gold in my pocket."

"Really, Popa! You're embarrassing me."

Unfazed, the earl pulled her close and bestowed a loud kiss on her forehead, before turning again toward Dare. "You have given my daughter her birthright. I could not be happier."

He linked arms with them both and propelled them toward the house. "Now then, the rest of the party is here, more or less. I will give you a chance to freshen up and then you must join us in the parlor."

They walked inside, and stopping in front of the staircase, the earl gave her another squeeze. "My girl, today you have given me the greatest present of all. I may be losing Caroline, but seeing you ride up, I feel as though a guardian angel has now blessed me with a whole new family member."

Dare leaned back and catching her eye, quirked an eyebrow. She gave a small, knowing shrug and headed up to her room. It was good to be home.

* * * *

It wasn't long before Nivea slipped into a bath to wash off the dust of the travels. As she was drying off, her maid, Emma, brought in a fresh dress for the evening. After pulling the garment over Nivea's head and beginning to work the buttons, Emma exclaimed, "Oh, Miss Nivea, this gown will not do. Look how much room it has. Have you been sick? I cannot pull it tight enough to wear."

"No Emma, I have not been sick. I think I have finally found an advantage to riding. After years of attempted starvation, I found a little exercise helped me slim down a tad."

"Oh, this is more than a tad, my lady. You've dropped almost half a stone. I will need to take in this dress afore you can wear it. Let me find another one that we can make work."

She prowled through the closet and retrieved another gown, rose-colored, with a pale overskirt of mauve. Pulling it over Nivea's head, she cinched it up to make it fit. "There, much better. It may be a few years old, but it looks lovely. Now, let me add a little curl to your hair and you'll be perfect."

Feeling rather triumphant, Nivea headed downstairs to join the guests. She could hear the chatter of conversation before she'd made it down the stairs. Entering the room, she saw it was packed full of guests, eager to join the celebration of Caroline and Nicholas's nuptials. She recognized most of the faces, but sought out her sister and mother first. They were standing to the right of the doorway and waved her over.

"Nivvy, there you are! I was starting to worry about you." Caroline greeted her with a hug. Her sister was most visibly a Horsham, with a stocky figure and plain brown hair. But her face was aglow with love.

Nivea returned the hug and then gave her stepmother a light squeeze. Slender and elegant, with blond hair that fell in well-tamed waves around her shoulders, there could be no doubt Amelia was the earl's second wife. She had known the earl when they were children. It was only when she'd brought her daughters, Abby and Constance, to London, following the death of her husband, that the two had been reunited. With a demeanor as sweet as her face, the Horshams had been happy to welcome her into the family.

"I heard from the earl you had quite an adventure," Amelia said.

"Yes, the carriage broke down outside of Norwalk and we had to proceed without it."

"And you had to ride a horse for three days? How on earth did you survive?" her sister exclaimed.

"I'll admit, the first day was agony, but by the end, I'd quite gotten the hang of it. In fact, after seeing Popa's expression when I rode up, it was almost worth it!'

They all giggled at the thought.

"What are you three laughing at?"

"Abby! How good to see you." Nivea turned as her stepsister and her husband, Lord Godwin, joined them. "Thomas, welcome. I'm glad you both could come."

"We wouldn't have missed it," Abby responded. "It is a wonderful excuse to bring our families together."

"Speaking of family, Mama, I was hoping you could go upstairs and sit with Lizzie and Jamie," Abby said. "They refuse to take a nap without a kiss from grandmamma."

"Certainly. If you'll excuse me." Amelia smiled and darted for the door.

"She loves spending time with those two. No matter what trouble they cause, she treasures them. I don't know why she's so tolerant," Abby mused.

"Probably because they remind her of her own darling daughter," her husband responded with a wry smile.

She looked at him sweetly and patted his cheek, oblivious to the scar that crossed his face. "You may be right." Turning to Nivea, she explained, "I was a bit of a wild child growing up, always outside running and riding. It drove Mama crazy. Now, my two are no better."

Thomas took her hand and squeezed. "But she loves you all, and so do I." Despite social convention, he kept his hand wrapped around hers as they stood there.

They were a handsome couple. Both had rich chestnut hair, piercing eyes, and an athletic grace that Nivea envied. They fit in well with the Horsham family. Abby loved horses and Thomas had been friends with William since they were schoolboys. The couple had met the year Thomas had resigned from his regiment to assume his title as Earl of Devonshire, and they quickly had become inseparable.

Well used to their displays of affection, Nivea returned to her conversation with Caroline. "So, who else is here, Caro?"

"Almost everyone. Nicholas's family and friends are here, including Lord and Lady Wilshire." She made a face. "It's not *him* I mind so much, but his wife is awful. Then there's Briar and Joseph, William and Betsy, of course. Betsy looks quite marvelous considering she just had a babe."

"I'm sure the joy of having the first son in a generation has made things much easier for her."

"Yes, her da' could never accept that he had four daughters and her ma' never forgave her for being a bluestocking. Until now, that is."

They all smiled, except for Thomas who obviously wasn't paying any attention.

"If you don't mind, luv, I am going to go join the men so you and your friends can talk." Thomas gave his wife a squeeze and headed off.

"I hope Nicholas still looks at me like that after we get married," said Caroline wistfully.

"I just hope I can get someone to look at me that way *ever*," mourned Nivea.

Abby hugged her. "Don't worry, your time will come. Someday a fine, young gentleman will be smart enough to see your amazing qualities."

Nivea sighed, not at all certain. Considering no one had noticed in her first five seasons, there was no reason to believe anyone would appear now.

Feeling a little uncomfortable with the conversation, she excused herself to greet her brother. William was standing near the window with his friend, Lord Duxbury. In the past, Joseph had favored the brightest of outfits, but since he had settled down with Thomas's sister Briar, he had developed a more sedate appearance. Tonight, he was attired all in gray, but as she approached, an enormous ruby pin sparkled in his cravat. It appeared he was not completely reformed.

The two men could not have looked more different. As always, her brother appeared as though he'd just rolled out of bed. His grey houndstooth jacket was patched and baggy, his brown hair loosened from his queue, and his boots hadn't seen a brush in over a fortnight. Nivea loved him, but was amazed how cavalier he was about fashion. How easy it was to be a man.

She returned his hug as he greeted her. "Nivvy, welcome home! I trust you survived the trip from London all right. Lord Landis was no doubt a perfect gentleman?"

He did not notice the flash of pain his teasing caused. Nivea knew she was virtually the only woman Dare would treat respectfully, and that wasn't a compliment.

She was tempted to snap a retort, when a male voice behind her responded, "Yes Horsham, your sister was in good hands. We had a bit of an adventure, but arrived intact."

As he joined the circle, Dare took a pinch of snuff from his jeweled box, his attention fixed on his male cohorts.

Would it kill him to acknowledge her? If she had been any other woman, he would have cast a sly glance at her, perhaps brushed a hand over her arm, letting her know he'd enjoyed the time with her. But no, he found her invisible.

Oblivious to her irritation, William chuckled. "Yes, yes, I'd heard. Father said you had to ride here…on horseback, no less. Nivvy, I never would have expected it of you. Quite the shock I must say. Landis, you must have had the fight of your life getting her to agree to that. What did you do, douse her with laudanum and toss her over your saddle?"

Dare gave a half smile before responding. "No, nothing quite so dramatic. After some initial protest, she handled herself quite ably."

"Initial protest, my arse. She must have cursed a blue streak at the prospect."

Oh, dear Lord. Nivea flashed her brother a look of annoyance. Couldn't he, for once, build her up in front of Dare?

Too embarrassed to remain, Nivea forced a smile and excused herself to join her favorite aunt, Mildred, at the other end of the room.

A few minutes later, warm fingers stroked her elbow and she jumped. Turning to see who had startled her, she fell into Dare's dark, hooded gaze. Her pulse kicked up.

"Excuse me," he purred silkily at Aunt Mildred, "I would like a minute to speak with Miss Horsham. Do you mind?" Then he flashed a devilish grin at the old dear, bringing a definite blush to her cheeks. Nivea had to choke down a smile as Mildred stuttered her response. "No…not at all. I'm sure she would much rather talk with you than me."

Now it was Nivea's turn to stammer. "Oh, no Auntie—you know—"

"Hush, just go," ordered Mildred as she waved her away.

Dare took her arm and drew her aside. Once alone, he leaned close enough for her to feel his breath on her ear. "I owe you an apology."

"What do you mean?" Her heart raced at his nearness.

"All that with your family. I realize you may have been right regarding your family's opinion. Trifling with the footman might have been less of a shock than your horse riding."

She chuckled. "I did warn you."

"Well, I'm pleased I was able to restore your honor within your family."

"Yes, you will forever be a legend in Horsham family lore. You have my deepest gratitude." She curtsied.

"That has always been my most sincere desire in life." With a twist of his lips he offered her a quick, sardonic bow, before turning to join the other guests.

Flushing with pleasure, Nivea stood there a moment, watching him. That was one of the nicest conversations she'd had with Dare in years. Maybe the trip *had* been a success. With a light heart, she rejoined the party.

Chapter 7

Dare congratulated himself.

He'd done quite well showing William nothing improper had occurred with his sister during their travels. It hadn't, of course, but he did have to admit to certain uncomfortable thoughts about her, as unexpected as they were unappreciated. She was a nice enough girl, but it wasn't as though she was his usual fare. She was an unmarried miss, not to mention his best friend's sister. He couldn't very well go lusting after her.

Determined to put her out of his mind, he turned his attention to more appropriate quarry. While the Horshams were known more for their sportsmanship than their love of fashion, they still had managed to invite a promising crop of ladies. Some were acquaintances from London, and others were fresh faces, no doubt from nearby land. A number were sneaking glances at him from behind fans or around shoulders, twittering with glee. Sometimes, it was almost too easy.

Secure in the knowledge he would have no trouble finding someone to warm his bed, he turned his attention to more conventional pursuits. "Well, Horsham, where are you keeping the best brandy? If I have to drink anymore of this blasted lemonade, I will throw myself through the window."

William turned with a smile. "One moment, Landis. Let me introduce Nicholas Beecham, my soon-to-be brother-in-law. And this is Sir Beecham, Nicholas's father."

Dare dipped a bow at each of them. They were obviously father and son, both with thinning sandy hair and ruddy cheeks. While Nicholas had a slender frame at the moment, he was sure to descend into stoutness in time, like his father.

"This scoundrel is Adair Landis, one of my oldest friends. Since you have no daughters, Sir Beecham, I can refrain from my usual warning, although I'd still suggest you keep a fair distance between him and Lady Beecham."

William chuckled, while Dare inclined his head in silent acknowledgement. No point in arguing with the truth. Married women were often his most enthusiastic conquests.

"You'll be joining us tomorrow for the hunt, won't you, Landis?" William inquired.

"Naturally. I wouldn't miss it."

"Be careful out there," warned Sir Beecham. "You'll want to keep an eye out for poachers this year."

"Poachers? How strange," said William. "It's been a good season this year. No need for poaching when the weather's good."

"Still, we've heard some shots at odd times. Found a few winged birds that weren't properly taken."

"Last time we had poachers was during the drought of 1811. Remember how bad things got? The lake damn near dried up."

"Good God, yes," Dare exclaimed. "The stench was horrendous. Half-dead fish flopping around in the muck. Smelled like a London wharf."

"We had to send our horses to Franklinshire to graze. Nothing here but stubble." William sighed. "Couldn't ride for almost a month." Turning to his left, he said, "Not a bad summer for you though, eh, Godwin? Weather was much nicer in Scotland, from what I heard. Very fruitful."

Thomas nodded before turning to shoot a smile in his wife's direction. "It was a very nice summer indeed."

"I sense there's a story here," said Nicholas.

"Yes, that was the summer Thomas went up to his estate in Scotland with his sister, thereby depriving me of her treasured company for almost two months," Joseph moaned.

Thomas rolled his eyes. "You survived quite well, and her absence probably helped your suit more than your constant presence."

"Yes, well, regardless of that fact," William continued, "Thomas took his sister Briar and her two friends, Abby and Constance, to Scotland. After their lives were threatened by a disreputable land agent, he acted the hero, saved Abby's life, and managed to make her fall in love with him."

"What I don't understand is why she continues to feel that way, now that you're back home. I thought surely she'd come to her senses," Dare said.

"Now don't be such a humbug, Landis. Just because you weren't able to pull off the same trick with her sister, don't begrudge Thomas his happiness," William retorted.

Dare flashed his friend a look that would terrify most people, but William took no notice.

Abby chose that moment to join them.

"Good evening, sirs. I had the strangest feeling I was the subject of your conversation and wanted to know if the sentiments were good or bad."

Thomas laid a gentle hand on her waist. "Always good, my dear. We were discussing our first trip to Scotland."

"Oh yes, what an adventure. We thought we were being very discreet, trying to refrain from a courtship to protect our sisters' sensibilities, and all the while Constance and Briar were plotting to throw us together."

"Where is your sister, Abby? Surely, Constance will be joining us for the wedding," Joseph asked.

"No, I'm afraid not. She has found she is with child again. She had a bit of a difficult time with Emmy, and Jonathan urged her to stay home to rest."

Dare was unable to prevent a flare of disgust at the thought. "Breeding more peasants, I see."

Thomas took a menacing step toward him. "I'll thank you to remember that is my sister-in-law you are referring to. Don't think for a moment the fact we are *friends* would prevent me from running you through." At that, he rested his hand on the sword that he wore, a holdover from his days as a soldier.

Unperturbed, Dare returned his stare. Thomas was fully capable of striking him down without a second thought, but Dare had no interest in ruining his evening over a distant memory. Turning to Abby, he executed the slightest of bows, and with as minimal scorn as he could muster, responded, "My apologies. Please offer your sister my felicitations."

Without waiting for a response, he turned and left the group.

He strolled to the opposite corner of the room, and had just taken a pinch of snuff, when a hand squeezed his arm. He glared down into the face of a dark-haired beauty.

"Don't worry, milord, I'm not going to take you to task. Quite the contrary. I couldn't be in more agreement with you regarding your disgraced ladyfriend. Why in heaven's name she would settle for a servant when she could have had"—her eyes took a long slow walk over Dare's form—"you. That, I will never understand."

"Ah, Miss Berkshire. How are you?"

"Lady Wilshire, if you please. You'll remember I have been married for three seasons now."

"As you say. Difficult to remember as you are never seen together in any pursuits."

"Yes, it works well for us. I now have a fortune, he has respectability, and we are both free to pursue our own interests." She ran her small gloved hand over the sleeve of his jacket. "Do you have any interests here, Lord Landis?"

The seductive smile and sweep of her thick lashes across her rosy cheeks left no doubt as to her meaning. Her red dress was rather bold for a country gathering, but it set off her creamy skin, and the red ribbon threaded though her dark hair made a striking contrast. While Dare had avoided the lovely Miss Berkshire while she was searching for a husband, she now presented a delightfully unencumbered opportunity.

Perhaps it was time to take advantage of a longing that had simmered for years. He pitched his voice low. "And the respectable Lord Wilshire…?"

"Is most decidedly occupied…as long as the spirits continue to flow." She gave a pointed glance toward a rotund gentleman at the far end of the room. Said gentleman was flushed and unsteady, draining a glass of Madeira as if on cue.

Dare leaned closer to whisper in her ear, "You do know that *respectability* is not something I value. In fact, I find it quite dull. Are you certain you can suppress that element of your personality, at least for the evening?"

She gave a throaty chuckle. "That should not be a problem."

She took a step toward the door and then raised her fan up to her face. Two flicks of the wrist were followed by a sigh. "La, I fear this room is getting warm. I believe I may need to lie down for a few moments before dinner. Will you excuse me?" Her eyes brazenly roved over his figure before she turned and glided out the door.

Dare watched her leave, noting the sway of her hips. He sipped his drink, enjoying the anticipation. When the glass was empty, he placed it on the footman's tray and slipped out of the room. He headed up the staircase to the guest rooms. A quick glance at the row of doors showed that Lady Wilshire was a woman with experience. The red ribbon that had been weaved through her hair peeked out of a doorway on the far left of the hall. *Perfect.*

He pressed open the door, taking the ribbon with him. Lady Wilshire was stretched out on the bed, a shapely calf peeking out from under her skirt.

"I understand you are feeling a bit warm. Perhaps I can help you out of your dress, so you'll be more comfortable."

With a wicked smile, she raised her arms and drew him to her.

* * * *

In the distance, a dinner bell stirred them from their lethargy. "Well, my dear, it appears we have other appetites that need sating. I fear that the Horsham's chef will have quite a time topping my last meal."

"Mmm. No need to go. I can ring to have a tray brought up." Lady Wilshire snuggled closer to his chest, gripping the fine lawn of his shirt. "Much as I enjoyed the blindfold, I'd like to see you this time."

He grabbed her hands before they could remove the red ribbon he'd tied around her head. Sitting up, he smoothed his shirt down with one hand before slipping the cloth from her eyes. "I think not."

In fact, that was definitely not going to happen. He climbed out of bed and reached for his breeches.

She hadn't gotten the message. She sat up and raised an arm to stroke his back. "I'm sure we won't be missed."

Before she could touch him, he twisted away to don his pants. "You may not be missed, but I most certainly will be."

As expected, that did not sit well with her. She glared up at him, her eyes narrowed to slits. "So, what they say is true. You use women for your enjoyment and then leave without the slightest care."

He raised an eyebrow. "You appeared to gain some enjoyment, Lady Wilshire. I cannot imagine you expected us to form a lasting entanglement."

Giving him her finest pout, she responded, "Not a lasting one perhaps, but I'm sure a repeat performance would be mutually satisfying."

"Perhaps another time. For now, I require some proper nourishment." He pulled on his boots, grabbed the remainder of his clothes, and strolled out the door.

By the time he reached the bottom of the staircase, he'd tied his cravat, straightened his cuffs, and run his fingers through his hair, assuring it was neatly arranged. Entering the dining room, he took his seat without a word. When William caught his eye, Dare raised his glass and gave him a satisfied smile. His friend chuckled and returned to his soup.

Chapter 8

The morning was overcast, but that wouldn't deter her. Nivea had been awake for quite awhile, listening to the sounds of the men as they prepared for one of the Horsham's favorite pursuits—hunting. Yet another passion Nivea did not share nor understand. But their absence provided her with a perfect opportunity to pursue her plan. Now that she had overcome her loathing of horses, she had decided to become a more proficient rider. She donned a riding habit she'd found buried in the back of the wardrobe and headed toward the stables.

"Why, Miss Horsham, what can I do for you?" The stable hand gaped at her in astonishment as she approached the stalls.

"I would like you to saddle a horse please. Something fairly tame, perhaps like Buttercup's Bloom, here," she answered, pointing to a mare even she could tell was well past her prime.

The groom scratched his head. "You want me to saddle a horse...for you?" He glanced around for another possible rider.

Nivea couldn't fault the man for his confusion, although it did sting. Except for dragging her brother from the building, she hadn't set foot in the stable for years. And until Dare insisted, it had been over a decade since she'd climbed on one of the beasts. But she was determined to go through with this.

"Yes. I would like you to saddle a horse. For me."

He shrugged and did as she bid. He led a sedate Buttercup to the mounting block, and after a few attempts, managed to shove her up onto the saddle.

Wiping his brow, he looked up at her with concern. "Would you be likin' Seth to ride with you?"

Answering with far more confidence than she felt, she said, "No, that won't be necessary. I won't go far."

Turning the horse away from the house, she nudged Buttercup forward, hoping no one would spot her. She knew her father had been surprised to see her riding the other day. What she wanted now was to gain enough skill so she could join the family for a ride. They were as comfortable riding as walking and could travel for hours without complaint. She used to joke that if her father could find a way to sleep while riding, he would live on his horse.

Her aspiration was much less lofty. She would be happy if she could mount the thing with a modicum of grace, keep it from eating grass, and maybe even coax it into a trot, if necessary. Of course, if she managed to slim down a teeny bit more in the process, so much the better.

She headed toward the lake, where the view of the house would be blocked by trees. The sun was warm on her face, but a cool breeze blew off the water. Buttercup was well behaved, requiring the bare minimum of instruction. Once she made it into the shadowed area, Nivea looked for a stump or log to begin her first lesson. On the left, she spotted a large stone and steered her horse alongside it.

Patting Buttercups's neck, Nivea whispered, "Now, don't be afraid. I'm new at this. I promise not to hurt you, but you have to be patient. If you are good, I have an apple in my pocket for you."

She positioned herself in front of the boulder and took a deep breath. This was the part she hated. How was she to contort her body to get out of the saddle and onto the rock? If she lifted her leg off the pommel, she was sure to drop like a stone. Then she would either fall under the horse's hooves and be trampled, or smash against the rock and bleed to death. Neither alternative appealed to her.

She shifted in her seat, feeling a trickle of nervous sweat behind her knee. Buttercup snorted her impatience.

"All right, girl. Don't fuss. I'm going to do this." Having said it out loud, she found the courage to dislodge her leg from the saddle. Her heart was pounding so loud in her ears, it drowned out all other sounds in the forest. She inched her weight forward keeping a firm hold on the horse. There was a moment of panic when she could feel nothing under her feet but air. But then her feet touched the stone's surface and she could breath once again. In her excitement, she turned back toward the horse, and nearly fell when her skirt got tangled around her legs. Flailing, her hands braced against Buttercup's solid flank, and she managed to regain her balance.

"There!" With a triumphant smile, she stood on the rock like a conquering hero. Buttercup turned her head toward Nivea and snorted, making her laugh. "Yes, I know, for most people it's not much of an achievement, but for me, it's quite a milestone. Now, you will have to be tolerant old dear, for I am going to try and get back up."

Nivea gave herself a moment to savor the victory before steeling herself for the real challenge. She leaned her torso over the saddle, kicked her skirt out of the way, and tried to tug herself up.

That didn't work.

She gave a little hop. That didn't work either.

Buttercup shifted her weight and turned her head to see what was going on.

Nivea blew a loose piece of hair from her eyes and reached up to pull the horse closer. "I know. I told you to be patient. I'll get it." She leaned into the horse and jumped harder. It wasn't enough to get her all the way up, and she slid back down onto the rock.

"Uuuurg! Why is this so hard?"

She once again reached over and flung herself upward. With an ungainly twist, and a most unladylike grunt, she managed to pull herself up onto the saddle.

Buttercup took two steps forward before Nivea could grab the reins and get herself settled. She took a deep steadying breath and patted the horse's neck. "Good girl. That wasn't so bad."

The horse nickered, but Nivea let it pass. "Enough of that for one day. Now we can take a stroll." She prodded the horse forward.

Really, this wasn't so bad. The woods were colored with a multitude of greens, hiding happy birds chirping to one another. Buttercup strolled along, her hooves drumming out a muffled beat on the packed dirt path.

Just as she reached the open field and decided to turn back home, she heard a whoop and turned to see whom it was. Abby and Thomas were galloping across the field; Abby's dark hair streamed out behind her, no sign of a hat. They waved at Nivea and slowed to approach at a sedate pace.

"Good morning. How are you today?" Abby asked as she drew alongside her. Her face was glowing with excitement and exercise. Thomas looked happy as well, but settled his features into more of a stoic expression. With the scar on his face, he looked almost fierce, but Nivea knew better.

Smiling, she answered. "I'm fine. It was such a nice morning, I thought I'd take a ride."

Thomas shot her a questioning look. Nivea was sure he realized in all the years he'd known William, he'd never seen her on horseback. Fortunately, he was too polite to comment.

"Did you have a nice race?" Nivea asked.

Abby smiled and the look of love she exchanged with Thomas was almost embarrassing. "Yes. These horses are wonderful. I could not wait to stretch their legs. They are magnificent creatures. Thomas, you are going to have to talk to William about selling this one to me. She's perfect."

His eyes crinkled in amusement. "I thought Arabelle was perfect. And Mystic. How may perfect horses do you need?"

Abby shrugged and patted the horse's shoulder.

"So, Thomas, the other men are all off hunting. Didn't you wish to go with them?" Nivea asked.

His eyes grew dark and shuttered. "I do not enjoy the sport. I have seen enough killing, thank you."

Recalling that his scar was a result of a battle wound, her face warmed. "Oh—yes—I see—well—" she stuttered.

Taking note of her embarrassment, Abby reached over and patted her husband's leg. "Let's go, luv, I'll race you to the stable."

He smiled and whipped his horse to a gallop, but Abby had already sprung ahead.

If she were a betting woman, Nivea would put her money on the lady.

By the time she reached the stable, grooms were already rubbing down the pair's horses. One of them stopped to help Nivea dismount. She almost felt graceful as she slid onto the mounting block.

Guests were starting to stroll around the yard. Hoping they wouldn't notice her riding habit, she darted up to her room. Changing into a delicate pink morning dress, she headed outside where the women and children were talking and playing games. Her sister-in-law, Betsy, was holding little Anthony under a giant parasol, querying Nicholas's sisters about teething.

Caroline was playing leapfrog with five rambunctious boys who were soon to be her nephews. Nivea joined her sister, helping the littlest ones climb onto the backs of their much larger brothers so they could spring off with glee. Over and over, they would push off the giggling lumps, before curling up at the front of the line to await their turn.

Little Daphne, one of Briar's twin girls, came up to Nivea and tugged on her skirt. "Aunt Nivvy, I'm tired. Will you pick me up?"

"Certainly, poppet. I'm a little tired too. Would you like me to carry you over to the shade and tell you a story?"

The girl's eyes lit up. "Oh yes! I love stories. Can you tell Eloise, too?" The little girl's face was full of hope, eager to share the moment with her twin.

Nivea's smile widened. "Of course. Let's gather up all your friends."

Nivea invited the youngest children and their wilting mothers to join her on a bench in the garden under the cooling shade of a crabapple tree. "Why don't you stretch out on the grass, while I tell you a story?"

"What kind of story, Aunt Nivvy?"

"Would you like to hear a poem I wrote about my cat, Samuel?"

"Yes, yes!" they all cheered. "Tell us about Smanuall."

Nivea smiled at their enthusiasm. Drawing Caroline's youngest nephew, little Colin, onto her lap, she began.

Tabby Cat, fat and lazy
lying in the sun.
Eyes blink,

you stretch and yawn
and make to get up
before falling back down,

content to pass another hour
In slumber.

They clapped, their faces alight with joy.

"Another! Tell one about horses! We love horses." Of course it was Abby's little ones who shared their mother's obsession for riding.

Nivea had attempted to write some, long ago, as it was the central theme in her upbringing, but had always found the subject challenging. After giving it some thought, she remembered one.

"How about this? I call it 'Another Day at the Races.'"

Horses flash past,
all brown and frothy,
thunderous hooves and slaps of whips
kicking up clods of dirt.

Cheering crowds surround me

as the winner is announced.
No surprise,
as it is once again
a Horsham mount.

She was delighted when the women laughed.

"Too true! I didn't know you had such talent, Nivea," Abby said.

Before she could respond, Caroline said, "I used to love when our governess assigned writing projects. My attempts were always dreadful, but your poems, Niv, were always so imaginative. It has been so long since I'd heard them. Have you written anything lately?"

Nivea shook her head. While relating silly poems from her youth was fine, she didn't wish to express her deeper thoughts with this crowd. Especially since most of them referred to her desperate yearnings for a certain black-haired rake.

"Nothing of importance. We'll save my ramblings for another time."

Seeing the children were beginning to drift off, she used them as an excuse to change the subject. "It appears Colin is not as fascinated with my poems as all of you. He's fast asleep. Would you like me to carry him in for a nap?"

"Yes, please. I think it's time for everyone to rest," answered Colin's mama.

Despite protests from the children, the mothers gathered up their drowsy darlings and escorted them inside.

Chapter 9

Dare had left for the hunt in high spirits, happy to enjoy the day with close friends and fine horseflesh. He was disappointed to find the earl had included his future son-in-law, as though he were a true member of the family, not only providing him with a superior mount, but including him in the conversation.

"Nicholas, my boy, I expect you will have a little more luck today. I remember the last time we went out for a hunt, you nearly got yourself killed. Surprising, since I'd always heard you were a steady sort of fellow."

Nicholas went red around the ears. "Truth be told, sir, I was pretty damn intimidated riding with you. Never thought I'd be able to keep up, not on my little horse. Next to your stallion, he looked like a pony for criminy's sake!"

"Nonsense. No need to be intimidated. We're always happy to have new blood joining us. William here could never keep up with me, and Landis, well, he's a moody sort. Not much for conversation, unless the fairer sex is around. I'm happy to have you with us."

Dare ignored that comment, keeping his eyes straight ahead on the path. He could never quite accept the earl's jovial manner around his family, even after all these years. It seemed unnatural, and Dare had maintained a wary distance. If the man saw that as moody, well, there was no help for it.

Nicholas did not display a similar affliction. With a wide smile, he gushed, "I appreciate that. This horse I'm riding is an absolute marvel. It's almost like he knows where to go before I tell him."

"So you like him, do you? Good. Consider him a wedding present."

"What?" Nicholas's jaw dropped, and he pulled the horse up short. "Oh, no, sir, I could not accept that. Just having your daughter is generous enough."

"Don't be silly. Can't have you traipsing around the countryside on a half-breed. How would that look?"

"Besides," William added, "it will give us a chance to spread the bloodline out and ensure our dominance in the county."

"By the time my grandsons can ride, you'll have your own mini-dynasty," chortled the earl.

Dare snorted. The best thing about hunting with the Horshams had always been their complete focus on the pleasures at hand...horses and hunting. Now, he was forced into listening to all this inane babble about family.

In the hopes of salvaging the day, Dare decided to issue a challenge. "Now that the young pup has a proper mount, what say we have a contest? William and me against Nicholas and the earl. The first to score three birds wins."

Confounding him, William announced an alternative. "How about I take Nicholas for a partner, and you and the earl can hunt together."

In all their years together, Dare had always paired with William. They were the dominant team, always prevailing over the group. He tried to suppress the sting of abandonment as Nicholas, beaming with pride, nudged his horse to join William, but it annoyed him to hear the two men nattering away at each other as they branched off.

Brushing off the insult, Landis tugged on his reins, forcing his horse to rear slightly before prancing back towards the earl. He ignored the sharp look the earl shot him—after all there were few greater sins with the Horshams than mistreating a horse. Attempting to make the best of it, he spit out a brief apology, and they headed into the woods.

Determined to put young Nicholas in his place, Dare forged ahead, doing his utmost to win. Being a good host, the earl made several attempts at conversation that Dare rebuffed. His father had always made it painfully clear that hunting required absolute silence. He'd learned at a young age to follow that ironclad rule to avoid the consequences. He wasn't going to change now to suit his congenial host.

By providing no more than one word answers, the earl soon learned conversation was unnecessary and, once quiet prevailed, the two men managed to bag a grouse within the first hour. They almost had a duck soon after, but it took flight behind a copse of trees. It was quite a while later that Dare had a quail in his sights when they heard the blast of a horn, startling the bird.

"Blast," Dare growled. William and Junior had won.

"Huzzah," crowed the earl. "My sons have bested us. Caroline will be quite pleased with her young man."

Dare looked over, baffled. The earl seemed genuinely pleased that he had lost. How was that even possible? Wasn't winning everything? The only thing?

Anything less was…failure. And Dare could not abide by failure.

It was obvious that the earl was not burdened by the same sentiment. As the group reunited, and the victors displayed their kills, they all rambled on about who shot what and how well the other performed.

"We will have to serve these birds at the wedding tomorrow. It will bring luck to our table," announced the earl.

Dare could do nothing more than shake his head in disbelief. The man truly did not care he'd lost to a lesser adversary. And William, he just rode alongside, acting as though he'd never had a better partner. As though all those times they'd been a team didn't matter. It was infuriating.

By the time they reached the house, Dare's mood was beyond surly. After handing over his horse to the stable boy, he strode into the entrance of the hall, determined to stew alone in his room. Everyone else could go to hell.

"Milord," he heard a footman call.

He didn't bother to slow down.

"Milord! I have good news for you."

Irritated, Dare stopped and turned on his heel. The sneer on his face gave the footman pause.

"Well?" he snapped.

"Oh, yes, sir—well, your carriage and luggage have arrived. Your man is unpacking it at this very moment. Oh, and there is a letter for you."

The footman scuttled back to the table, swept an envelope off, and handed it to him. Dare took one look at the handwriting and snatched the paper from the startled servant before storming up to his room.

His man, Jackson, was in the room arranging his things.

"Good day, milord. I have put your belongings away and can prepare your clothes for dinner now."

"Yes, do it with all haste and then get out. I'm in no mood for your chatter."

Well used to his master's curtness, Jackson took no offence to the insinuation that he "chattered." Instead, he helped him out of his riding clothes and into a clean linen shirt, dove-gray trousers, and spotless boots. That being done, he gathered up the dusty clothes and closed the door behind him.

Anticipating unpleasantness, Dare stretched out in a chair by the window to read the missive from his sister.

Adair,

While I am usually able to overlook your abhorrent behavior, this time I must protest. I urge you in the future to unleash your baser instincts on women raised for that sort of behavior. What business have you abusing my friends so callously?

Poor Victoria has been widowed for a mere six months, as you well know. In her fragile state, you have no right to use her and then toss her aside. It is not as though she is that attractive and has any self esteem to begin with (although I would never admit so to her).

Would it have been too much to ask her to join you at the Horsham's affair? Now, I shall have to invite her to come to Shavely to restore her spirits. With her moping around, it is sure to be much less pleasant than I had hoped.

I do not understand how you can be so selfish. Just because Miss Abbington broke your heart does not mean you should take it out on the entire female species. You do not have to be as cruel as father.

Regards,

Anne

He threw down the letter in disgust. *You do not have to be as cruel as father.* As if that were even remotely possible. The devil himself could take notes from the marquess on ways to torment people.

Picking up the letter again, another line caught his eye, further stoking his anger.

Just because Miss Abbington broke your heart, does not mean you should take it out on the entire female species. As though Constance Abbington had any effect on his behavior! The idea was ludicrous.

As for breaking his heart? Relieved was more the word. If anyone was suffering, no doubt it was she. She could have had a peer of the realm. And yet she threw him over for a peasant. The man had been a servant in the Abbington household, for God's sake! He comes back from war with a mangled leg and a pathetic title, and suddenly the wench decided being a marchioness wasn't good enough.

He fumed as he paced the room.

And now that William's father had married Constance's mother, he had to be polite and magnanimous whenever the woman was mentioned. If William hadn't been such a good friend, he would not stand for it.

Growling in frustration, Dare banged on his desk, causing the writing instruments to jump.

He had expected the wedding party to be boring but tolerable. Instead, it was one irritant after another. He merely wanted to enjoy life with no baggage, no ridiculous delusions about love and family. That shouldn't be too much to ask.

At least he could set his sister straight. He dashed off a quick yet cutting response to her correspondence and slammed it on the desk, ready for the morning post.

Vowing to make the best of it, he yanked on his jacket, took a large pinch of snuff, and headed down to do some serious drinking.

Chapter 10

Pausing at the bottom of the stairs, Dare steeled himself. Before he could drown out his irritation, he must first suffer through another supper held before the sun was down. He would never get used to country hours. Still, he took his place at the table, bestowed a few witticisms on his companions, offered a few set-downs when necessary and, after a healthy serving of wine, began to feel more like himself.

That is, until they finished their meal. He was almost through the doorway when Nivea stopped him with a touch of her hand. The warmth of her fingers penetrated the thin sleeve of his silk coat. Strange that he didn't mind, as he didn't particularly like to be touched—outside the bedroom.

She looked up at him with an enchanting smile. "Lord Landis, thank you for delivering my luggage. I was afraid my clothes would not arrive in time for the wedding."

Her sweet expression made him feel strangely benevolent. "I am happy to have put your mind at ease, Miss Horsham. I regret I cannot take all the credit. In truth, it was my coachman who returned your possessions."

Issuing a dramatic sigh, she responded, "I suppose that's true." Then she flashed him a saucy grin. "In that case, perhaps I should seek out Weldon. I am certain he would be grateful of my appreciation."

He was bemused by her flirtatious response. Without missing a beat, he slipped into his rakish persona. "I will pass along your appreciation, milady, and let him know you are in his debt. He will be most honored to hear of it." With a flourish, he bowed over her hand before raising it to his lips. At her gasp, a rather entrancing blush warmed her cheeks. Enjoying the sensation, he held on to her fingers a moment longer than was necessary. In fact, he found that he didn't want to let go.

When her eyes darted to his right, he realized others were watching. *Good lord, what was he doing?* He dropped her hand. Spinning on his heel, he found himself skewered by Lady Wilshire's incredulous glare. She must be irritated that he was showing attention to another female. Perhaps he would make it up to her tonight. She was certainly a more appropriate quarry.

With a lascivious wink in her direction, he headed into the study to join the other men. There, he grabbed a glass from the sideboard, filled it with amber liquid, and took a satisfying gulp.

Ahh, brandy. The magic elixir. Crossing the room, he sat down in his favorite mahogany chair at the card table and nodded to his friends. Joseph was lounging to his right, Thomas, ever the soldier, sat stiffly erect on his left, and Nicholas, the nit, sat across from him. William had been chatting with a few other gentlemen around the room, but strolled over to join them.

This was comfortable. Familiar. Dare just hoped they would behave as they ought. The rest of the day had been quite a trial.

Eager to set things to rights, he placed a stack of notes next to his glass. "I am in the mood to play a bit of chance. Are you gentlemen ready for a little wagering? *Vingt-et-un*, perhaps?"

"I am," stated Joseph eagerly. "I still need to recover the funds you stripped me of last month at White's."

"And what makes you think you'll have any more success tonight?" Dare taunted as he gulped down his glass.

"Well, I'm more sober this evening, and it appears you'll be in your cups in no time." Joseph grinned.

He fixed his friend with a steady gaze. "When have you ever found me to be a poor gambler as a result of drink?"

William laughed, slapping Joseph on the shoulder. "He has you there. Never seen a man more able to hold his liquor and his cards at the same time. It's almost mythical." He grabbed a deck of cards from the drawer and sat down with the others.

"Perhaps tonight's the night we can take down the mighty Zeus," chuckled Nicholas as he pulled up a chair.

Dare gave him a cold stare. "You can try, but the odds are against you." He had achieved most of his wealth through card playing, supporting himself after his father turned him out. And this pup imagined he could win? It was laughable.

In no time, coins and notes covered the table, each man with a glass of liquor at his elbow.

Predictably, Nicholas was the first to surrender. "This game is too high-stakes for my blood. In the future, I will stick to whist with the ladies. I fear you lads from London are too skilled."

"Maybe you're just distracted by the upcoming nuptials," William responded, affably.

"That could well be. I appear to have used up all my good luck attracting your sister."

"Well said. You two should have a very happy life together."

"It is my greatest wish. With that, I will adjourn, gentlemen. Tomorrow promises to be a more fortuitous day."

At the sound of the door closing, William said, "Nice fellow, Nicholas. Caroline is a fortunate girl. It's too bad Nivvy hasn't made such a match."

"I suppose she's the only one unmarried now, eh?" Joseph observed. "Does it bother her much?"

"She's holding up well, but with Caroline being so much younger, it must sting. All those years on the marriage mart and not so much as a nibble. It's a shame. She's always been good with children. I'm sure she's keen to have some of her own."

More interested in the game than the conversation, Dare stated, "Why not find her a widower or lonely vicar and make him come up to scratch?"

William shot him an insulted glare. "Come, now, Nivea deserves better than that. She's a good sort and the Horsham name should ensure her a title. Wouldn't you agree?"

Dare had begun to enjoy himself and had no interest in being drawn into a discussion of marriage. "Maybe she's better off as she is. After all, marriage is naught but a prison."

He should have known better. All he did was stir up a heated reaction.

"Ho, ho! I don't think that theory holds much water here," William proclaimed.

"That's right. We are quite content with our lives," added Thomas.

"Ah yes, I'm sure you think so now. But the thrill will burn out soon enough and you'll be joining me in rakish pursuits in no time. Of that, I am certain." Then turning to his left, he added, "Well, not you, Godwin. You always have been a bit of a stick. Now you're just a sappier stick."

Thomas shrugged his shoulders. "I have no regrets. In fact, I think I'll retire and join my wife for some marital bliss."

"Ha! There is no marital bliss, just people in heat."

Thomas didn't rise to the bait. He scooped up his pile of coins and took his leave.

Dare threw back another drink, warming to the subject. "Come now. You know marriage is no more than a business relationship. Even if it begins with some attraction, the hands of time cause it to sour."

Joseph shook his head. "That is not true. You're just bitter because Constance threw you over."

With a scornful snort, Dare answered, "I only pursued her because she would have been an obedient wife who stayed in the country, bearing my heirs, while I continue my lifestyle. My heart was never involved."

"That may be why she chose someone else," Joseph pointed out.

"Ridiculous. There is obviously a flaw in her character. It is just as well I didn't introduce her blood into my family." He banged his glass down on the table.

William growled, "Be careful now, Dare. You forget that blood is now in my family. Amelia was the best thing to happen to my father."

Dare waved his hand dismissively at his friend. "Yes, well, she won't be bearing you any heirs, will she? You'll be the next earl, and your son after you. All I can say is that I must be very selective when finding a wife to carry on my bloodline. It will be a business decision, not anything as illusionary as love."

"Illusionary? Landis, you couldn't be more wrong. I love Briar," Joseph protested, with William joining in.

"And I, Betsy. Surely, you can see if you stopped treating women like interchangeable playthings, you might be able to form an attachment."

Dare glared at them. "But why would I want to? They *are* interchangeable. The only difference is how long it takes for me to find their cloying behavior to be a bore."

"You need to consider the possibility that the right woman is out there," Joseph urged.

"The right woman, meaning faithful and obedient? It's not possible."

"There are any number of happy marriages."

"Bah! My parents cannot tolerate each other, with good reason. My sisters? They just hope their children's parenthood is never called into question. Do you know how many women come to my bed, bemoaning the fact that their husbands are too old or difficult, or unable to satisfy? It's a stifling union that is guaranteed to tarnish with time."

He shoved back his chair to get another drink. Spotting a laggardly lump in the corner, he called out, "Wilshire, how much time do you spend with your enchanting little wife, Elizabeth?"

George raised his bleary eyes from his glass, as though awakened from a deep sleep. "Eh, my wife? I keep her in frills and she leaves me alone."

Dare waved his glass in the air. "There, you see."

"That means nothing," Joseph said. "Someday, you'll think differently. A woman will catch your interest, and God help you when she does. You will never let her go."

"The only thing I'll never let go is my gold," he announced, sitting back at the table, running his fingers over a stack of coins.

George muttered, "If you want to keep hold of your gold, definitely don't wed."

They laughed, but he continued, morosely. "Lady Wilshire is striking, but she's an expensive piece. As if clothing isn't enough, she's always wanting to buy damned jewels. I gave her my grandmother's rubies and she acted insulted. Said they looked old. Old! Of course, they're old. Ain't that the point? But no. She wants to go out and drop all my coin on her own baubles." Following that outburst, he slumped back into his chair. "I make her wear the demned rubies to remind her she doesn't need others," he mumbled before lapsing back into sodden silence.

Dare smirked and tossed back another drink. "My point exactly. Marriage is an institution that pleases no one."

"But don't you want somebody to talk to? To discuss your day's events?" asked Joseph.

Dare stared at him. Discuss things with a woman? Why on earth would that be an incentive to marry?

"Come, now. Surely you've had conversations with women," he prodded.

"You mean ones that didn't involve begging for compliments or hinting at marriage? No, not a one."

Suddenly, the image of Nivea sitting on the rock as they pleasantly chatted over a picnic lunch came to mind. Chalking that up to an aberration, he continued his argument. "Much as this conversation bores me, I'd much rather be sitting around with you gentlemen, drinking and gambling, than spending more than five minutes with a woman. Any woman. Although once her skirts are off, I'd happily reorder my priorities."

With that, he turned his attention back to the cards.

Chapter 11

The day of Caroline's wedding dawned sunny and warm. Nivea once again arose with the sun and snuck out to the stables for her daily ride. The stable hand was less surprised to see her this time. She didn't ride long, knowing guests would arrive soon for the celebration. As the dew was drying on the grass, she returned and headed up to her room where Emma helped her on with her dress.

"You look so pretty, miss. That color truly suits you."

Nivea beamed at her reflection. "Thank you, Emma. I feel pretty."

The dress was a soft, flowing creation in burgundy silk with a sash of pink roses, and matching flowers in her bonnet.

"I finished the alterations last night. It's a good fit, now." Emma smoothed the sash down, settling it along her waist. "I have Sarah working on your other clothes. Don't go starving yourself or we'll have to redo all our work."

Nivea smiled. "Don't worry, Emma. With all the treats Cook has prepared, I'll probably be back where I started by nightfall."

But looking at her reflection, and seeing the subtle changes, she knew she'd be able to tamp down any cravings. Her cheeks had a little more definition, making her eyes seem larger. Her waist had a slight curve, emphasized by the sash under her bustline. It was a heady experience knowing she wouldn't be Nivea, the frumpy wallflower, today.

Best of all, she was finally making progress with Dare. He must feel the growing attraction between them. He had talked and laughed with her that first night of their return. Then, last night he had kissed her hand, right there in front of everybody. And he could not have missed the spark that sizzled between them as he squeezed her fingers.

Heading toward the stairs, her thoughts were buzzing. Once he saw her in this beautiful dress, surely he would take notice.

Nivea found the entire house party ready to enter carriages. She scanned the bright array of colors, hoping to catch a glimpse of Dare. Tall as he was, he was sure to stand out, but she did not spot him. It appeared the magical moment would have to wait.

Upon reaching the bottom of the stairs, William tugged at her arm. "Nivvy, there you are. Popa and Amelia have already left for the chapel with Caroline. You are to ride with Betsy and me." Not giving her a chance to answer, he escorted her into their carriage.

The sanctuary was a beautiful structure, built by the Normans. Amelia had arranged for the entranceway to be decked in flowers and ribbons. Flanking the path, footmen, bearing the family's burgundy livery, sat astride two white horses with matching ribbons braided into their mane and tail.

The Horshams had been generous supporters of the church for centuries and it was equipped with comfortable pews and plenty of room for the swarm of guests. Taking her seat near the front, Nivea tried to be subtle as she looked around the church for Dare. She finally caught a glimpse of him tucked in the back.

Even without his acknowledgement, her heart skipped a beat. The sun, streaming through the window, glinted off his sleek black hair while throwing his face into shadows. He appeared an entrancing contradiction of a heavenly devil.

With a sigh, she turned back and tried to focus on the ceremony.

It was a beautiful service, and Nivea brushed away a few happy tears as the couple took their vows. The peal of bells proclaimed their marriage to all, and their guests streamed out of the church into the courtyard. Nivea spotted Dare near the carriages talking to Joseph, but she was surrounded by family and unable to get closer. Still, she was able to drink in the sight. His charcoal grey jacket, silver waistcoat and spotless white breeches molded to his form like a second skin.

She stopped breathing when, catching her gaze, he crooked a rare smile her way. Oh, good heavens. She hadn't imagined it. He, too, felt the growing connection between them. Maybe her dreams would come true.

Dizzy with delight, she managed to finish greeting the remainder of enthusiastic well wishers, before racing to her carriage to take her to the wedding feast.

* * * *

Cook had outdone herself. The buffet tables were laden with tasty treats. Nivea plucked a few slices of seasoned pheasant from a silver tray and turned to survey the room. Friends and family created a living kaleidoscope. Dresses of all colors swirled in an ever-changing pattern around the more sedate tones of the gentlemen's attire. The terrace doors were open wide, allowing a light breeze to circulate. The scent of fresh flowers filled the air, and musicians played softly in the background. It was the most perfect of all days.

Caroline appeared in the doorway and Nivea strode over to give her a kiss.

"Oh, Caro, it was a superb wedding. You looked so happy."

"I am happy. Nicholas is so sweet. He keeps telling me how beautiful I am and saying how lucky he is to marry me.

"He's right you know. You are beautiful and he is lucky."

Amelia joined them, wrapping them both in a hug. "I don't even need to ask you if you're happy, Caroline. Your smile lights up the room."

"It has been a wonderful day. The decorations at the church were as striking as you'd planned and my dress makes me feel like a princess. Thank you Amelia." She twirled with a giggle, showing off the cream-colored dress with rosebuds embroidered along the hem. Pale pink strips of lace crisscrossed her bodice, encircling her waist and streaming down her back.

Smiling, Nivea adjusted a piece of lace on her bodice. "There, now you're impeccable."

"Thank you, Niv. You are beautiful, too, you know."

The pink in Nivea's dress was a perfect complement to her sister, as Betsy pointed out when she and Abby strolled over. "The two of you look like a picture. I feel like a frumpy aunt next to you." She glared down at her shapeless lavender gown .

"Don't be silly. You just had a baby. You look radiant. Especially when holding little Anthony. He is precious."

"Yes, he is. I am so blessed."

"As am I," said Amelia. "I never dreamed I would become part of such a wonderful family. First Abby and Constance, then you girls getting married. Now we just have to get Nivea settled and our family will be complete.

"You should have invited the vicar. They could have made a match," said Elizabeth Wilshire with a smirk as she strolled up to the group.

"Excuse me?" Nivea sputtered.

"Last evening, Lord Landis suggested if no one else would have you, perhaps you could get lucky and marry a vicar or a lonely widower. Of course, if you were really lucky, you'd have a husband *and* a man to warm your bed." At that, she glanced over at Dare, who was looking in their direction.

Nivea's heart stopped. No. It couldn't be. Was she implying that Dare was involved with her? The thought was too much to bear. Elizabeth had always been a spiteful creature, mocking others without care. Surely, Dare wouldn't stoop to bedding her.

Elizabeth took no note of her dismay and continued, "Yes, while they were playing cards last night, your brother said you would never marry, but Adair commented that you should at least be able to attract a vicar, desperate for a helpmate."

"What?" How could he say such a thing?

"I don't think it was phrased like that," protested Caroline.

"That's right. William argued that you were an upstanding girl and deserved better," said Betsy.

"But Lord Landis said no one but a vicar would agree to marry me?"

Abby cut in, "Landis was being his pompous self, declaring love and marriage to be a sham. Thomas said he was quite intractable."

Nivea blinked back tears as she stared at her family. "So, am I to understand the men spent the evening talking about how I may never get a husband, and then relayed all the embarrassing details to you?" It was too degrading to even consider.

"Oh, it wasn't like that at all." Caroline patted her arm in an attempt to comfort her, but Elizabeth piped up once again.

"No, of course not. They did not waste much time discussing _you_. It was simply noted that you are the only unmarried female now, and he provided a solution. Most of the conversation involved Adair explaining how he prefers to limit his associations with women to _livelier_ activities than marriage." Waving her fan, Elizabeth let out a merry laugh before mincing away, leaving no doubt as to her meaning.

Nivea sucked in air, trying to steady her breathing, but she couldn't stop the tears that burned her eyes. With an angry swipe of her hand, she brushed them away. What a fool she'd been. Not only did Dare not find her the least bit attractive, he didn't even think her worthy of another man's attention.

Amelia pulled her into a hug. "Don't listen to that nasty woman. You know she likes to stir up trouble."

"Are you saying that Lord Landis would not insult me in front of his friends?" she choked out.

"Of course he would. He insults everyone." Caroline had never understood her infatuation with Dare and was always eager to disparage him. "Truly, what does it matter what he thinks? I have no doubt you will find someone who appreciates you as much as Nicholas does me."

"That's right," said Betsy. "I never expected to find a husband until William came along, and now I couldn't be happier."

"Please don't let that bitter woman ruin this day for you," Caroline pleaded.

"For you, Caro, I will forget it. I don't want to cast a shadow on your day."

Nivea forced a wan smile and marched over to the terrace doors for some air. Taking a deep breath, she resolved to show the unconscionably rude Lord Landis just how wrong he was. She could be charming. She could attract suitable gentlemen.

She smoothed her hands down her skirt and tucked a few stray hairs back into place, ready to dazzle all the eligible men in the room. Turning to face the room, her resolve almost crumbled. Dare was staring straight at her, dark eyes blazing with anger.

She gasped. *What does* he *have to be angry about?* He wasn't the one insulted in front of friends and family. She glared back at him, and he turned away.

Pain shot through her. Why was he acting like this? They had been getting along so well together. She didn't really expect him to marry her, but for him to say she was worthy of no prospects beyond a lonely, desperate vicar was heart-wrenching.

But since she'd promised Caroline she'd enjoy the day, she squared her shoulders and returned to the party.

Chapter 12

First on the dance floor were the bride and groom, followed by the earl and Amelia, and Nicholas's parents. Then the whole family joined in, laughing as they twirled across the floor.

Soon the ballroom was filled with the sounds of celebration. Having two neighboring families joined in a love match brought out a heightened joy amongst the guests. It was obvious that Caroline was marrying a fine fellow who would treat her with respect and affection. Dare could barely look at them without retching.

It could be the amount of spirits he had indulged in the previous evening, but that seemed unlikely. He'd been taught at an early age a man was expected to handle his liquor.

The real question was, how could everyone be so blind to the fact that this was all a mirage? Once the celebration was over and the marriage began, there would be no happiness. It was best to live life to the fullest, take what pleasure you could, and then leave with a minimum of fuss.

To that end, Dare turned to notice Miss Yorklyn standing near the open window. She was a comely neighbor of William's, who he had met a few times over the years.

He strolled over and asked her to dance. She shot a smug look at her companions, before grabbing his extended arm and tucking it into hers. Beaming up at him, she pressed the curve of her breast against his sleeve. Not one to ignore an invitation, he appraised her form, noting how the jade green dress enhanced her eyes, and the tight-laced bodice emphasized a generous cleavage. Offering her a seductive smile, he bowed in appreciation.

As the music began, he found her to be quite graceful, matching his steps with a minimum of effort. Unfortunately, that left plenty of opportunity for her to talk.

"Look at her…could that shade of yellow make her look any more sallow?" Followed by, "What has she done to her hair?"

This one's dress was too tight, that one's waistcoat was too loud—on and on she went, barely taking a breath between insults as she assessed the other guests. Dare was never one to avoid a proper set-down when necessary, but the key was to be well-placed and clever. Simply spewing comments against her friends and neighbors was bad form.

Driven to desperation, Dare let his attention wander around the room. His gaze happened to settle on Nivea. She was greeting guests and chatting with friends, a contented smile lighting up her face. Firmly on the shelf, she had no husband, no prospects, her younger sister newly married, and yet there was no bitterness or resentment. How was that possible?

The only time she'd appeared troubled today was when Lady Wilshire had spoken to her. No doubt the woman had said something spiteful, because Nivea had turned quite pale. Who did that woman think she was to make Nivea uncomfortable? There was no excuse for such petty behavior. With her looks, charm, and a husband, what right did she have to insult the poor girl? Of course, just as he had been silently cursing Elizabeth to perdition, he had realized Nivea was staring at him. He had turned quickly away, not wanting to add to her embarrassment.

"Wouldn't you agree, Lord Landis?" Miss Yorklyn asked with a slight tug on his arm.

Realizing he'd been ignoring his companion, Dare nodded his head and flashed her a roguish smile. Content that she once again had his attention, she returned to her diatribe.

Dare divested himself of her as soon as the music finished and moved on to speak with his friends. Finding William and Wilshire by the buffet, he loaded up a plate and spent a pleasant few minutes making plans for an upcoming hunt.

Once he finished his meal, Dare took a pinch of snuff and scanned the floor for a dance partner. A quadrille had begun, so he approached Joseph's wife, Briar. She was a nice enough woman, and a capable partner, able to master the complicated pattern.

He led her to the floor where they joined the first set. When it came time to switch partners, Lady Wilshire wound up on his arm.

"You look very handsome today, sir," she purred, waiting for a compliment in return. The half-smile she gave him was no doubt designed to draw his interest, as was her crimson dress that clung to her curves. Oddly, it had the opposite effect. He felt nothing but disgust.

Remembering how she made Nivea uncomfortable, and always happy to stir up trouble, he decided to set her straight. Without the courtesy of a glance, he inclined his head and responded, "Good day, Lady Wilshire. Are you enjoying the festivities? There is no better way to spend an afternoon than celebrating the cherished bonds of matrimony. Don't you agree?"

Eyes narrowed, she snapped, "Oh yes, nothing like watching two people dedicate themselves to each other for eternity. Their future is sure to be filled with nothing but joy and happiness."

"I sense that you do not find it so. Nor do I. It is much preferred to spend just enough time with someone 'til you are weary of their company and then part ways." He plucked her hand off his arm and unceremoniously passed her off to the next gentleman.

Her eyes widened with surprise, and then narrowed in anger.

How delightful. *Truly, timing was everything.*

Suddenly, Nivea flew into his arms. Nicholas, as inept on the dance floor as he was on a horse, had spun her off before stumbling over to his new partner, almost knocking the woman over. Judging by her expression, Nivea hadn't minded his bumbling. Her cheeks had a rosy glow and her laughing mouth gave evidence of pure joy.

What was it about Nivea that enabled her to find such delight in the most tedious of circumstances? How long had it been since he'd experienced such a lighthearted emotion? Had he ever?

Inclined to explore the matter further, he glanced down at Nivea and was disappointed to see her smile disappear. In fact, she was glowering at him.

That was unusual.

Even more odd, she refused to acknowledge him as they twirled in circles, first left then right then promenading across the floor. Only her fingertips brushed his arm as he guided her through the steps.

"Is everything all right?" he asked.

With her eyes fixed on the couple in front of them, she responded, "Of course. Why do you ask?"

He could hardly miss the belligerent tone. Puzzled, he pulled her closer, whispering in a seductive tone, "You seemed to be having a much more enjoyable time with Nicholas than with me."

She shrugged, unconsciously drawing his attention down to her bosom.

God's blood, it was an attractive bosom.

Forcing himself to ignore *that* detail, he glanced over to the man in question, just in time to witness him stomping on the lady's gown, almost dragging her to the floor. With a snort, he asked, "What exactly would make partnering with Nicholas so appealing?"

"I find him pleasant and kind and he treats me with respect. It is more than I can say about some people." At that, she jerked her arm out of his grip and sailed on to the next partner.

Unsettled by the exchange, Dare finished the dance and headed over to the closest footman for a drink. Pulling two glasses of champagne from the tray, he downed one in a gulp. The bubbles produced an unpleasant sensation, but he hoped the jolt of alcohol would clear his head.

It had been such a strange day. Here he was, with his closest friends, surrounded by attractive women, and yet he was irritated beyond measure.

Sipping the second glass of champagne, he observed all the mini dramas playing out amongst lovers and friends—squabbles, flirting, and rebuffed advances. Women pranced by him with an expectant air, waving their fans or tossing their hair, hoping to catch his eye. In the past it had been enough. He'd been content. But something was different today.

Nivea. She was ignoring him.

Not that it should matter. He didn't need her attention. After all, she was…well, she was just Nivea.

They'd had an amenable relationship until now—in fact, recently it had become more than cordial. But today, she wouldn't look at him. What the devil was going on?

As he finished off the glass and placed it on a table nearby, he sought her out, hoping to solve this unusual enigma. He spotted her near the terrace doors, where a rather plump fellow tapped her on the arm. "Nivvy!" he heard the man exclaim and was annoyed to see her respond with a broad smile.

"Winnie!" she cried, making the fellow laugh.

They talked briefly before the cheeky fop gave her hand a kiss, and they began strolling around the room, arm in arm.

Anger tightened his chest. She could fall all over this countrified buffoon, but couldn't spare him the time of day. And after he had escorted her up from London for the bloody wedding.

Staring at her, he finally drew her attention. In response, the infuriating chit pursed her lips and turned away. Why did she deign herself important enough to treat *him* with disdain? True, she was looking rather attractive today in her stylish pink gown, but she was still Nivea.

Deciding to set things right, he grabbed two glasses of lemonade and pressed through the crowd. He found her talking to another gentleman, this time a young pup with starched points and an outrageously styled cravat.

Why wasn't William keeping a closer eye on his sister? She appeared to be throwing herself at men today.

Marching up, he wedged himself between them and thrust the glass as her. "Here," he announced, "you looked peaked."

Her eyes flew to his face, wide with surprise and something else— distaste. "Thank you."

Without taking a drink, she leaned past him and said, "Sir Morrell, this is Lord Landis, a friend of my brother. Sir Morrell is Nicholas's cousin."

"Pleasure to meet you," answered Sir Morrell with a short bow.

Dare merely glared at him. As he'd hoped, the man grew flustered. After stammering out a few platitudes to which Dare offered no response, the man beat a hasty retreat.

"That was rude," Nivea snapped.

"Hmmm. I just thought you might need rescuing from the young popinjay. I was afraid if he asked you to dance, he might poke out your eye with his collar."

She must have been thinking the same thing, because she was unable to smother a smile. Well, that was a start. Trying to figure out his next step, he decided to ask her to dance. That usually did the trick with women. She gave his ego another little poke when she hesitated before answering in the affirmative.

God's blood, what was going on here? He would set things straight once and for all. He shot her an alluring smile and pulled her close. Closer than he'd ever remembered holding her. It was then he noticed her scent. Not the cloying smell of roses that clung to most ladies. This was something sweet, like a lemon cake or vanilla.

He inhaled deeply, causing Nivea to cast a wary glance his way.

He responded with a deep penetrating look that always caused ladies to sigh with delight, and was encouraged by the heightening color of her cheeks.

Still, she was not fully engaged.

Dare was unable to hide his irritation. "Who was that you were with? A suitor?"

"What? You mean Sir Morrell?"

"No!" he snapped with unusual vigor. "That man you were parading around the room with. Nivea followed Dare's gaze into the crowd.

"Do you mean Edwin Corknell? Surely, you remember him. He lives in nearby Northumbria."

He gave a quick shake of his head. "I don't remember."

"No? He was here frequently. His father, Lord Corknell, was close friends with Popa. In fact, it was assumed Winnie and I would become betrothed."

Dare frowned and looked closer at the man. "Hmmm. Really?"

"Yes, really! That is until he went to Cambridge and fell in love with a classmate's sister." Her gaze drifted over toward the ridiculous pup, and she sighed. "He's quite happy now."

"So he married someone else?"

She stiffened in his arms. He was shocked by the angry fire in her eyes.

"Yes, milord, he married someone else. I guess that's not surprising, though. After all, he's a lord, not a vicar! Obviously, no one as decent as Edwin would want to marry *me*." At that, she tore away from him, leaving him alone on the dance floor. Stunned, he stood there for a moment before heading for the nearest tray of spirits.

That clinched it. For whatever reason, women were even more incomprehensible today than usual. He resolved to spend the rest of the evening conversing with the more sensible sex.

Chapter 13

The next morning, the celebration continued, with most of the party heading to the races. The Horshams had several horses entered and their guests were eager to cheer them on. Nivea was only too happy to stay behind. She managed to have an enjoyable time at the wedding by putting Dare out of her mind, more or less, but she was now exhausted.

Pleading a headache, she spent the better part of the morning in bed. Wallowing in self-pity. How could she be so stupid? Dare didn't love her. He would never find her attractive. No one would. She was nothing but a dowdy toad. That's all she'd ever been.

Reaching under her bed, she pulled out a box, secured by a scrap of ribbon. It contained a hoard of poems documenting all the heartbreak of her life. She unknotted the ribbon and lifted the sheath of papers.

The first few, written in girlish handwriting detailed the grief she'd felt at her mother's death. As she'd grown older, the poems began to detail her youthful insecurities—her loneliness, her weight. After that, there were numerous pages dedicated to Dare and his handsome form, his entrancing eyes, his dancing prowess, each one more mawkish than the last. Then she came to the most recent poem, written after visiting with Nicholas's sister last year.

"Godchildren"

Laughing, smiling, climbing,
Screeching, chattering, toddling,
tripping, crying, eating,
Falling asleep in my arms.

"Did you have fun?"
"Aren't they sweet?

She asks, returning from her walk.

Maybe you'll have some of your own
one day," she says.
"Maybe," I say.
With no more conviction than she.

Forever Miss Horsham

Tears blurred the words on the page. With a loud sniffle, Nivea stuffed the poems back into the box and flopped against her pillows. She was a pathetic ninny. She'd wasted all these years pinning her hopes on a man who saw her as a wretched charity case. Fit for a widower and nothing more.

She deserved better. She deserved a man who loved her and would give her children and a home of her own. It was time to put away the silly dreams of her youth and find a man worthy of her love. From this point forward, she would become someone interesting enough to attract the attention of a noble suitor. Mastering her riding skills would be a good first step.

Resolute, she wiped away her tears and climbed out of bed. She threw on her riding habit, twisted her hair into a loose bun, and headed downstairs. As she approached the door to the rear of the house, she heard sounds coming from the music room. That was odd. All their guests had gone to the races. Who could it be?

Creeping to the doorway, she found Dare sitting at the piano, playing furiously. His eyes were closed, and his lips were pressed together, almost angrily. As his fingers dashed over the keys, the music rolled out of him like a storm. He looked positively magnificent.

She stood there in stunned silence. When the last notes of the sonata drifted away, she entered the room, her boots clicking on the floor.

His eyes flew open, and he jumped up from his seat. "Where the hell did you come from?"

Shaken by his tone, she took a step back. "That was beautiful. I didn't know you played."

"I don't," he snapped. The look of pure fury was so powerful, she was unable to respond. Before she could gather her wits, he shoved back the bench and stormed out of the room. Shaking, Nivea stood rooted to the spot. Through the windows, she could see him marching to the gardens.

What was he talking about?

She raced after him as he strode down the stone path, past the boxwood hedges, and into the rose garden.

When she caught up to him, he was staring into the fountain. The sun flickered light and dark shadows over his face as clouds blew across an uncertain sky. The flowers were in full bloom, encircling the fountain with their crimson beauty, but he didn't seem to notice.

Attempting to diffuse the situation, she offered softly, "We are putting on a musicale at the end of the week. Perhaps you'd like to play a song for us?"

He jerked his head up. "I don't know how."

But he *did*. She had been right there in the room listening to him. "Don't be silly. You play better than anyone I have ever heard."

"No!"

"Yes, you do," she insisted.

He took a menacing step toward her, his eyes blazing. "I do not play. It is Not. Who. I. Am."

She wanted to take a step back, but was riveted in place.

"What do you mean?" she asked, her voice barely a whisper.

"I am a man. I'm the future Marquess of Raynsforth. I do not play the piano like a traveling minstrel, begging for coins."

Abruptly, he turned, leaving her staring at his broad back. A strong breeze tugged at his glossy black hair, but it remained neatly pulled into a queue. Hers was not so obedient. Puzzling through that statement, she thrust an errant lock behind her ear. "That doesn't make any sense. Who put such an idiotic idea in your head?"

"Why, the current Marquess of Raynsforth, of course. May God have mercy on his soul," he muttered.

Nivea had never seen him like this. Dare never mentioned his father; it was obviously a sensitive subject for him. What had the man done to provoke such anger? Unsure of how to proceed, she stood behind him, waiting for Dare to explain. When he didn't, she couldn't help but probe further. "I don't understand. What did your father do?"

The sound of his bitter laugh shook her. "You do not want to know. With your close, loving little family, you would not understand. No one can."

The words stung her heart. As he stood there, the picture of a tortured soul, she couldn't help but wonder what exactly had happened. She had to know.

"Please. Tell me."

* * * *

He turned, strode to the nearest bench and sank down. The pain and rage churning inside were both fierce and unyielding.

He couldn't believe she'd caught him playing. He had been certain the house was empty. But no, she had to be the one to hear him. And now she stood there, asking for an explanation. Delving into his personal life. As though she could even begin to understand his shameful past.

Raising his head, he stared deeply into her eyes, willing her to back down. To go away. When she didn't move, he barked out, "Fine."

He didn't know what he was going to tell her, or even why. But at this moment, he found himself powerless to stop. Anger simmering in his voice, he asked, "What do you know of my family?"

"Not much," she admitted. "You have several sisters, but they are older than me, so I am not well acquainted." She didn't mention that they were considered rather horrible, but he could see the truth in her eyes.

She continued, her voice hesitant. "As you have spent most of your holidays with my family over the years, I imagine you are estranged."

"Estranged?" he choked out. "Hmm, yes, that is an innocuous word to use."

"But why? And what has that to do with the piano?"

He fixed her with a fierce stare, the muscle in his jaw jumping as he battled for composure. Could he really do this? Could he say it aloud? His throat convulsed at the thought.

Nivea sank down next to him on the bench. Without a word, she waited for him to continue. Not speaking to him, not looking at him. Just waiting. It appeared there was no way out. Why not just tell her? Shock her. Show her the world isn't the pretty little fairy tale she imagined.

Keeping his tone deliberately casual, he began. "I was the youngest of five, the only boy in a gaggle of girls. My mother was surprisingly involved and we all took our lessons together, learning to dance, paint, arrange flowers, and become accomplished musicians. Everything a young lady of gentle birth needs to be a successful wife."

"But…but, you were a boy. You can't have been expected to do everything your sisters did"

Dare sneered. "The fact that I was a boy did not affect my mother a whit. You would no doubt be amazed at my talent for embroidery."

"Oh, no,"—she stifled a giggle—"really?"

He nodded, closing his eyes at the embarrassment that welled inside him.

"How did your father feel about that?"

The question started his blood pounding. Unable to sit still, he leapt to his feet and began pacing. "Ah, there's the rub. My family's once vast estate had been decimated over the years by poor management and uncontrolled gambling. My father was determined to return our title and our fortune to its former glory. He learned of an opportunity in the New World and decided it would be the best way for him to earn untold riches without other nobility knowing he was getting his hands dirty, so to speak. He left for the West Indies when I was in swaddling clothes and rarely made an appearance." He hesitated.

"Go on," she urged.

Yes, go on. Why not share the most traumatic moments of his life with her? What harm could possibly come of that?

His heart was pounding in his throat, choking him. No, he couldn't do it.

Then he looked into her soft, pleading eyes, and the words tumbled out. "My father returned for good when I was seven. He had established a profitable empire in the islands and wanted to flaunt his success."

Resentment clogged his throat. "He had been a slave owner there. A cruel taskmaster, earning his money on the backs of his human chattel. You can imagine he was none too pleased to arrive home and find his son on the pianoforte serenading the neighbors."

Nivea's hands flew to her mouth as she realized what his reaction must have been.

"Yes. He was furious. The beatings began almost immediately. As the sounds of applause drifted through the hallway, my father ordered me outside. The first punch knocked me to the ground."

"What? He *hit* you? With his fist?"

Dare nodded.

"But you were just a child."

"Not a child…a son. His son. And he wanted me to be a man."

"Surely not by use of his fists!"

"Oh, I was to learn that was not his most painful weapon," he snarled.

"Please do not tell me." Her face had gone pale and she rose from the bench and tried to turn away.

"Oh, no. You wanted to hear." He swung her back to look at him, forcing her chin up with his fingertips. "He had a special treat for me in his bags. Luckily, he had not yet unpacked, because his fury was so great that day, I likely would not have survived. "

Fear and tears filled her eyes. He could tell she didn't want to ask, but was powerless to stop herself. "What was in his bags?"

He dropped his hand and stared off into the distance. Nivea chewed on her lip but remained silent. Even the wind had stilled, as though it, too, was waiting for him to answer.

Taking a deep steadying breath, he answered, "His whip."

Her eyes widened in horror. "His *whip*? Surely not."

Dare did not move.

"He did not whip you," she choked out. When he didn't answer she asked in a desperate tone, "Like a riding crop?"

"Oh, no, a full-length, corded rope." He extended his arms six feet apart before calmly continuing, "Everything I learned in the first seven years of my life was now a shameful embarrassment to my father. Every joy, every talent, every soft emotion displayed my inability to become a man. My father spent the next few years beating me into the type of son he wanted. And he succeeded. I am a man." He crossed his arms, daring her to disagree.

When she didn't respond, he added, "So, you see, my piano playing is not an option. I never play. For anyone."

Nivea crumpled onto the bench, her head bowed. He'd shocked her well and good. She didn't move until the sun ducked behind a cloud and she shivered, breaking the spell. Then she blurted out, "Didn't your mother help? Did she try and protect you?"

He snorted. "My mother? One could not ask for a worse ally. Angry at my father's abandonment for all those years and his attitude toward her childrearing abilities, she attempted to punish him…through me, of course. She would complain about how she missed me and wanted us to stay close. She would charm me into playing for her or helping in the garden. Invariably, my father would find out. The mandatory punishment would be followed by an arduous lesson in manly pursuits—broadswords, hunting, or boxing. Only gambling was excluded, as a disgraceful waste of money. That was how we lost our fortune."

Dare realized that was what stung the most. His mother, who he had loved and trusted, hadn't protected him. While his father's treatment of him was physically painful, at least he had a reason—he wanted Dare to become a man. Her attitude was selfish, caring about no one except herself. As difficult as that was to accept, it had taught him a valuable lesson. Women were not to be trusted.

And yet, he was here talking to a woman, spilling his secrets. It made no sense. He had no reason to trust her. He should leave before he made an even greater fool of himself.

But before he could get away, Nivea drew his attention once again. "You say you weren't allowed to gamble, yet I know you do. In fact, I've heard you are quite skilled."

He couldn't help but smirk. "Yes, that's true. I do take perverse delight in gambling."

A bitter smile crossed her lips. "I don't blame you."

Her response was unexpected.

"So," he growled, "you are not adverse to breaking the fifth commandment? Honor thy father? I am surprised at you."

Her eyes flashed a fiery blue. "He forfeited God's protection the first time he laid a whip on you."

"Interesting interpretation but I'm certain he would disagree. Still, it is no matter. I am no longer under his thumb and can do as I please."

A strong breeze loosened her hair and sent it tangling around her face. With a frown, she gathered it in a messy bundle and pinned it back into place. He hoped the matter was now closed, but when her hands stilled and her brow furrowed, he knew she wasn't done tormenting him.

"So, is that why William invited you to spend your holidays here? To protect you?"

Fury surged through him again. With one quick step, he leaned into her face and hissed, "Absolutely not! William knows nothing about this! Nobody does."

At her horrified expression, he straightened and stepped back. He would have to pull himself together. Forcing a smile, he said, "I was fortunate that William enjoyed my company. Whenever he offered me the option of joining him here, I took it. Gladly."

"But didn't your family want you home once you'd proven yourself a man grown? Wasn't your father impressed by who you had become?"

The question further sparked the anger that simmered, always.

"Proud? Proud of me?" he snarled. "No, that is not an emotion that has ever been expressed."

"I simply don't understand. You are smart and accomplished. William has repeatedly confessed he would not have gotten through Harrow without your help. What more did he want?"

"Nothing. He wanted nothing from me. He accomplished the task he'd set out to do and could move on. He turned his attention to a steady stream of mistresses, which he paraded in front of my mother."

"Oh, goodness. How did she tolerate that?"

His laugh was dark. "Her response was to hurl every valuable we owned at him. God, he hated that. He valued his possessions above all else."

For years, decades really, he had hidden this. Now, he was assailed by the memories of the hideous battles he'd witnessed on a regular basis. His parents couldn't be in the same room without violence erupting. One sister had almost lost an eye when a shard from a shattered vase sailed over the dinner table.

His legs weak, he lowered himself onto the bench.

There was no reason he should be sharing any of it with Nivea. All his suffering was in the past and would remain there. Eager to restore his composure, Dare flicked his wrist in dismissal. "As long as my father received good reports from the school, he had no interest in my activities. I was free to come and go as I wished. It will not surprise you that I wished to go.

Nivea rested her hand on his. "Oh, Dare, I'm so sorry. No one should suffer like that. I'm so glad you found solace here."

He was so stunned by her reaction, he didn't even remove his hand. He had been weak and worthless, never good enough to please his father. Knowing he was tainted, he'd erected a wall around himself and vowed to block out all emotion. No one would guess he was anything less than the image he'd perfected—the most arrogant and imperious, Lord Landis. Revealing his secret should have provoked scorn, not sympathy.

But chancing a glance in her direction, her clear blue eyes were filled with concern. Her thumb stroked his knuckles, shooting warmth up his arm. And a breeze stirred her hair, setting it to dance along her generous décolletage. One curl even had the temerity to dip inside the bodice of her cambric riding shirt.

It was quite a picture. A very sweet, desirable picture.

And it caused him to lose his mind.

Kiss her.

He was so startled by the thought, he leapt up from the bench.

Nivea's eyes flew open wide. "What's wrong?"

God in heaven she must think I'm a complete bedlamite.

Here, she had just pried his most shameful secrets from him and now he wanted to kiss her? Ha! She'd probably slap him for being a pathetic coward. Not to mention, the Horshams were the closet thing he had to a family. And she was William's sister. His sister! He had very little morality when it came to women, but he could never damage the friendship he had with William. Obviously, desire, interest, lust, or whatever crazy reaction he was experiencing must be squelched immediately.

He had to get away. Now.

Taking a deep breath, Dare summoned his most imperturbable expression. "Forgive me. I should not have burdened you with this. It was nothing. Ancient history. We need never speak of it again."

With that, he gave her a curt bow and strode back toward the house without a backward glance. By the time he made it to his room, he was in a fury. He slammed the door and pounded his fists on his head until it throbbed.

What, in Devil's name, was wrong with me? What was it about that woman that made me open up and bare my soul to her? Hell and damnation, I will never be able to show my face here again.

No doubt, Nivea was tracking down her brother right now, relishing the fact that she had gossip on the indomitable Lord Landis. This information was too delicious.

He groaned out loud. *Now, I'll have nowhere to go on blasted holidays… Good God, I can't even eat dinner here tonight.*

Letting out a growl, he decided to pack up and leave immediately.

He rang the bell for his manservant. Then he rang again. God's blood, where *was* he?

At that, a timid knock came at the door.

"Come in!" he bellowed.

An unfamiliar young man peered in the door.

"Where is Jackson?"

"Begging your lordship's pardon. Jackson is indisposed at the moment. Bad pudding, he claims, although Cook won't hear a word of it. May I send up someone else to assist you?"

Dare growled in frustration, causing the young man to take a step backward into the hallway. "No. I am fine. Never mind," he answered sharply.

"Yes, sir." The servant darted from the room.

Dare threw himself down on the bed and tried to determine how to make the best of this. He could claim he had a fever. He could accuse Nivea of having a fever. He could laugh it off as a joke. But he was fairly certain none of those would work. His thoughts grew more and more sluggish as his eyelids grew heavier. Before he could come to a suitable conclusion, he drifted into a deep, dreamless sleep.

* * * *

The sound of someone repeatedly clearing his throat brought Dare around. The darkness confused him, and he sat up in alarm.

"I am sorry, milord. It is time for dinner. Do you wish to join the Horshams downstairs? Or should I make your excuses?" Jackson stood near the bed, an anxious look on his face.

What time was it? Why was he lying on his bed with his boots on? Dare shook his head to clear away the cobwebs of sleep. Oh yes. He'd confessed his deepest darkest secrets to Nivea, and she had probably spent the better part of the afternoon regaling everyone in earshot with his embarrassing tale.

There was nothing to be done about it now. He would face his doom with all the grace and elegance he could muster. And arrogance. He could hide a world of sins with a mask of arrogance.

Chapter 14

Most everyone was already seated when Dare entered the dining room. Pasting on the sardonic sneer that had held him in good standing all these years, he walked to his seat with studied grace. Accepting the large platter of meat handed to him, he placed a small strip of venison on his plate, although the thought of food sickened him. Nervous about what he might find, he glanced to the head of the table. The earl and his wife were chatting with Nicholas's father. Next to them, William was excitedly discussing horses with Abby. And Nivea, damn her to hell, was talking to Briar.

Well, that was good. No one was remarking on his arrival. There were no scornful glances or goading insults. Apparently, Nivea hadn't had time to unveil his secrets. Yet.

But she was watching him. Their eyes met, briefly, and she gave him a hesitant smile. There was no look of triumph in her face. Still, a prickle of fear danced down his spine. It was only a matter of time before he became a laughingstock.

Focusing his attention on the plate in from of him, he gulped down some food, eager to escape and strategize his next move.

As soon as the meal was over, he darted for the door. Just steps away from the exit, he flinched when a gentle hand settled on his arm.

"Are you all right?"

It was Nivea, with her sweet, sympathetic eyes, probing, always probing into his life. Dare slid his patented sneer into place. "Of course. Why wouldn't I be?" He hoped his haughty expression would drive her away. It had in the past.

He stifled a groan when, instead, she continued, "I did not mean to upset you. Please accept my apology."

He stared down at her. *Surely, she must be mocking me.* He'd bared his soul to her and now she was the one to apologize? But, as always, her face was masked with concern. *She's good. Very good.* Who knew that William's sister was such an accomplished actress.

Struggling to keep all inflection out of his voice, he replied, "It is of no consequence. I haven't given it a moment's thought. Now, if you'll excuse me."

* * * *

Nivea wasn't fooled. How horrible that Dare had reverted to his usual harsh facade. He must be truly hurting now that she had opened old wounds. She wanted to help, but one look at his face, tight and forbidding, told her that sympathy would not be appreciated. He hadn't spoken with anyone at dinner. No witty repartee, no banter with his friends. What had she done?

Sleep did not come easily that night. Thoughts of Dare's painful childhood haunted her as snatches of memories flickered through her mind. Now, all his odd behavior made sense. His relentless control. His remoteness. And his utter disdain for marriage and family. How could he possibly imagine a contented home life after such a brutal upbringing?

As she tossed and turned in bed, the clock on her mantle chimed two. Then three. Still she could not reconcile he had suffered this pain all these years without anyone suspecting.

As she was finally dozing off, another memory emerged. She recalled Dare's fierce reaction several years ago when Joseph made the mistake of introducing him once as Lord Landis, Earl of Havenshire.

Dare had exploded. "Never refer to me as earl again! My father extends me no respect, and I refuse to accept so much as a courtesy title from him. Until his death, when I am saddled with the Raynsforth title, I answer to Lord Landis and nothing else." Then he had stormed away, leaving everyone staring in stunned silence. Joseph had made light of it, of course, but Dare had barely spoken to him for days afterward. Now Nivea was afraid of what his reaction would be to her.

She'd finally drifted off around four o'clock. As a result, instead of rising early as she'd hoped, she woke up well past breakfast. She raced downstairs, desperate to see him, yet having no idea what she would say once he did appear. How did you restart a conversation about such a traumatic event? Were there any words that would help?

In the end it didn't matter. Only her brother was in the dining room, enjoying a hearty plate of kippers and toast.

"Good morning, Nivvy, you're up later than normal," he greeted her, waving a fork in her direction.

She couldn't very well tell him why she'd had such a restless night, so she made up an excuse. "I think all the excitement over the last few days has caught up to me. I decided to take advantage of the quiet morning and stay in bed." Putting a few slices of toast on her plate, she joined him at the table. "Did I miss anything? Has anyone left this morning?" she asked, trying to sound nonchalant.

"No, the Abbingtons may head home later today, but you can still catch them before they go."

She tried to look interested, but feared she failed miserably. Fortunately, William did not notice anything amiss. It was blatantly obvious to her now how unobservant her brother really was. She could not imagine being friends with someone for over a decade and not having an inkling about his past.

Chapter 15

After spending the morning contemplating his options, Dare decided it was in his best interest to leave. He could not risk having all and sundry learn about his past.

He'd return to London where he would taunt some poor unfortunate sot into a fight. This would solve several problems. First, by exerting himself, he could work off some of his anger. And second, he could laugh off any rumors that arose, inferring that he was a pathetic weakling. Lord Whomever-Irritates-Me-First with the blackened eye and bruised ribs would no doubt attest that Dare wasn't buried in the country, confessing any embarrassing secrets.

Not to mention, if he was no longer around to remind Nivea of their discussion, perhaps some other event would catch her interest and she would put it out of her mind. Yes, that would work. He'd announce his departure at the lunch, charge back to town, beat the living daylights out of someone, and return to his normal routine.

It seemed like the perfect plan, only to be foiled by Nivea's stepmother a few minutes into the meal. "Lord Landis, I fear today will be a trial for you. The children have decided to host a sporting challenge this afternoon. We are all to pick sides and compete. I seriously doubt that sort of thing would interest you."

He graced her with a tip of the head, waiting to see where she was going with this.

"Perhaps you would like to spend the day on the lake. It is quite a bit cooler there and the solitude can be soothing."

While he agreed it would have been a more attractive alternative, he preferred to escape entirely. "My apologies, madam, I am planning to depart today."

"Oh! I thought you were to stay through the weekend."

"Yes, we were counting on you for another hunt this week," William exclaimed.

"Surely, you can tolerate us for a few more days."

He cringed at Amelia's cajoling tone. Wonderful. If he made an issue of it, he was certain to attract unwanted attention. Forcing a tight smile, Dare bowed his head in her direction. "I supposed I can rearrange my schedule."

"Splendid!" Then after a slight pause, she added, "Nivea does not take pleasure in sporting events either. Perhaps she can accompany you. She has always enjoyed the lake."

The look of surprise on Nivea's face no doubt mirrored his own, and convinced him that she did not have a hand in this arrangement.

Now he was exceedingly torn. Spend the day with rambunctious children or be trapped on a small craft with Nivea. Hell would be a more comfortable location. She would no doubt wish to continue yesterday's conversation. Could this day get any worse?

Trying to keep the frustration out of his voice, he responded. "That would be delightful. Nivea, are you interested in joining me?" He did not think she would refuse, but he'd at least give her the opportunity.

He discerned a blush as she lowered her eyes. "Yes, I will join you."

As the conversation turned to other matters, Dare considered how to best address the situation. If he dazzled her with his charm, perhaps she would forget yesterday's conversation. Or maybe he could pass it off as some twisted, ill-conceived joke. It was often noted that he had a warped and unpleasant sense of humor. Fitting, considering he found the world to be warped and unpleasant most of the time.

Attempting to put off the inevitable for as long as possible, Dare polished off not just one plate of food, but two. Once every speck was devoured, he wiped his mouth and stood. Holding out his arm to Nivea, he flashed his most irresistible smile. "When would you suggest we make our escape?" A small herd of children were, at that moment, racing across the front hall and out the door.

"I would imagine right now would be best. Otherwise, the little ones will try and wheedle us into joining them."

Shuddering at the thought, he quickly steered her to the right and they headed out the side door unnoticed.

As they reached the dock, one little girl came streaking down the hill screaming, "Don't you want to play cricket with us, Aunt Nivvy? It will be so much fun!"

Nivea smiled. "Sorry, Lizzie, but I promised Lord Landis a boat ride."

"I could come," she piped up.

Good God, no. He handed Nivea into the rowboat before casting off the rope and climbing in. Putting his back to her, he grabbed the oars and nudged them against the dock.

"Maybe next time, darling." Nivea waved goodbye as the boat glided away.

Little Lizzie stood there a moment, the picture of disappointment, before running back up the hill.

"Thank you," Nivea murmured behind him. "I love my family, but never really understood their love of sports."

Dare remained silent. Sports, he could understand; it was children that he abhorred.

It would be much more tolerable here. He took pleasure in the pull of the oars, the sun on his face, and the quiet of his companion. He just hoped she would remain so and allow him to enjoy the day.

That hope was quickly dashed.

"I do love being out on this lake." Nivea announced. "I remember when my mother died, I would drag William out here with me. Somehow, floating on the water under the giant open sky, she seemed closer, like she could look down and see me." Her voice trailed off.

Surprised, he glanced backward at her. This was not the direction he had expected the conversation to go.

She was leaning back, hands resting on the sides of the boat, staring up into the clouds. Her lips, red and plump, were curled in a sad smile. Her bonnet was pushed back, creating a halo of sunlight shimmering around her hair. And her gown, made of peach muslin, gave her cheeks an innocent flush of color.

That quick glimpse sent an unwanted jolt to his nether region. It was not unusual that gazing upon a woman would cause such a reaction, but he had not been able to figure out why Nivea was now causing it. He turned back, determined to keep his focus on the shoreline as it drifted from view.

They had traveled to the deepest part of the lake and were now gliding toward the wooded side when Dare decided to resolve the odious issue at hand.

Charm and surprise had always been helpful in gaining the upper hand. With that in mind, he drew the oars into the boat and removed his jacket, folding it meticulously onto the seat in front of him. Stretched his muscles. Pulled at the tips of each finger to remove first his left glove, then his right. And ran his fingers through his hair to re-secure his queue.

Certain he had her attention, he spun around. Noting Nivea's wide-eyed expression, lips shaped into an admiring O, he knew he'd succeeded. He chuckled inwardly. "It was warm. I hope you don't mind," he crooned.

Caught staring, she quickly shifted her gaze.

Now that he had her off guard, he would press the issue. Clearing his throat, he began, "Yesterday…I…"

She cut him off before he could finish his thought. "Do not worry, Lord Landis. Your story is safe. I shan't say a word. Unless you wish to talk more about it…"

"No," he barked. Embarrassed by his vehement tone, he repeated "no" more quietly. "I prefer never to speak of it again."

The matter settled to her satisfaction, Nivea closed her eyes, a serene smile on her face. Her thick lashes rested on cheeks warm and rosy from the sun. When she leaned back, the fabric of her dress pulled snugly over her bosom. A row of silver buttons ran between her breasts, creating delectable twin globes.

He couldn't take his eyes off her. His gaze ran from her neck, across to her short, capped sleeves, and over the creamy expanse of skin jutting from over the lace trimming of her bodice. His blood began to pound.

Dammit to hell, what was wrong with him? Here he was trying to ensure she did not destroy his reputation, and he couldn't think of anything but the blasted woman's breasts.

Unaware of the effect she was having, Nivea abruptly spoke up. "I was sitting here wondering how you and William become friends. I don't think he's ever mentioned it."

Dare sucked in a deep breath, hoping to clear his head. Unsure if she was mining for more information to help ruin him, or just being pleasant, he took his time responding. He studied her intently, but could sense no malice, no sly edge to her voice, no focused stare weighing every nuance of his response. Nothing. She was simply leaning back, idly watching the clouds overhead.

What could be the harm in answering? It happened as his life was starting to turn around. Blessedly, his father had agreed to send him away to school, convinced he would learn the discipline needed to make him a man. At Harrow School, the regulations were strict and the curriculum grueling, but Dare found it considerably better than being at home.

It seemed harmless enough to discuss.

"We met at school, of course. I had been at Harrow for a week when we were given time at the stables. My father had allowed me to bring one of our finest horses, Valiant, and I was thrilled with the opportunity to ride. He was a difficult horse, hot tempered and strong. I was quite certain there would be no horse his equal. Just as I had mounted him and turned him toward the field, a pudgy boy, dressed in ill fitting clothes, hair in disarray and boots covered in mud, entered the yard. I would have thought he was a stable hand if not for the obvious quality of his boots. Always careful of my horse, I proceeded from the yard with the utmost caution and headed toward the fields. Suddenly, a black streak went tearing past me. That rumpled, pathetic excuse of a boy was atop the finest piece of horseflesh I had ever seen. I whipped Valiant into a gallop to catch him and we have been friends ever since."

Nivea smiled. "That must have been Captain. He was a handsome horse. William raised him from a foal."

"Yes, he did. He told me. There is not a man in England who knows horses better. I consult him whenever I purchase a new mount."

"It is his passion. I don't understand it, but I can appreciate it. It filled a large hole when mother died. Father was so overcome, he spent virtually no time with us. William found solace in horses. He could always be found in the stables." Her lips curled up in a gentle smile, her eyes soft at the memory.

Dare could not help noting the sadness that hovered around her. Never very interested in delving in other people's emotions, he was surprised when he felt the need to probe further. "And you? What gave you solace?"

"Me?" she looked up, surprised. "I—I wrote."

"You wrote?" he repeated.

"Yes. Poetry. I would sit in my room, writing my thoughts, pouring out all the angst a young girl can generate."

"Did it help?" He leaned forward.

"I suppose it did—" She raised her eyes to his and blushed. From her cheeks to her hairline, she flushed crimson before returning her gaze to her lap.

How odd. What was that about?

Sounding more than a little flustered, she blurted out, "Do you write?"

"What? Like poetry? God, no." Dare sat back and tipped his face toward the sun. "I leave that to the pathetic pups who moon around ladies' drawing rooms."

"Ah yes, no need for that. You merely have to walk in a room to gain a woman's attention," she retorted with a grin.

He quirked a quick smile. "True."

They both laughed and then slipped into a companionable silence, enjoying the rocking of the boat.

Out of nowhere, he announced, "I like numbers," surprising both himself and her.

He wasn't sure why he felt the sudden need to share, perhaps because he didn't want the conversation to lag.

"Numbers," Nivea repeated, waiting for him to continue.

"Yes," he responded, trying to find the right way to explain. "Words can be twisted...but numbers are solid. Real. And they come surprisingly easy to me. I have built a sizable portfolio with very little effort. Frankly, I don't understand why others can't. Even gambling is easy if you watch the cards and play the odds."

"I wish I had that talent. I can barely play a hand of whist without losing count of the tricks."

"Well, if it's any consolation, William isn't much better. I have had to save his skin a number of times when he got in over his head."

Nivea stared at him. "Really? I thought he was quite adept at gambling."

"God, no. Horse racing, yes, but put him at a card table and he's hopeless."

She appeared amused to learn of her brother's shortcoming. "I had no idea. I shall have to tease him about that."

At her tone, something shifted inside him. A knowledge that her teasing would be lighthearted, not at all spiteful. Not like his own family.

He responded in kind. "Oh, please don't mention it. It is quite a shameful secret, and we wouldn't want to betray any of those would we?" His kept his expression bland, but didn't disguise the hint of self-mockery.

He must have caught her off guard. Her brows hovered between amusement and disbelief as she puzzled through his response. Once she decided he was joking, her lips twisted into a wry grin. She opened her mouth, as though preparing to speak, but it turned into a gasp. "Oh, no! We've sprung a leak."

She pointed down. Water was pooling at her feet, covering the bottom of the boat. Dare sprang into action. He spun around, intending to paddle back to the dock before realizing they had drifted closer to the opposite side of the lake. Grabbing onto the oars, he headed toward the woods instead. Once they reached the shallow water, Dare climbed out of the boat and pulled it onto the rocky shore.

Chapter 16

"We shall have to walk home from here. I hope you don't mind," Dare said, taking Nivea's hand and helping her from the boat.

"No, I don't mind." Quite the contrary, she was barely able to suppress the joy that bubbled inside her. Dare had rolled up his sleeves, her hand resting on his muscled forearm, sending tingles through her palm. She was near enough to him that she could luxuriate in his irresistible scent. Unlike her family, who always smelled of horse and leather, Dare emanated a clean, manly aroma all his own. She longed to wrap her arms around him and bury her nose into his deliciously firm chest.

When he had taken his jacket off in the boat, it had taken all her will not to reach out and run her hands over his broad shoulders and muscled arms. Truly, he was the most perfectly-formed man on earth. She had forced her attention elsewhere, hoping he wouldn't detect the desire that flashed through her. But now, touching him, she once again felt the familiar flush of warmth.

It brought to mind some of the more scandalous poems she had composed. Recalling her tributes to his gleaming black hair, his beautiful form, his full, sensual lips, an involuntary shiver ran through her.

"Are you all right?" He looked down at her with concern.

Going hot with embarrassment, she dropped her eyes to the ground. "I—erm—yes, well—" Seizing on the first thing she could think of, she blurted, "This terrain is rough on my feet. I fear my shoes were not designed for tramping over stones."

"My apologies. I forgot ladies' slippers are so delicate. Let us move up into the woods where the ground will be softer." He curved his arm around her waist and guided her away from the shoreline.

While it was infinitely better on her feet, his intimate touch didn't help her regain her equilibrium. Having him so close was exquisite, but had a disastrous effect on her pulse.

For better or worse, once they reached the trees, he once again tucked his hand in the crook of his arm, allowing her to breathe again.

It was delightful, walking with him in such a manner. She could almost pretend they were lovers out for a stroll, rather than accident-prone travelers, struggling once again to get home.

They followed an overgrown path that skirted the lake. The surface was softer, but the path was a difficult one and they were forced to climb over roots and branches. Nivea was breathless and her feet sore.

Looking around for a place to rest, she spotted a familiar structure. "Oh, look, it's our old hunter's cabin. Remember when we used to play Rescue the Princess there?"

His brows furrowed. "Do you mean Knights and Soldiers?"

That made her laugh. "Yes, Knights and Soldiers." As she'd suspected, their childhood game had a completely different objective in his mind. She wanted to be saved by a handsome prince, and he just wanted to wage swordfights.

Eager for an excuse to spend more time with him, she asked, "Would you mind if we stop there for a moment? My feet are quite uncomfortable."

"Whatever you wish." He led her to the cabin and opened the door. Inside, utilitarian furniture was scattered around the room. The cabin had been unoccupied for years, and all that remained were a few tables and chairs and a narrow bed, all covered in a fine layer of dust.

"Wait here," Dare commanded. He strode over to the bed and yanked off the counterpane. Using the fabric, he dusted a nearby chair before tossing it on the floor. Then he came back to the door where Nivea was leaning against the frame. She gasped when he lifted her in his arms and carried her over to the bed. The muscles in his shoulders felt safe and powerful under her hands as she wrapped them around his neck. And his smell…it was nothing short of divine. Sadly, the bed was only a few short steps away.

As he placed her gently on the mattress, she flushed, overcome with both excitement and embarrassment.

"Comfortable?"

Breathless, she could do little but nod.

"Good." He drew the chair next to the bed and sat down. Unsure what to say, Nivea peeled off her left slipper and waved it at him before rubbing her tender foot. "These are totally useless for walking. Men have it so much easier with their sturdy boots."

"Ah yes, but they are designed so we can't get them on and off without the help of a valet. Who dictated that dressing oneself should be a team activity? I have my boots specially made to allow me to disrobe in private when I feel the need."

With the tantalizing image of him disrobing etched in her mind, Nivea swallowed hard and released her foot.

"Here, let me." He reached over to take her right foot in his hand, slid off the second slipper with the other, and let it drop to the floor. With warm, strong fingers, he started to slowly stroke the sole of her foot. She leaned back and sighed as he drew circles around the balls of her foot, pulling on the toes, cupping her heel, soothing away the pain.

"I'm beginning to think we should stop traveling together," Dare mused. "We seem to run into an unusual number of problems."

Her heart was beating so rapidly, Nivea was barely able to choke out a response. "Perhaps we should limit ourselves to walking. Very few accidents can occur that way."

"Walking? Oh, that can be most dangerous. You could turn an ankle…" He gave her foot a teasing twist. "Or we could be set upon by footpads. Or caught in a downpour and catch a killing cold."

"True." She tried to mirror his lighthearted tone, despite the turmoil his touch was causing. "It is no doubt safer for us to stay where we are and pray the roof doesn't collapse."

He looked up in mock horror. "I will keep a keen ear out for the sound of creaking timber and rush you to safety in such an event."

"Thank you, sir. You are too kind."

They were quiet for a moment, while Nivea savored the delicious sensations running up her leg. It was quite the most pleasurable feeling she'd ever experienced. Once again, he was her hero. She wondered if he even remembered the first time. Pulling herself up onto her elbows, she said, "You know, we shared another boating incident."

His brow wrinkled. "Did we?"

"Yes." She flopped back onto the bed. "You had just arrived for a summer visit. William and I were out on the lake when the wind kicked up with alarming force. Realizing it was going to storm, William did his best to row into shore, but the water had gotten very choppy. He lost his grip on an oar and it slid into the water. Reaching for it, he lost his balance and fell out of the boat. He must have hit his head and knocked himself out." She took a breath before confessing, "I thought he'd been killed."

Dare nodded. "Oh, yes, I do remember. I heard you screaming as soon as I arrived and ran down to the lake to see what was the matter. You were waving at me so frantically, I thought you were going to capsize."

Pulling herself back onto her elbows, she couldn't quell the fear in her voice. "I was in such a panic. I couldn't get William back in the boat and, with only one oar, I couldn't get us to shore. I grabbed his arms to keep him above water, but was unable to pull him in without overturning the boat. When I saw you running down the hill, I was so relieved."

She could still picture Dare, athletic and commanding, bounding out to the dock to assess the situation.

"You whipped off your coat and boots and dove right in. The waves were so rough, but you cut through them as though it were a calm summer day. I was so thankful when you reached us."

"Yet you refused to let go of William. Kept yelling at me that he would drown."

She laughed. "That's right. You barked at me to stop screaming and yanked him out of my grasp. I watched helplessly as you dragged him to shore and started pushing on his chest. But he wasn't moving. He wasn't waking up."

The memory still upset her. She felt her stomach clench remembering the fear that had coursed through her.

"It only took a few moments for him to recover."

"That's true. But by then the waves had blown me even farther away from shore. I confess. I was worried you'd leave me out there."

Dare rubbed her calf as though soothing a scared kitten. "Oh, come Nivea, I wouldn't have done that."

She smiled ruefully. "No. I suppose not. As soon as he was able to sit up, you dove back in to get me. I was never so happy when you reached the boat and pulled me to shore. You were my hero."

Refusing to look at her he said, "I'm certain it wasn't that impressive. Frankly, I'd forgotten all about it. I remember now that William was so embarrassed, he kept begging me not to tell anyone what happened. I guess I never did."

Nivea hadn't forgotten. Dare had saved her brother's life. From that day forward, she had loved him. Totally, endlessly, and irrevocably.

And now, they were alone together in this cabin, where they had played Rescue the Princess. And he had saved her once again. But this time was different. He was sitting next to her, massaging her with his strong, firm fingers. His touch was making her flushed and warm. She would have liked to close her eyes and enjoy the sensation, but she was afraid he would think she was bored and decide to leave.

So she kept up the conversation, sharing stories and even making him laugh on occasion.

Her heart felt as though it would burst the first time he laughed, tossing back his head and letting out a deep chuckle. With his soft hair waving around his face, the harsh planes of his face relaxed, she caught a glimpse of him she rarely saw. The sneer, the arrogance, the bored expression was completely absent.

If he looked handsome in the ballroom, it was nothing compared to this relaxed, heart-stoppingly beautiful man in front of her.

Nivea wracked her brain for interesting stories. She was in the middle of one when she felt his hand glide up to her knee. She smothered a gasp. Fortunately, she did not yank her leg away in surprise, because the sensation was too delicious. Trying to remain calm, she continued her story.

A moment later, he leaned forward in his chair and his hands drifted up, up, up toward her thigh. This time she did gasp. This was beyond inappropriate. She should put a stop to it right now.

Rubbing her sore feet was one thing, but this was…yes, it was definitely a caress. And they were alone…in a cabin…and she was on a bed. And he was rubbing her…Ohhh! Now, that was a sensitive spot at the back of her leg.

"Did that tickle? I'm sorry. Is this better?" Instead of removing his hands, he simply increased the pressure.

Watching him from beneath her lashes, she expected to see the seductive smirk she'd witnessed a hundred times as he lured in his willing prey. But no. Instead, his face appeared…peaceful. There was no other word for it. His eyes were calm and unfocused, his full lips curled into a tender smile. Dust motes were floating through the patches of sunlight like fairy dust, and he sat there like a handsome prince, caught in a spell.

Her breath caught and she stopped talking all together.

She watched him as he focused his attention on her legs, rubbing her newly formed muscles. They had been sore from her horseback riding, and the massage was soothing. She had hoped to stutter out a few more words of her story, but realized coherent thought was beyond her.

Dare did not notice her distress, and in a soft, beguiling voice began recounting a story about William when they were boys. She remembered William writing her about it at the time and she enjoyed hearing it from Dare's perspective. Not that she was really able to listen. Her brain had turned to mush.

Still, his hands continued their ascent. They pushed up her gown to mid thigh and were touching her soft inner legs. A strange pulsing began, and she closed her eyes, giving in to the pleasure. There was no sound now, except the rustling of the leaves outside.

Merciful heavens, this felt good. Sinful and decadent, but delightful beyond words.

She bit back a whimper when he removed his hands from her thigh, but then he picked up her hand and continued his massage. He rubbed each finger...the palm...her wrist and a slow path up her forearm. Her skin was tingling and her breathing ragged. She was certain he could hear her heartbeat, it was hammering so hard.

But no, he still sat there, lost in a peaceful daze, seemingly unaware of what he was doing. He reached for her other hand and repeated the pattern—fingers, palm, wrist, and forearm, and then continued up to her shoulder, rubbing her skin in slow sensual circles.

Never looking at her face, never saying a word. It was as though he were in a trance.

He reached as high as he could on her arm before the sleeves of her dress impeded his path. Undeterred, he trailed a finger over to her neckline. He drew a delicate swirl over her collarbone and down to her bodice.

This was completely improper. Yes, she'd loved him forever and wanted him to notice her, but she never expected he would touch her like this. Nor did she imagine just how glorious it would feel. Oh yes, this was wholly inappropriate, but she refused to interrupt this magical moment.

He remained in an almost dreamlike state, trailing his finger back and forth on her exposed skin, his full lips curved in the slightest of smiles. She'd seen him in countless situations over the years and never witnessed this expression before. She closed her eyes, vowing to let him continue as long as he liked. After all, he was William's best friend...a gentleman. And she was Nivea...a respectable over-the-hill spinster who did not inspire lust or attraction in any man. She could not be in any real danger, could she?

Then he murmured, almost to himself, "You are so soft. I did not think you would be so soft. Not that I thought about it much at all, but it is truly remarkable...softer than any other woman I know."

He ran his fingers down to the top button on her pale pink bodice.

And popped it open.

She stopped breathing. No, she must have imagined it.

Then another button popped open.

Her eyes flew wide. No. This was not possible.

He was not... Oops, there went another one.

While her brain struggled to respond, her body rebelled. Her hand did not fly up and grab his. Her mouth did not form the words, "no" or "stop." All she was able to do was lay there, eyes wide open, watching him begin to push the fabric aside, exposing her thin white chemise. And slowly, carefully, oh so delicately, he lowered his hand to her breast.

That got her breathing started with a sharp gasp. He looked up at the sound, his eyes black and unfocused. He smiled at her, bemused.

"You are so lush and pale. It's quite intoxicating." And he returned his attention to her breast.

Her skin was on fire, tingling from this new sensation. She watched in fascination as he leaned closer, closer, closer to her, dipping his head until his lips touched her breast. She jerked in surprise.

"Shh," he whispered, sliding next to her and resting his hands on her shoulders. "Shh, I won't hurt you."

All rational thought flew from her brain as he lowered his head and kissed her hardened tip. First one side, then the other. His hands kneaded her breasts as he nuzzled the skin through the fabric.

"I just want to taste it. I'll bet you taste like fresh cream. I have to know," he said, his voice tight and strained. His fingers untied the ribbon of her chemise and pulled it apart. Her white flesh was now exposed, topped with two hard red buds. He sighed and lowered his head again.

The feeling was exquisite. Her heart was beating so fast and strong, she was afraid it would come out of her chest. Her breathing was labored, and now she could hear his breath, too, coming more rapidly. His hands started to explore her body, roving up and down her waist, arms, and hips. She squirmed, wanting more, but unsure what *more* meant.

But he knew. He knew exactly what she wanted. He pulled her dress up higher on her legs and palmed her thighs with a groan.

"I never expected you to feel so good...to taste so delicious," he whispered.

Unable to resist, Nivea raised her hands and ran her fingers through his hair. It was as soft and silky as she'd imagined. She pressed his head to her, refusing to let him go.

He moaned again and nudged her over, stretching out next to her on the bed. His warm, masculine scent enveloped her. He was so hot, it seemed to scorch her skin.

As his hands continued to roam, he began to thrust against her. She could feel a large ridge pressing against her hip. Having been raised with horses, she was well aware what that appendage meant. She froze.

Oh, God. This had gone too far. He was actually in need of her. That could not be. She had to put a stop to this. Her hands stilled and she was going to push him away when he slid his fingers up under her dress and touched her, *there.*

Her hips twitched, and he gave a low chuckle. "Shh," he repeated. "Don't worry. I won't hurt you. I'll just—" He again moved his finger over the center of her being.

The feeling was exquisite. She could not have him stop no matter what happened. He rubbed again. Harder.

Then he drew little circles around the area, his thumb caressing her. She could feel a strange, wet warmth growing as he increased the pressure. She was panting now.

Then he slid a finger inside her and she moaned.

"Yes, that's it. Don't be shy. Let me know that you like this."

He lowered his head to her breast again and licked her nipple as his hand increased the pressure between her thighs. She wrapped her arms around his head and pressed it to her, knowing that whatever he was doing, she never wanted him to stop.

Ever.

She was pulsing, convulsing, trembling with need. And then a firestorm flashed through her and she screamed. Not a squeak of surprise, but a full, enthusiastic scream. She clutched him to her like a drowning woman. The feeling was overwhelming and awe inspiring. Only when the shudders of excitement had stopped did she loosen her grip.

Once she did, Dare slid up her body and kissed her. His full, warm, soft lips pressed against hers and her heart nearly exploded with joy. He kept his hand between her thighs and continued the delicious tickling sensation, while kissing her lips, her cheeks. He moved to her earlobe and nipped it gently.

"I am so stiff, I cannot stop. I must—I—." He kissed her hard and sat up. When he removed his hands, she gave a little sob of protest. He smiled and bent down to kiss her again.

Then he yanked off one boot, and it fell to the floor.

Then the other.

She watched with equal parts horror and fascination as he drew off his breeches. This could not be happening. She could not let him do this! But before she could utter a sound, he lay down beside her and replaced his hand on her curls. He brought his head to her chest and licked her nipple until she could not breathe. She felt his weight shift and then he was lying over her, nudging her legs apart.

"I'm sorry. I must. I shouldn't, and I may never forgive myself for this, but I must. Please forgive me," he gasped.

He rubbed his hand faster and faster over her mound before lowering himself down. She felt something hard, pressing against her sensitive skin, pushing forward, inward, an uncomfortable stretching and then a moment of harsh pain. She stiffened as reality permeated her brain.

He had done it. Dare had taken her maidenhead.

How could she have let this happen?

She lay there in horror, unsure what to do. Then he shifted his weight and his hand returned, rubbing and teasing her.

The haze of desire returned and she gasped for air. She could almost inhale his warmth, his beauty, his masculine power, and she sighed with delight.

"That's it. Concentrate on the pleasure. It won't hurt again." He nuzzled into her ear.

He began sliding in and out, in and out, causing her discomfort at first, but it quickly dissipated. Then he increased the pace, rubbing his finger faster in time with the stroking, in and out. In and out. Harder and more urgent with each thrust. As the pleasure built, she thrust back, increasing the pressure, the friction, the incredible building sensation.

"Yes. That's right. Oh, yes," he groaned and lowered his lips to hers. His tongue forced its way into her mouth and he swirled it around hers. She was surrounded by him, inside and out. He tasted wonderful. She was so overwhelmed by the sensations, she couldn't breathe. He kissed a path across her cheek, down her neck, and paused for the briefest of moments at her breast. Then with a deep, thrilling groan, he flicked his tongue over her swollen, aching nipple, and she exploded once again. Barely aware of what was happening, he drove into her with fierce precision before emitting a loud shout. He pulled out of her sending a warm burst of wetness against her leg.

They lay there for a moment, without saying a word. Until Dare rolled away from her and groaned. "Oh, my God. What have I done?"

Embarrassment flashed through her like fire. There was no moment of tenderness. No words of endearment. Just heartbreak.

Now that it was over, he was consumed with remorse. Of course. How could he have sunk so low as to sleep with her? She was a cow—a dowdy toad. He didn't even think her suitable to be a vicar's wife. What had she been thinking?

Dare moaned again and sat up. Reaching around, he grabbed the counterpane on the floor and dropped it on her, refusing to meet her eyes.

"Here, you can clean yourself up with this." He dropped his head in his hands and ran his fingers through his hair. Then he yanked on his breeches and drew on his boots.

"That was inexcusable. I—I'm so embarrassed. I...have no words," he said, his voice strained.

Nivea swallowed hard in agony. Only seconds ago, her life was like a slice of heaven. Now, she was in hell, never to recover. He was embarrassed to have touched her. She would never be able to face him again. As though *he* would ever want to face *her*.

She pulled down her dress and pushed him away so she could rise. Her legs were as shaky as a newborn colt's. He took her elbow to steady her and she snatched it away.

"I must go," she choked out, hoping to make it to the door before the tears of humiliation started.

As she ran out the door, she heard him moan once again, "Oh, God, what have I done?" before laughing darkly.

* * * *

A few guests waved hello to him as Dare entered the hall, but his blackened expression drove away any attempt at conversation. He headed straight to his room and collapsed on his bed, unmoving.

His boots were still on. He leaned over once, then a second time, intending to remove them. They were dirty and scuffed and would not do at all.

But then he would picture his boots on the floor of the cottage, right before he had stretched out on the bed. He remembered the soft, seductive sounds Nivea made as he touched her. Imagined the warm, delicate skin under his fingers, running over her legs, her breast, and face. He had been with more women than he could remember, and no one had felt like her. Or made him feel like he had with her. She was so soft and womanly, and he had lost all control.

But why? Why Nivea? What had possessed him?

She made him warm. *Inside*. Sitting with her on the boat had brought him the most unusual sense of serenity. And when they were together in the cabin, talking, and she relaxed under his touch, he couldn't help reaching higher and higher. He hadn't even noticed that he was crossing a line until he was so mesmerized by her, he hadn't been able to stop.

My God, maybe I am no better than my father. Maybe worse. While the marquess would flaunt his mistresses in front of his mother, at least they were women of a certain sort. He had never trifled with an innocent.

But Dare had. With Nivea, of all women. His best friend's sister. How could he?

A week ago, he wouldn't have considered it. But now, it was not so preposterous. Her skin was so soft. Smooth. She did not drown herself in scents, and yet she smelled enchanting. Like vanilla. It was delicious. For the first time in decades, she made him feel...he wasn't even sure how. Safe?

It had taken him a lifetime to become impenetrable. It was the only way to avoid pain and betrayal. But when his boots dropped to the floor of that dusty old cottage, and he lay down next to Nivea, something happened. He felt...worthy. Vulnerable, even. It felt nice.

Suppose when he removed his boots, he lost that feeling? That serenity.

He snorted. God's blood, what was wrong with him? He was the infamous Lord Landis. He took his pleasure whenever and wherever he chose. He didn't need Nivea to make him whole. That was ridiculous.

In fact, he was being ridiculous.

Determined to regain some sort of equilibrium, he sprang off the bed and headed out onto the grounds to join the others, still wearing his boots.

Chapter 17

"Broken"

A touch, caress,
a kiss, the heat.
His mouth, my skin, the warmth.
As senses tingle, words elude,
he casts a spell that
I am loathe to break.

Up my ankle, calf,
and knee, his fingers slide
oh so deliberately.
A familiar path for him
but new to me.
All new to me.

The fire, the heat, and up it went
until the word
I know I must yell out,
the simple word, to stop it all
was in my brain
but not across my lips.
"Oh, no, stop, no."

I wanted more
from him, just him.
Don't stop, your lips, your touch, your skin
on mine.
Oh God, don't stop

the heat, the thrill, don't stop.
Oh no, not that.
Don't stop, oh Yes!

There are no words
from me, no words, the joy too great.
But him,
from him, just words of pain.

"Oh God. What have I done?"

Hidden in the deep recesses of Nivea's wardrobe was a hatbox,
containing seemingly random items—a gold button from a man's
waistcoat, a soft, black velvet ribbon used to tie back a handful of equally
soft, black hair, a ladies glove that once rested on a broad masculine
shoulder during a dance that, just for a moment, elicited a smile from his
full seductive lips. Nivea carefully went through the items, before adding
the hastily scribbled poem, pouring out her agony of the afternoon.
Folding it time and time again, to appear as small and inconspicuous as
possible, she tucked it into a playbill from the first show she had ever
attended, escorted by her brother and his devastatingly handsome friend,
Lord Landis. Then she slammed the wardrobe shut and threw herself onto
her bed, sobbing like a child.

Finally, he had noticed me.

That was all she had ever wanted. He'd taken virtually every other
woman in London to bed except her. But now that he had, what had she
gained? His final words kept ringing in her head. *My God, what have I
done?* No loving whispers, no promises, just an outburst of horror. As
though the very thought of touching her disgusted him.

She dropped her head into her hands. How unfair that the most magical
experience of her life could turn into a horrifying embarrassment, in
the blink of an eye. Or to be more accurate, in the utterance of a single
sentence.

How could she have been so stupid? So gullible? She had lost the
man she loved and now she was ruined. How could she pledge herself to
another man? He would expect her to be untouched.

But she had been touched. And it was wonderful. But not for him.
Dear God, she would never be able to face him again.

Her best hope was that he would return to London. Then she could remain at Vincent Hall for the rest of the summer, and put this whole degrading experience behind her.

* * * *

Despite her best intentions, every time she turned around the next two days, Dare was there. She had tried to sneak out to the stable to ride, and he had come walking up the path. She arrived late to lunch, only to find him filling his plate at the buffet. When she had entered the study with Amelia to plan the next evening's entertainment, he had been there, playing chess with William. Still disgusted with her, he would quickly excuse himself.

After each episode, she had to fight back the fiery blush of embarrassment. The final time, when he swept past her without a word, she must have gone pale, because Amelia laid a gentle hand on her shoulder, asking, "Has something happened, dear? Lord Landis looked rather angry when he left."

"No," she stuttered, "nothing happened. It appears we just won't suit. I'm sorry all your efforts were wasted."

"Don't be silly, darling. They weren't wasted. I enjoyed spending time with you." Amelia gave her a hug. "At any rate, we have the musicale tomorrow. We'll invite Sir Morrell and a few other more amenable gentlemen. No doubt you will charm them all."

Nivea tried to smile, but was certain the result was unconvincing.

Chapter 18

The musicale began well. There wasn't much talent to draw from, but the guests were eager to participate. Briar and Joseph played a melodious duet on the piano. Betsy borrowed a recorder from the nursery and played a Scottish jig. William and the earl encouraged everyone to join them in a rousing hunting song.

Next, it was Nivea's turn. She was not all that comfortable performing, but Amelia had convinced her to sing, while she accompanied her on the piano. She made it through without butchering the song too badly and the crowd gave her a supportive cheer.

She was still standing at the front of the room, when the earl asked, "Would anyone else like to entertain us?"

There was a pause and then a women's voice rang out. "Lord Landis, I've heard you are a talented pianist. Why don't you play us something?"

Nivea's eyes flew to Dare. He'd gone rigid, before turning toward Elizabeth Wilshire. The woman was pure evil. Her smirk made Nivea's blood run cold. How could she know that? To his credit, Dare assumed his most bored expression and responded, "Sorry, my dear, but you are mistaken. I don't play."

She tossed her head, setting her curls bouncing. "That's not what I've heard. I understand that you are quite an accomplished musician. You used to love to entertain your family."

Nivea's heart sank as Dare turned to her with unmitigated fury. Her legs threatened to give out, and she slumped against the piano. Dear God, he thought she let out his secret.

Pulling himself together, Dare pulled out his snuffbox, took a pinch, and ground out the words, "Again, I insist that you are mistaken. I do not now, nor have I ever played an instrument."

Luckily, William came to his rescue. "Elizabeth, I have known Adair for more than fifteen years and I have never heard him play a single note.

If he had any talent at all, you can be assured he would use it mercilessly to attract members of the fairer sex."

* * * *

Everyone chuckled and the tense moment passed. After the next song, Dare excused himself and stormed into the hallway.

He was hardly able to contain himself. His body pulsed with rage. So, Nivea decided to take out her revenge by spilling his secrets to the *ton*. How stupid could he have been, giving her this ammunition? He could be furious with Elizabeth, but while she was the one swinging the blade, Nivea had handed her the weapon.

She was no different than any other woman. True, he'd tumbled her once, and that was inexcusable. But that did not mean she had the right to betray his confidences.

He darted into the study and poured himself four fingers of William's finest brandy. Tipping his head back, he gulped down half the glass, savoring the burn.

He should have expected it. After all, the wench had practically been stalking him these last two days. Everywhere he went, she would appear. Was she hoping he'd seduce her again? Or more laughably, was she looking to become his wife? God's blood, she was the antithesis of what he expected in a wife. She would need to be beautiful, elegant, sophisticated, cultured, and, to fit in with his family, cruel. Only on that score, would she be perfect.

Still, her duplicity had taken him by surprise. What else had she confided to her friends?

Hell, he didn't even think Nivea and Elizabeth *were* friends. She must be telling everyone his shameful history— how weak and pathetic he was to have let his father whip him like a dog. How he was afraid to go home. It was beyond infuriating.

Realizing that a mere glass of alcohol would not have the desired effect, he grabbed the bottle and headed up to his room. Maybe there he could drink enough to convince himself this was all a bad dream.

He had just stripped off his jacket and collapsed into his chair when he heard a faint knock on his door.

"Dare? It is Nivea. Can we talk?"

She was not to be believed. Hadn't she done enough damage already? Did she really think he would *ever* speak with her again?

"Dare? Please. I need to see you. Please let me in."

He wouldn't dignify her with a response—the treacherous, two-faced charlatan.

"Lord Landis, I need to…"

"No!" he bellowed.

Surely she would take the hint. But instead, he heard her shuffling around on the other side of the door. Ah, so she required a direct confrontation. He hauled himself out of the chair, stormed over, and threw open the door. She stood there, frozen, with her hand raised in mid-knock.

"Still here?" he barked. Not wanting to create a public spectacle, he grabbed her arm and dragged her into his room.

The look he gave her was so ferocious, she took a step back. *Good.*

"Let me make myself clear. After tonight, I will not speak to you again. I do not know why you felt the need to discuss my past with others, but I can promise you this. If you do it again, you will be eternally sorry. I will see to it that you are shunned by every family in the *ton*. You are not to speak *to* me or speak *of* me *ever.*"

Nivea stood there shaking. "Dare, I did not. I swear. I would not have told that to anyone, little yet Lady Wilshire."

"I suppose she just guessed? Is that what you expect me to believe?"

"No, I mean—I don't know!"

He put his face in hers and hissed, "I do not believe you."

She stood there without another word, her eyes wide and dilated, her breaths gasping through parted lips. The need to punish her was overwhelming. He could not remember being more angry at another human being. Or disappointed in himself. After all, he had brought this on with his ridiculous confession.

Furious, he grabbed her and slammed his lips on hers.

The searing kiss was designed to intimidate her. And it did.

Not done, he pushed her up against the door and wrapped his arms around her.

"Were you angry because I shunned you? Were you hoping for more?" he growled. "Is this what you want?"

His lips began a trail down her jaw and neck, where he nipped at her throat. "You're just like all the others. Selfish and petty, stopping at nothing to show your displeasure. I should have known better than to trust you."

But as he continued, desire coursed through him. When he dug his fingers into her arms, continuing to nibble her neck, she gave a low moan of pleasure.

She was enjoying it. Well, so was he. Her scent was intoxicating. Unable to resist, he pressed his growing desire against her leg. When she tried to pull away, he tightened his grip. "Oh no. You'll not escape me. I plan to show you exactly what happens when someone toys with me. You will pay."

* * * *

She wanted to fight him. She wanted to stop this madness and convince him she wasn't the one who had told Elizabeth. But she couldn't. She was powerless to resist. While his words were ugly, they were whispered in a lover's tone that excited rather than scared her. So, when he brought his hand up to her breast and squeezed, she did not stop him. Instead, she leaned into him, yearning for his touch. Then he brushed his thumb over her peak and her knees buckled.

"Oh yes, you like that?" he taunted. "You may like this more. Maybe it will help you hold your tongue." He lowered his head to her other breast and suckled.

It was sweet agony. She wrapped her arms around his shoulders just to remain upright.

"Feeling unsteady are you? Perhaps you should lie down." He gathered her in his arms and with three long strides dropped her onto his bed. Shucking off his jacket, he covered her with his long, lean body and reclaimed her breasts with his hands and mouth. Quivering with sudden need, she rubbed against him.

"Yes, that's it," he coaxed.

She whimpered when he removed his hand.

"Don't worry, I'm not done." He moved his hand to her legs and pushed up her skirts. His touch was hot and made her ache grow, sending warmth throughout her body. It was reprehensible, but she prayed that he would once again touch her between her legs.

As if reading her mind, he worked his fingers slowly up and pressed them against her undergarments. Even through the fabric, the sensation was magical.

"Oh, yes. Right there." She dug her fingers into his back to hold him in place. Instead, he jerked away.

"Perhaps this will help." He flipped up her skirts and slid her pantaloons down, tossing them on the floor. Before she could register a protest, he'd unbuttoned his breeches and pressed his bare legs against hers. The coarse hair scratched against her thighs, unusual and intimidating, yet not unpleasant. In fact, it was exciting. She had just begun to adjust to the feel when Dare drove a finger inside her. She bucked her hips off the bed.

"Oh, are you are ready for me so soon? Who would have thought shy, dowdy Nivea would be capable of such passions," he murmured.

She should have been shocked. Or insulted. Or embarrassed. But his fingers were pressing against her delicate skin, circling, probing, shooting sparks to her very core.

How could he reduce her to a wanton being with just his hand? She was teetering on the edge, desperate for release. Then Dare shifted without warning and thrust into her.

God in heaven, the feeling was exquisite. There was no pain this time, just a blinding flash of bliss. She felt as though she were drowning, unable to take a breath. Showing no mercy, Dare continued his onslaught, roughly kneading her breasts. His hands were everywhere. She was so weak from desire she could do little more than grab at his shirt, feeling the solid muscle of his arms as he drove into her again and again.

When she thought she could stand no more, he raked his teeth down her neck and nipped at the sensitive peak of her breast. *Yes, yes!* Waves of pleasure crashed over her. She buried her face into his neck to stop from screaming. He thrust a few more times before emitting a loud groan. She was still quivering when he collapsed on top of her, shooting his seed up her thigh.

She was enveloped by his scent, his weight, his heat. It was glorious. Then he rolled to her side and cool air chilled her skin. Instinctively, she leaned into him for warmth, but he raised his arm to cover his face. Saying nothing. Blocking her out.

As the fog of pleasure dissipated, reality returned. How could she have allowed this to happen? She had hoped to convince him of her innocence, but instead she let him seduce her again. And to what end? He was still furious with her. How could she make him understand?

"Dare?" she whispered.

She reached over and placed a hand on his chest. Feeling his heart hammering under her palm, she knew he couldn't be as unaffected as he appeared. Maybe she could reach him. Maybe he would understand.

He flinched as though she'd branded him. "Go," he growled through clenched teeth.

"Dare, please listen—"

"Go, now!" and rolled to his side, facing the far wall.

Humiliated, Nivea rolled off the bed. Her legs were so shaky, she could hardly stand. Pain gripped her heart and squeezed through her chest. There was no hiding from the truth—all her dreams, all her illusions were dead.

With tears in her eyes, she grabbed at her undergarments, tugged her clothing into place and fixed her hair as best she could. All the while, Dare didn't move. He hated her. After all he had been through, he thought she too betrayed him and there was nothing she could say to convince him otherwise.

She walked to the door and paused.

"I'm sorry," she whispered, without knowing exactly what she was apologizing for, and crept out of the room.

Chapter 19

The next day, Emma was flitting about the room, eagerly sharing gossip about the evening's events. Nivea couldn't bear to be around her. Feeling the worst sort of fool, she needed some place to hide. Knowing few people would venture into the library, she headed there and closed the door.

The room was warm, but there was a light breeze coming through the open windows. Crossing to the sitting area in the corner, she curled up into a worn, comfortable chair and tried to sort out the last few days.

She loved Dare. She knew it was irrational, but that was the truth. She knew her family and friends didn't understand her lifelong devotion to a man who rarely paid her any mind at all. But it wasn't as though she'd had a line of suitors vying to woo her.

More importantly, they didn't appreciate his finer points. He'd been a devoted friend to William for *years*. He'd saved his life, for goodness sake.

To her, he had appeared to be the perfect man—handsome, strong, and controlled—confident of his place in the world. She had always envied him that.

Now, she realized it was all an act. He had no control or confidence. His father's abuse had caused an anger and resentment so deep, he would never be able to trust her or anyone.

She wanted to help him heal, but he would never let that happen. He hated her, thinking she, too, had betrayed him. That was why he was acting so cold. To punish her.

The worst thing was, she now craved him more. The things he did to her, the way he made her feel—it was unimaginable. Even thinking about it made her flush. She could almost smell his scent on her. Feel his hands running over her skin, his fingers stroking her throbbing core. And his lips…now she knew why women were always twittering about his lips.

They trailed fire down her skin. How could she live without ever feeling his touch again?

She would have to. He thought she betrayed him. He would never forgive her. Never forget. They would never be together.

She closed her eyes in defeat. Tired from a restless night sleep, despair swirling through her head, it didn't take long for the warmth of the room to lull her to sleep.

* * * *

Nivea awoke to the sound of women's voices. They were settling on the terrace right outside the window, chattering like magpies. Their topic of conversation brought Nivea fully alert.

"Did you see how angry Lord Landis became last night at the musicale? I thought he was going to burst into flames. La, that was amusing."

That was Elizabeth Wilshire's catty voice. Nivea would recognize it anywhere.

"So, is it true? Can he play piano?"

"Oh yes, but he considers it some shameful secret."

"How do you know about it, Elizabeth?"

Nivea held her breath waiting to hear the response.

"His sister, Anne, told me. She was so mad that Dare dallied with her friend, she wrote and asked me to extract some revenge. She informed me that he had been quite proud of his talent as a child. But her father found it embarrassing and tormented him until he gave it up. Anne said he would be mortified if people knew he played," Elizabeth gloated.

"It most certainly worked. Did you see how quickly he left? How embarrassing for him. Adair Landis, the great rakehell of London, is afraid to play the piano," snickered another voice.

"Well, *I* don't care if he's afraid of his own shadow. I would still be eager to invite him to my bed," giggled another female. The others murmured their agreement and they moved on to other subjects.

Nivea sat there, hot with anger. She did not expect any better from Elizabeth, who had always been a mean-spirited shrew. But how could Dare's sister betray such a confidence? His family was insufferable.

Sickened by their behavior, Nivea spent the better part of the afternoon trying to figure out a way to break the truth to Dare. She was still upset about the way he had treated her, condemning her without any proof. But how could he think otherwise? His parents had both betrayed him, and now his sister. How could he ever have faith in people?

Restless, she went to the window, hoping a cooling breeze might clear her head. She leaned out the casement and sighed.

A hawk glided overhead, lazily floating on the still air above. No other movement was visible. The guests must all be in their rooms, resting up for the evening activities. She decided to do the same when a figure strode across the yard.

It was Dare, heading for the stables. His hair sleek and black in the sun, appearing almost wicked, as did the stark, forbidding planes of his face. Even at a distance, she marveled at how handsome he appeared.

She had to set things to right. She had to make him understand.

As soon as he had ridden away, she ran out to the stable. Finding the groom, she asked him to remain out of sight when Dare returned. Then she headed back to the house and waited.

For the next hour, she paced and fidgeted in her room. She fussed with her gown, pinned and re-pinned her hair and doodled at her desk, stopping every five minutes to peer out the window. Finally, she saw Dare charging across the field back toward the house.

Rushing down the back stairs, she raced outside, arriving just in time to hear him yelling for the stable hand. Then he yelled again when no one appeared. Uttering a string of curses, he leapt down and led the horse into the stable himself.

She heard a stall door slam. Around the corner, the groom peeked out and waved at her. She mouthed the words "thank you," and he returned to the rear of the stable.

This was it. This was her one chance to make things better. If only she could get him to understand. Her heart hammering, she took a deep breath and crept over to the stall where Dare kept his horse.

He had removed his jacket and flung it over the side of the stall. His shirt, loosened from his tight breeches, clung to his broad shoulders. Judging by the horse's lathered coat, they must have had a hard run. It snorted emphatically as Dare began to brush him.

Cautiously, Nivea opened the stall's door and cleared her throat. Dare whirled around, glowered at her, and promptly returned his attention to his horse.

Dear Lord, this was harder than she expected. Her insides were twisted in knots.

"I need to speak with you," she said, trying to sound firm.

"You have nothing I care to hear."

She could see the angry set of his jaw as he continued to tend to his horse but refused to let it deter her. "Regardless, I will have my say."

He stilled, but did not look at her. "Fine. Talk away. You'll excuse me if I do not respond. I have no doubt anything I say will be thrown back in my face."

That stung. The pain in his voice was almost too much to bear. But at least she knew she had his attention.

Squaring her shoulders, she said as calmly as she could, "I know you think I betrayed your confidence. That is not true. No matter what you think of me, I would never hurt you so."

He snorted. "Am I to assume that Elizabeth just guessed that I play the piano?"

"No," Nivea whispered.

"So, you admit you told her?" he growled over his shoulder.

"No, it was not I."

He stormed over, stopping inches away, and bellowed, "Who then? Who? After years of hiding my disgrace, one person finds out. One person! And then suddenly my secret is guessed by a virtual stranger? Is that what you expect me to believe?"

Anger radiating off him. His breath was hot, intimidating, on her face. But she couldn't back away. Not yet.

Locking eyes with him, she said, "No, she didn't guess. And I didn't tell her."

He slammed down the curry brush. "Then who did?"

"I—I—." Nivea did not want to admit his sister's role, knowing it would cause him more pain.

"That's what I thought." He tried to brush past her. "It's hard to feign innocence for your betrayal after apologizing for it."

"What do you mean?"

"As you left my room, I heard you. You apologized."

She shook her head, confused. "I did no such thing. I—I—"

Then she remembered. "I said I was sorry…not for betraying your confidence, but because I was sorry to see you hurt."

He took a step toward her and looked her dead in the eye. "But *you* didn't betray me? So, tell me, Miss Horsham. Who. Did?"

Knowing she had no choice, she breathed one word. "Anne."

He rolled his eyes at her. "Anne who?"

"Your sister."

He stopped. Some of the fire seemed to go out of him.

Closing his eyes, he exhaled deeply. "Explain yourself."

"This morning, I overheard Elizabeth say she received a correspondence from your sister. She'd been angry with you—something about dallying with a friend of hers. She asked Elizabeth to extract some revenge for her. She told her how you played piano, and that your father…disapproved. If she asked you to play, it was sure to upset you."

Expressions flitted across his handsome face. Anguish, anger, and shame all took a turn as the words sunk in. She wanted to embrace him and soothe away his pain, but he looked so forbidding, she didn't dare move.

After a moment, he composed his features, stood up tall, and faced her. "It appears I misjudged you. Please accept my apology."

Nivea felt a small flicker of hope. "So, you believe me?"

"Do I believe that you can be trusted? No. That will never happen. But do I believe that my sister would reveal my darkest secrets to an outsider just to punish me for a deed that had no bearing on her whatsoever? Yes."

Nivea breathed a heavy sigh. That was not the reaction she had hoped for, but at least it was a start. Maybe she could make this right. If only she could find the words.

"I'll have you know I find it outrageous how your family treats you. No one should be made to suffer as you do."

Unimpressed, he bent down to grab the feed bucket, placing it in front of his horse. "My family is of no consequence. Do not let them concern you."

"But—"

"No buts." He grabbed her wrist. "This does not concern you. Forget everything I've said. I do not want it mentioned again."

Pain was evident in his eyes. He tried to hide it behind anger, but it was there, along with a hint of fear. The poor man was terrified his indomitable facade would be torn away.

She covered his hand with hers. "Dare, you can trust me. I give you my word that I will never disclose details of your youth."

* * * *

He let out a snort. Trust. What a ridiculous concept. He trusted no one. Opening his mouth to tell her so, he stopped, startled.

Nivea stood there, eyes wide and earnest, brow creased with concern. God's blood, he could almost believe her. So, instead of a flippant retort, he responded, civilly, "Thank you. I would appreciate that."

At his response, Nivea's expression transformed—her blue eyes darkened with pleasure and a smile, wide and soft, lit up her face.

His breath caught in his chest. She really was an engaging thing. Not a beauty in the classic sense…her features too soft, her shape too curvy, and her hair pulled back in a careless style *no* one would emulate. But her unaffected air made him feel…comfortable. Almost as though he *could* trust her.

It was an amazing sensation. Before he had time to assimilate his feelings, she surprised him again. His horse curved his neck toward Nivea and nudged her hand. Instead of drawing away, she turned to pet his muzzle. "Hello there, handsome," she cooed, "did you have a nice run today?"

He stared in disbelief. "What is this? I thought you hated horses."

She giggled as she stroked the horse's neck. "I have come to learn they are not the horrifying beasts I had thought. They are actually quite sweet. I will never be the horsewoman my sister is, but I am learning."

Dare remember the greeting they received upon their arrival. "That must be quite a pleasant surprise for your father."

"Oh, I have not told him yet. I…"—she paused and lowered her voice—"I have been riding in secret every day since we arrived. Once I am fully comfortable, I will make my 'debut,' as it were."

He raised an eyebrow. "Really? You have been practicing alone, just to please your father?"

"Yes," she replied with a hint of embarrassment. "For once, I would like to truly feel like a Horsham."

That statement hit Dare like a blow.

He was a heel. A total, inexcusable cad. The girl did not have a mean bone in her body. She wanted nothing more than to fit in with her family, not even realizing how much they already loved and accepted her.

And how had he treated her?

He'd taken her innocence, accused her of betrayal and, when she tried to make amends, he'd assaulted her in his room. He had abused her abominably. Guilt washed over him, clogging his throat and sending a jab of pain through his chest. He had to make amends. As if it were possible.

Deciding to extend an olive branch of sorts, he cleared his throat. "Perhaps I could help you become more proficient," he offered. "If you would like, I could accompany you on your ride tomorrow."

Joy lit up her face. "Would you?"

"I would be honored," he said with a bow.

"That would be lovely. Do you promise to keep my secret?"

She was teasing him. After all he'd done to her, she bore him no ill will. No matter what happened, she remained cheerful, guileless. It wasn't an act—she was truly a nice woman.

He felt a strange lightness in his chest, like a knot bound too tight, loosened.

He'd been so upset, thinking he'd trusted her and she'd played him falsely. Learning it was his sister who stirred up such mischief was not only expected, it was comforting. He would deal with her later. For now, he would try to make amends to Nivea. She deserved no less.

He smiled at her. Not the forced, insincere ballroom smile he usually gave, but one that bubbled up from his chest. "Of course, I will keep your secret." Taking her arm, he breathed in a deep, satisfying breath and escorted her out of the stable.

* * * *

Now that he knew who was responsible for embarrassing him at the musicale, Dare decided to extract some revenge. That evening, while the guests were socializing in the parlor, he drew Nivea aside.

"Would you agree to a favor?" he asked.

"Certainly," she responded, with a hint of hesitation. "What do you need?"

"Pretend I have offended you and act outraged at my behavior."

"What? Why?"

"I have a score to settle."

Turning toward the rear of the room, his eyes settled on Elizabeth Wilshire. Anger flared as he watched her casually flirting with an enamored young whelp. He'd settled on a plan that would make her think twice about toying with people's emotions.

Nivea must have guessed who his target was as she wasted no time embracing the ruse. Planting her hands on her hips, she snapped, "Fine. I'm sure if you simply act like yourself, I'll find some reason to take exception."

The contempt in her voice was disturbingly convincing. His surprise must have been evident as she attacked him again.

"That's right, you have not always been the most pleasant of escorts, you know. Your charm is offset by your scorn, set downs, and insults. It is amazing anyone would socialize with you."

Unable to help himself, he glared down at her.

"See, just that expression. I have done nothing to merit such a look, yet it has skewered me on more than one occasion. In fact, I don't know why I even waste my time talking with you, sir." Her shrill tone reverberated around the room. "I have done nothing to you and yet you continue to treat me as a nuisance. I will stand for it no longer!" Then she twirled on her heel and stormed away. As she reached the door, she turned back, gave him a saucy wink and she was gone.

Well, that was unexpectedly well done. Dare's heart was pounding, and he felt as though he *had* insulted her.

Realizing all eyes were upon him, he gathered his wits, and went along with the charade. Smirking at the closest gentleman and bestowing a glare on the remainder of the room, he pulled out his snuffbox. While taking a pinch, he spotted his quarry over near the window. Lady Wilshire shot him a smug expression. He quirked his lips into an arrogant smile and approached.

She brought up her fan to shield her smile. "It appears you are not as irresistible as you imagined, Lord Landis."

He sneered at the door where Nivea had made her escape. "'Tis a pity certain women don't appreciate a well-intentioned bit of advice."

Elizabeth fanned herself, slanting a knowing look at him. "Then perhaps you should limit your attention to the women who appreciate your…intentions."

He forced a husky laugh and pressed closer, nudging her into the folds of the thick drapes, obscuring their view from the room.

"I admit you were very appreciative," he purred, reaching up to caress her neck.

She flashed him a wicked smile. When he leaned in closer, she tilted her head and her eyelashes fluttered down, anticipating a kiss. Perfect, he thought. With a quick tug, he removed both her ear bobs.

Elizabeth let out a screech that Dare covered with a loud well-timed cough. Gazing into her furious eyes, he leaned forward and growled, "What I would appreciate, my dear Lady Wilshire, is for you to discontinue any and all correspondence with my sister. And if I ever suspect you of spreading evil gossip about me and my personal family relationships, you will suffer devastating consequences, I can assure you."

He waved her ruby earrings at her and then slid them into his trousers pocket.

"Although your husband is not a doting spouse, I have no doubt he would be quite distressed to learn you had left his grandmother's jewels in my quarters, following a night of debauchery. I have several acquaintances that would be happy to share personal details of the evening, right down to the distinctive mole on your left thigh."

She narrowed her eyes and hissed at him.

"That's right, your respectability would be quite tarnished with a tale such as that."

"I need those back. He is sure to notice if I don't wear his blasted jewels."

He tapped his finger to his lips, thinking. "When the time comes that I believe you won't cause any mischief, I will return them. Until then"—he patted his pocket twice—"they will remain safe with me." With a wink, he sauntered off.

Well aware he may have stirred up a dangerous hornet's nest, he decided to reinforce his warning. Stopping to get two glasses of port from the sideboard, he went to Lord Wilshire.

"Sir, you appear a bit parched. Care to join me in a drink?"

George gave him a bemused look, but was more than happy to take the drink. They clinked glasses and Dare launched into a conversation about the upcoming hunt. As they chatted, he feigned amusement at one of Lord Wilshire's comments and patted him heartily on his back.

That should keep the nasty shrew squirming.

Chapter 20

Greek statues could have been carved from that man. Nivea sighed as Dare approached the stable the next morning. His black hair gleamed in the morning sun, his perfectly-tailored forest-green riding coat emphasized his broad shoulders. And his legs? The muscles, straining against the soft fabric of his tight fawn breeches, inspired all sorts of wicked thoughts.

"Good morning, Miss Horsham," he called out, flashing her a brilliant smile. "Are you ready to ride today?"

Ready? She had barely been able to think of anything else since he'd invited her.

"Yes. It is kind of you to accompany me." Not to mention, thrilling and nerve-wracking. She was so jittery, she wasn't sure how she would manage to climb on her horse. Fortunately, with the help of the groom, she was able to haul herself up with a moderate level of grace and join Dare, who was already astride his enormous black stallion.

"You have made some improvements," Dare remarked as they headed off toward the trees. "You still have a long way to go to be considered a true Horsham, but at least I no longer fear you will plummet off the back of your trusty steed."

She laughed, patting her horse affectionately on the neck. "Thank you. She is more of a plodding puddinghead than a trusty steed, but we suit each other well."

As they entered the woods, Nivea pointed to a nearby boulder. "This is where I have been practicing my dismounts. Buttercup was quite disgruntled at first, but I think I'm learning the way of it now."

"Maybe I can be of some assistance," Dare offered. He pulled his horse to a stop and swung himself to the ground with the grace of a dancer. She stifled a sigh of pleasure as he stopped a mere arm's length away and flashed her a roguish smile.

"I will steady Buttercup," he stated, rolling his eyes at her name, "while you adjust your weight to one foot. Then shift your, ah, lower half toward me and I will help you down."

She wanted to trust him, but her skin pricked with nerves at the thought. Other women drifted daintily down into their escort's arms. But all she could picture was plummeting like a stone and knocking them both to the ground, breaking an ankle or rendering one of them unconscious.

Unaware of the perilous situation he was putting himself in, Dare stood there with his arms raised. It took her a moment, but determination won over fear. Taking a deep breath, she followed his instructions and slid out of the saddle. Remarkably, he grabbed her around the waist and lowered her to her feet unscathed.

Nervous tension heightened her senses, and his touch sent an immediate spark of desire through her. His hands lingered on her hips, his fingers burning through to her skin, tormenting her. Dropping his hands, he pinned her with deep onyx eyes and a lazy grin. Then he leaned in and whispered in her ear, "Well done...for a novice."

It sounded...well, it almost seemed like he was flirting with her. It was hypnotic, rooting her to the spot. Memories of him touching her, caressing her, flashed through her mind and set her heart pounding.

As if he were reading her mind, he leaned in again and purred, "Now we can practice mounting, if you'd like."

Nivea took a step back and shook her head in disbelief.

Dare laughed. "The horse, my dear. Practice mounting your horse." And he gave her a wink.

He *was* flirting with her. What had she done to deserve this sudden change in attitude? It sent a delightful buzzing through her brain, and she almost missed what he was saying. "Riding sidesaddle is a little trickier to master than sitting astride. But once you put your foot in the strap and reach up to the saddle, you give a little hop, and I will lift you up and into position."

"You will lift...wait! What?" She jerked back to reality.

He looked at her, eyebrows raised. "You will push up and I will lift you into the saddle."

She balked. "Oh, no. Certainly not. Shouldn't we use the stone to help, at least for the first few times?"

"No need. We'll manage."

She wasn't sure which was wreaking more havoc on her nerves, having Dare so near, or the thought of him throwing her up onto a horse. He must have seen her tremble, for he placed a hand on her shoulder and said, "Come now. You'll be fine."

His dark, entrancing eyes bored into her, lending her strength. Wishing to make him proud, she took a deep breath and nodded. She raised her foot to the stirrup. He placed his firm hands around her waist and yelled, "Jump!"

She gave a little hop and he heaved her up, twisting her squarely into the saddle. She grabbed the sides to steady herself and then looked down in stunned delight. "I did it!" she crowed.

He quirked a brow at her and she laughed.

"All right. *We* did it. Oh, thank you ever so much!"

"My pleasure," he answered with a bow. "Now come, we will try it again until you are comfortable."

It was unbelievable. She'd mounted a horse. Why had she ever thought it to be difficult?

Beaming, she gave Buttercup a pat before shifting her weight forward out of the saddle. Dare reached up and she glided into his arms. As soon as her feet touched the ground, she spun back toward the horse and raised her leg. She couldn't believe she had been able to scale a horse so easily.

"Ready?" Dare grabbed her waist. When she nodded, he lifted her up into the saddle, this time exerting far less effort.

Throwing back her head, she laughed with joy. "I cannot wait to show Popa. For years, he and William tried to convince me I could do this without a mounting block. But I refused to consider it. I just *knew* I'd flail about so much it would spook the horse, who would go rocketing off, most likely dragging me to my death."

Shaking her head in amazement, she sighed. "Oh, Dare, this is simply wonderful."

His smile bespoke amused tolerance. "Come now, let's try it again to make sure you've mastered it." He reached up his arms and she slid into them. This time, when she reached the ground, he didn't let go. His eyes darkened and he lowered his lips to hers. Enthralled, she threw her arms around his neck and eagerly returned the kiss.

"Thank you," she whispered when he raised his head.

"For what? The kiss or the lesson?" he rumbled.

She smiled. "Both."

At that, an odd look crossed his face. To her disappointment, he stopped and took a step back. "I think we should continue our lessons."

Hmm. Frankly, she would rather continue with the kissing, but it appeared he was no longer interested. Had she done something wrong?

With a sigh, she let him return her to the saddle and they headed up the path.

After a few moments, Dare asked, "Do you think you could prod Buttercup into a trot?"

Surely, he was joking. This slow easy gait was quite enough for her; she couldn't imagine bouncing around any faster on the beast. "Oh, I don't know about that. I think we are happy to walk."

"Come now. There's a bit of a clearing up ahead. We can safely pick up some speed without threat of injury. I promise not to press you past your level of comfort." He must have noticed the fear in her eyes, because his look grew soft. "Look, here's the meadow. We'll just nudge them a little until we reach the other side."

He was serious. *Just nudge them.* And not expect them to go tearing across the countryside in an unbridled panic? How was that even possible? Trying to sound reasonable, she squeaked out, "What if I can't get her to stop?"

"There's nothing to it. When you're ready, pull back on the reins a little. She'll probably turn to a walk herself as she gets near the woods on the other side." Still sensing her hesitancy, he pressed her ultimate weakness. "Your father would be so proud to see you trotting up the path...."

That was unfair. But effective. "Fine. But stay close, just in case," she agreed.

With a nod, he steered his horse closer. "Take a steady grasp of the reins and give her a light tap with your heel. It will feel a little bouncy at first, but you'll settle into a rhythm in no time."

She found that highly doubtful, but did as he said. It took two or three taps to convince Buttercup to speed forward. It was quite jarring, in fact, and Nivea almost bit her tongue on the first few strides. But, by the time she was halfway across the field, she was able to brace herself to counteract the motion. As he'd promised, Dare kept his stallion close enough to grab hold if she started to slide off. As they neared the woods, he called out, "Now, very slowly begin to pull back on the reins. Just light pressure, don't tug at her mouth."

Like magic, her horse slowed down and reverted to a walk.

"That's it. Now give her a pat. I'm sure that was as surprising for her as it was for you."

His smile was genuine and it made her giddy with pleasure. This was one of the best days of her life—and it was occurring while riding a horse. Remarkable.

"Are you ready for a bit more of a ride? We can go to the ruins and then head back."

She nodded, eager for more adventure. The ruins had been one of her favorite spots as a child. It was nothing but a tumble of stones from an ancient abbey with vines crisscrossed through the remaining walls, weaving a perfect hideaway for children. She would love to see it again.

They entered the cooling forest, surrounded by thick green foliage and a happy chorus of birds. The sound of the horse hooves was muffled by the dirt trail they followed. A few moments into the trees, they approached a stream and stopped to give their horses a drink.

Nivea was delighted to see small blue flowers dotting the bank. "Oh look, forget-me-nots! My favorite flower." She bent down to touch their petals. Dare strolled over to stand beside her.

"Forget-me-nots. Truly? Not roses or lilies or some other exotic bloom?"

As she straightened, she took in the tantalizing fit of his breeches, the finely tied cravat, the wry twist of his lips.

Sigh.

Hoping to hide the blush that now warmed her cheeks, she returned her focus to the flowers. "Oh, no. Forget-me-nots are so delicate and unpretentious. Roses are beautiful, but far too much work. I prefer the simplicity of wildflowers."

Dare shook his head. "You are an unusual woman, Miss Horsham."

She lifted her eyebrows, unsure whether to take that as a compliment or not.

He raised his hands in defense. "I beg you, take no offense. In a society such as ours, unusual can be an appealing quality."

It took all her willpower not to snort. "I have not found it to be a particularly attractive trait."

"I have been called many things—unusual is one of the more complimentary."

"Well, of course. You are a man with unnaturally good looks, a title, and deep pockets. Being dissimilar is no detraction."

With an indolent grace, he leaned against a tree, crossed his arms and flashed her a seductive smile. "So, I have unnaturally good looks, do I?"

She rolled her eyes at him. "As though you need me to tell you that. Most notorious rake in all of London, most sought after prize at every soirée, it's no wonder you are as arrogant as a king."

Realizing how rude that sounded, she blushed in embarrassment. She should apologize. Risking a glance at him, she feared he would be glowering at her. He was indeed staring, but instead of anger, a mocking smile curled his tantalizing full lips. That was unexpected. She was more surprised when he pushed himself away from the tree and strutted toward her, his polished boots crunching on the undergrowth. Upon reaching her, he clicked his heels, sketched a bow and drawled, "I confess, I am all that and more."

She laughed. He was magnificent. His posture was languid, his eyes soft, and his mouth tantalizing. Unable to tear her eyes from his face, she got the distinct impression he was going to kiss her once again. Really, this day was proving to be far too delicious. There must be fairies in the woods, sprinkling a magical spell over her. There was no other explanation for his behavior. Her pulse fluttered as his gaze swept over her.

Then he straightened, uttered an appallingly colorful curse and stormed away, stopping at the edge of the clearing.

What just happened? What did she do that could have upset him so? Before she could build up the nerve to ask, he turned and took two large strides toward her. His jaw set, his dark eyes glared at her.

She held her ground, convinced he was going to yell at her, yet baffled as to why. Consequently, she was quite unprepared by his response.

"Miss Horsham, I beg your forgiveness. I have been subjecting you to grievously ill behavior this entire visit. I can offer no excuse. You are a lady of gentle birth and the sister of my truest friend, and for me to have abused you so horrendously these past few days is beyond the pale."

His gaze rose above her head, and he rocked back and forth on his heels as he sought to continue. "I may be a disreputable rake, but I do try to maintain the code of conduct befitting a peer. God knows, I have violated that, and you, on several occasions."

He gave her a searching look before raising his hands in a gesture of defeat. "I had vowed to come out today and make amends. To treat you as a gentlewoman. Yet, for some inexplicable reason, I am unable to maintain any level of decency with you. I find myself going out of my way to bring a smile to your lips or a blush to your cheeks. You are not the sort of woman I should dally with, and yet it is all I can think of at the moment."

He began to raise his hand as though intending to touch her cheek. But then his face hardened and he snapped his arm back down to his side. "But I will stop. Rest assured, from this moment on, I *will* behave as a gentleman. You deserve no less. Can you find it in your heart to forgive me?"

She stood there shocked into silence. Adair Landis was *apologizing* to her? True, his behavior had been abhorrent and she should...wait, had she heard him correctly?

The world seemed to freeze in time. There was no breeze, no sound, just Dare, the handsome, arrogant man of her dreams, who admitted that *she* was all he could think about. Her heart soared with joy and she couldn't help breaking into a smile. "Yes, of course I forgive you."

Their eyes locked and she felt the sizzle of attraction flash between them. Then his face went taut and a muscle jumped in his jaw. "Good," was all he said, before turning crisply on his heel and heading toward his horse. "Then let's put this behind us and continue our ride."

He wasn't going to get away from her that easily. Reveling in her newfound power, she called out, "Ah, Lord Landis?"

Dare stiffened, waiting for her to continue.

"Can you help me up onto my horse?" she asked, smothering another smile.

He stalked back and held out his arms. Facing the horse, she grinned as he wrapped his hands around her waist and hoisted her up. She was giddy with delight. True, he had said he was going to act the perfect gentleman, but as he hadn't found the fortitude to control himself today, she imagined he would once again lose control.

Since she was already ruined, what harm could there be in another few indiscretions before he came to his senses and she returned to being plain old Nivea?

Chapter 21

Nivea nudged her horse forward, eager to catch up with Dare as he progressed down the trail. Buttercup was slow to get moving, but had almost closed the gap when a shot rang out.

Horrified, Nivea saw Dare jerk upright and then slump forward. She screamed and leapt off her horse. As she approached, he grimaced but managed to rasp out, "You have made amazing progress dismounting."

Too stunned to give any response, she grabbed his horse as it pranced about in alarm and tried to soothe the beast. Dare gingerly reached down to rub its neck and murmur a few sounds until it settled down. Then he lowered himself from the horse and collapsed on the ground.

Nivea sunk to his side. "What just happened?" she squeaked.

Dare's face was pale. "I think I've been shot." He reached his right hand into his jacket and pressed it to his side. As he withdrew his arm, blood coated his palm.

Nivea looked about in panic. "Good heavens, why would anyone shoot you?"

He shrugged before closing his eyes. "I don't think it's bad, just grazed me," he ground out from clenched teeth.

Pressing a hand to her throat, she could feel her heart racing. "What should I do? Do you want me to bandage you up or go get help?"

He stretched out his legs, shifting uncomfortably. "I'm fine. Just give me a moment." He reached his hand back into his shirt and pressed on the wound. It was obvious he was in a lot of pain. She had to do something. "Here, take your coat off and let me see."

He shook his head.

"I need to see how bad it is."

"No!" His face hardened and his eyes blazed black.

Well, he was being ridiculous. His flare of anger did nothing to dissuade her. She was terrified for him and would do whatever was required to make certain he was all right.

Sucking up her courage, she leaned over and put her face nose to nose with his. "Listen to me. You will take off your jacket, and you will let me examine your wound. Or I will leave you here to rot."

He must have realized arguing would be futile, for he reached up to slide the jacket from his injured side. Seeing him wince, she helped ease it off his shoulders and crouched beside him. Giving him a tight smile, she peeled his hand away from his side. There was blood staining the side of his snowy white shirt below his silver embroidered waistcoat. Not a lot, but enough to make her feel a bit queasy. She sucked in a breath and said, "Now we'll remove your shirt."

* * * *

"No!" he barked, slamming his hand back to his side. The burst of pain was so severe he almost blacked out. He clenched his jaw, trying to regain his breath, before opening his eyes again. Her expression was so fierce, he didn't bother to fight. He wanted to. After all, he knew this was the end. All his subterfuge…all his deception would be lost. The final humiliation was upon him. It was infuriating, but he could see no resolution.

"Fine," he snapped and began tugging off his cravat. Stumbling to his feet, he slid off his waistcoat and attempted to remove his shirt. His shaky fingers fumbled with the buttons until Nivea brushed him away. She made quick work of it and stood back as he tugged it from his breeches. With a deep exhale, he slowly lifted off his shirt, bracing himself for her reaction.

It took a moment longer than he expected since Nivea's attention was first focused on his wound. "This isn't too bad," she assessed, her fingers probing the spot. "Just a graze really. When we get home, I'll have cook make up a poultice for you."

To Dare, it burned like fire every time she touched it, but he submitted to her inspection without making a sound.

It wasn't until she straightened up that she gasped. He closed his eyes, clenching his jaw, dreading what was to come.

"Dare! Heaven above what—? How—?" Her voice dropped to a whisper. "Your father?"

He swallowed, forcing down the lump in his throat. Steeling himself, he opened his eyes. With a defiant tone, he spat out, "Yes."

Her fingers brushed over the scars that crisscrossed his back. Some were faint licks that had barely broken the skin. Others remained an angry red, where the lash had cut deep into his flesh and ripped muscle. The majority centered between his shoulder blades, but a few trailed over his right shoulder and down his waist.

There. His shame was complete. He had managed to hide them all these years. And now, all his careful maneuvering was for naught.

"What kind of a man—?" Nivea sputtered, unable to even finish a sentence.

The horror in her voice made him even angrier. "Go on, say it! What kind of a man allows his father to whip him, like he's no better than a mongrel dog," he snarled, stumbling to his feet.

"No!" she gasped. "Is that what you think?" In her anger, she grabbed his arm to twist him around to face her. Unfortunately, she forgot about his injury. He let out a groan as the pain almost dropped him to his knees.

"Oh, God," she screamed, grabbing him around the waist to steady him. "Sit down. Ho, what is wrong with me? Let me patch you up. Then I can tell you how ludicrous you are."

Not looking forward to that, Dare sat clumsily on the ground. The sudden movement opened his wound farther. Nivea looked around for something to staunch the blood. Without a word, he handed her his impeccable white cravat. She yanked a bit of trim from her bodice to make a bandage and wrapped the cravat around his waist to secure it.

"There. I think that should hold until we get home."

That would be a challenge. While he was certain he could handle the ride, getting into the saddle would hurt like the devil. He closed his eyes, attempting to shore up his energy.

Before he had a chance to move, Nivea settled next to him and drew him into her arms. "Don't worry, you'll be fine," she crooned into his ear, rocking him as she would a babe.

He waited for the sharp bite of anger to take hold. First, she forced him to expose his most humiliating secrets, then she nursed him like a child. It should be infuriating. But when she ran a soft hand across his shoulder and down his bare arm, he relaxed into her embrace.

Her voluptuous curves pressed against his torso and he could feel her heart racing. Her hair, silky soft, was tickling his cheek as he rested against her. Opening his eyes, he found he was inches away from the entrancing swell of her breasts. The view was both soothing and arousing. Each time she moved her hand to stroke his arm, it exposed a tantalizing gap in her bodice.

Inhaling, he smelled her distinctive vanilla scent. He could remain here forever. It was so peaceful. So quiet. As though there was no one else in the world but he and Nivea.

Then he stiffened. Yet someone had shot him. Why? And where had they gone? Maybe there were still out there. He tried to rise.

"Are you all right?" Nivea tightened her grip on his arms.

"We should go. Since we don't know who shot me, we must move away from here."

"Oh, you are right. Let's go." She rose to her feet and held out her hand.

Ignoring her help, Dare found his feet and straightened. No longer wrapped in Nivea's warm embrace, he shivered. Grabbing his shirt off the ground, Nivea handed it to him. He was able to slip it over his head, but his fingers refused to work the buttons. *When had he gotten so bloody feeble?*

Nivea once again brushed his hands aside, this time fastening the material. It felt rather intimate, having her dress him. Judging by the flush that settled on her cheeks, she must have felt it too. Either that or pity, knowing he was such a disfigured coward.

As she retrieved his jacket and turned toward their horses, she asked, "Do you need any assistance getting up?"

There was his answer. She pitied him. What a lowering thought, that Nivea, of all people, thought he needed help mounting his horse. Well, he would move heaven and earth to get on the beast unaided.

He thrust his foot into the stirrup and threw himself into the saddle. A crippling jolt of pain sliced through his side and radiated across his chest. Letting the sensation wash over him, he managed to relax enough to grab the reins, betraying only a hint of distress. It was a skill he'd perfected long ago.

Ready to show Nivea how unaffected he was, he turned and realized he'd forgotten to help her mount. To his surprise, he saw her balancing on a fallen log, before pulling herself up onto her horse. Issuing him a triumphant smile, she asked, "Are you ready to proceed?"

"Yes," he spat out through gritted teeth.

It was a quiet ride. Thankfully, she didn't expect him to speak until they returned to the stable and were heading back toward the house. Dare did his best to walk with the confident stride of a gentleman, but it cost him greatly. Nivea, damn her eyes, was not at all fooled by his posturing.

She patted his hand that rested on her arm and said, "As soon as we return, you go to your room and I will send Cook up to treat your wound."

She must know now that was not an option. "No, I'll be fine. I'll have my man tend to me."

Not content, she pressed, "Please, let Cook help, she's well trained in the healing arts."

Obviously, he would have to spell this out for her. Unable to prevent the bitterness from seeping out, he said, "Jackson will handle it. He has nursed me through many injuries."

Nivea blanched as understanding dawned. "Was he...? That is to say, has he been with you long?"

Anger coursed through him. She shouldn't know so much about his shameful past, but there was nothing to do about it now. "Yes. Jackson has been with my family since I was a boy. He was the one called upon to patch me up when circumstances required it."

At that, he dropped her hand and stared her in the eye. "He is one of the few people I trust."

He didn't trust her. He couldn't. That was something she would need to accept.

He could detect the note of remorse in her voice when she nodded and said, "All right. I'll have the supplies readied for him in the kitchen."

"Thank you." Eager to change the subject, he took her arm again and walked her toward the front steps. "Please allow me a few minutes, and then I would like a word with William. I don't know who shot at us, but we must have them apprehended."

"Oh, yes. Certainly. We must make sure no one else is injured." With a final squeeze to his arm, she gathered up her skirts and ran into the house. Finally alone, Dare let out a deep groan and dragged himself to his room.

Chapter 22

Jackson patched up Dare's wound with a minimum of fuss and then doused him with laudanum. It helped him sleep through the night, and when he finally roused himself by mid-morning, the pain was bearable.

As Jackson reapplied his bandage and helped him dress, he briefed Dare on the recent events. "You had a steady stream of visitors while you were sleeping, milord. Lord Horsham and the earl were quite distressed to learn you had been shot on their property. They are arranging a search party for this afternoon to investigate the area. If you are up to it, they would like your assistance."

Dare flinched as he drew on his shirt. "Yes, I will join them. I look forward to finding the bastard who shot me and giving him a taste of his own medicine."

"Yes, sir. I will inform them of your interest. You were also visited by Lord Duxbury, who was relieved to hear that you are sound with only a minor injury. After learning of your state, he proclaimed it likely perpetrated by a jealous husband, and returned, unperturbed, to his room."

"Jacksnape."

"Yes, sir. The most frequent visitor was Miss Horsham, who expressed great concern and made me promise to update her on your progress and remind you that you should not go riding alone, as it can be very hazardous."

At that, Dare looked up to examine Jackson's expression in the looking glass. As he was focused on adjusting Dare's cravat, he did not notice Dare's flash of interest.

It was comforting that Nivea was worried about him. Although, given her cryptic message, she wished her riding lesson with him to remain a secret. That might be difficult to pull off, considering the increased scrutiny caused by the shooting. But he would do his best, if that's what she wanted.

Once dressed, Dare headed out for a walk around the grounds. He wanted to clear his head of the laudanum before heading into the woods this afternoon. He did not have to go far. It was a clear day with a gentle breeze and the fresh air quickly restored him. He took a leisurely stroll to the lake, before circling back toward the stables. He had happened upon a patch of forget-me-nots and thought to make Nivea a small bouquet. Although he tried to tell himself it was a simple gesture to thank her for her concern, he knew the truth.

He was using the flowers as a ploy. He imagined handing her the bouquet, causing her to smile and coo. Perhaps she would even agree to a kiss or two. He had been unable to think of much else since she had leaned over him to bind his wound. Even as he'd shuddered in pain, her scent had both soothed and taunted him.

She was just so...sweet. Everyone had said so, but he'd never considered it a complimentary trait in a woman. Sweet implied bland, insipid, perhaps even a bit dim. Yet yesterday, watching her joy as she learned to ride—it was inspiring. It made him happy. He wanted to see her sparkling sapphire eyes light up, and her plump, red lips curve in a wide, unaffected grin. He'd spent the past day craving a taste of those lips.

Once he handed her the flowers, he would not let it get out of hand. Only a quick peck to get her out of his system and he could move on with his day. Confident he was in control, he entered the family wing. Making certain there were no others about, he knocked on her door.

No answer.

He knocked again. Still nothing.

Disappointed, but undeterred, he turned the knob and slipped inside. Placing the flowers on her pillow where she was certain to notice them, he decided to pen her a brief note. Nothing too risqué, just letting her know he had been there. It was certain to bring a blush to her cheeks. Considering he preferred more experienced women, he was surprised at how enticing that image was.

He crossed to her writing desk. Opening the drawer, he found a stack of papers already written upon. He was not intending to pry, but as he happened to glance at the top page, his heart clenched.

In disbelief, he scanned the page once, then gripping the back of the chair, he read it again.

"Betrayed"

Crisscross welts given

by a man who should only be giving
love
and guidance.

Inflicted, why?
Upon a boy
whose only guilt was what?
Malice?
Or evil schemes?
No, his sin was nothing more
than being born, and young, and a son.

I lost my mother
as a girl
and thought that must be
the greatest sadness to be felt.
But no.

To be betrayed by those
who should give love,
not pain.
'Tis unimaginable.

No wonder
he dare not love
when love has brought him nothing
but anguish.
And welts.

Nivea Horsham

Shaking with emotion, he dropped into the chair. His rage was so great
he thought he might explode. How *dare* she put his deepest secrets on
paper! What right did she have to summarize his life, so stark and cold it
made him weak?

He'd thought her sweet. Bah! More like a feral cat. You lean over to pet
it and the damned beast sinks its teeth into your hand.

Oh, he would wring her neck for mocking him. For opening his secret
to the world. Hell, she even put his name in the poem. Right there, to

erase any doubt. He *dare* not love! Of course he did not love. There is no such thing as love—only pain.

He dropped his head in his hands and tried to stop the shaking. Suddenly, scenes from his youth, scenes he had buried deep into the corners of his mind, came flooding out.

Playing piano at his mother's request, watching her smile with joy, then stepping in the hall and being knocked to the ground.

Falling from a horse and struggling to remount with an injured leg. After ridiculing him for poor horsemanship, his father rode off with the horses, leaving him to stumble home alone in the dark, only to collapse with exhaustion and terror hours later, long after the family had retired.

His sisters, with their triumphant sneers, eagerly relating his transgressions at dinner. They had quickly learned their punishments would be lessened if their father had someone else to focus his attention on.

He trembled as the agony from days long gone flooded through him. Then his eyes fell back on Nivea's poem, and the anger surged back. What was her motivation for putting his deepest shame onto paper? Was she truly as sympathetic as she appeared? Or would she use it to betray him? She was a woman, after all.

He had to find out for himself. He would have to confront her, look her in the eye, and study her reaction. Regardless of her response, he would make clear this was his business alone. He did not need nor want her sympathy.

Placing the poem back into Nivea's desk, he slammed the drawer shut. Taking a deep breath, he stood and crossed to the door. He would have to find her. Now.

Striding downstairs, he saw the other gentlemen waiting for him in the entrance hall. He signaled that he would join them in a moment and headed into the parlor where Lady Horsham was serving tea. Spotting Nivea near the window, he crossed to her.

"I would like a word with you in private," he hissed.

The smile that had lit her face changed to worry at his tone. "What is wrong? Are you all right?"

"Not now," he emphasized. "I want to make something clear to you. When we get back from the woods, I'll come to your room."

She looked up in surprise.

He gave her a sardonic smirk. "Have no fear, I will not tarnish your reputation, milady. I am perfectly capable of sneaking in and out of a bedroom without detection."

She looked at him with a steady gaze. That did not appear to sit well with her, but she nodded her head in assent.

With a curt bow, he strode back into the hallway.

There. He would deal with that issue when he returned. For now, he would focus on discovering who shot him and why.

Chapter 23

As they rode, the earl chatted amiably with William, never raising his voice or casting aspersions. They were so bloody *nice* to each other.

Listening to them, the truth of Dare's past took hold of him. Damn it, he *had* been deprived of a normal upbringing. Instead of support or encouragement, he had been taunted and abused. It was no wonder he kept himself isolated. Who among his associates had ever experienced even a sliver of the torment he had?

None.

They had been raised with kindness and guidance, not whips and straps. They were able to love and laugh and enjoy their families and friends. Nivea was right, he had suffered. Through no fault of his own, he was left to wallow in this black pit of despair.

The question was, could he move past it? Could he learn to trust? Could he, in fact, trust Nivea?

No! the voice inside shouted. Look at the poem. She was mocking you! She will betray you.

And yet images of Nivea flitted through his brain, a soothing blur of laughter, concern, and passion. She didn't flirt with him like most women, with mooning eyes or calculated glances, but instead talked to him like a friend. He felt so damn peaceful around her. How was that possible? She was a woman! While a man might inflict physical injury, it was the insidiousness of women that caused the most pain. What exactly did she want from him?

Unable to arrive at an adequate conclusion, he returned his attention to his companions. "We're almost there. I was around the bend a bit, planning to go as far as the ruins, but I never made it."

"I cannot tell you how incensed I am that you were injured on my land. I don't understand how this could have happened," said the earl.

Having no explanation, Dare shrugged. A few steps farther, he drew his horse to a stop. "This is it. We were right here when I felt the shot."

William's head shot up. "We?"

Damn. He must still be muddled from the laudanum. So much for keeping Nivea's secret.

"Ahhh, did I say we?" Dare faltered.

"You most certainly did. And judging by the hoof prints, there was definitely more than one horse here," confirmed Joseph with a smirk. "Looks like I may have been correct. You were out on a clandestine interlude, weren't you?"

"Come, sir. If you were out here with a woman, we need to know," barked the earl. "If this was in fact the result of a jealous husband, it is a completely different matter."

Fixing a glare on his friends, Dare considered how to resolve the situation. By admitting he was with Nivea, he would have to divulge her secret. But if he said it was another woman, they would end their search. Dare definitely wanted to learn who shot him, he decided it best to come clean. He hoped she would understand. "I was riding with Nivea yesterday."

William shot him an angry look, while Joseph fought back a grin. "I told you he had been up to no good."

William turned his glare on Joseph before growling, "What in God's name were you doing out here with my sister, Landis?"

Dare knew he had to give a careful answer. Affecting a dispassionate air, he answered, "I was doing her a favor."

"Oh, is that what we're calling it now?" William sneered, edging his horse closer to Dare's.

"That's enough, William," the earl cut in. "Lord Landis, give us the details, if you please."

With his mouth set in a grim line, Dare turned his attention to the earl. "Well, sir, following our mishap on our trip from London, Nivea decided to increase her proficiency on a horse. I offered to assist."

The earl's brow furrowed as he considered this surprising response. "But why would she come to you for help? Why didn't she ask one of us?"

"She had hoped to keep it a secret, in order to surprise you, once she mastered her riding skills."

"And why did you agree?" asked William, eyes narrowed in suspicion.

Ah, he would have to dance around the truth on that one. Sliding into a haughty drawl, he answered, "Perhaps, I felt I owed her after making her arrival here so uncomfortable. Or perhaps because she was so determined to make you proud, I thought it noble to help. But most likely, I was bored and she caught me in a rare moment of weakness."

Then, while fighting back the images of Nivea, lying under him, soft and flushed with passion, he fixed an arrogant stare on his oldest friend and boldly stated, "Regardless of my motivation, I can assure you, I did not molest your sister during our ride."

The truth had never been so thoroughly strained. But it worked.

He was a bit unnerved by the earl's intent stare, but then the man proclaimed, "Well, as Nivvy has not expressed any concerns over your behavior, I think we can assume you have behaved as a gentleman."

The others appeared satisfied for they dismounted to survey the surrounding ground. Dare let the matter drop, but their attitude irked him. Dammit, why did he have to explain himself? He was the one who'd been shot. Sore from the injury and angry with himself for betraying Nivea's secret, Dare watched them in silence as they scoured the area.

"I don't see anything here. Let's proceed toward the ruins and look for anything unusual." The earl remounted and urged his horse forward.

As soon as they arrived at the ruins, it was obvious the area had been in use. Footsteps crisscrossed the dirt trails and the brush surrounding the abbey's structure was flattened.

They spread out, and it wasn't long before Joseph called out. "Ho, look here. I found a hideaway tucked into the wall. It appears a small group of mischief makers have been making themselves comfortable."

"Mischief makers?" Dare snapped. "I hardly think being shot off my horse can be qualified as mischief."

The others tramped over to the area and found the remains of a fire, a blanket stuffed behind a rock, and a satchel covered by twigs and leaves.

Dare strode over and dumped the satchel on the ground.

Out fell a hardened lump of bread, a small bag of gunpowder, a handful of misshapen round metal balls, flint, and a penknife. Picking up the penknife, Dare examined the handle. "It has initials carved in it. K.D. Does that mean anything to you, gentlemen?"

William turned around from the edge of the woods and called back, "Could be Kirby Dugan, the blacksmith in town. While I doubt it's him, he has a passel of boys at home." He walked closer, holding an object in his hand. It was a piece of white bark with holes in it. "I found this too. Looks like boys were up here taking target practice. There's a bunch of metal pieces along the ground—not well-made bullets, but maybe bits left over from the smithy."

The earl shook his head. "Damn fools must have been out here practicing. Chances are a shot went wide and managed to clip you, Landis."

"Who allows their children to run wild like that?" Dare growled. It was intolerable to think he'd been wounded by a pack of unruly brats.

"I seem to recall Dugan lost his wife last year, leaving him with half a dozen boys under the age of twelve. It's difficult for a man to keep all that in line," recalled William. "I think Nivea went to visit a few times to bring them food and supplies until they could get back on their feet."

"And they repay her by shooting at her? She could have been killed!" Dare flailed his arms, only to wince from pain as he jolted his injury.

"Very true. We must remember that they are still young and may not realize the implications of their actions," soothed the earl.

"That's no damn excuse for letting them shoot at people. We need to teach these Dugans a lesson on how to behave!"

"Most assuredly. We will go to the village and have a word. But we will behave as gentlemen and not go flinging accusations about," the earl stated.

It was easy for him to react so calmly to the situation. He wasn't the one with a bullet hole in his side. Pulling himself back into the saddle sent another burst of pain through him, and he grew more bitter.

When they arrived in town, William took a look at Dare's incensed expression and announced, "I'll go talk to Dugan and see what we can find out. Wait here."

He headed to the smithy and disappeared inside. A few moments later a large, burly man came flying out of the door.

"Ian! Robbie! Where are you, you little hellions? I'll beat you both bloody." He stormed into the house next door and grabbed two thin, mangy-looking lads, dragging them outside. Shaking them violently by the scruff of their necks, he bellowed, "You two have some explaining to do. Yesterday, when you should have been out helping Miss Irma tending her garden, you were up by the ruins where you shot a lord! These gentlemen tell me they found your satchel and my knife there."

His face was as red as a blazing sun and his thick-corded arms rippled as he shook his sons. Their long, black hair whipped around their dirty faces, eyes wide with fear.

"Now, you stand here and beg forgiveness while I get the strap to beat you." He shoved them forward and they stumbled toward the horses. With a growl, he thundered into the smithy, then emerged clutching a thick piece of leather.

The boys looked up at Dare with terror in their eyes. As he sat there, high above them on his horse, he remembered how horrendous this situation felt. His own father had towered over him, waving his whip, yelling at him over some transgression. He didn't always know what had caused the anger, but that didn't matter. There would be no escaping the pain.

"Speak up boys! Come clean before I beat you bloody!" yelled Dugan as he barreled over to them.

In that instant, Dare's anger drained away. "Enough!" he yelled, immediately grimacing from the effort.

Dugan looked up. "I beg your pardon, milord. Would you like to do it then?" He turned back to his sons. "He's within his rights, you know. You deserve no better." He held the strap up to Dare. "Here, tire yourself out, if you like."

The other gentlemen looked on with horror as Dare dismounted and headed toward Dugan. Most of them had been on the losing side of a boxing match with Dare when he was in a temper and were well aware of what he was capable. But just as they were on the verge of calling to him to be merciful, he announced in a strained voice, "That won't be necessary. I would prefer to take the boys inside and have a few words with them in private."

That brought Dugan up short. He opened his mouth to protest, but the look Dare shot him brooked no argument. The boys stared at him in terror, totally unable to imagine what fate might befall them inside.

"Come!" he barked at them and pointed toward the house. As he strode forward, they began babbling their apologies.

"So sorry, milord. We didn't know, milord. An accident, to be sure. We were just—"

"Landis," shouted the earl in a warning tone.

Dare dismissed his concerns with a flick of his wrist and headed inside.

After a few moments, he called Dugan into the house. It didn't take him long to settle the matter, and he left pleased with the outcome.

Dugan followed, bowing and scraping in his wake. "Thank you, milord. You are too kind, milord. Your mercy will not be forgotten."

Brushing a speck of dust off his coat, Dare climbed back onto his horse.

The two boys stumbled outside. Where they had previously cowered in fear, they now stood straight and tall, nervous smiles hovering on their lips.

Dare withdrew his snuffbox, took a pinch, and glanced down at Dugan with a fierce look. Dugan bowed his head. Content the man was sufficiently cowed, Dare gave his horse a rap with his heels and set off down the road.

His friends trailed behind, remaining quiet until they reached the edge of town.

Joseph could no longer contain himself. "What in bloody hell was that all about?"

Dare kept his gaze on the road ahead. "The matter has been handled to my satisfaction. I have faith that there will be no more incidents regarding the Dugan clan."

"But Dare—" began William, but his father cut him off.

"If Lord Landis is satisfied with the situation, so am I. Let's go home," said the earl, ending the conversation.

* * * *

Nivea spent an anxious afternoon in the parlor awaiting Dare's return. Tea with the women was a tense affair, listening to them gossip about the possible scenarios that could have caused Dare's injury.

She hoped the men were able to discover what had happened out there. Being with Dare when he had been shot had been terrifying. But not wanting to publicize their growing relationship, she couldn't share her concerns with anyone.

So she moved to sit in the far corner of the room, where she gazed out the window, sipping on her umpteenth cup of tea. She rested her head against the cool pane of glass, as though it could soothe her heated thoughts.

She couldn't get the images from yesterday out of her mind. Dare dropping from his saddle in pain. Blood staining his shirt. And then his scars! They had made her physically ill—puckered ridges stretching across his back, some blotchy red and brown, while others curling around his shoulder and ribs had faded to a translucent shine. They were horrendous.

She couldn't fathom how a man could do that to his son…a child. And to think no one in his family had tried to protect him. Instead, they had provoked even more punishment.

Restless, she got up from her chair to pace. How was it, after all these years, no one else knew of Dare's torment? Not even her brother. How had he managed to keep this secret from everyone? She desperately wanted to let him know that she cared. That she loved him and nothing he had told her would change that. But would he believe her? Probably not.

She sighed.

"Nivvy? Are you all right?" Betsy reached out a hand, her brow creased with worry.

"What? Oh, yes, I'm just…erm…worried. About the shooting." Casting about for a way to deflect her preoccupation with Dare, she blustered, "I hope the men are safe out there today."

Betsy's eyes teared. "Yes, I don't know what I'd do if anything happened to William. I would be…"

She couldn't even finish the thought. Instead she dabbed at her eyes and then gulped down another sip of tea. Nivea tried to offer a comforting response, but the effort was too much. "This waiting is exhausting. I think I may go lie down."

Betsy forced a smile, "Yes, that's a good idea. We will let you know when the men return."

Desperate for solitude, Nivea headed for her room. As she walked up the stairs, she began to catalogue the remarkable turn of events that had occurred over the past fortnight. There had been so much to comprehend.

First, Dare had insinuated that she was so unappealing, she was incapable of finding a husband. Then he'd ravished her, the second time while berating her over a supposed betrayal. And once she'd convinced herself that their relationship was completely ruined, he had a complete about face and announced he found her irresistible. How was that even possible? Then, he had gotten shot right in front of her eyes.

Shot! As though he hadn't been through enough.

Exhausted, she rubbed her hand over her eyes. She couldn't wait to lie down. Walking into her room, she was just steps away from her bed when she noticed something near the headboard. Leaning in for a closer look, her heart stuttered.

Forget-me-nots.

On her pillow.

Had Dare been in her room? Had he left forget-me-nots for her? No one else knew of her preference. In fact, no one had ever given her flowers before, not in such an intimate fashion.

She gathered them up and pressed them to her face. No longer tired, she twirled around the room. Dare had been thinking about her. He had deliberately slipped into her room. How romantic.

Wait. Hadn't he been angry with her earlier, barking that they needed to talk?

She stretched out on the bed and tried to remember. Had he been irritated with her? And if so, why had he left her flowers?

Perhaps he *hadn't* been angry. Maybe it was his pain that made him seem cross. That had to be it. He said he would sneak into her room to see her. It was dangerous, but she wasn't about to dissuade him. After all, she was already ruined. And maybe, hopefully, it would turn to something more.

More eager than ever to see him, she scrambled to her feet and set to making herself presentable. After she rinsed her face and tidied her hair, she tucked his flowers into her bodice.

There, that was better. Now she just needed him to return. Perching on her dressing chair, she rested her chin in her hand and closed her eyes.

Tick tick tick went the clock on the mantel.

Tap tap tap went her fingers on her cheek.

Tick tick...sigh.

Tap tap—argh!

Just when she thought she could take no more of the waiting, she heard voices in the front hall.

Chapter 24

Oh, thank God. Nivea raced down the stairs and searched the faces of the men as they appeared in the entranceway. She was pleased to see they were in good spirits. But Dare was not among them. Where was he? Was he all right? Just as an unreasonable panic started to build, the door opened and he strolled in.

Before she could approach him, Amelia waved everyone into the parlor. "I'm so glad you've returned," she said, drawing her arm through her husband's. "We were so worried. Did you find anything out?"

"Nothing to fear," the earl answered, kissing her fondly on the forehead. "Let me get a drink and we'll explain what we found."

Amelia poured him a cup of tea and after taking a sip, he announced, "The shooting was an accident. The blacksmith's boys had gone into the woods to practice their aim and must have shot wide. They have been made to understand the unfortunate consequences of their actions. It should not occur again."

There was a palpable sigh of relief throughout the room, and then the women gathered closer to ask questions. Seeking an excuse to speak with Dare, Nivea poured him a cup of tea and crossed over to where he was leaning against the doorjamb. Judging by the tight lines around his mouth, she could tell he was suffering.

In a gentle tone, she asked, "Lord Landis, how are you feeling?"

"I'm perfectly all right," he answered, straightening. The ruse cost him, and he flinched. She ached to hold him, comfort him, but this wasn't the time or the place. Tonight. In her room. That was what he'd requested. But noting the weary slump of his shoulders, she wasn't so certain.

"Do you still wish to speak with me this evening?"

His eyes closed as though the thought pained him. When he reopened them, his gaze was focused, intense. "No, it can wait. I think I will head upstairs for the evening."

That was disappointing. She wasn't sure she could get through the night without talking to him...making sure he was all right. That *they* were all right. When he moved to take his leave, she placed a hand on his arm. "If you don't mind, I would like to check on your wound."

When she saw he was about to refuse, she blurted out, "Please, I feel partly to blame. If we hadn't gone riding, this wouldn't have happened. I will bring up another poultice to your room. I won't stay long, I assure you."

He must have been too tired to argue, as he shrugged in agreement.

As she turned back toward the room, she saw her brother was watching her, his brows drawn and his mouth pinched. Had Dare told them that they had been riding together? If he suspected there was anything untoward between them, it would not go well. Determined to paint an innocent picture, she approached her stepmother and announced rather loudly "Amelia, Dare said he was tired and would like to have supper brought up to his room this evening. Would you like me to inform Cook?"

"Yes, dear, that's a good idea. I'm sure today was a strain for him."

Nivea rushed out the door and headed toward the kitchen.

* * * *

Upon entering his room, Dare slowly pulled off his jacket, unable to stifle a gasp of pain. Jackson reached for the garment and laid it aside. "My lord, were you able to discover who shot you?"

Dare felt a bit foolish, admitting that he'd been shot by a mere child, but word would spread, so he might as well play it off as best he could. "Nothing too dramatic, I fear. Although it would have been more scintillating if it had been an act of bitter retribution over a lifelong grudge, it was in fact village boys practicing their shots. It will not happen again."

"Very good, sir." Thankfully, Jackson knew better than to ply him with sympathy, so he returned the conversation to matters at hand. "Will you be joining the Horshams for dinner? I can lay out your eveningwear."

"That will not be necessary. The Horshams are having a tray sent up. I will just wash up and retire for the evening."

"I would like to change your bandage—"

Dare cut him off with a silencing glare. "There is no need. Cook is sending up a poultice that I will apply after I wash. You are dismissed for the evening."

Jackson may have been surprised by his self-reliant behavior, but that couldn't be helped. Knowing Nivea was on her way, Dare wanted his manservant to be off as quickly as possible. Although Jackson had been the soul of discretion during his service, Dare did not want him privy to this situation.

Dare was beginning to feel very protective of the girl. It was not a sensation he was familiar with. If women wished to risk their reputation to be with him, he considered it their own affair. He was a well-established rake, and if they did not understand the consequences, the blame lay fully at their door.

But tonight there was no need to set tongues wagging. He would merely put Nivea's mind at ease and then send her on her way without the slightest taint to her reputation.

First, he needed to get cleaned up. He strode over to the bath closet, removed his shirt, and ran a damp cloth over his face and down his chest. Twisting with care, he checked his bandage, pleased to see it hadn't bled through.

Crossing to his expansive four-poster bed, he sat back against the pillows, intending to relax for a moment before donning a new shirt.

He considered discussing the outcome of today's events with Nivea. She, of all people, would understand the magnitude of his actions. The restraint he'd shown when dealing with the Dugan boys was remarkable. He could imagine her eyes growing warm with pleasure when she learned of his newfound control. Perhaps she would wrap her arms around him, press herself against him, and he would draw her down—

No! He could not think of her that way. He would honor his vow to cease all unseemly behavior toward her. She deserved respect. Resolutely, he closed his eyes and forced himself to imagine the most unpleasant and non-erotic situations possible.

The next thing he knew, Nivea was above him with a cool hand placed on his brow. "You don't have a fever. That's encouraging," she said.

He jerked upright, startled to discover he had fallen asleep. He tried to swing his legs off the bed, but she pushed him back down.

"No, rest for a moment. I would like to check your wound and then you can eat."

He swept away her hand. "I'm fine. It's just a scratch."

With her hands on her hips, she fixed him with a defiant stare. "It's not a scratch. You were shot and that can be very serious. I know men are irritable when they are injured, but you will not deter me from this. I *will* be removing the bandage and applying Cook's poultice. Now lie still and let me look."

Dare did not like to be ordered about. In fact, more likely than not, if he was ordered to do something, he would do the complete opposite. Yet when he tried to fix a rebellious glare at the woman beside him, he found himself unable to resist. She stood there, like a defiant angel, feet planted, mouth firm, but her eyes filled with concern. For him.

Imagine that.

Noticing a spray of forget-me-nots tucked in the bodice of her dress, he allowed a faint smile. He had forgotten he'd left them in her room earlier. It seemed a long time ago.

Relenting, he growled, "Fine. Take a look. But I assure you, I need no nursing."

She unwrapped the bandage and drew her fingers over his tender skin, ignoring his slight flinch.

"It looks quite well. No sign of swelling or infection. I should like to sponge off a little blood and reapply the bandage."

He nodded his head once, so she rose to pour water on a clean towel. Very carefully, she patted his wound before dabbing some of cook's yellowish brown concoction onto a strip of cloth and placing it on his side.

"There, that should help," she said, tucking in the ends of his bandage with a tender smile.

He was surprised to find that it did. Her touch was much more soothing than Jackson's brusque treatment. Letting out a breath, he found that it was nice to be taken care of, spoiled even.

"Are you hungry now? I'll bring you your tray." Without waiting for a response, she crossed to the table near the door.

He watched her hips as they swayed rhythmically away from him. He had always found a woman's derriere to be an entrancing sight. Granted, hers was a little more rounded than most, but for some reason, that didn't detract from her appeal.

She turned and he quickly dropped his gaze. It wouldn't do for her to catch him ogling her like a common doxy. It also wouldn't do for him to let his thoughts continue in that vein.

Unaware of the effect she was having, she handed him the tray and a tall glass of lemonade before turning once again to seize a decanter of brandy. Thankfully, she placed it within reach on the nightstand, and then sat on the chair next to the bed.

The scent of food reminded him how hungry he was, and he downed a few bites of poached salmon. When he finished chewing, Nivea handed him the glass of lemonade and asked, "Would you like to tell me what happened today?"

Did he? Now she was there, he wasn't certain he wanted to tell her. Maybe it wasn't so impressive. He'd already proven himself embarrassingly weak in front of her, hadn't he? Best to stick to the Earl's summary. "You heard. It was just some boys from the village."

She appeared to consider his response before announcing, "No. There was more to it. I can tell." Sitting there, serenely, one would think she'd spent hours chatting with partially clothed men in their bedrooms.

He longed to invite her beside him on the bed. To bury his face into her bosom and breathe in the faint flowery scent of forget-me-nots as it mingled with her essence. He would nibble his way down to her sweet rosy peaks hidden by her gown.

Damn it all. He was supposed to maintain control, but doing a damn poor job of it. Instead he was in danger of upending his tray of food. He would relay the events of the day and get her the hell away from him before he caused any more damage.

Leaning back against the headboard, he began, "As your father explained, we went out to the ruins and found a small campsite of sorts. It appeared young boys were attempting to practice their shooting skills. Having discerned it was the Dugan boys, we headed to town to inform their father of their actions. When William told him what had occurred, Dugan flew into a rage, dragging his two sons into the yard and threatening to beat an apology out of them."

Dare paused as unbidden memories surged forward, along with the latent pain and humiliation. He remembered his own efforts to maintain a stoic visage in the face of such anger, just as the two Dugan lads had, and only now realized how badly he must have failed. It was humbling.

"I saw myself at that age. It was so disconcerting to witness the rage and hear the words that had permeated my childhood coming from this complete stranger. I watched the boys as they struggled to understand their transgression. All the while, having the unerring knowledge that the pain of the beating would linger for days."

He took a deep breath, but found he couldn't banish the painful sensation haunting him. Hands shaking, he reached for the bottle of brandy on the bedside table. He splashed it into a glass on his tray and downed it in a gulp.

Lord, this was difficult. He couldn't look at her, afraid what he might see. But he pressed on. "I couldn't allow that to happen, Nivea. I remembered how desperately I had prayed that someone would intervene on my behalf. That something would happen to protect me."

Pouring another glass of brandy, he took a sip, savoring the slow burn. It cleared his head and brought him some semblance of control.

"I realized I could provide that protection for these boys. They had no intention of hurting me. It was an accident. So, I led them into the house as they babbled their apologies. A few younger boys with dirty faces and tattered clothes peered out from the doorway. From what I could tell, they had no guidance, no order to their lives. Their home was unkempt and neglected."

Picturing the scene in his head, he absently took another sip.

Nivea leaned forward in her chair. "So, what did you do?"

"Oh, yes—well, I advised the boys that I would not have them arrested if they promised to honor their mother's memory. I instructed them to sweep and polish the house 'til it shone, then dress in their finest clothes and offer to apprentice with the baker, thus earning their keep and becoming men of honor. They stared at me wordlessly until I waved my hand and they scattered, each grabbing a rag to begin cleaning."

"That was very kind of you." She smiled, reaching up to twirl a loose lock of hair around her finger.

"Yes, well, they were happy to have escaped punishment from me, but were still expecting one from their father. Determined to prevent that, I decided to fix it as any lord of my standing would."

"What does *that* mean?"

He raised his glass in mock salute and answered, "I threw money at him."

Her hand dropped to her lap. "You what?"

He savored the look of surprise that flashed across her face. "I called him into the house and explained that he was not to whip his children. I told him if I ever heard that he laid a hand on them again, I would come to his house and run him through."

Beginning to enjoy the account, he continued, "Quite insulted, he began to argue, insisting that I had no right to interfere. That there was no other way to survive. I poured out a handful of shillings and advised him to use it to convince the baker to apprentice his two oldest sons. It would teach them the value of work, keep them out of mischief, and help put food on his table."

"Oh Dare, what a wonderful idea!"

"I then threatened him again, saying if I found out he had used it for drink or other personal vices, I would hear of it and convince the constable he had shot me and stolen my purse."

He grinned at the memory of Dugan's face at that proclamation.

Nivea sat back in her chair, a look of astonished joy on her face. "Oh, Dare, you will be their hero. I am so proud you were able to overcome your anger."

As he had hoped, she leaned over to kiss him on the cheek.

"Surely, such noble behavior deserves more reward than that," he teased and turned his head, catching her lips with his. Oh, she tasted so sweet. Then he caught her scent, that subtle, entrancing essence of vanilla. He couldn't resist gliding his tongue into her mouth.

"Ohh," she breathed.

At her reaction, he deepened the kiss, teasing her tongue with his. Dipping in and out of her lips, he tasted her essence, sensed her passion. His desire spiked with surprising alacrity.

Grabbing her shoulders, he trailed kisses down to her neck. His gaze strayed to her bosom, overflowing her gown as she leaned forward. Her skin was so impossibly white and soft. He remembered how her skin had tasted in the cabin, how responsive she'd been, and he needed more. Sliding the tray off his lap, he pulled her down to sit next to him and wrapped his arms around her waist.

When she let out a breathy moan, his unreliable conscience resurfaced. He pushed her back and took a deep steadying breath.

And then another, damn her.

"That is enough. We shouldn't be doing this. You need to leave, now, before I dishonor you once again."

But she didn't. She settled next to him and leaned over to nibble his earlobe. "But I like doing this. I know it's wicked, but I don't care." Her voice was low and husky. With a sinful smile, she let her fingers creep across his chest to skim his nipple.

He yelped and grabbed her hand. "God in heaven, Nivea, don't do that!"

Taking no pity on him or his noble efforts, she pulled her hand free and repeated the motion, rubbing the right nipple and then the left, while nibbling on the taut cords of his neck.

That did it. There was no turning back. All rational thought vanished into the ether. Ignoring his wound, he rolled her beneath him and plundered her mouth. His hands roamed over her body, pushing fabric out of the way to knead the soft flesh. The heat between them flared to a fiery pitch.

"Oh, Dare, this feels so wonderful," Nivea groaned. Her soft, warm hands caressed his shoulders before moving around to his back and touching the raised flesh.

Chapter 25

"Don't!" Dare bellowed.

Nivea's fingers had barely encountered the smoothed ridges of a scar below his shoulder when she was shoved backward.

Her heart clenched. She hadn't meant to touch his scar. Hadn't meant to upset him. She had been lulled into a haze of desire and hadn't even realized what she was doing; she was simply trying to pull him closer.

At the haunted pain lurking in his eyes, she stuttered, "I'm so sorry, Dare. I didn't mean to upset you. Here, let me…" She reached out to place a soothing hand on his arm.

He jerked away and hissed through clenched teeth, "Don't touch me. I don't need your pity. Just leave me alone."

That stopped her. "Pity?" she cried. "Is that what you think?" Then she froze as a horrible thought struck her. "Is that what your other women felt? Pity?"

"No!" he shouted, his eyes blazing. "Haven't I made myself clear? No one else knows about this."

Now she was truly bewildered. How was that possible? She sat there trying to puzzle through such an amazing revelation. "But surely, after all those women, how did you hide it?"

"I'd hidden it from you, hadn't I?" he jeered.

Still stunned by the implications, she managed to respond with only a slight edge, "Well, yes, but I was an innocent, as you well know. Not all your women were."

He sat there, arms crossed rigidly, his expression fierce.

Curiosity overcame desire. Sitting up, she tucked a loose lock of hair behind her ear and pondered this paradox. How was it possible that he'd bedded dozens of women without them discovering his secret?

"I don't recall asking you to make yourself comfortable," he growled.

She couldn't help but smile, "Yes, I know. You want me to leave. But please, you have to tell me. How did you keep it a secret?"

Digging the heel of his palms into his eyes, he sighed. "Please, don't ask. You would not think well of me."

At that, she laughed. "After all I've heard about the infamous Lord Landis, I dare say I won't be shocked."

Clenching his jaw, he looked at her steadily, as though taking her measure. Then narrowing his eyes, his demeanor changed and the unrepentant rake appeared.

"I had a few tricks," he drawled. "You would not appreciate them, I'm certain, but others did. Many, many others."

She knew he was trying to drive her away, but she couldn't help but be fascinated by this side of Dare—the sensuous, dangerous, Lord Landis. He'd definitely peaked her interest now. "Tricks? What kind of tricks?"

Given his exasperated expression, he did not want to tell her. But she had to know. Feeling reckless, she pressed her advantage. Placing a hand to his chest, she leaned over and cooed as she'd seen other ladies do. "I would like to know your tricks."

He huffed angrily and glared at the ceiling.

She leaned closer and paused, her face only inches from his. "Please?" she breathed, surprised at the silky, sexy tone she was able to affect. He returned her gaze, but still did not move, except for that compulsive tightening of his jaw.

Silently, patiently, she waited until he finally relented.

"All right, if you must know," he growled, shoving himself into a seated position. "In most cases, I would simply keep my shirt on, my waistcoat too, if circumstances allowed. It seemed more like uncontrollable passion than an unwillingness to disrobe."

Nivea felt herself blush. That was how he had taken her, not once but twice.

Warming to the subject, his voice turned silky as he continued, "Sometimes I preferred to take my time, savoring the moment. In that case, with a less experienced woman, I may blindfold them, keeping their hands pinned down, so they couldn't see or feel the scars. They usually found the suggestion titillating and never questioned me."

She should be horrified, disgusted even, but instead she was more aroused. "And the more experienced ones? What of them?" she breathed.

Dare's deep hooded eyes bored into hers, and she knew he could sense her longing. An odd, calculating expression crossed his face, only to be replaced by the gleam of a perilous predator. "If you must know, I will show you."

Pulling her into a hard embrace, he drove his tongue into her mouth. Eagerly, she kissed him back. He was so delicious, tasting of brandy and spices and Dare. His soft, full lips nipping and sucking, his tongue probing and tickling.

She could feel the heat of his skin and wanted more. She ran her hand through his silky, dark hair before inching toward his shoulders. He suddenly rolled over her, locking her in place with a long leg. Then he grabbed her wrists and stretched them above her head. Now trapped, she could do no more than moan as he trailed kisses down her neck, collarbone, and into the expanse of skin above her bodice. As she sighed with delight, he straddled her, and rubbed his hardened member against her skirts.

His eyes were black, hypnotic when he purred, "Darling, you drive me to distraction. If you wouldn't mind, I would love to treat you to a little excitement."

He leaned forward to press a warm, lingering kiss on her lips. "It's a little daring, but I think you would like it. In fact, I *know* you will like it."

Thoroughly intrigued, she managed to nod her head in agreement.

"Good. Now, close your eyes and don't move," he crooned. His hand trailed across her breast before she felt his weight shift away from her. In an instant, he settled back on the bed.

Once again, he grabbed her hands resting above her head before wrapping fabric around her wrists. Alarmed, she tried to tug them free.

She felt his laugh rumble against her. "Now, now darling. I won't hurt you. Just lay still and I promise you will not be disappointed."

She opened her eyes and watched him loop the end of a cravat around his bedpost, restraining her. Confident she was secured, Dare nibbled her ear and ran a possessive hand down her breast. Rolling over, he extinguished the candles beside the bed. Now the room was bathed in shadows. The beautiful planes of his face were barely visible from the lone candle located near the dressing area.

His hands roamed over her gown, growling as it prevented him from reaching her skin. "Usually," he confessed, "I would have my partner disrobed before this point. I admit this order poses as bit of an impediment."

Divining a solution, he flipped her over onto her stomach. Straddling her once again, he rubbed rhythmically against her bottom, cupping it in his hands. Then he brushed away the hair at her neck and slowly, methodically, began popping open the buttons of her gown. After each button, he would place a kiss on her exposed skin, first her neck, then shoulders, then down her spine.

She shivered with delight. "Oh Dare, this is exquisite."

"Yes, it is," he groaned. He licked and nipped his way down her back, now fully exposed. While it was a trifle unnerving to be at his mercy, she found the prickle of uneasiness heightened her senses. As desire swirled through her, she pressed deeper into the mattress, aching for friction.

He slipped the sleeves of the gown off her shoulders and murmured, "We won't be able to remove it entirely, but I think I can manage to work around it." Proving his point, he rolled her onto her back and nudged the loosened neckline down, exposing her torso. Lowering his head, he took a nipple into his mouth.

Fire shot through her veins and she bucked wildly in response. *God in heaven that felt good.*

"Easy, darling, this is only the beginning," he cooed. Picking up the flowers that had fallen out of her bodice, he raised them to his face and inhaled. "Ah yes. A delicate scent, but not as enticing as yours, my dear." He began to trace the flowers over her skin. Starting with her cheek, he trailed them down her neck and across her chest. It was tender yet erotic, especially when he followed their trail with his lips.

She sucked in a breath as though it were her last on earth. Desperate to touch him, Nivea tugged at the bonds.

"That feeling of helplessness is quite erotic, is it not? No matter what I do, you are completely at my mercy." To prove his point, he reached his hand down and dragged the hem of her skirt up, over her ankle, knee, and thigh, his hand leaving a fiery imprint in its wake. Releasing the fabric, he untied the ribbon on her undergarment. Flashing her a devilish smile, he eased them down.

Torn between desire and embarrassment, Nivea tried to squirm away, but the bindings on her wrists held firm.

"Don't be shy, darling. There is nothing more beautiful than a woman opened to her man."

Squeezing her eyes shut, Nivea braced herself.

Nuzzling her ear, he whispered, "No need to be afraid. The best part is just beginning." He kissed her deeply and placed his large, warm hand on the juncture of her legs. She shivered. Pressing up toward his palm, she could not help when a moan escaped.

"That's it, my dear, tell me if you like it." He moved his hand, slowly gliding his fingers inside her, rubbing her sensitive skin until little sparks of pleasure jolted gasps from her.

Just when she thought she could take no more, he lowered his head to her nipple, suckling the tip as he drove his fingers inside of her. She forced down a scream, trembling with anticipation. Eager for what was to come.

Then he lightened the pressure, barely touching her throbbing skin. When she whimpered, he chuckled. "Not yet, my impatient lamb. You wanted to know my tricks, remember?"

He sat up. "First, let's get this clothing out of the way. I want to see you. All of you." Sliding her stockings and undergarment down her legs, Dare stroked the newly exposed skin. Then, crawling over her, he tugged her gown over her hips, torso, and arms before flipping it inside out over the headboard. "That's better."

His gaze was so hot and appreciative, Nivea felt her embarrassment abate, replaced by burning desire.

Settling next to her, Dare nuzzled her throat while his hand skimmed over her ribs and the underside of her breasts. She could do more than lay there quivering with need, shifting her hips, rubbing her thighs together in a desperate effort to gain release. Twisting to her side, so his hand rested on her breast, she wiggled against his fingers. When he chuckled and palmed her flesh, she let out a sigh of relief.

It didn't last long when he squeezed her rosy tip, causing even greater torment.

"Oh, yes, Dare. Don't stop," she cried, barely recognizing her own voice.

He shifted to take her other breast in his mouth as his hand continued to roll and pinch her sensitive peak. She was unable to breathe. Her eyes were shut tight, closing out the world to everything except the feel of his lips and fingers against her skin.

"Please, Dare, I need…I need more," she whimpered.

Thankfully, he began to slide his hand down, over her stomach, through the curls and into the hot, wet center of her being. He stilled for a moment, pressing his palm against her aching skin. A long, agonizing moment.

"I think you're ready now," he crooned and flicked his thumb against her nub of pleasure. She exploded in ecstasy. Lights flashed behind her eyes, and her body jerked and quaked. Still tied to the bed, her arms yanked at the restraints.

Sweet lord in heaven, she would never survive this.

He continued to stroke her through the ripples of pleasure, until the final tingle subsided.

Unable to open her eyes, she felt Dare roll to the side of the bed and remove his breeches. "Now, my dear, perhaps you won't mind if I take some pleasure as well." His voice was so low and rough, she barely recognized it. It didn't matter. Still incapable of speech, she gave a tired nod.

Dare stretched over her, his skin hot and feverish. The solidness of his bones and muscles crushed against her, pushing her deeper into the mattress, and she reveled in his divine maleness.

Overcome with the urge to touch him, she tugged against the restraints to no avail. Her eyes popped open and she found Dare smirking at her. His eyes dark and glazed with desire, his mouth firm and his jaw clenched."You are mine."

Then he swooped down and engulfed her mouth with his. Unable to do more, she writhed against him. He moaned and ran his hands over her hips.

"You are so responsive," he breathed, "I can't wait to bury myself inside you again. Are you ready?"

She was so ready, she couldn't breathe.

He didn't wait for an answer. Just as she had hoped, he slid his hand across her stomach and between her thighs. She pulsed upward, and swallowed a scream of desire.

He looked into her eyes and gave her a smile more sultry than she had ever imagined. He raised himself over her and slid his hardened shaft between her legs. He began a slow steady pace, pulsing within her. Nivea breathed in the smell of him, overwhelmed by the mixture of love and lust. This was how it should be. This is what she had dreamed of. This and more.

She kissed him desperately, frustrated by the bonds at her wrists. How she wanted to hold him close to her, caress him, comfort him, draw him nearer. All she could do was rock her hips as he plunged into her. He lifted up her breast and suckled it, causing her to explode once again. She could feel her inner walls quivering. Tipping him over the edge, he gasped, and with several powerful strokes, shuddered before jerking himself free. Warm wetness spilled over her legs as he collapsed to the side.

It was a few moments before either of them spoke. Once their breathing had started to return to normal, he rolled towards her and said with a smug expression, "That is how I concealed it."

As her body was still warmed by the lingering tingles of pleasure, she let out a sated chuckle. "Mmm, I can see that would be quite effective."

He smirked and tapped her on the nose, before reaching up to loosen the knots at her wrist.

Rubbing her arms, Nivea laid there for a moment, mulling over all the things he'd told her. Another thought popped into her head. She knew she shouldn't ask, as the answer would no doubt be painful, but she had to know. Hesitantly she whispered, "What would you have told your... wife?"

He didn't respond.

"Would you..." she started, "would you have explained things before you were married?"

He sighed heavily and turned away. "No."

"But..."

With a resigned tone, he answered, "She would be a country girl, sweet, untutored. I would set her up in a country house and take her quickly and infrequently, just enough to ensure an heir. She would never be the wiser. Once she had done her duty, I could leave them buried in the country and return to town to continue as always."

He didn't mention Constance's name, but Nivea could see she would have fit into his plan. How horrible for her to marry Dare, only to be cast aside. She was glad that hadn't occurred. For all of their sakes.

She turned toward the man beside her, her heart swollen with love and desire. "I'm glad you don't have to hide them from me. I look forward to touching every inch of you next time," she murmured, snuggling against his chest.

* * * *

Dare froze.

Next time? There most certainly would not be a "next time." This absolutely, positively had to stop. Surely, he had gotten her out of his system.

But as he lay there, stroking her skin as she curled against him, he began to consider his future. What *would* happen between them? Would they have any sort of relationship after this? After all, men like him did not have women friends. It didn't happen. And it was not as though she could be his mistress. He could hardly set her up in a house, awaiting his nightly visits. She wasn't that sort of woman.

Nor could he marry her. That thought was even more ludicrous. He had no desire to be tied down to one woman. Not to mention, his future marchioness would need to be beautiful, elegant, the perfect hostess. Nivea, on the other hand was...not.

So, what did that leave? Nothing.

That thought made him more anxious than he would have imagined. Just a fortnight ago, he had dreaded spending a few days in the carriage with her, yet now, he was unsettled at the thought of not having her around.

With a sigh, he closed his eyes. He was tired and satisfied and did not wish to think on it further. They would just continue as they were and work it out when the time came. Dropping a soft kiss on Nivea's head, he drifted off to sleep.

Chapter 26

Dare bolted awake. A nightmare had set his heart pounding and even now the images were horrifyingly clear.

The dream had started out quite stimulating. Dare had been in his family home at Raynsforth, wrapped in a passionate embrace with an entrancing woman. She had been soft and willing, and he had been taking great delight in nibbling his way down her neck and into the delicate lace of her bodice. Aroused and content, he had suddenly heard a most distracting sound.

He had found himself surrounded by a handful of children, a mass of black, tangled hair and large pleading eyes, tugging on his coat. As he tried to block them out, he had heard them calling to him, "Father, watch me. Father, see what I can do? Can you teach me to ride? Come here, father."

He had fixed them with a killing glare, designed to drive them into retreat, but it had no effect. They had continued to pull at him, entreating him to pay them heed. As a result of the interruption, his curvaceous companion had stepped away. His temper flared, and he had raised his hand to issue a slap to the closest child.

The woman screeched at him, "How dare you threaten our children! I knew you would be just like your father." It was Nivea. With a swirl of her skirts, Raynsforth family sapphires twinkling from her neck, she had darted toward the door. When she reached the hall, she had called out, "I'm ready, dearest Winnie!"

Dare had tried to chase after her, but was trapped in place by the children, clinging to his arms. Pinned, he had been forced to watch as a smiling, rotund fellow had minced over to Nivea's side and had placed a kiss on her cheek. Arm in arm, they'd walked to his curricle and had headed down the drive.

The anger that had exploded in his chest nearly killed him.

Betrayed!

The emotion had been so raw, it snapped him out of the dream, leaving a crushing weight on his chest. When he tried to sit up, he realized the weight was actually Nivea. Her head was resting on him, a contented smile curling her lips.

The reality of the situation hit him like a blow. If he wasn't careful, he'd find himself trapped into marriage with her. And there was no doubt at some time his temper would get the best of him, and she would leave. Once she fully saw him for the monster he was, she would turn on him without a second thought. Just like everyone else.

By God, he would not let that happen.

Dare needed her gone. Now.

He nudged her rather harshly. When she rolled over, he withdrew his arm and swung his legs from the bed.

"Nivea. It is late. You should go to your room, before your absence is noticed."

She awoke and sat up against the pillow. As she did, the covers dropped to her waist and Dare was treated to a glimpse of her soft, curvy torso. This time, it was not enough to distract him.

"Let's go, Nivea. You fell asleep. You cannot be found here."

Suddenly, realizing where she was, her eyes flew open in a panic. "Oh, yes. I must go." She yanked the covers up to her neck in embarrassment. "Can you hand me my gown?"

Only too happy to speed things along, Dare gathered her clothing and deposited it on the bed. Paying her no mind, he crossed to the dressing area and pulled on his robe. He turned back to see her struggling with the gown.

"Here, let me help," he snapped, yanking down the fabric, and then buttoning it in place. As she turned to thank him, the look on his face must have troubled her.

"Dare? Are you all right?" She raised a hand as if to stroke his cheek. He caught it and squeezed her hand in his. Dredging up as much sincerity as he could muster, he said, "I'm only worried about you, dear. Now hurry before your reputation is destroyed." Then he kissed her wrist and hustled her towards the door.

She shot him a look of concern, but nodded in acceptance before peering out the door. Finding the hallway empty, she dashed out toward her room. It was only then that Dare let out a sizeable breath.

There. She was gone.

He closed the door.

Expecting to feel relief, he was instead struck by a looming emptiness. His room had lost all manner of life.

That had never happened before. He always had been perfectly content in his own company. Preferred it, in fact. But now, for the first time in decades, he was...lonely.

God damn Nivea Horsham and everyone else on this bloody planet. Why couldn't they all leave him alone? Crossing to the table by his bed, Dare raised the bottle of brandy to his lips and proceeded to drink himself senseless.

Chapter 27

Nivea slowly opened her eyes, giving a long luxurious stretch. Sunlight streamed in the windows and fluffy, white clouds floated across a brilliant blue sky.

Had there ever been a more perfect day? Nivea gave another stretch, unable to temper the smile that lit up her face. Not only had last night been incredibly enjoyable on a physical level, but Nivea was sure it had been a turning point emotionally as well.

Dare had spared those boys a punishment and helped their lives for the better. It was wonderful to think she had a positive impact on him. And he had told her about his wonderful tricks. He trusted her as he had no other. Surely, that was a first step to building a relationship.

Never a fool, she knew full well he would not consciously acknowledge it yet. But she imagined slight changes to his behavior, a knowing smile, a touch of his hand, occasional moments of shared intimacy that would tie them together. Until the day he realized that they were meant to be together. Forever.

Maybe not today, but soon.

She couldn't wait. Nivea leapt from her bed and rang for her maid.

Bustling in a few minutes later, Emma exclaimed, "You slept in this morning, miss. Breakfast is almost over. Would you like me to bring up a tray?"

"No, thank you. I'd like to go down and see—" She caught herself from blurting out his name. No point in feeding the servant's gossip mill too blatantly. "And see if there are any outings planned for the day," she finished. "I know we have the dance at Lord Morrill's this evening, but perhaps Amelia has scheduled something for the afternoon."

Emma reached into the wardrobe and pulled out a dress of grey muslin. "Would you like to wear this today?"

Nivea wrinkled her nose. "No, I think I would like the green gown with the sprigs of flowers on the sash."

"Oh, that's a pretty one, for sure. Hurry and we'll have you ready in time to eat."

As Emma adjusted her gown and arranged her hair, Nivea could not help staring at her reflection. Her eyes bright with excitement and her cheeks flushed with pleasure. Surely, everyone would sense the difference in her today.

As if on cue, Emma murmured, "You look enchanting today, miss."

Nivea thanked her before dancing from the room.

When she entered the dining room, she was disappointed to find only William remaining. Especially once he began skewering her with questions. "What's this I hear about you letting Lord Landis give you riding lessons?"

Nivea sighed. She supposed it was too much to ask for Dare to keep her secret, although hiding *that* part of their relationship was the least of her concerns.

Giving her brother a shrug, she answered in a measured tone, "Well, once I was forced to ride, I discovered horses aren't so horrid. I wanted to become more proficient."

He waved his fork in the air, not assuaged in the slightest. "But why didn't you tell us? Or ask us for help? Why go to Landis of all people?"

She nibbled at a slice of toast. "I didn't want any of you to know. I wanted it to be a surprise!"

"But Landis? Really Niv, he's one of my closest friends, but that doesn't mean I trust him. He's a complete scoundrel."

That made her angry. What right did he have to talk to her like this? "Are you implying I'm too naive to handle my own affairs? Your poor, desperate little sister can't take care of herself? She'll simply fall at the feet of any man who speaks to her? Is that it?" Her voice had risen to a wholly unnatural octave, but she couldn't help it.

Nonplussed by her reaction, William just blinked at her. "No, Niv, you know it's not that. I…I just want you to be careful. Dare can't be trusted around any woman. They are just playthings to him. He can't help himself."

Nivea knew she was acting irrationally, but William had tapped into her greatest fear. Suppose Dare was just toying with her?

No, she shook her head. She was different. They shared a deeper connection. He trusted her. She was sure of it. But until the time came that Dare was willing to acknowledge their relationship, they would have to be very discreet.

"I'm sorry, Wills. I know you're just looking out for me. Don't worry. Lord Landis has been a member of this household for a long time and I well know what to expect from him."

At least she hoped she did.

Needing to reassure herself, she finished her meal and slipped outside in search of Dare.

Chapter 28

An incessant banging forced Dare to open his eyes. With a groan, he peeked through gritty eyelids and glared at the culprit.

Just as he thought. Jackson was stumbling around the room, slamming pitchers of water on his dressing table and boots into his wardrobe. He drew in a deep breath, preparing to bellow at the hapless servant, but that simple movement caused more pain than he could have imagined. He settled for a deep groan.

"Ah, milord, you are awake." Jackson crossed to Dare's bed. "From the smell of it, I'd say you spent the better part of the evening swilling brandy. Is your wound troubling you?"

Dare grimaced before growling, "No. My wound is not troubling me. I am fine. Or I would be if you would stop smashing my possessions around."

"Yes, sir. Terribly rude of me to bring in warm water and clean clothes. I should have known that you were choosing to spend the day in bed."

Dare watched as the arrogant fool crossed to the window and threw open the drapes.

"Argh! Are you trying to blind me? Close them," Dare screamed before sinking back into the pillows.

"So sorry. I had merely hoped to air out the room. It's a bit stale today."

"Well it will bloody well stay stale for the next several hours. I have no interest in being bothered. Go get me some coffee and then be gone."

Dare groaned one last time as the man deliberately and noisily slammed the door shut. Pressing his hands to his temples, he tried to piece together the evening. He remembered Nivea waking him with a cool hand on his forehead. They talked. They kissed.

He turned toward his headboard and saw his cravat still tied to the bedpost. Ah, yes, he definitely remembered their liaison.

Then his dream came back to him. Nivea watching in horror as he smacked one of their children. Her disgust driving her out the door and into the arms of that Corknell fellow. She was no better than any other woman in his life. She had judged him, found him lacking, and left without a backward glance.

The worst part was, he had actually started to believe she might be different. That she might truly be sympathetic. But deep down, he knew she would never understand the ugliness, the anger, the violence that simmered beneath his surface. At the first sign of his true personality, she would turn tail and run. He had no doubt of that.

Although their relationship had, until this point, been far more enjoyable than he would have ever imagined, he realized it must come to an immediate end. This ill-fated trip had gone on long enough and it was high time he return to London and his normal life.

Strange how that thought brought a surge of pain to his chest.

Putting that sensation aside, he opened his eyes once more determined to leave at once. But as his head threatened to explode, he quickly shut them again. His departure would need to wait until tomorrow. The thought of riding in a jolting carriage was far too unsettling.

* * * *

It was hours before he managed to pull himself together. Thankfully, Jackson had brought coffee and a headache powder that addressed most of his needs. After an extensive nap and a long soak in the tub, he decided to get dressed and attend the evening's dance. Although he had no interest in participating, he was loathe to give rise to any rumors that he was unwell from his injury, or God forbid, that he had managed to drink himself stupid.

Starting tonight, he would return to his old self—Lord Landis, notorious rakehell. That would dash any hopes Nivea may harbor about a "next time." She would learn she was just another in a long line of women.

He summoned Jackson to prepare an unrestricting, yet thoroughly rakish wardrobe. It took some doing, but the result was striking. He wore a midnight blue jacket that hugged his broad shoulders but did not need to be buttoned. His silver waistcoat, embroidered with indigo thread, was lightweight and flexible. His dove grey trousers sat low on his hips, below his wound. Setting off the ensemble was a deep sapphire blue pin embedded into his starched white cravat.

Jackson was just securing his queue with a blue ribbon when there came a knock on his door.

"Landis, you in there?"

"Yes, Horsham, what do you need?"

William opened the door and peered in. He was dressed in a drab brown jacket and trousers, only one step up from his usual riding attire, but what passed as fashionable for him. "We haven't seen you all day. Just checking to see if you are all right."

"Yes, yes, I'm fine."

"Good, happy to hear. We are all ready to depart for the evening's soiree. You will be joining us?"

"Would I be wearing this if I weren't?" Dare swept his hand over his attire.

"One never knows with you, my friend," William answered with a chuckle. "Would you like us to wait for you? You can ride in my carriage."

"No need. I will require a few more minutes. Go ahead and I will meet you there."

"Very well," he responded and started to pull the door shut. Then he popped his head back in. "Landis, just one more thing."

"Yes," he drawled.

"Keep away from my sister." And he pulled the door shut.

Dare glared at the door. As Jackson moved to give his cravat a final adjustment, Dare slapped his hands away. "I'll finish it myself. Go make yourself useful somewhere else."

As he walked out, Jackson didn't hide his judgmental smirk. Dare was not amused. Something had made William apprehensive. Had he seen Nivea leaving his room last night? Surely not. If William had the slightest suspicion his sister was ruined, Dare would be dragged to the church in irons.

It must have been a result of their ride together.

Well, there was no point in deluding himself anymore that Nivea was harmless. She was as dangerous as any woman he knew. Perhaps more so. He had been entirely too risky, dallying with her.

Good God, what had he been thinking? Obviously, there could be no more contact with her. Starting tonight, he would once again embrace the role of a devilish rouge, thereby crushing any of Nivea's ridiculous expectations.

"Next time," she had said. There would be no next time. No liaisons, no friendship, and certainly no marriage.

Giving his attire a final tug, he stormed out of the room. On his way to the front hall, he paused by Horsham's study to consider downing a glass of whisky. When his stomach lurched at the thought, he made do with a large pinch from his snuffbox.

Chapter 29

By the time Dare arrived at the blasted popinjay's estate, carriages jammed the circular drive. Morrill was in the House of Lords and had attracted more of a crowd than Dare had expected.

He strode inside and scanned the ballroom with the sole intention of keeping a sizeable distance between himself and Nivea. This odd fascination had gone on long enough.

"Landis, over here," Joseph called out, waving him over. He was standing with Nicholas's father. That was a safe enough crowd. Landis could listen to them with half an ear while surveying the ballroom for more interesting entertainment.

Leaning back against a column, he noticed many of the same faces from the wedding. A few more nabobs had been invited, at the behest of the young Morrill pup.

He spotted Nivea almost immediately. She looked radiant tonight in a turquoise gown, a satin ribbon of cream gathering the fabric under her bosom. It was more form-fitting than her usual attire, giving the guests a healthy view of her charms.

Damn her. She was drifting from group to group, smiling and chatting like a demimonde. Where was the shy, retiring girl, cowering in the corner, peering at others on the dance floor? Why couldn't she have crawled back into her ridiculously self-conscious shell? Instead, she seemed to be adopting a whole other persona right before his eyes.

He sneered as a thought hit him. No doubt she was bolstered by misguided dreams of the future. A future with him. Any minute, she would spot him, race over, and place a possessive hand on his arm. She would look up at him with adoring eyes and everyone would know.

Snap! The parson's trap would be set and sealed.

A burning rage flared through his chest. It would be a cold day in hell before he allowed himself to be manipulated like that.

Turning, he spotted a more agreeable companion. An elegant redhead was standing alone near the edge of the dance floor. Her deep violet gown skimmed her curves as amethyst jewels sparkled at her neck. Excusing himself from the conversation, he strolled to her side and bestowed his most appreciative smile on her.

She glanced up at him with an answering gleam in her eye.

"Good evening, milady. Are you having an enjoyable evening?"

"Yes, milord, I am." Her voice was low and husky as she asked, "Have we met before?"

He bowed low over her hand, before raising it to his lips. "No, I think not. I would certainly remember someone of your loveliness," he purred. "I am Lord Landis, Dare to my friends. And you?"

"Lady MacNair." She curtsied low enough to give him a full view of her décolletage. It was less impressive than some, but he was feeling generous enough to overlook that.

He locked eyes with her and said silkily, "I confess I was concerned the evening would be a trifle dull. But seeing you here has given me hope."

She leaned closer, slanting her face up towards his. "Has it now? In what way?"

He noted a slight Irish lilt to her voice that he had always found intriguing. One of his more adventurous liaisons had been with a Celtic lass.

With his interest suitably spiked, he responded, "I have been trapped in the country for a few weeks and desperately miss the pleasures of London. Perhaps a dance with a bewitching redhead would sustain me."

"A dance?" she answered, her eyes wide with feigned innocence, "Is that all you are hoping for?"

He chuckled. "It would be a start." Running his gloved fingers over her arm, he whispered, "I'm told that I'm quite a good dancer. In fact, some ladies declare that one dance is not enough."

She took a long slow look at him and purred, "Is that so?" Then with a sigh, she drew back. "Well, as intriguing as that sounds, I fear my husband would not approve. Here he comes now."

Reaching out her hand, she drew an oversized bear of a man to her side. He had two glasses of lemonade clutched in his giant paws. He handed one to his wife before glaring at Dare.

She smiled sweetly at her husband. "Milord, this is Lord Landis. He was keeping me company in your absence. Lord Landis, this is Laird MacNair."

MacNair growled as Landis bowed, as minimal as circumstances required. Never a stupid man, he realized there would be no benefit in pursuing this relationship. A large, possessive husband was rarely a good thing.

"Now that your escort has returned, I will once again join my friends. It was a pleasure making your acquaintance, Lady MacNair." He gave her a smirk, and she shrugged her shoulders and sipped from her glass.

He walked away, maintaining his haughty, unconcerned visage, masking the disgust that washed over him. How many more examples did he need to prove marriage was a ridiculous institution? Women were nothing but immoral hypocrites, keening for the respectability of a husband and hearth, and as soon as they have it, prowling for more excitement. Not one of them could be trusted.

Crossing the room, he kept a vigilant eye out for Nivea. He spotted her by the terrace doors. Even from this distance he could see her blue eyes sparkling with pleasure as she held an animated conversation with two older gentlemen seated along the wall. She leaned over to pat one of the gentlemen on the arm, treating Dare to a view of her rounded bottom, encased in a snug fitting skirt. He never remembered her looking so alluring. He could almost feel her soft curves pressed against him.

To his horror, he became aroused at the thought, right there on the ballroom floor. Good God, he hadn't the control of a green boy.

As though she could sense him, she turned to look in his direction. He deftly spun on his heel and headed toward the dance floor. A quick glance to his right showed Miss Yorkshire heading toward him. Remembering the dreadfully dull conversation they had at the wedding, he was determined to give her a wide berth.

Thankfully, Joseph's wife was only a few steps away, and he gathered her up and pulled her onto the dance floor.

She gave him the bemused look she reserved for him before politely asking, "So, Lord Landis, how are you feeling today?"

"Quite fine, madam. And you?"

"I am well, thank you." Both fell silent as they promenaded through the pattern.

She was a nice enough woman, but since she was unable to provide Dare what he was looking for tonight, he didn't feel the need to be particularly charming.

The dance was almost over when she said, "We missed seeing you at lunch today. I was afraid you were feeling poorly after your ride into town yesterday."

He kept his face expressionless as he twirled her left and then right. "No, milady, I was eager to catch up on my correspondence. Matters demanded my attention."

He kept his eyes on the couples in front of him and could sense her weighing the veracity of his response. But she didn't question him, and they finished the rest of the dance in silence. When it was done, he thanked her and turned his attention back to his quest.

It didn't take much effort. There was a delectable morsel standing a few steps away, waving her fan in his direction. Her soft blond curls brushed her cheeks, and her thick lashes dipped as she caught his eye.

Ahhh, this was promising. No chaperone in evidence, no husband nearby ready to sweep her away. "Good evening, Miss…"

She flashed a half smile, then cast her eyes downward. "Mrs. Fallows of Bristol, milord. Perhaps you remember meeting me at my husband's estate last fall. We took a stroll around his orangery. He had a great love of citrus trees."

He looked at her closer, trying to recall. She did appear familiar. It was then her word choice caught his attention. "Does he no longer have an interest in citrus?"

"He has no interest in anything, milord. He passed on soon after Michaelmas."

He looked at her sharply, trying to gauge her response. Was she in mourning? As her gaze slid from his face down to his chest, and settled on his thighs, he knew he had his answer.

"Dance?" he asked, pitching his voice low.

"Certainly," she purred and held out her gloved hand. He tucked it into the crook of his arm and led her onto the floor. The musicians had just struck up a waltz.

Finally, the stars were aligning for a more promising evening.

Dare pulled her into his arms, letting his fingers skim the silken lavender fabric encasing her slim waist. Taking a deep satisfied breath, he began dancing.

She glided along in his arms, a small smile quirking up the corners of her mouth. He gently squeezed her fingers, and she looked up at him with breathless anticipation, a slight flush dancing across her skin.

"Well, Mrs. Fallows, how did you come to be in Durham this evening?"

I have been staying with my cousin, just down the road at Hillshire."

"And are you enjoying yourself?" He asked, pulling her closer, watching the flush grow deeper. He inhaled to catch her scent and was dismayed by the strong rose fragrance that assailed him.

"Yes, milord." She leaned into him. "I am enjoying myself. Are you?" She leaned closer still.

"Oh, yes," he purred, letting his gaze dip to her bodice.

She was just the thing to take his mind off the clingy, unmarried, trickster sashaying around the room. He could almost feel Nivea's eyes boring into him, begging for his attention. Well, he'd be damned if he would give her the satisfaction of even meeting her glance. No point in feeding her ludicrous fantasies.

"I heard you had an unpleasant experience."

He drew back to stare at his dance partner. What? How could she know?

Mrs. Fallows looked up at him with startled eyes. "I had understood that you were shot, milord."

Oh, that! He relaxed, embarrassed by his overreaction. "Yes. It was nothing. Just a scratch."

Her face softened. "I would very much like to soothe your wound. I've been told I have very healing hands." She ran her hand down his arm, her fingertips straying towards his back.

He stiffened. God, no! He simply wanted a quick tumble and to be on his way. There would be no *soothing* involved. Inhaling sharply, he almost choked on her flowery odor. Good lord, the scent was excruciating. Had she been *rolling* in a hothouse garden?

"Are you all right, my lord?" she squeaked.

"No, yes…I'm…yes, I'm fine," he ground out. Fortunately, the waltz was ending and he was able to escape. "Please accept my apology, madam. I'm afraid I have had a trying week. Excuse me." He strode away, leaving her standing in the middle of the floor.

Before he was halfway across the room, Nivea's stepmother laid a hand on his arm, her face a mask of concern. He stifled a growl of frustration. She was the last person he needed to see.

"Lord Landis, are you all right? When you didn't join us for lunch or tea, we were concerned your injury had taken a turn for the worse."

Give me strength, he begged silently. Just how much meddling could a man be expected to stand?

Taking a deep breath, he repeated the same excuse. "I'm perfectly well, madam. Several matters demanded my attention, and it took the better part of the day to address them."

"Oh, good. I was afraid yesterday's outing to the village had caused you distress."

"Not to fear, I am fine." He turned to leave, only to find himself face to face with Nivea.

Of course.

He stopped so quickly, his waistcoat rubbed against his wound. Perfect. The pain was now excruciating.

She bobbed a curtsey, staring at his face with innocent eyes. "Good evening, milord. How are you feeling today?"

"I'm fine!" he barked. "Why won't everyone stop worrying about my well being?" He felt great satisfaction as Nivea took a step back, her eyes wide. *There, now perhaps she will leave me alone.*

Maybe everyone would just leave him alone. If they could, for one minute, stop reminding him about his wound, maybe he could ignore it.

He stomped away.

God in heaven, when did it get so bloody hot in here? Air. He needed air. And a few minutes of peace.

He strode to the terrace doors and stormed out into the garden. There were couples strolling along the well-lit patio, with the more daring sort walking down the darker paths. If this evening hadn't been so cursed, he would have been one of those men, in search of a dark corner with a soft, willing woman.

Instead he would settle for a quiet bench to rest upon, undisturbed. He headed for the most secluded trail, tromping loudly enough to give any licentious couples adequate warning. He had just entered the shadows when Satan took another poke at him.

"Dare?"

The scent of vanilla betrayed her.

He squeezed his eyes shut, drew a sharp breath, and turned around to face her.

"What?" he ground out between clenched teeth.

"Oh, Dare, what is wrong? I feel as though you have been avoiding me all day."

He could barely see her face in the shadows, but he sensed the intensity of her gaze. "Nothing. I am just weary of all this concern over my health."

Laying a hand on his arm, she asked furtively, "Is that all? Are you certain I have not done something to anger you?"

He jerked his arm free. It was time. He would adopt a cool demeanor and put an end to this insane attraction. "I assure you, Miss Horsham, I am fine. I don't need your sympathy and I don't need your concern. What I most especially don't need is to be caught out here in the dark with you in the hopes of becoming a marchioness."

She let out a gasp. "You know that is not what I am doing here. I thought we were friends. I am merely concerned."

He stared at her in disgust and spat out, "Is that why your brother warned me to stay away from you? Because he feared for your *concern* of me? Don't be coy, Nivea. It doesn't suit you."

"What? I'm not being coy."

"No, then why *are* you here? What do you want from me?"

She looked up at him, her blue eyes swimming. "I was hoping you might dance with me."

The sight of her tears almost caused him to relent. But he knew better. The price was too high. Instead, he would take this opportunity to end things once and for all.

He leaned closer and purred, "So, you want to dance with me. You know, I can usually be persuaded by your well-meaning friends to dance with you at least once an evening. *Pity dance,* you understand. But now that I think about it, I believe I've given you enough pity attention this week."

She stepped back as though he'd slapped her.

Adopting a condescending tone, he continued, "Oh, I beg your pardon. Did you think I was infatuated with you? Come, come, Miss Horsham. Do not flatter yourself."

"Dare! What's come over you? Stop being so horrid."

He stretched his mouth into a smile. "Horrid, am I? No, my dear, this is the real me. Perhaps you were just expecting too much. I'm not surprised, most women do."

Her chin quivered, but she said nothing.

"As pleasurable as this trip has been," he continued, allowing his eyes to rake over her, "I find I have grown bored in the country. I will be returning to London tomorrow. I have business to attend to."

Instead of crying or begging, as he had expected, she set her jaw, nodded briefly, and responded, "I see. Yes. I'm sorry to have disturbed you. Go back to London then."

He could see the glitter of tears reflected in her eyes, but she refused to let them fall.

"I will be remaining at Durham for the month. If you change your mind, you'll know where to find me," she choked, before turning on her heel and running back toward the house.

He let out a violent exhale.

There. It was done.

Over.

Chapter 30

Dare awoke early, restless and anxious. He needed to return to London and put this nightmare behind him. "Jackson! See that my things are packed up today. We will be heading home after the midday meal."

"Very good, milord."

"And ready my riding clothes. I would like to stretch my legs a final time before being cooped up in a carriage for days."

"Yes, milord. Anything else?"

"Yes. Keep everyone the hell away from me. I'm sick to death of people's company."

"Certainly, milord."

Once again, Dare caught the smirk on Jackson's face before he disappeared. At some point, he should probably discipline the man for his impertinence, but today, he just hadn't the energy.

* * * *

The sun was hovering over the trees as Dare rode up the main drive. He had considered heading into the woods, where it was cooler, but didn't want to run into Nivea practicing her riding. Not that there was anything special about Nivea. As he'd told Jackson, he didn't want *anyone's* company. There was no reason he spurned her presence more than others.

He gave the horse his head, and they streaked away from the house. As they neared the main road, a carriage came rolling up the drive. Dare gave way, slowing his horse and pulling him off to the side. No longer in motion, he realized both he and his horse were lathered. Not to mention there was a sharp ache in his side.

Giving into the feeling, he turned the stallion back to return home at a more sedate pace. He entered the yard and handed the reins to a groom. Careful to mask his pain, he took a deep steadying breath. At the sound of another horse entering the yard, he turned to see William's wife, Betsy, grinning like a fool, astride a large, prancing grey. She jumped down, unassisted.

"Oh that was marvelous. I have been waiting so long to once again be on horseback. If I didn't love little Anthony so much, I would have gone mad from the wait."

At that, a large woman came trudging up the path from the house, a crying, flailing bundle at her breast. Betsy rushed over and scooped the baby into her arms.

"Beg your pardon, milady. He was fussy from the time you left. Refused a nap or even a biscuit. You are always able to soothe him."

As Betsy cooed lovingly, the cries stopped.

The groom approached. "May I see the wee lad, milady?"

"Certainly, Ian."

Uncovering his face, Betsy allowed him to admire her son's round cheeks and strawberry blond fringe of hair.

"Oh, he's beautiful and strong, that he is. And look, he's blessed with the Irish mane," Ian declared, running his fingers through the child's hair.

"Look at me, boy. This is how you'll no doubt turn out one day." The groom laughed, running a freckled hand over his own flaming red hair.

Betsy laughed too and headed back toward the house.

Dare stood there, appalled by the level of familiarity between Betsy and her servants.

Shaking his head, he headed into the house only to find Nivea wrapped in the arms of another man.

"Oh, yes, Winnie," she squealed with pleasure, "I'd be happy to join you for dinner."

The gentleman's round, red face beamed with delight.

"Excellent, my dear Nivvy. Come by Valendeer next week. I'll show you my garden. It is wonderful this time of year." He bowed and grabbed her hand, kissing it with vigor as Nivea smiled at him as though her world was complete.

Dare could barely contain his rage as he watched the lobcock saunter out, a besotted grin plastered to his face.

It was only once the door was shut that Nivea noticed him. Feigning innocence, she said sweetly, "Oh, Dare, I'm glad you've returned."

"Are you?" he exploded. "Are you sure I didn't interrupt? I could go back and give you and your lover a few more minutes alone."

Nivea paled, obviously stunned to be caught. Dare couldn't believe how quickly she'd turned to another man.

"Now I understand why you were so eager for me to go back to London. I didn't realize you had a line of suitors, and I have overstayed my welcome. Please forgive my oversight."

He had taken two steps inside when Nivea found her voice. "Dare, you know that's not true. Winnie is…was…he's one of my oldest friends. We were just… He's married, for goodness sake!"

"I am not interested in him or you. I don't know why you think I would have any interest in your personal life whatsoever. You are free to act the whore with whomever you chose."

She just stood there, her face twisted in anguished horror. He didn't care. It was obvious his dream was more prophetic than he'd feared. She hadn't even waited until he'd left to betray him with her precious Lord Corknell. As fury ripped through him, he stormed toward the back of the house, almost running down William emerging from his study.

"Ho, sir, are you all right? I heard yelling?"

Dare strode into the room, sloshed a glass full of whisky, and downed it.

"Drinking at this hour? My, what has put you in such a temper?"

"Women!" He poured another drink.

William strolled over and said with a chuckle, "What is wrong with women? You are usually quite amenable to the fairer sex."

"They can't be trusted. Not a one. They are all disreputable, unfaithful liars."

"Yes, so you've said, but you know I have to disagree."

"Do you?" Dare turned with a growl. "You and your loving, devoted wife? You think you can trust her? Have you not noticed the striking resemblance between your son and the groom? I would attempt to put another heir in your wife's belly in the hopes the next one look more like the Horsham name he bears."

William froze, his face mottled with anger. "Take that back! You have no right to impugn my wife's honor like that."

"Don't be a fool. She was able to satisfy her family and their stable of daughters by finally getting a man, with a title at that. Surely, you don't expect her to be faithful, now that she has what she wants."

The next thing Dare knew, he was lying on the floor.

William had punched him square in the face and was looming over him, yelling like a deranged lunatic. "Damn you to hell, Landis. I have defended you for years. Everyone in the *ton* has questioned our friendship, and I have staunchly stood by you, explaining how it was just an act. That you didn't mean what you said. That you just enjoyed acting the pompous fool. But you have gone too far. Get out. You are no longer welcome in my house."

At that, William stormed out of the room, slamming the door.

Dare rubbed his jaw. *Well that was a surprise.*

He could almost pity the poor deluded devil. When the little brat grew to look just like their redheaded groom, he would see Dare was speaking the truth. Until then, he would have to give William time to calm down.

It was obvious to Dare that this entire trip had been a mistake, one horrible episode after another. Stomping out of the room, Dare flew up the stairs and bellowed for Jackson.

* * * *

Nivea heard Dare charging down the corridor past the door of her room. She had collapsed into a chair in her sitting area, shaking at the recent turn of events, trying in vain to suppress the pain.

How could he be so cruel to her? She hadn't asked for anything, hadn't expected anything. She only wanted his friendship.

But, no, that wasn't true. Even after learning all his secrets, she still wanted his love. A special place in his life.

Was it possible he'd had his fill of her and was now returning to the welcoming arms of more beautiful, experienced women? Were they better able to meet his needs? The thought shot pain through her heart.

No, she argued. No one else had forged a connection like she had. No one else knew the truth. Surely, that was something.

Agitated, she paced her sitting area, listening to the servants removing Dare's belongings. Once they had completed the task, she peeked out her door and crossed to William's room. From there, she could watch his carriage parked on the front drive.

It wasn't until she saw him storm outside, leap into the carriage, and drive off that the tears started. She ran back to her room, threw herself onto her bed, and let all the agony pour out. The only thing that kept her sane was the faint, slight, sliver of hope that one day he might return.

Chapter 31

Dare settled back into his life at his London townhouse. There was no need to reflect on any of the unpleasantness he left behind at Vincent Hall. None at all. He was home and ready to enjoy the pleasures in town.

While entertainment was limited during the summer months, he soon learned of a lavish rout that was certain to break up the summer doldrums. As he approached the house, Dare could sense the evening held countless possibilities. Designed like a gypsy camp, the grounds were surrounded by tents and bonfires. Jugglers, fortune tellers, and musicians strolled around, as did servants with trays laden with delicacies.

He'd barely stepped on the grounds, when he was greeted by a group of revelers.

"Landis, welcome back to civilization!"

"Hasn't been the same without you here."

Graves, Lazby, Highstone, and Courtlay gathered around him, eager for an evening of debauchery. They were the crème of the *ton*, wealthy, attractive, and titled, gaining them entrance to any ballroom, and most bedrooms, in London. Dare finally felt at ease.

"What do you say we stir up some excitement, Landis?" asked Graves, a devilish glint to his eye.

Dare took the glass of spirits handed to him and drawled, "What do you suggest?"

Lazby, the youngest of the crowd was eager to respond. "Let us head down to the tent on the water's edge. I understand there's a tasty morsel doing a gypsy dance."

They turned to Dare for approval, and he nodded his head agreeably. Delighted, Lazby stumbled forward toward the tent and the others followed. He smiled as Lazby grabbed a tray of drinks from a startled footman before distributing them to his compatriots. Throwing himself into the festivities, Dare gulped down two in rapid succession, earning himself cheers from his friends.

Letting the younger men roam ahead, he paused at a table to sample a skewer of roasted boar. Graves joined him. "So, were you able to find a few willing wenches in the country to keep you amused?"

Dare had been friends with Graves since his early days in London. Together, they had embraced the rakish lifestyle, exploring the gaming hells and clubs in search of fights and women. They had often waged contests to see who could attract the more beautiful or scandalous conquest. Dare could imagine the reaction of his friend if he told him of his experience with the formerly virtuous and overly voluptuous Miss Horsham. It would hover between disbelief and horror.

Now that Dare was back home, he found it difficult to believe himself. Knowing that Graves expected some sort of tale, he resorted to an unusual and rarely called upon strategy. He lied. Extravagantly. "Actually, old man, it was quite an enjoyable interlude. Scored a winning hand—four queens."

"You did not!" Graves shouted. "Two brunettes and two redheads? Quite a feat, even for you. Tell me more."

Dare shrugged, warming up to the tale. "The first was Miss Berkshire, now Wilshire. A nice enough piece, to be sure, and hair as black as spades."

"Ah yes. She has been cozying up to you since her first season. Was she worth the wait?"

"She had some talent. Unfortunately, she crossed me and won't get a second chance."

"Pity for her," Graves smirked.

"Too true. Next was a wedding guest from a nearby shire. I fear she was hoping for a nobleman's title, but only wound up with his staff."

"Ho, Landis, you are the devil himself, aren't you? And was she a redhead?"

"No, my queen of clubs had rather ordinary hair, brown and curly. The redheads were a special treat the night before my departure. Would you believe cousins, visiting from Galine? I managed to persuade Fiona to take a tour of the library. After sharing a glass of sherry, I discovered the couch, and the redhead, to be quite accommodating."

Graves just rolled his eyes at this and waved at him to continue.

"After that, I strolled in the gardens with the delightful Miss Brynwyn, where we located a secluded temple. We found the Greek statues to be quite inspiring and she eagerly explored my ionic column."

At that, Graves laughed. "You are a master at the double entendre, my friend, quite the turn of phrase. I'm sure you understand that I will need collaboration before I let you win this hand."

Dare raised an eyebrow in silent rebuke.

"Surely, you were not so discreet as to go completely unnoticed, especially when the ladies in question came stumbling back to the party rumpled and sated."

"I'm certain they were sated. As to the rest, I cannot say." He waved a dismissive hand in the air and headed down the path, content that his tale included enough of the truth to quell any rumors regarding his true exploits.

It didn't take long to locate the desired tent. It was surrounded by a bawdy crowd of gentlemen, eagerly expressing their appreciation. Undeterred, Dare strode through the throng and secured himself a key vantage point, with Lazby and the others following close behind.

The woman in the center was quite magnificent. Lean and dark, with thick black hair and shadowed eyes, she spun and swayed in a circle. She had four veils draped over her lithe form, with others scattered about on the grass. A chain of gold surrounded her waist, and she held tiny cymbals in her fingers that were barely audible over the catcalls of the crowd. As a dancer she was well skilled, alternating between slow sensuous movements and a more fevered pitch, twirling in mad circles, causing her gold jewelry to flash in the lamplight.

A portly fellow next to Dare gave him a nudge in the ribs. "Called the dance of the seven veils." Without taking his eyes off the entertainment, he licked his thick lips. "Three are gone and the next few promise to be quite revealing."

The dancer's hand trailed along the edge of a gauzy blue scarf, draped from shoulder to hip. The shouts grew louder as the crowd implored her to remove the draping. Once she sensed their attention was maximized, she once again slowed down and loosened the knot at her shoulder. Catching both ends in her hands, she slid the scarf across her body, tantalizing them with flashes of skin.

The tension mounted. Only three scarves remained, covering two scraps of strategically placed gold fabric. She once again picked up the tempo, whipping the scarf above her head before letting it sail to the ground near Dare's feet.

"God's blood, she is magnificent," Lazby slurred at his side. "She would be a ride no man could forget, I'd wager." Then, to everyone's dismay, he reached out and grabbed a hank of hair as the dancer twirled by. The sudden tension yanked her from her feet and she collapsed in a heap in front of them.

The crowd erupted with shouts. They were not happy to have their entertainment interrupted. Dare reached over and pried the pup's hands out of her hair. "Lazby, that is no way to treat a lady."

"She's no lady. She's mine. I saw her look at me. I know what she wants."

"Here now, Lazby. You must be nice and share."

The cur slapped Dare's hand away and grabbed once more for the woman. "I don't wanna share. I caught her. I keep her."

Dare was disgusted by his ill-mannered behavior. "No, she's here to entertain everyone. Perhaps after the show you can seek her out. For now, I think it's time to leave."

He motioned to his companions to grab Lazby's arms and together they dragged him from the tent. The sot flailed around, trying to break free, but they held tight. As they headed up the path, they heard the music in the tent resume.

"Damn," muttered Graves, "I was really looking forward to the next veil."

Dare grunted his agreement before turning to the others. "Highstone, see that Lazby doesn't get into any more trouble. I have no interest in rescuing him again this evening."

Gravely, Highstone nodded, dragging his disgraced friend off to get some food.

At that, a trio of ladies entered the path ahead of them and Dare thumped Graves on the shoulder. "I'm sure we'll be able to find adequate replacements this evening. Let's get a drink and begin our search."

Putting that unpleasantness behind him, Dare spent the rest of the evening in flirtatious conversation with uncomplicated women, accompanied by sly smiles and eager touches. It was just what he wanted. Superficial and uninspired as always, with no mention of his injury, no deep, personal probing into his upbringing. Just unfettered enjoyment. Dare was finally able to relax.

As the evening grew later, exotic fortune tellers appeared, wandering between groups. Draped in gauzy skirts and glittering jewelry, they invariably offered the same predictions. "You will find happiness. You will be blessed with children. You will have a successful night at cards in the near future." It was all in good fun.

It wasn't until Dare was heading out that he felt a prickle of anxiety. Turning around, he was startled by a gypsy woman in darker clothes, appearing more ragtag than sparkly. She grabbed his arm with her strong, narrow fingers, looked deep into his eyes, and whispered, "Your pain is ending. Allow it to happen. Don't let fear stop your destiny."

He froze. What sort of odd entertainment was this? He shook off her hand. "Quiet, old woman. I don't need your ridiculous pronouncements."

She gave him a steady look, her coal-black eyes boring into his, and then turned away without another word.

Dare felt a shiver run down his back. "Your pain is ending," she had said.

Well, indeed it was. He had left his pain in the country. And he had returned to his destiny, his life, in London. While that interpretation made perfect sense to him, he could not shake the eerie sensation her words had caused. Determined not to let it overshadow his evening, he did his best to put her out of his head.

Chapter 32

The next evening, Dare and Graves settled into one of their favorite gaming hells. They cordially greeted the other gentlemen gathered around the table, wasting no time joining their card game. It started as a casual pastime, but as the evening wore on, the play became more intense. Upon the arrival of Lord Barley and his more desperate cronies, the stakes rose with alacrity.

"I'm out," said Graves, after a bad turn of the cards cost him a tidy sum. "I'm going to head to the club. Do you care to join me?"

Dare was having an unusually difficult time playing cards. Every so often, he would hear Nivea's voice in his head, ruining his concentration. He recalled the morning when he'd told her about his childhood and she pointed out, *You gamble.* And then, when he mocked her disregard for honoring his father's wishes, she shot back, *I don't blame you for breaking the fifth commandment.*

Her support gave him a queer feeling inside. Why couldn't he just block her from his thoughts?

But he couldn't. In fact, she'd been rattling around his brain for the past week. Every time he saw a pair of pretty blue eyes or noticed flowers in the park, he thought of her. Tonight, when nothing in this godforsaken place should have had the remotest connection to her, he still couldn't get her out of his head. And it was ruining his game.

Determined to end this once and for all, he responded to his friend, "You go on ahead. I'm certain to redeem myself. This run of bad luck can't continue."

"Are you sure?" Graves leaned over. "You sound like one of them."

Dare sneered. "You know better than that. I will never be like them— in *any* form."

Graves raised an eyebrow, but didn't press the issue. Dare waved him away and turned back to his cards.

The stakes rose rapidly as others did their best to recoup their losses. After a few more hands, Dare considered walking away. He had not expected such an intense session and was running low on funds. He would play just one more hand and then move on.

Picking up his cards, he did his best to remain focused. Here was a hand that could not lose. Apparently, others felt the same way, and after a particularly aggressive round of betting, Dare found he couldn't match the pot.

Well, that was a disappointing turn of events.

He withdrew his jeweled snuffbox and took a second to consider his options. He could leave the table, but it seemed a damned shame given his spectacular hand. His companions sensed his situation and, anticipating his continued bad luck throughout the evening, began to press their advantage. "Landis, old man, it appears you are a bit out of pocket. No worries there, we are happy to take a voucher from you."

Like hell they would. Betting more than he could cover was a rule Dare never broke. It was such foolishness that resulted in his family losing their fortune and led to the unfortunate circumstances of his youth.

No, he would leave it up to them to divine another alternative. He leaned back in his chair, assuming his most bored and dispassionate pose and drawled, "Sorry, gentlemen, I fear I may just call it an evening. No point in pressing my luck any further."

Desperate not to lose his mark, Barley's eyes roamed over his opponent. "Perhaps you have something else you'd care to wager." His eyes lit up as they settled on Dare's snuffbox.

Affecting a nonchalant tone, Barley stated, "We don't want to end our fun quite yet. Perhaps you have a bit of jewelry you'd like to toss in, like your stick pin or a watch." He paused a beat before continuing smoothly, "Or maybe that snuffbox would fill in the gap, to let you finish the hand."

Resisting the desperate urge to recoil, Dare slowly placed a hand on the box and slid it off the table into his pocket. Having seen the speculative light in his companion's face, he knew that was what he was after. But Dare would go to great lengths to protect that box. The thought of losing it sparked a slow burn of anger that made him want to quickly win this hand and depart.

"The box is nothing but a trinket," he answered, keeping his voice level. "But you are correct. I am not ready for the fun to end. Perhaps I will wager my...ring." Sliding the heavy gold piece from his finger, he held it up so the large sapphire sparkled in the candle light.

"It has been in my family for a century or so, and I *hate* to part with it. You must promise that if I do lose, you will give me a chance to win it back at a later time. I am certain my father would be…perturbed to find it missing." With that he cringed, giving all indications that he'd filched a valuable family heirloom.

Eager to take advantage of the situation, Barley agreed, "Of course. We are all gentlemen here. We can make an arrangement for you to regain your bauble, should the need arise." With his answering smirk, Dare knew he was thinking *at a hefty price.*

The smile disappeared the instant Dare laid down his cards. In silence, the others followed suit, knowing that they'd been bested.

"Thank you for an enjoyable evening," Dare said, scooping up his winnings. "I fear my luck has reached an unexpected peak. I should take advantage of that and look for another sort of entertainment to finish my evening." With a jaunty wink, he strolled from the room.

As he climbed in his carriage, he withdrew the snuffbox and stared at it, twinkling in the lamplight. The thought of risking it in a card game was so ludicrous he actually laughed out loud. It was one of his most valuable possessions.

His mind turned back to when he was a young man, just graduating from the university. His father had come to town and they were strolling past some shops when Dare noticed the jeweled snuffbox in the window.

With the brash surety of youth, he announced, "That's quite the thing."

"Pshaw," growled the marquess. "Nothing but a useless play toy for the idle. No son of mine would waste his time with snuff…and certainly not with such a foppish box as that."

Determined to exert his independence, Dare declared, "I disagree. I think I might get it."

His hand had not even reached the latch to the shop's door when his father's fist slammed into Dare's head, leaving him with a familiar dizziness.

"You bring that into my house and I'll bounce you out on your arse, make no mistake," he bellowed and strode down the street without a backward glance.

Dare could vividly remember the shame and humiliation of his father's abuse right there on the sidewalk for all the world to see, and anger roiled in his belly.

He had stood there for a moment, gathering his wits, before turning on his heel and marching back to his rooms. The next day, he had gathered all the coin he could find and purchased the snuffbox. It was with great satisfaction that week, upon returning to his home in Raynsforth, that he had sat as his father's dining table and pulled it out of his pocket.

True to his word, his father threw him out on the spot. It was five years before he was forced to lay eyes on his sire again. Five blessed years. That snuffbox was a symbol of Dare's freedom and he treasured it above all else.

Feeling restless, Dare instructed his groom to take his carriage to Madame Amora's. He was certain to find ample entertainment at her elegant and exclusive accommodations.

As he walked in the door, he realized it had been almost two weeks since he'd had a woman. No wonder he was unsettled. That was an extraordinary oversight on his part.

Madame Amora welcomed him as soon as he entered the oversized parlor. The room was filled with a plethora of attractive ladies draped across comfortable furniture and amused gentlemen. Madame pressed her abundant figure against him and asked, "Lord Landis, my pet, we have missed you. What sort of entertainment would you prefer this evening?"

He stared at her, realizing he had no idea. That was odd. Waving a hand, he proclaimed, "I care not. Pick me something new."

She pondered a moment, tapping a finger to her lips before proclaiming, "I have just the thing. We have an exotic creature from the south upstairs. Quite talented."

"From the south, you say? Sounds intriguing."

"Quite," she answered, stroking his arm.

He followed her upstairs and paused as she knocked on a door to the right. A husky female voice called out, "*Si?*"

"I have a gentleman who would like to meet you."

The door opened and a lithe young woman appeared in the doorway. Her even white teeth flashed at Dare as she leaned her slim hip against the frame. Her long black hair hung in a thick curtain around her scantily covered body. The candlelight illuminated the gauzy fabric, turning it transparent.

"Welcome, milord. My name is Marita. Please come in." She let her eyes walk slowly over his form as she gestured toward the room.

"Is she to your liking?" asked the madam, silkily.

He nodded and crossed the threshold.

Marita directed him to a chair and slid his jacket off his shoulders. As he sat down, she whispered in his ear, "First we will relax and get to know each other a little, *mi amor*. It is important to soothe the mind as well as the body."

"Hm," he grunted.

She crossed to the sideboard and poured him a glass of brandy. Crossing back, she knelt in front of him, and placed her small, warm hands on his thighs. "Do you have any troubles you would like to tell me about? I am a good listener." She stroked his tight breeches and looked up at him with a coquettish smile.

No.

No, he did not want to talk. Nor confess any troubles. Or be touched, for that matter. Which didn't bode well for the evening. So Dare took a good long pull of brandy and tried to put himself in the proper frame of mind.

When he didn't answer, she let her fingers brush the placket of his trousers and slide open the first button. She licked her lips and slanted him a look of lust.

"No? That is all right. Perhaps you would like to take me to bed, then?" She took his hand and pulled him up from the chair before heading toward the bed. When he didn't follow, she stopped and gave him an alluring glance over her shoulder.

She was sensual and erotic. She was here to give him pleasure, and, judging by her movements, he could expect considerable enjoyment. Yet Dare was dismayed by his complete lack of interest.

Determined to shake off the unsettling mood, he bestowed an appreciative smirk on Marita and strode toward the bed. When he reached her side, she raised her arms to the buttons on his shirt. He snatched her hands and pulled them to his lips. Just because he had let Nivea see his scars, he wasn't going to open that door to everyone.

Adopting a tone that implied he was sharing a secret of utmost importance, he whispered, "Indulge me, darling. In my line of work, I prefer to keep on as many clothes as possible. It allows for a safe and speedy exit, if needed."

Like all women, she looked suitably impressed. Having dodged that issue, he took her into his arms and began to stroke her long, silky hair. He inhaled her scent—a spicy, exotic mixture filled his head. He ran his hands down her spine and pulled her close, allowing her flat stomach to press against his manhood.

And nothing.

He felt nothing. What the hell? Normally, he would be primed and ready to throw her down and take his pleasure, but not tonight. Determined, he reached down to knead her derriere while burying his face into her neck.

She ran her hands through his hair and undulated her hips against him. Then she pressed him down onto the bed and began to unbutton his trousers, her knuckles brushing his thighs.

He pulled open her silky robe and stroked her coffee colored skin. And felt…nothing, absolutely nothing. It just felt…wrong.

She was too bony and small. Her skin wasn't smooth and pale. She tasted wrong, spicy and exotic, not like sweet English cream.

Unbidden, visions of Nivea flashed through his mind. His hands stroked her skin, translucent and voluptuous in the flickering shadows of a single candle. Breathing in her delicious vanilla scent as he buried himself inside her soft willing thighs. *That* was what he wanted.

He froze. *My God, no. Why was she tormenting him here of all places?* He was being entertained by an experienced, exotic beauty ready to serve his every desire. How could he even be thinking of Nivea?

She was clingy and needy and constantly pressing him to discuss things he had no intention of sharing. She was certain to be his downfall, either trapping him into marriage or subjecting him to a public betrayal. Or both.

Suddenly the room seemed stifling. Hot and stuffy, with an overwhelming foreign smell.

This was lunacy. As Marita leaned down to remove his boots, he decided that this would not happen. Could not happen. It was time to leave. Which put him in a quandary.

How would he get out of this?

Should he claim too much to drink? He scoffed. Surely not. That would be too lowering.

He could get rough with her and scare her from the room. No. That sort of behavior was not allowed in Madam Amore's. And frankly, the thought made him ill.

Then it occurred to him. *I need no excuse. I am Lord Landis. I don't have to explain myself to this woman.* With that, he rolled off the bed, threw down some banknotes and strode from the room without a word.

As he burst through the door, he took a deep breath. *What the hell is happening to me?*

Chapter 33

Dare slowly raised his gaze to find Joseph standing over him, smiling. "You look like hell"

"Thank you. You may go."

Naturally, Joseph sat down. The man's gold waistcoat and green breeches were far too much color for his pounding head, and he groaned.

Dare had come to White's this afternoon to regain his equilibrium. He needed to be around normal things, manly things, to stop that infernal woman from burrowing into his thoughts. She was like a splinter that had slid under his skin, starting to fester and throb.

Of course, most of the conversation at the club centered around horses, horse racing, and women. The horseracing reminded him of his fight with William, which pained him. All the rest reminded him of William's blasted sister.

What was she doing now? Scheming a plan to ensnare him into a "next time?" Or plotting revenge over his sudden departure, eagerly disclosing his secrets to any and all who would listen? Fully irritated, he had retired to a table, alone, to nurse a bottle of brandy.

Or he *had* been alone, until now. Joseph leaned back in his chair, folded his hands on his stomach, and smirked. "Still upset about your fight with William?"

"Sod off. The man's an idiot. At some point he will realize that and apologize."

"You accuse his wife of cuckolding him and think *he's* the one who will apologize? That's rich."

"Women cannot be trusted. He should know that."

"Women must be watched closely, that is true. But once you find the *right* one, they are both trustworthy and wonderful."

"Even the *right* ones can't be trusted," Dare mumbled, disgusted by the thought. Then, realizing what he'd said, he stiffened. He must be drunker than he'd imagined. It wasn't as though Nivea was the right one. God's blood, if Joseph had heard him, no doubt he would misinterpret *that* slip of the tongue. Warily, he raised his eyes and groaned.

Oh, no.

Joseph was staring at him. He watched as the jacksnape inched forward in his chair with a slow, spine-chilling smile creeping up his face. Dare returned his attention to his drink, determined to ignore whatever rubbish was forthcoming. It didn't take long.

"The right one, eh?" Joseph drawled. "Well, well, that explains an awful lot."

"What explains an awful lot?" Dare sneered.

"You, the infamous rake, Adair Landis, have met your match. You have fallen ass over teakettle for a woman."

Dare snapped his head up and glared at him. "What bloody nonsense are you spouting?"

"You. Classic symptoms. Miserable, drunk, fighting with friends, condemning all of womankind, and losing all sense whatsoever. I heard you wagered your ring in a card game, almost losing to Barley of all people. Good God, man, you never lose, especially to that wastrel."

Dare waved his jewel-encrusted finger in front of Joseph's nose. "That is true. And as you can see, I won both the hand and the pot."

"Yes, but it was apparent to all that your concentration was abysmal. I heard they were circling you like sharks. Graves tried to drag you out, but you insisted on remaining. In fact, he said you've been acting queer all week."

Dare shook his head, but Joseph was just warming up on the subject.

"It's so obvious now. You have lost your heart, and either can't win the woman—highly unlikely, I know—" he added, airily, "or she has demanded more than you think you can give. You want to forget her, move on, prove that she's wrong. But you can't because there's no hiding from the truth. You are in love."

Dare looked at him as though he'd lost his mind. Love? Preposterous! He was distracted, maybe. Unsettled. And oddly fixated on a woman he had no business thinking about. But love?

Joseph was an idiot. Of course, that didn't stop him from prattling on.

"Lord Landis in love. Remarkable really. I never would have believed it. Now, who could it be? Who could bring down a confirmed rake such as yourself?" He tapped his fingers to his lips. "Was it a delicate debutante who caught your eye? Most likely, no. Maybe a mature woman, a wealthy widow perhaps, who has no need of a husband. That would be quite rich.

After years of shunning marriage, to be attracted to a woman who turns the tables on you."

As no answer was forthcoming, Joseph narrowed his eyes at his friend. "Come now, man, who is it?"

"You're ridiculous," Dare growled.

Joseph shrugged. "Come up with a better conclusion, then. What else would explain your behavior, you morose dragon."

"Morose drag—?" Dare banged his fist on the table. "Who do you think—?" Before he was able to sputter out a suitable retort, Lazby sauntered up to their table.

"Good evening, gentlemen. We are getting up a game of *vingt-et-un* in the front room. Would you like to join us?"

"Laz, that sounds like a fine idea." Joseph rose languidly from his chair and flashed a mocking grin at Dare. "Will you join us, Landis?"

Dare just gave him a sneer.

Joseph laughed, "Well then, I'll let you stew awhile. When you are ready to admit the truth, come to me. Perhaps I can help. We men must stick together. Women are baffling…but they are definitely worth the effort." He strutted off with a wave.

Idiot.

Pompous fool.

Overdressed jacksnape.

Each time Dare thought about Joseph's proclamation, he devised another insult.

He wasn't out of sorts because of a woman. The idea was laughable.

He was simply irritated by life. His life.

No, that couldn't be right. He loved his life—the parties, the women, his horses, his freedom. He had no obligations other than the ones *he* wanted to have. It was just as he liked it.

Although, he couldn't explain the unexpected sensation of dissatisfaction he'd been feeling since he'd returned to London. Or even during the Horsham's visit. The only time he'd truly enjoyed himself was…with Nivea.

No. That could not be.

The ride to Vincent Hall had been pleasant, but not because of *her*. His rendezvous with Elizabeth Wilshire had been…no, actually, he found that rather unsettling. The boat ride on the lake had been relaxing, when he and Nivea… *No, stop that.* How about the day he went riding in the woods with… Damn, it had all involved that infernal woman.

He contemplated long and hard about the time he'd spent with her.

She was a surprisingly passionate woman, and he enjoyed that aspect. But there was more to it. There was more to her. He felt *comfortable* around her. Safe and normal and comfortable. And now, for some inexplicable reason, uncomfortable everywhere else.

What did that mean?

Certainly not love. After all, the damned woman had ripped open long-healed wounds and shoved unwanted memories back into his consciousness. He just wanted to forget them. And forget her.

Love was a silly fairy tale. Joseph was just a damned fool who fancied himself in love and imagined everyone else was too.

Gulping down the last of his brandy, Dare banged his glass on the table and stormed out of the club in disgust.

Chapter 34

Nivea did her best to entertain herself in the country, shopping with friends, taking long walks, and improving her riding skills. All the while hoping Dare would reappear. Day after day, she would watch the horizon, praying he would race up the road, spot her in the doorway, and sweep her into his arms.

He did not.

She kept replaying that final night in her head, watching him from across the dance floor, flitting from woman to woman, all the while avoiding her. He must have been terrified. Never before had he opened himself up to anyone. He'd confessed his secrets to her and even let her touch his scars.

He had started to trust her, which must have been highly unsettling. It was unsurprising that, in light of such unusual feelings, he would run. No doubt he expected her to betray him as well. She could forgive him for his lack of faith. How could he feel otherwise with his family's history? Still, she assumed after he spent some time away, he would acknowledge his mistake and, realizing they were meant to be together, come back to her.

Perhaps he was so embarrassed by the things he'd said to her, he couldn't bring himself to return. He had been quite horrid. But as deep as her love was for him, Nivea would forgive him without question. If only he'd come back.

It was difficult to wait at Vincent Hall with so many memories taunting her at every turn. Joining friends for a picnic near the lake brought a blush to her cheeks, as she pictured their first liaison in the hunter's cabin. Just the thought of him touching her made her flush with desire.

Spotting forget-me-nots in the garden reminded of the little bouquet he'd given her, now pressed inside a book of poems.

Riding in the woods was the most difficult. That was where he had confessed that he couldn't keep away from her. Adair Landis found her irresistible. Or so he had said. Now she wasn't so sure.

When she couldn't bear his absence any longer, she would go into his room, lie on his bed and remember—his touch, his lips, his scent. The way he looked when he confessed to intervening on behalf of the Dugan boys and providing them the protection he never had. That was the moment when he transformed from an arrogant rake to the kind, caring man she knew he could be.

But she had gotten too close.

He opened up to her, and it was scary and difficult and he ran.

At least she hoped that was the problem. The alternative was far too painful.

What if he had simply used her for his own pleasure, grown bored, and returned to his rakish lifestyle? After all, she was just...Nivea. And he was the irresistible, untamable Lord Landis. *Maybe*, he had just moved on.

When those thoughts would emerge, she would lay her head on the pillow where they had spent that final, magical night together, and let the tears flow.

* * * *

By the end of the third week, the last of the wedding guests headed home and she returned to London with her father and stepmother.

She now realized just how big a fool she'd been. For years, her entire existence had revolved around trying to attract the attention of a man who was miles out of her reach. That had been painful enough. But it didn't begin to equal the heartbreak of experiencing his love, and then losing him. That was a hundred times worse.

As the days passed, sadness had given way to anger, directed more at herself than at him. She knew exactly what he was, how he was. She was just a passing phase, no better than all his other women.

Why did she think she would be any different? Just because she had spent her entire adult life loving him, did not mean he would love her back. No doubt, every woman he met felt she was special. That was part of his charm.

The question was, could she give up on him? Was she ready to accept reality? She wanted a husband, and now she had to accept that Dare would never be that person.

Yet she missed him. Desperately.

She had to see him, one last time, to convince herself it was over. That was the only way she could move on.

Determined not to embarrass herself, she had come up with a plan. When she next saw him, she would not risk her pride by groveling. She would not appear sad, but rather filled with *joie de vivre*. Let him see what a wonderful, charming woman he had let slip away. And if he didn't fall at her feet and beg her forgiveness, she would move on.

With that in mind, she accepted every invitation in town. She rode through Hyde Park, went to the theatre, and attended every musicale.

Yet there was no sign of Dare.

He never called, never attended the same events, and never apologized. All the while, she waited in vain for him to appear.

Then, one day, he did.

Chapter 35

Rifling through his invitations, Dare drew a weary hand through his hair. Motram's Ball—full of debutants and watery lemonade? No.

Glouster's musicale? Certainly not.

Lazby's country house? While the company might be entertaining, the pup was undisciplined and irritating, so no.

No.

No.

And no.

Ever since talking to Joseph, he had been unable to shake the uncomfortable feeling that something was wrong. Determined to prove he was fine, he'd thrown himself into his regular routine with a vengeance, seeking out his most salacious friends and immersing himself in the most hedonistic pursuits.

All to no avail.

He was bored. And lonely.

He missed the Horshams. Since his abrupt departure from Vincent Hall, he had not seen nor talked to William. Although the man could be dreadfully dull at times, they had been best friends for over a decade. And the Horshams had been the closest thing to a family that Dare had. But now it was over. He had ruined it.

The worst part was there was no one he could talk to about it. Joseph would mock him and call him a fool. The only other person he'd ever talked to about his feelings was Nivea, and now she was part of the problem.

That was why he found himself sitting in his study, alone and miserable.

Throwing down the invitations in disgust, he stormed toward the front hall. "George! Bring me my coat," he roared. "And have Spartacus saddled up. I'm going to White's."

He should be able to find someone at White's whose company was worth keeping. Play a game of cards perhaps, or just sit in a quiet corner and drink.

* * * *

Caroline had returned from her honeymoon and Nivea was eager to show off her new skills as a horsewoman. She'd suggested they go for a ride in the park.

Amelia had been so excited her stepdaughter was now riding, she'd insisted on purchasing several outfits. Today, Nivea donned her favorite habit, green with silver buttons, and white lace at her bodice and cuffs. Her jacket was fitted just under her bodice, emphasizing a waistline she hadn't had in years. And to top it off, she had a matching hat with a peacock feather tucked into the brim.

The combination of exercise and lovesick depression had definitely impacted her figure for the better, and Caroline was quite surprised at the transformation. "Nivvy, you look wonderful!"

"Thank you. You look wonderful, too. I take it marriage agrees with you?"

"Oh yes. Nicholas is such a dear. He took me to see his family's home in Coelburn. It is a quaint town, surrounded by beautiful rolling hills and the most amazing waterfall nearby. I almost hated to leave."

"Well, I'm glad you're back. We all missed you."

"I missed you too. I'm looking forward to spending time with the family again."

"We may have a chance to see Betsy today. She brings Anthony to the lake most mornings. She said he likes the ducks."

Caroline laughed. "He's still a baby, isn't he? Does he even know what ducks are?"

"I admit it sounds a bit funny to me, too. Why don't we race over and see. I'll lead the way." Nivea tapped her horse's flank to spur her into a trot.

Caroline let out a cry and urged her horse to catch up. "I can't believe how comfortable you are on a horse. It's marvelous to see. Who would have thought—my sister trotting through the park!"

They were giggling to each other when Nivea felt her heart catch. A tall figure was heading toward them. Judging by his elegant posture, astride an equally elegant horse, there could be no doubt who it was.

Dare.

Nivea scrambled to control her emotions. This meeting was so unexpected, she couldn't remember how she had decided to behave.

While she'd hoped to be calm and collected, her heart was pounding so hard, she could scarcely breathe. What a disaster. He was so unbearably handsome, and she was all windblown and disheveled.

It didn't take long before Caroline spotted him too and groaned. "Ugh, there's Lord Landis. Arrogant sot. I have no interest in being pleasant to him. You don't mind if we just nod and go on our way, do you Niv?"

Gathering her self control, Nivea smiled. "That would be fine. I think my infatuation with him has finally run its course."

"I'm glad. You were always too good for him, you know."

Nivea laughed at her sister's ridiculous favoritism, but it didn't stop her stomach from doing somersaults.

* * * *

Dare had spotted Nivea bouncing along on her horse with her sister by her side. The women's faces were wreathed in smiles as they chattered away.

He took in her attractive riding habit and the soft glow of her cheeks. *My God, she looks...beautiful.* The sudden tightening in his chest was unexpected. He hadn't realized just how much he had missed her. It was like seeing the sun peek through the clouds after a long, dreary winter.

When he heard her laugh, it sent a shiver of desire straight to his groin. He shifted uncomfortably in his saddle. Was it possible that this is what had been missing from his life? No. That was preposterous.

And yet...

The women approached.

"Good day, Lord Landis." Caroline was the first to acknowledge him in a clipped tone.

He nodded his head in her direction. Hearing no greeting from her companion, he turned his attention to Nivea. The happy countenance he had witnessed moments ago had vanished.

"Good afternoon, Lord Landis," she murmured. He was dismayed to see a flash of pain in her soft blue eyes before she lowered her lashes, her gaze centered on her hands.

It was then that he remembered their last meeting. He'd charged into the house and called her...my God, he'd called her a whore! He had forgotten until just this minute just how cruel he had been. He'd taken her virtue, accused her of betrayal, and then left. My God, what a bastard he was.

And why? What possessed him to act so abysmally?

Ah yes, the dream. She had walked out of his life and into the arms of another. Did he really believe she would do such a thing? Was it possible? He frowned as color flooded her cheeks.

No. No, he did not. She had showed him nothing but kindness, and he behaved like…well, like his father. It was unforgivable.

"We were on our way to the lake," announced Caroline. "I'm sure you have somewhere important to go, Lord Landis. Please don't let us keep you."

He raised an eyebrow at her tone, but she just smiled coolly at him and waited. It appeared he was being dismissed. He deserved it, without question. He looked once again at Nivea still cringing at his presence, and he sighed. "Yes, I'm off to the club."

He wanted to say more. He wanted to apologize. He wanted her to look at him and smile as she had always done. Seeing her so uncomfortable in his presence made his chest ache. But most of all, he wanted her to make him feel happy again.

But there was nothing he could do. Not with her sister glaring at him. So, he tipped his head and murmured, "Good day." Tugging the reins, he started his horse up the path.

Chapter 36

"Yes, there is a woman," Dare choked out, unable to look at Joseph as he confessed the truth.

He had walked through the door at White's and, spotting Joseph, almost had turned to leave. His thoughts were in turmoil and he didn't think he could face the man. But sitting there, the man seemed so content and serene, Dare felt…jealous.

How had his friend managed to transition from dandy to husband, and yet appear so satisfied?

Was it really possible?

Without making a conscious decision, Dare stalked over to him and dropped into a vacant chair. At Dare's proclamation, Joseph looked up at him, startled. Then he waved to the steward to bring another glass and waited for his friend to continue. Unsure how to begin, he shifted in his chair, damned uncomfortable.

"Don't look so distraught. We've all been there. How can I help?"

Dare ran his fingers through his hair. "I don't know. This woman…she affects me. I don't want her to, but she does. I can't stop thinking about her. I have tried staying away, but it's no good. Then I see her, and it's still no good."

"And does she return the sentiment, this woman of yours?"

"No. At the moment, she hates me. With good reason."

"I see. What did you do to her?" Joseph leaned forward.

Dare buried his face in his hands and groaned. "I said some horrible things to her, and now she is disgusted by me."

"You need to apologize," Joseph said simply.

He growled with annoyance. "No. It won't matter."

"Of course it would matter. That's the only thing you *can* do if you want to get her back."

He slammed down his fist. "Don't you see, I don't want her. I just want to stop thinking about her!"

Joseph gave him a level look and repeated, "If she makes you feel this way, then you want her. You have to apologize."

That was not possible. Dare knew there were no words that would earn him absolution. "No."

Joseph snorted.

"I can't."

"You must. If you wait too long, she may realize you're nothing but a pompous, arrogant ass and turn to someone else."

"What?" Dare slammed his chair legs back onto the ground.

"Well, you are a pompous, arrogant—" Joseph started with a grin.

"That's not what I meant."

The thought of Nivea with another man—soothing him with her touch, entrancing him with her scent, her soft blue eyes, full of passion, gazing into his—it made him furious. His dismay was eminently apparent to his friend.

"I know. The thought is galling. That is why you must apologize. The bigger the accusation, the bigger the apology needs to be. So, who is it and what did you say to her? Just how rude and boorish were you?"

There was no way he could admit who it was. Nivea. The woman they all agreed was a plain, plump wallflower. His best friend's sister. Or formerly best friend's sister, which made it even worse.

In absence of a response, Joseph continued, "It would make it easier for us to plot your strategy if I had a clue as to your intended. A young miss would require flowers, a picnic, sweet-talking her mother. An older woman will be more expensive—jewelry, a visit to a modiste, followed by a trip perhaps."

"Neither," Dare ground out.

"Surely not a barmaid or demimonde?"

"God, no!" Dare barked. What could he say? Nothing. There was no way he could make Joseph understand. He barely understood it himself. "Never mind." Dare scraped back his chair. "I will figure it out."

"All right. I'll be here if you change your mind. Oh, and don't forget about my birthday celebration on Friday. Everyone will be there," Joseph called after him. "Maybe you could bring your secret lady friend."

At the sound of the fool cackling, Dare growled and stormed out.

* * * *

Friday morning, Dare awoke, humming with excessive energy. Loathe to admit it, he was nervous about the evening. Joseph's soirée promised to be quite an endeavor. The Horshams were sure to be there. He would have to make peace with them. All of them.

He'd missed William's companionship more than he'd ever thought possible. He had taken him for granted all these years, just assuming the fellow was a comfortable stand-in, but after spending time with Graves, Highstone, and the other dandies, he found himself irritated by their prattle. Although William's conversation could not be construed as sparkling, he would never be accused of prattling.

And then there was Nivea. He could simply not deny the his attraction for her. He needed to set things right between them, whatever that meant.

He had not desired another woman since his return from Vincent Hall. That was particularly troubling. Maybe if he could bring her to bed a few more times, he could get her out of his system. This evening could provide the perfect opportunity. He would lure her into a quiet room, beg her forgiveness, and charm her into a quick tumble. Then he could finally move on.

He snorted at his own absurdity. She would probably not even acknowledge him, little yet raise her skirts for him.

But if she did…if he could get her to listen to him. If he could once again get her to smile at him, her wide, generous mouth tilting up in delight as he swooped down for a kiss, feel her shiver with anticipation as he nuzzled her neck.

He relaxed at the thought of being in her presence. Was it possible he could once again find serenity in his life? Dropping his head into his hands, he cursed, "God's blood, when did I become so maudlin?"

In need of a distraction, he retreated to his study to review his financial accounts. After a half hour of calculating the same figures over and over again, he slammed the book shut. Normally, he found working with numbers soothing, but today he was unable to concentrate.

He should do something physical. Perhaps a round of fencing with Joseph. Surely, the helpless sot would be eager for a chance to escape the mayhem at his house as they prepared for his party.

Happy to have a plan, he called for Spartacus to be brought around and headed out.

* * * *

"I'm sorry, Lord Landis. Lord Duxbury is not at home at the present time," informed the butler when he rapped at Joseph's door.

Damn, where was the fool?

He was on the verge of leaving, when a female voice called out from the parlor, "Carrick, has the florist arrived with my arrangements?"

"No milady. It is Lord Landis."

Briar appeared in the hallway. "Oh, Landis, we weren't expecting you. I'm afraid Joseph has gone out with the children. They were getting underfoot and he agreed to help them feed the birds." She smiled indulgently. "They should be back in a few minutes. Would you care to wait?"

As he had nowhere else to go, he bowed and crossed the threshold.

Briar drew near and whispered, conspiratorially, "Actually, I sent him away so I could prepare for the party. He was getting underfoot just as much as the children."

"How are the preparations going?" he inquired, politely.

"Quite well. We have musicians, a sumptuous dinner planned and—oh, you have to see this. It will be the talk of the season."

She grabbed his arm and dragged him in front of a door just off the dining area.

"We have a new chef who is enamored with pastries. When he mentioned he'd like to do something special, I agreed, never imagining this!" She threw open the doors and pulled him inside.

Tables lined three sides of the room, covered in desserts—large and small pastries, white and chocolate confections, sugared baskets of flowers and fruits—there were treats everywhere. In the middle of the room stood an enormous three-story cake, elaborately decorated in swirls and twirls of colorful icing.

Briar giggled. "It's quite amazing, isn't it? I wasn't certain about it, but chef described it with my girls in the room, and they insisted we go forward. They have been so infatuated by the designs, the chef had to bake them each a little cake to eat."

He took in a deep breath to respond and froze. The most luscious scent surrounded him. It was delicious. Arousing even. The response was surprising, since he'd never had much of a sweet tooth. He had seen women go into throes over desserts, but he rarely gave them a second thought. He took another inhale and felt his skin flush. The scent. It was intoxicating.

Briar didn't notice and continued to extol on the chef's elaborate preparations. "He said he discovered a new process. He takes an exotic vanilla bean and soaks it in brandy to bring out a stronger flavor, then he…"

Vanilla! That was it. The room smelled of Nivea. After filling his lungs with the scent, his groin tightened. He could picture her under him, tied to his bed as he unbuttoned her gown.

"The icing is a special blend of..."

He couldn't focus on her words. Image after image of Nivea slammed through his brain—her whimpering at his touch in the cabin, pressing him to her breast once he'd been shot, moaning in pleasure as he buried himself into her in his bed. It was enthralling.

This was the smell he'd been craving. Not the exotic, contrived smell at Madame Amora's, but the sweet, delicious scent of vanilla, of Nivea.

His manhood began throbbing, pressing against his breeches. He could barely breathe. Running his hand through his hair, he was surprised to find it shaking. Oh, good God, this was ridiculous. He had to get away, now, before Briar noticed his obvious state of arousal.

"I'm certain our guests will be..."

"I have to go," he choked, stopping her in mid sentence.

She gave him her usual bemused expression. "Excuse me?"

"I have to go. I forgot. I have to—to—" Oh, he was stuttering like a school boy, glancing around for some sort of excuse. "I have a surprise for Joseph's birthday. I must check on it."

Her face lit up. "Oh, that's wonderful. What is it?"

"I can't tell you. It would ruin the surprise." He tried for a charming grin, but feared it came out more like a grimace. He had no idea what he would be getting. None, whatsoever. He just knew he had to get out before the smell of vanilla made his arousal embarrassingly evident.

Unperturbed, Briar walked him to the door. "Well, I'm certain Joseph will be pleased. I'll let him know you were here."

Barely able to contain himself, Dare bowed and rushed out onto the street. As soon as the door closed, he inhaled large gulps of fetid London air. *Ahh, that was better.* God in heaven what had happened in there? Obviously he had gone too long without a woman.

Far too long.

And because of his lapse into lunacy, he now had to come up with a present for Joseph. Damnation, he had no talent for that sort of nonsense.

Leaping up onto his horse, he flicked the reins and darted out into the street. He would ride around and pray an idea came to him. As he passed the park, a flash of color caught his eye. It was a gentleman driving a curricle, wearing a coat of lemon yellow, silver buttons flashing in the sun. It could only be Joseph.

What a jacksnape. Imagine if everyone dressed as he. The result would be ghastly. Appalling.

Then it hit him. The perfect gift!

Chapter 37

"No."

"Excuse me?" Dare gaped.

"No. I absolutely refuse. I will not let you ruin my reputation with this preposterous request."

Dare stared at his tailor in amazement. The man had never talked to him like that. "Francis, be reasonable. It is just one outfit. Your reputation could not possibly be tainted that easily."

"No." He stood immobile, arms crossed in defiance.

Dare decided to take another tack. "Let us pretend it is a masquerade. I will simply be assuming another's persona for one evening. It will be amusing."

One look at Francis's expression assured Dare there would be no possibility of amusement coming from that quarter. Well, Dare couldn't very well push the man. He was, after all, his favorite tailor. "Fine," he exclaimed with a flick of his wrist. "I will find someone else to accommodate me."

Without waiting for a response, Dare exited the shop and headed down the street. Locating a smaller establishment a few blocks down, he went inside and explained his desire.

The tailor gasped at him in dismay. "Impossible!" he cried. "I cannot create what you wish by this evening."

Dare glared at him. "Surely, you could come up with something suitable. I will pay you handsomely for your effort."

"My lord, I would love to assist you, but a request such as this would take four days at least. We are a small shop and simply do not have the resources. If you allowed me till the end of next week, perhaps…"

"No, it must be this evening."

The man held up his hands with a shrug. Dare was on the verge of berating the man for his incompetence when he had a sudden flash of inspiration. "Do not concern yourself, sir. I know just where to go."

* * * *

Glancing up at the sign, Dare gave a nod of satisfaction. *LeFleur's Emporium for Discriminating Gentlemen.* Yes, he was fairly certain Joseph frequented this shop.

When the man flounced out of the back room and gasped appreciatively at Dare, he knew he'd come to the right place. Dare assumed his most imposing posture and got right to the point. "I have a special request for you. I believe you are familiar with Lord Duxbury."

"*Oui, monsuier.* 'E is one of my favorite customers." The man beamed.

"Today is his birthday. To help him celebrate, I would like to procure an outfit…for me…that is more in keeping with his fashion."

The man paused for a moment, and then his eyes lit up.

Alarmed, Dare held up a restraining hand. "Not one of his more extravagant creations. I would just like something a hint less…restrained than my usual attire."

The man nodded with a grin. "Yes, milord."

"And I would need it completed"—he paused a beat—"for tonight."

The man's mouth dropped in alarm. He quickly snapped it shut and narrowed his eyes in thought. "Tonight?" Circling Dare with measured steps, he evaluated his form, seeming to take special note of his broad shoulders straining the fabric of his charcoal grey jacket. "An outfit for tonight that is daring, yet restrained, hmmm…" He returned to face front, crossing his arms and tapping his chin with his long slender fingers.

"You are not the usual shape for such clothes, *non*? This fashion is more tailored for a man less…how you say…solid. They are usually more effeminate, no?

Dare shrugged, uncomfortable at the man's intense scrutiny. Perhaps this wasn't such a good idea after all. He was on the verge of withdrawing the request when the tailor suddenly clapped his hands. The eager glint in his eye sent a cold shiver down Dare's spine.

"Ah, yes, Pierre has just the thing! Wait here, *s'il vous plait*, I will return."

He flew into the back room and emerged a moment later with a coat the color of grape hyacinths.

He held it up and explained, "This was specially designed for a certain gentleman of larger proportions. His lady friend had a penchant for purple, and I created several suits for him during their...ah...how you say...association."

He shrugged. "The relationship recently ended and he no longer requires the jacket. I think it is quite large enough to fit your physique with very little alteration."

He removed Dare's jacket and helped him into the coat. "We nip it in at the waist here and we shorten it like so." His hands tugged at the fabric briskly.

"Ah, then we add this..." He darted over to a chest of small drawers and pulled out a handful of buttons and gewgaws, and skipped back. Pursing his lips, he held up the various options for consideration.

Feeling quite embarrassed, Dare just stood there trying not to flinch... until the Frenchman let out another squeal. "*Mon dieu!* Pierre, you are a genius. Why did I not think of it sooner?" He sashayed back into the storeroom and returned dragging an assistant with a monstrosity of color over his arm.

"Come. We will create the perfect look for a friend of Lord Duxbury. Nothing too extravagant, I assure you," he said with a smirk. "Except for the price, no? Such a rush job, it will cost you, *comprenez-vous*?

"*Oui, je comprends.* Just make sure it is ready for this evening."

"*Oui. Oui* my lord."

Chapter 38

Lord and Lady Duxbury were greeting late arrivals to the party when Dare made his entrance. Briar was conversing with an elderly gentleman and Joseph was standing idly by. As Dare approached, Joseph gave him a vague smile before gasping in surprise.

"Landis! Good God, is that you? What are you wearing?"

Dare smirked, bowing to his friend. "Why Joseph, this is my new wardrobe. Do you like it?" He affected the pose of a preening dandy, enjoying the shocked expression still affixed to his friend's face.

Then Joseph broke out in a grin. "I adore it! What possessed you?"

"It's your birthday. I thought I might give homage to your fashion sense. Is it too much, do you think?"

"No, no, it's perfect." He tugged on his wife's arm and announced, "Darling, look at what Landis has worn for me."

Briar turned and burst into laughter. "Oh, is that is why you had to run off today? Now I understand. You look quite remarkable."

That was certainly the word for it. He was wearing the purple jacket with blue silk buttons. His starched white cravat billowed from his chin to a multi-hued waistcoat made up of blue, green, and purple ribbons. It appeared he'd been entrapped by drunken maypole dancers. He'd finished off the outfit with dark blue breeches and tasseled boots. Pierre had declared him *"tres magnifique!"* Dare could only imagine what Francis' horrified response would be.

Tugging on his arm, Joseph urged him, "Come, let us join the festivities. I cannot wait to see everyone's reaction. You have ensured that people will be talking about my party for months."

Yes, they would. Dare shuddered. He pulled out his snuffbox to steady himself and then headed into the crowded room.

Graves was the first to approach him. "What the deuce have you got on, Landis?"

"I thought I'd give Duxbury a taste of his own medicine."

"Poison, is more like it," he scoffed.

"Well, I love it," Joseph interjected. "In fact, I may have something similar made."

"Too bad it won't look as attractive on you as it does me," Dare said with a smirk.

As Joseph feigned a pout, Dare excused himself and crossed the room. He had spotted William near the terrace doors and was eager to get some of the evening's unpleasantness out of the way. He pretended not to notice the stares his presence caused, rippling through the room as he swept through.

Planting himself boldly in front of his oldest friend, he glared, as though daring him to walk away. Judging by the look on the man's face, he was considering just that.

"Yes?" William spat out a single word.

Willing his voice to remain steady, Dare looked into his eyes and gave the speech he had been rehearsing for hours. "William, I am a blackguard of the first order. Your wife is a charming woman who loves you dearly and I had no right to accuse her of treachery. I realize I behaved abysmally and the only excuse I can offer is that, after a week of endless romance and familial affection, on top of being shot, I succumbed to a moment of insanity. Regardless, I have no excuse for insulting you or her. I pray you will accept my apology and forgive me."

He swallowed hard, watching his friend, trying to gauge his reaction. He was fully prepared to take a blow if it came to that. He deserved nothing less. Therefore, he didn't flinch when he saw William's arm come towards him. But instead, he found himself engulfed in an uncomfortably solid hug.

"You insolent bastard. I have no idea why I put up with your outrageous behavior, but I confess, I've missed you beyond measure. God help me." He released his grip a moment before pulling Dare back into a hug. "Betsy will be furious, and I may spend a month sitting alone at the dinner table, but yes, I forgive you."

Dare knees went weak. Never had he expected to feel such a flood of relief. He smiled and thumped his friend on the back. "All right you pathetic sot. Now keep your hands to yourself or I'll have to go insult another family member," he growled, causing William to chuckle.

Drawing back, an unexpected sentence burst from his lips. "Would it help if I apologized to your wife?"

"Ho, no!" A grin crossed William's face. "I never told her what you said. She just knows you crossed a line, and she thought nothing of giving you a cut direct on my behalf. I think it best if I smooth things over with her."

Dare breathed a sigh of relief. "As you wish."

Grabbing two glasses from a passing footman, he asked, hopefully, "Friends?"

William clinked his glass. "For now, you rotter."

Eager to put this unpleasantness behind them, Dare gave an abashed grin and steered the conversation onto more familiar ground. "Now, William, tell me about Hades. Is he truly faster than Acheron? I've never won with a grey horse and I hesitate to place too big a wager on him."

As anticipated, William launched into a description of his colt's bloodline, detailing the advantages over its closest foe. Dare stood there, content, as the ordinariness of the evening washed over him. He exhaled with relief. Knots in his shoulders he hadn't even realized were there, slowly released. It didn't take long before his friends followed William's lead and joined the conversation.

Dare struggled to maintain a dignified demeanor as they took turns taunting his attire, but eventually even he succumbed to laughter. He'd never enjoyed humiliation more.

With that trial over with, he was anxious to address his other problem. He spotted Nivea across the room. Wearing a brazen gown of bronze, her bodice was low enough to display a tempting expanse of succulent white skin. Not the only one to notice, a few conniving gentlemen had circled her. And worse yet, she was smiling back at them.

Joseph's words echoed in his head. *If you don't apologize, she may turn to someone else.* He could not allow that to happen.

Making his excuses, he skirted the room and placed himself in an alcove, strategically located between Nivea and the lemonade. It was a warm evening and she was sure to need a drink soon. He just hoped she was alone when she decided to approach. He wasn't at all sure what her reaction would be, but he was fairly certain it wouldn't be pleasant. He just hoped he could find the words to make it up to her.

For once, luck was with him. He heard her ask her companions if they cared to join her for a refreshment. They declined, choosing instead to go mingle.

As she headed toward the table, Dare stepped forward and she barreled right into him.

"Excuse me, milord. I didn't see anyone there," she exclaimed into his chest.

It wasn't until she stepped back and realized it was him that she recoiled. He couldn't have her escape before he could apologize, so he hastily grabbed her arm.

Ahh, the scent of vanilla. That's what he'd missed. What he'd craved. As she gazed up at him, her eyes wide with alarm, he realized just how lovely she was. Curvy and soft and sweet. He *had* to make her forgive him. Somehow.

She tugged her arm once. Twice. Then her lips compressed and her lashes fluttered shut as she struggled to regain her composure.

Then she slowly raised her eyes, taking in his tasseled boots, beribboned waistcoat, and violent purple jacket. Once her gaze fixed on his face... she burst out laughing. "Lord Landis, I did not realize this was a costume party."

That was embarrassing. He'd forgotten he was attired like a frivolous fop. With a sheepish shrug, he responded, "I thought I'd give Joseph a birthday treat. I had this made up in his honor."

Nivea's brows flew up in surprise. Then her eyes grew soft, and an engaging smile curled up the corner of her mouth. "What an uncommonly nice gesture. It is rare that you would risk your dignity for a friend. I'm sure he loved it."

Dare flushed. She was pleased by his actions. A whole host of unfamiliar emotions washed over him—happiness, even contentment. This is what he had been missing.

He *had* to put things to right. "Nivea," he started, his voice low and urgent, "please allow me a moment of your time."

She looked wary, but didn't step away. Encouraged by that, he held out his hand and guided her into the alcove for some privacy. His heart was pounding so hard, it was like horses were galloping through his chest.

As she stared up at him with those wide, blue eyes, he tried to remember the words he had carefully crafted through the week. But once he had her hand in his, felt the warmth of her touch, he knew he must speak from the heart. "Nivea, I hardly know what to say. I have no excuse for my behavior. I had no right to speak to you as I did, and once again, I must beg your forgiveness."

He paused, hoping she would say something. Give him a hint as to whether she was amenable to his apology or squaring up to slap him. But her gaze had fixed on his hideous beribboned waistcoat, and he couldn't read her expression.

Well, there was no getting around it. He would have to press on. "Nivea, you have been nothing but kind to me, and yet I have treated you abominably. I had no right to accuse you of the things I did, and I am deeply sorry."

Now came the truly difficult part. "As I'm sure you have guessed, I am not comfortable speaking about my personal life, and confiding in you was very...disconcerting. There are precious few people I trust in this world, and I foolishly decided you were not worthy of that honor. I now realize it is I who am unworthy. I hope you can forgive me. I...I value your friendship and do not want us to be on bad terms."

There. He'd done it. He'd laid his soul bare.

Afraid it had not been enough, Dare was unable to face her. So, he stood there, focusing on her gloved hand resting in his. How he wished he could touch her skin, feel her pulse, know if it was racing as fast as his. He could hardly breathe.

Then she reached up and stroked his cheek. "Oh Dare, of course I forgive you. Who knows better than I what you've been through? I'm just glad you've come back to us."

Oh, thank God. He exhaled so violently, the wisps of hair around her face stirred.

She chuckled at that, her smile inviting. She looked at him with such a warm, gentle expression, he wanted nothing more than to sweep her into his arms and kiss her senseless. But then, she stepped back. "I heard that you made up with William."

Her pink cheeks betrayed her. She was affected by him too. But she was determined to keep their conversation proper. He could play that game too. For now.

"Did you? Word travels fast."

"Yes, it does. I was also informed that no one had ever heard you apologize before, and they were quite sure you were going to choke on your tongue."

"Oh, really?" He attempted to glare at her, until he saw the delightful smile that had crept up her face. "Did that please you?"

"That you almost choked? A little." She laughed, before confessing, "But I am so glad you did. William has missed you dreadfully, you know."

"And you? Did you miss me?" Dare was appalled at the neediness in his voice. He could not remember ever missing a woman before. Or caring whether she had missed him.

Thankfully, she whispered, "Yes, I did."

Keeping his eyes averted, so she wouldn't see the remnants of fear in his eyes, he asked, "So, we can be friends?"

"I'd like that." And she squeezed his hand.

Euphoria washed over him, driving away the odd prickly feeling that had seeped into his bones. It took every ounce of self control not to crush her to him. How could he have stayed away from her for so long? He wanted more. He wanted to wrap around her, press her against the wall, and plunge into her once again.

Fortunately, the butler took that moment to announce that dinner was being served. He could escape without causing any more harm. Or so he thought, until Nivea leaned forward and in a surprisingly sultry voice asked, "Lord Landis, do friends escort each other into dinner?"

Yes, exclaimed his long-dormant libido.

No, begged his self control, afraid he would find himself leg-shackled by midnight.

"Certainly, milady." His libido had resolved the situation before he could mount a sensible argument.

Chapter 39

Nivea could hardly contain her delight. Adair Landis was sitting next to her.

He had apologized to her, escorted her to dinner, and was now seated so close, she could have rubbed her leg against his, if she wished to. And she wished to in the worst way.

When she had seen him arrive tonight, it had taken all her self control to ignore him. She'd refused to reveal herself as a pathetic love-struck sycophant, willing to excuse his outrageous accusations. But then, when he had cornered her, and she'd observed his ridiculous attire, well, all her defenses had crumbled. He was trying to make amends, to her, to William, to all their friends. It was an enormous step forward. She had to forgive him.

And now, sitting next to him, she was trembling with excitement. What would happen now? What would be his next step?

Around the table, she noticed a number of her friends staring at them outright—their expressions ranging from bemusement to outright shock. Lord Landis never escorted an unmarried female to dinner, unless directed by their hostess. But he had strolled in with her as though it was an everyday occurrence.

True, he wasn't talking to her, but she could sense that he was casting occasional glances her way. It was…well, it was an irrevocable step forward in their relationship. Although, he did not appear to notice it. He was too busy trying to deflect a large amount of good-hearted ribbing, on account of his clothing.

"Lord Landis, did you lose a bet?"

"Adair, were you attacked by an outraged ribbon merchant?"

"I think you need to let your manservant go. He was obviously drunk this evening."

He was smiling in remarkably good humor, but Nivea could tell he was uncomfortable. He was not used to playing the fool.

He looked quite handsome, in spite of the outrageous fashion. How could one overlook his intense dark eyes or silky black hair? Or those tantalizing full lips. She imagined them pressing against her neck, his tongue trailing fire along the sensitive skin of her collarbone. She shivered. Oh yes, she could forgive him for not speaking to her, as long as she could be alone with him once again.

Embarrassed by the direction of her thoughts, Nivea tried to focus her attention on the neighbor seated to her right. Fortunately, Joseph's uncle was happy to ramble on, requiring virtually no response from her.

It wasn't until the fish course was being removed that Dare turned to her. "Did you enjoy your meal, Miss Horsham?" His face was an impassive mask, although his eyes traveled over her form. That was certainly a good sign.

"Yes, it was delicious." In truth, she couldn't recall a single course. "Did you?"

"Yes, actually," he responded. "I haven't had much of an appetite lately, but I found tonight's meal very satisfying."

They lapsed into silence. Dare's eyes roamed around the room a moment before he abruptly announced, "Briar has had a special treat prepared for dessert. I think you will enjoy it." Then he seemed to flush and shifted away from her.

"I'm sure I will like it. Briar is an excellent hostess. Would you care to offer me a hint?"

He turned his head toward her, but his eyes were fixed on the back wall, as though deliberately avoiding hers. "No, never mind. Forget I said anything." He shifted again in his seat before turning toward his neighbor.

That was odd. What about dessert would make him uncomfortable? Fortunately, she didn't have to wait long to learn about the treat. As soon as the dishes were cleared, Briar stood up and called for attention. "For dessert this evening, I have prepared a special surprise for you all. Please come with me as we adjourn across the hall."

They walked to the closed doors. Briar pulled her husband to the front and flung open the doors. "Happy birthday, darling!"

Joseph let out a hoot of laughter and raced inside.

Nivea was so pleased to find Dare still by her side, she didn't notice the room at first. Then he leaned over and murmured in her ear, "Well, what do you think?"

It was then she became aware of the myriad of treats around the room.

"Oh, Dare, it's divine! Look at it all. It's like a confectionary shop. Oh, and just smell the heavenly scent!" She closed her eyes and inhaled deeply.

When she opened her eyes, she noticed his pained expression. "Are you all right?"

He nodded. "I'm not much for sweets. I think I will go join the other men for a port." With that, he turned and disappeared through the doors so quickly one would think his feet were on fire.

She sighed. *And so continued the mysterious behavior of the elusive Lord Landis.*

Trying to push it out of her mind, she filled her plate and indulged in a comforting array of pastries.

Chapter 40

Dare avoided Nivea as much as he could that evening. His ridiculous attire made him the center of attention, and he knew it would be hazardous for both of them if he spent too much time in her presence.

Besides, if he got too close to her, there was no guarantee he could stop himself from touching her. Nuzzling her. Devouring her. That would be a catastrophe of epic proportion.

He had hoped that once he'd apologized, he could go on his merry way, but apparently this odd obsession had not yet run its course. So, he contented himself talking with William and watching her from afar. At ease in this small gathering of friends, she flitted among guests like a queen bee enjoying a garden of roses. But her tender smile, her boisterous laugh called to him.

When she joined the dance floor, escorted by a young relative of Joseph's, he had to fight back an overwhelming urge to march over and yank her away. No doubt the undisciplined pup was trying to charm her with ridiculous tales while peeking down her bodice. And the trusting girl was probably fascinated, hanging on his every word.

As they spun past, Nivea caught his eye, gave him a shy smile and waved two fingers in his direction. And just like that, jealousy turned to joy. He inclined his head and sent her an answering grin.

God's blood, he was acting like a love-sick swain. Forcing a languid sneer to his lips, he returned his attention to William, enjoying the man's simple banter. He was amazed how much he'd missed the old goat. Their conversation was nothing of consequence, but there was no annoying bluster or foolish posturing. It was so refreshing.

The only person at the party who was not pleased with his return to the proverbial fold was Betsy. Sidling over to her husband, she tugged on his sleeve. "William, may I speak with you,"

"Yes, dear. Of course. Are you enjoying yourself this evening?"

"Not precisely, no. I fear I am not feeling quite the thing. Would you mind if we left soon?"

William grabbed her hand. "Are you all right? Is it anything serious?"

She flashed a scowl at Dare, indicating she desired some privacy. Happy to oblige, he took a step away and shifted his attention to the dancers. Still, he heard Betsy whisper, "I'm just a little bilious. Perhaps it was too much dessert."

"You poor dear. I know exactly how you feel. I am a little unsettled myself. We can leave immediately if you'd like."

"Oh, but what about Nivea? We were to take her home."

Just then, Nivea swished by, her fingers entwined in her partner's. Dare choked back a growl.

"Are you all right?" Betsy exclaimed.

"What? Oh, yes, just clearing my throat." He forced a cough to cover his embarrassing outburst. "Did you say that Nivea needs a ride home? I have a carriage."

"Oh, no," Betsy answered. "You do not need to do that. I'm sure she will not mind leaving with us."

William may have forgiven him, but it was apparent his wife was still aggravated.

Taking a cue from her, William hastily added, "No, we don't want to impose. I'm certain you have plans for the evening."

As a matter of fact, he did. And having Nivea all to himself would fit those plans nicely. But first he would need to convince her meddling family that he was doing them a favor, without appearing too eager.

Summoning up his most contrite expression, he murmured to William, "I would be happy to escort her home. It's the least I can offer, as penitence for my earlier behavior. Don't worry. Your sister will be in good hands."

Betsy snorted. "That's what I'm afraid of."

Damn. She didn't trust him. With good reason. He would have to address the problem head on. "No need for concern. I'm certain, dressed as I am, no woman will fall victim to my charms," he said with a depreciative shrug.

Even Betsy had to smile at that. "You are not up to your usual snuff, are you?"

"It was for a good cause. Joseph enjoyed my humbling tribute to him."

Unconvinced, she gave him a long hard look. "Perhaps we should ask Nivea what she would prefer."

Dare assumed his most indolent expression. He just prayed they didn't notice the sudden pounding of his chest at the thought of getting her alone.

As the dance ended, William motioned to Nivea to join them. "Nivvy, Betsy is not feeling well and would like to go home."

"Betsy, are you all right?"

"Oh yes. It's nothing serious," she reassured her. "We were wondering if you are ready to leave yet."

The corners of her mouth dropped in dismay. "Oh, I confess I was hoping to stay a little longer."

Betsy shot William a fretful glance before stating, "Dare has offered to escort you home." Her lack of enthusiasm spoke volumes.

"Would that be acceptable?" Dare asked in a measured tone, doing his best to keep his expression impassive.

Noting the telltale flush that crept up her cheeks, Dare was certain that Nivea would accept. She felt the pull between them as strongly as he did. Still, sensing the tension in the air, she managed to answer coolly, "I suppose I could tolerate a short ride in his presence."

Betsy fixed her with a steady stare, willing her to reconsider. When no other response was forthcoming, she gave a wan smile and held out her hand to her husband.

"Well, it's settled then. If you're certain it won't be an imposition, we'll be off." William took Betsy's arm and then paused, narrowing his eyes at Dare. "Remember, Landis, we have just made peace." He cast a meaningful look at Nivea.

Dare bowed in silent acknowledgment and the Horshams took their leave.

"I don't think they were comfortable leaving me in your care," Nivea murmured.

Dare laughed darkly. "No I don't imagine they were. Do you mind?"

Nivea grinned without reserve. "No, not at all."

"Good," Dare exhaled. Then holding out his arm said, "Perhaps I can claim you for a dance?"

Her eyes clouded and her smile disappeared. Turning away, she mumbled, "No, that's quite all right. You needn't bother."

How odd. Why the sudden about face? She'd danced with other men that evening. Seemingly countless men. Then he remembered. That evening at Morrill's party. *A pity dance.* That's what he had offered her. God, he was such a cad! He would burn in hell for the way he'd treated her. It was a wonder she'd ever spoken to him again.

The most distressing part was tonight he truly did want to dance with her. It was a deep and primal instinct. He wanted to touch her, claim her. But first, he would have to convince her that this was a sincere invitation.

Bowing low, he wrapped her hand in his. Raising her fingers to his lips, he stared deeply into her eyes. "Nivea, there is no one here that I would rather dance with. I would be honored if you would join me."

He could sense the conflict raging through her, trying to reconcile the pain he had caused.

This was an important moment. He had danced with her all those years out of a sense of duty. That's what gentlemen did for their friends with undesirable relations. But this time he truly wanted it for himself.

"Please," he said, softly, urgently, his heart thudding with anticipation.

She scanned his face, and he could tell she was weighing his words, judging their sincerity. With a slight nod, she murmured, "Yes. If you truly wish to, I will dance with you."

Whoosh, he could breathe again. "Yes, Nivea Horsham, I do wish to dance with you." He grabbed her hand and they both laughed as he dragged her onto the dance floor.

* * * *

The rest of the evening, Dare hummed with pleasure. It was funny how comfortable he was once again surrounded by friends. There were no outlandish amusements, no outrageous performances, yet he was happy. Content.

How was that possible? Didn't he thrive on rakish pursuits? Wasn't that his *raison d'etre*? If he wasn't the arrogant, contemptuous, derisive Lord Landis, who was he?

"Dare?" He heard Nivea call his name.

Was that the answer? Could he just be Dare? Not Lord Landis. Not the bedamned future Marquess of Raynsforth, but simply Dare? For once, the thought was intriguing.

"Yes, my dear?" Turning towards her he must have bestowed a more seductive expression than he'd intended. Her eyes grew wide with wonder and her skin flushed crimson.

"I—I—that is to say…"

She looked so adorably befuddled, Dare couldn't help but laugh. The urge to draw her into his arms was overwhelming. Despite her brother's warning and his own sense of self-preservation, watching the candlelight illuminating her skin, her scent tantalizing his senses, he had to get her alone. If only for this one night.

"Let's go outside." Wasting no time, he grabbed her arm, and guided her through the door and into the small enclosed garden.

"Dare!" she gasped, stumbling behind him. "We shouldn't. People will—"

"I don't care what people will do. Come quietly and we'll be fine." He tugged her behind a privacy hedge, plunging them into darkness.

"Dare!" she squeaked once more, but he silenced her by pulling her into his arms and kissing her. What started out as a controlled maneuver, turned into a slow, entrancing dance. He slid his tongue into her mouth and felt her relax in his arms. After a few moments, he broke off the kiss, buried his face into her neck and inhaled.

"Finally." He sighed, reveling in her vanilla fragrance.

She giggled. "Finally, what, milord?"

"I have been craving a taste of your skin all evening. All day, in fact. Since I saw the dessert room."

"The dessert room?" She sounded confused, and rightly so.

He wasn't about to admit what had occurred this morning, his embarrassing surge of lust at the vanilla smell, so he attempted to distract her by nibbling on her neck. She was as delicious as he remembered. He nipped his way across her shoulder before trailing his tongue back to her earlobe. She sighed with delight.

But, being Nivea, she wouldn't be content until she'd delved into his private thoughts. "What happened in the dessert room?" Her words vibrated in his mouth as he sucked the sensitive skin at her throat.

He sighed and pulled back. In the darkness, he could just make out her eyes, filled with curiosity. "Well, my dear, you may not know this, but you have the most alluring scent of vanilla about you."

"I do?" she squeaked.

He nodded. "I find it quite irresistible."

She smiled, lowering her lashes.

He continued softly, "When I visited the house this morning, Briar bid me to enter the room. The smell of vanilla was overwhelming, and while she was rambling on about her chef's culinary talents, I was growing hard as a pillar thinking about you."

Nivea's eyebrows shot up and her mouth turned into a perfect O of surprise.

"It was not at all welcome at the time," he admitted, "but now that I have you, the sensation is much less uncomfortable."

He pulled her closer, making her fully aware of his condition. Unperturbed, she reached up and wrapped her arms around his neck and kissed him with an eagerness that tickled his heart. "I am so glad to hear you have been thinking about me."

He would not disclose how much. Not now, not ever.

Besides, the time for talking was over. He only had one thought in mind—touching and tasting every inch she would allow. He stripped off his gloves and tucked them into his jacket. Stroking her arms, he reveled in the feel of her skin. It was as smooth as he remembered and compelled him to explore further.

He teased her mouth, playfully sucking at her lips and tongue while inching the small cap sleeves off her shoulders. Sensing no resistance, he trailed his fingers along the top of her bodice and let his thumb dip down to skim her nipple. He felt her gasp in his mouth and deepened the kiss. The skin puckered and swelled beneath his palm as she pressed closer to him.

Oh, she was so responsive. It amazed him that a quiet, reserved gentlewoman would be so eager for this lascivious behavior. He squeezed a handful of flesh under the frothy fabric and she moaned. It was nearly his undoing.

Grasping the sleeves, he tugged down, pulling her bodice to her waist and exposing her bountiful breasts. Growling, he buried his face between the soft mounds of flesh and inhaled. He ran his nose along her chest and settled his mouth on her rosy peak. It was so intoxicating, he almost released on the spot.

As he suckled, she slid her hands from his shoulders and down his waist. "I want to touch you, too," she begged, freeing his shirt from his breeches and placing her hands on his back. In the deep recesses of his mind, he realized she was touching his scars, but it didn't upset him in the slightest. They were a part of his past and no longer mattered. At least not with her.

He licked and teased her left side while gently tugging her right nipple between his fingers.

"Oh Dare, oh yes,"

He pulled her close, rubbing his form against her skirts, enjoying the friction, the heat. When her knees buckled, he whispered, "I believe there's a low wall just behind you. Come."

Placing his lips on hers, he scooped her up in his arms and carried her to a wide slab of marble. It stood two feet from the ground, surrounding a raised bed of hollyhocks. Dare dropped down onto the wall, and settled Nivea on his lap, savoring the feel of her voluptuous bottom pressing against him.

He returned to the sweetness of her lips, his hand trailing down to her bared bosom, fondling the soft, warm skin. His desire was painful, straining against his breeches.

"I want more," he growled into her mouth. Sliding his hand down her leg, he then raised her skirts until he could feel the bare skin above her stockings. She buried her face into his neck and moaned once again.

"Yes," was all she said. She nipped his neck, sending a flash of fire through him. Losing all reason, he moved his hand to the slit in her undergarments and plunged into the silky wetness. She was exquisite. There was no other word for it.

As he stroked and teased her delicate flesh, sliding his fingers in and out of her, she wrapped her arms around him in a vise-like grips. "Oh, yes, Dare! Don't stop. Please."

He loved the passion in her voice, the desperate ache that echoed inside him.

"Nivea, I want you. Right here. Right now. Do you understand me?" His tone was brusque, but he couldn't help it.

She looked at him with unfocused eyes and nodded solemnly. "Yes. I want you too. But how?"

In no time, he dragged them both to their feet. Giving a quick kiss to her adorably befuddled face, he spun her around to face the hedges surrounding the house. Then he unbuttoned his breeches, dropped down onto the wall and pulled her back onto his lap. This time, her legs were straddling his, her back resting against his chest.

"Dare?" she asked, a nervous hesitancy in her voice.

"Don't worry, darling, I'd like to show you another one of my tricks." Reaching one hand around, he palmed her breast, while the other rifled under her skirts to find the sensitive nub between her legs.

"Oh!" she cried out.

Oh, indeed. He smiled into her neck.

Bracing her feet on the ground, she began to rock up and down. Her scent so intoxicating, her sounds so arousing, he was barely able to control himself.

He nudged her upward and guided his manhood into her silky wetness with a groan.

"Oh, yes, Dare." Easing down, she began thrusting her hips, setting a blistering rhythm.

Teetering on the edge, he moved his fingers faster and faster over her pleasure spot, kneading her breast, urging her to completion. She squealed with delight and her shudders pushed him over the brink into heaven.

With a final pulse, he fell backward into the hollyhocks, his arms sinking into the damp soil. It didn't matter. Nothing mattered, except trying to breathe.

Nivea recovered quicker than he. She wiggled her hips and turning flashed him a wicked grin. "I *liked* that trick."

He barked out a laugh. "Did you?" Pulling her against his chest, he sucked her earlobe. "I did too. In fact, at the moment, I think it's my favorite."

Before he had time to suggest another alternative, strains of the final waltz drifted through the garden followed by the sound of voices.

"Ho, the party's over! People will be coming!" Nivea leapt to her feet and yanked up her bodice."I must look a mess. What will we do?" She frantically brushed at her skirt trying to smooth out the wrinkles. "I can't possibly go back inside looking like this."

He buttoned his breeches and pulled her into his arms. "Shh, it will be all right." Taking one more satisfying inhalation of vanilla, he drew away. "We'll wait here until the guests depart. Then, I will sneak out to the mews and have my carriage brought around back. No one will notice your delightfully disheveled state as we escape out the rear alley."

"But…I have to say goodbye to Briar and Joseph! It is their party. To do otherwise would be rude. They are certain to question me on it."

"Tomorrow we will make our apologies. We will tell them that you had to leave suddenly," he answered, thinking through the excuse as he spoke. "We can say that you, too, were feeling sick. Just like Betsy. And you had wanted to say goodbye, but the feeling was quite strong and the final waltz had just started, and you didn't want to interrupt their final dance."

That sounded quite plausible.

"I, of course, did not wish to deal with a female of questionable health in my carriage and urged you to leave immediately before you could ruin the interior of my carriage." He ended with a haughty, supercilious tone.

Nivea giggled, as he hoped she would.

"Yes, well I think that part would be entirely believable. It is well known that you have no use for sickly females."

"Quite so."

"I confess I don't like having to admit to an ailment such as that. It is quite embarrassing. And I *certainly* don't like having to lie to my dearest friends…"

"Well, you can always tell them the truth," he drawled and paused for the expected gasp.

Instead, she snorted. "Oh yes. Can you imagine? Briar, dear, thank you so much for the delightful party. I apologize for not bidding you adieu last evening, but you see, I accompanied Lord Landis into your garden. You know that garden wall where your daughters like to play. Well, I hiked up my skirts and used it to ride Lord Landis like a stallion. And you know we Horshams always win the race. It was quite exhilarating, really."

Rode him like a stallion? Lord, she was funny. Unable to help himself, he pulled her into his arms and kissed her soundly on the cheek. "You, Miss Horsham, are a remarkable woman." Setting her back, he looked into her face and said, "As much as I like the sound of that, I don't think it's our wisest course."

"No, I suppose you're right. Fine, we'll go with your story and hope for the best."

"That's a good girl. Now come over here and wait for my whistle. I'll pull up close to the door and you can dart in without being seen."

Giving her one more ardent kiss on the lips, he slipped out the gate and headed toward the mews.

Chapter 41

Dare bowed and lowered his foil.

"Well done, Lazby. Your technique is much improved."

The young dandy flushed with pleasure. "Thank you, Landis. I have been practicing. Not that I will ever match your skills, but I appreciate your encouragement."

Dare did his best not to laugh. He was finding it much easier to be tolerant of the overeager sycophant. Last night's soiree had been such a success, he was feeling positively benevolent today. He strode to the back of the fencing studio and chatted with him as they removed their protective gear.

"Will you be back again tomorrow? I have a noon engagement, but could be here by two," Lazby offered.

All right. Maybe there was a limit to his benevolence. "I think not, good man. Perhaps sometime next week."

"Next week. Yes. That would be better. I'll work on my parries in the meantime." Grinning like a fool, the silly sot gathered up his equipment and sauntered away.

"Been dipping into the brandy again?"

Dare hadn't notice Joseph emerging from the neighboring *piste*.

"Excuse me?"

"Since when do you encourage that rattlepate?" Joseph was leaning on his foil, his expression intent.

He chuckled. "You are just jealous you aren't able to attract such adoration."

Joseph snorted and removed his padded vest. "Yes, that must be it." Once he stowed his equipment in his case, he turned to Dare. "Do you have your carriage? I am in need of a lift to Bond Street."

"Certainly. Are you going to visit my new friend Pierre? His talented transformation of me on Friday is sure to increase business."

Joseph laughed. "How did you know? I plan to advise him to place a sizeable order for Landis Lilac. Once word gets out regarding your new fashion preference, Pierre will be hard pressed to keep the fabric in stock. No doubt, Lazby will wish to recreate the entire ensemble."

"Good Lord. Please, do not let that become my fashion legacy," he moaned, pulling on a subdued midnight blue coat.

"It would serve you right."

Glaring at his friend, Dare sauntered out to his awaiting carriage with Joseph following closely at his heels. Tired from a morning of dueling, he would have been content to ride in silence, but Joseph had something on his mind.

"So, it appears you have resolved your recent dilemma."

Dare closed his eyes. "What do you mean?"

"You've changed. You're much more relaxed than the time we talked at White's. I take it you've resolved your issue with the woman in question."

Dare shrugged.

"So. Nivea Horsham, is it?"

His eyes flew open. Good God, how had the man arrived at that conclusion? Forcing his voice to remain steady he asked, "Why would you say that?"

"At my party...I was watching you. You couldn't take your eyes off her."

Dare snorted. "Surely, you are mistaken."

"No. It was quite obvious." Leaning forward, he speared Dare with a penetrating gaze. "Now, tell me why was she so upset with you? Was it because you insulted her brother?"

He could blame it on his fight with William, but that did not seem fair. Taking a breath, he decided to come clean. "Truth be told, the day I insulted William, I was in a foul mood. I was unforgivably rude to Nivea as well. At your party, I decided to make amends with the entire Horsham clan. Fortunately, she is an immeasurably tolerant girl and she accepted my apology."

Hoping to end the conversation, he added, "That was why I was being so attentive toward her at your party. I was just seeking to earn her forgiveness."

Joseph nodded his head. "So, that was all—you hoped to earn her forgiveness?" he restated in a less than convinced tone. "So, the two of you are just..." He paused.

"We are just..." Dare struggled to come up with an appropriate word and settled for "friends." He shrugged, thinking the subject closed.

"Hmm. Friends. Well that will certainly help matters when you ask the earl for Nivea's hand?"

He flinched. "What? Why would I be doing that?"

Holding up one gloved finger, Joseph said, "You escorted her to dinner."

That was a ridiculous point. "Can't I be polite to my best friend's sister?"

"You can, but you never have before." He raised a second finger. "You have showed her an increase in attention. And you danced with her."

A third finger appeared, which irritated Dare to no end.

"I've danced with her before without damaging her reputation."

"Yes," said Joseph, leaning in and lowering his voice, "but have you ever snuck into a garden unescorted with her before?"

Dare's stomach dropped. They'd been seen.

Joseph nodded. "There. Now you know you must marry her. That is the end of it."

"No."

"Yes!" shouted Joseph. Then he calmed himself and continued. "Come now, Landis. Enough playing games. You must marry her. She is a lady, not one of your doxies. You cannot have a dalliance with her."

"I know she is a lady. But, I cannot *marry* her. It's...it's Nivea!" Dare choked out as panic seized him.

"Yes," Joseph growled, stony-faced, "It is. She is *Miss* Nivea Horsham, unmarried daughter of the sixth Earl of Cheltenham."

The carriage stopped, but Joseph remained seated. "I don't know if anyone else was aware, but if they were, and you don't offer for her, she will be ruined. Forever. She doesn't deserve that."

"I understand that," Dare admitted. He did. Truly. But for some reason it hadn't prevented him from doing just that. But marriage? *No.* He couldn't breathe. There had to be a way out. "What about me? What about what I deserve?"

To which Joseph softly responded, "I think you are getting exactly what you deserve."

With that, he climbed out of the carriage and walked away, leaving Dare to face a very uncomfortable truth.

He had to marry Nivea Horsham.

No, surely not. He would not be marrying anyone, anytime soon. He had made that perfectly clear. Once he did decide to become leg-shackled, it certainly wouldn't be to someone he cared about. That would just lead to trouble, impeding his lifestyle. As his wife, Nivea would no doubt expect him to accompany her places—riding together in the park, dancing with her at balls, disappearing into secluded gardens to tempt her into some more scandalous tricks...

No! His libido was once again getting the best of him. He had to think with his mind, not his body. But that was impossible when it came to this particular female.

Dropping his head into his hands, he tried to imagine the *ton's* reaction to this unprecedented news. They would be appalled at the thought of Lord Landis marrying a plump, plain wallflower.

His family...well, he really didn't care what his family thought. Frankly, he didn't care what the *ton* thought either, but he didn't want to become a laughingstock.

Ouch.

That was a painful realization. How petty of him to think that marrying a sweet, generous woman like Nivea would embarrass him. Shame choked him and he swallowed hard. He'd spent most of his life worried that *his* secret would be discovered. That he would be ridiculed for his cowardice. Yet when Nivea learned of it, she stood by him without judgment, without reproach.

Society had never given her the same courtesy. And why? What was her sin, after all? Being larger than was fashionable? That she wasn't able to deliver a well-timed quip or set down? Is that what was important?

His father had spent years trying to make him a man, and until this point, he only had a superficial understanding of what that meant. But now, he understood. Nivea had shown him it meant doing the right thing. Caring for others and treating them with respect. And not expecting the worst of everyone.

Which was exactly how Nivea behaved.

She was kind and loving and beautiful and had made him a better person. He felt safe with her. When he was with her, he felt at home. The truth was, he trusted her.

And that was all that should matter. That was love.

Holy God in heaven, he loved her.

He shook his head in wonder. He loved Nivea Horsham.

He couldn't control the smile that crept up his face. Love. He was in love. This was what he'd been fighting all these years. Remarkable. And now, sitting here in his carriage, he couldn't for the life of him understand why.

Chapter 42

A rare sight treated Londoners strolling through Hyde Park. Adair Landis, the future Marquess of Raynsforth, one of the most arrogant, supercilious, notorious rakes of their time, was skipping.

Well, perhaps that was a bit of an exaggeration, but he was definitely walking with a jaunty bounce, tipping his hat to passersby and smiling like a bedlamite.

"Such a pity," a stately matron whispered to her companion, "that such a refined gentleman as Lord Landis would succumb to drink so early in the day. It is quite unseemly."

But Dare didn't notice the stares of surprise. Or if he did, he simply didn't care. He'd made up his mind to marry Nivea. He was going to her house to ask for her hand. He could not believe how eager he was.

He would meet with the earl and state his intentions and...

Dare froze.

Good God, when had he ever given the man a reason to think he'd make a good husband? The earl would reject his suit. Of course, he would. For that matter, so would Nivea. It would serve him right if she rejected him. He had been a complete scoundrel after all.

As he slowed down to a virtual crawl, passersby were forced to skirt around him. He stepped out of the way, located a nearby bench, and threw himself down.

She would never agree to marry him. Why would she? He'd made it perfectly clear that he would only marry to beget heirs. And once that was accomplished, he would abandon his wife in the country, while he continued his debauched lifestyle. What woman would agree to that?

He dropped his head into his hands.

She would throw him out on his head. Or even worse, decide he was only marrying her out of pity. That, having taken her virtue, he was once again doing his duty as a so-called gentleman. He couldn't have that. He had to convince her that he loved her, respected her, and would treasure being with her.

Obviously, this proposal would require more finesse than he'd anticipated. Rising from the bench, he reversed direction and headed back home to consider his options.

* * * *

"Horsham? How's your colt? Will he be ready for the Derby next week?"

"Yes, yes." William beamed. "He's fully healed now, good as new."

"Excellent to hear. I'll make sure to place my bets."

Dare had had an inspiration. He would reestablish himself with the Horsham family, join them for casual events, and slip in admiring comments about Nivea. He would act the gentleman, well and true, and convince them all that he was a worthy suitor. And more importantly, prove to Nivea that he was reformed.

So, he had spent the past two weeks accompanying Nivea and his friends to all sorts of entertainment—the theatre, musicales, picnics. While these outings had always bored him beyond tears, he was astonished to find himself looking forward to each engagement with anticipation. They gave him a chance to see Nivea. To kiss her hand, to watch her smile, to give her an improper leer and watch the blush creep over her cheeks.

He ached to do more—touch her, smell her skin, taste her lips. To his dismay, more often than not, Joseph was hovering in the background, monitoring their actions, preventing any further familiarities. After uncovering their tryst during his birthday party, he had become extremely vigilant, making sure Dare did not tarnish Nivea's reputation any further.

This was becoming rather challenging, given the lady in question appeared to have no regard for her reputation whatsoever. She had been taking every opportunity to lure him into a secluded location and press against him.

"Lord Landis," she would coo at him, "would you accompany me to get a lemonade during intermission?" Or "Oh, I left my reticule in the carriage. Can you help me retrieve it?" Or, most distressing, she would offer him a plate of treats, bending low enough to afford him a tortuous view of her delectable bosom. He could tell she was dismayed by his repeated rebuffs. And he was getting painfully tired of returning each night to an empty bed.

But with remarkable discipline, he evaded temptation and continued his campaign to becoming a respectable, respectful suitor.

Hopefully, once she learned why he was being so elusive, Nivea would forgive him.

He had determined his next maneuver would take place on Thursday. With Horsham's colt racing at Epsom Derby, he could accompany friends and family to cheer the horse on. It should be a simple matter to draw Nivea off to a private spot and declare his intentions. If he was as persuasive as he hoped, perhaps Nivea would agree to do more than just talk.

The day dawned clear and cool, perfect for the races. The entire Horsham family was joined by Briar and Joseph, Abby and Thomas, and a hodgepodge of other friends. The group was in high spirits as they strolled the grounds, visiting tents with assorted entertainment. Dare managed to act the solicitous gentleman once again.

It was late afternoon when he spotted a gathering of fortune tellers. With sudden clarity, he remembered the eerie message he'd received from the gypsy soon after his return to London. "Your pain is ending. Allow it to happen. Don't let fear stop your destiny."

His gaze settled on Nivea. The old crone had been correct. His pain was ending. With a simple smile or a longing gaze, Nivea soothed him. She was his destiny.

Now, he was desperate to get her alone. But every time he attempted to pull her aside, someone would interfere. It was maddening. The day was ticking away, and he hadn't declared his intentions.

He couldn't bear to wait another day. He invited his friends back to his townhouse on the premise of celebrating the Horsham's victorious colt. Surely, he could get Nivea aside there.

They had just entered his foyer when there was a knock at the door. Expecting to welcome another friend, Dare was surprised to find a dusty, road-weary rider on his doorstep.

"Lord Landis?" asked the man.

Dare inclined his head.

"I have an urgent message from your father."

He grunted in disgust. "I'm not interested. Please be on your way."

Dare's footman started to close the door, but the man braced it open with his dirt-encrusted boot. "Milord, you don't understand. Your father is very ill. I must speak with you."

Noting the man's grave tone, Dare waved him into the foyer. His friends were still gathered there, exhibiting a concern that Dare himself did not feel.

"Well?" he barked.

The man eyed the mass of onlookers and whispered, "Milord, this is a family matter. Perhaps we should discuss it in private."

Dare glared at him. "How private?"

He crumpled his cap in his hands. "As I said sir, your father...is...that is to say...he's not well. In fact, he may not...there's a good chance he may...perish."

"Finally." Dare spat out. "So, tell me, what is it that will take the bastard out?"

His friends gasped.

"Dare," Betsy exclaimed, "surely you should be more respectful of your father."

He waved her off. When Betsy tried once more to speak, Nivea placed a hand on her arm. "Let him be."

Dare turned back to the messenger and, raising a haughty eyebrow, silently bid the man to continue.

"My lord, the marquess appears to have"—his voice dropped low—"the French disease. He rallied this summer, but now he is weak. Very weak. He is not expected to last through the month."

While the others murmured their condolences, Dare stood there, unmoved. When it became evident the messenger expected a response before continuing, Dare replied, "That is fitting. What am I expected to do about it?"

The man, troubled about the way this was unfolding, continued to mangle his cap, trying to decide how to proceed. Then he marshaled his courage, squared his shoulders, and continued with the message.

"The marquess has decided that you must be married before he passes on. It has been a great disappointment that you have not already done so. He has made arrangements with the Billingston's on the adjoining property. Their daughter was to be introduced this spring. Now, a contract has been made with Lord Billingston, and you are engaged to be married."

"What?" Dare barked. That was ridiculous. The man had no right!

His jaw was so firmly clenched, he was barely able to spit out a retort. "I am of majority now. My father cannot enter me into such a contract."

The hapless man took a step back in the face of such powerful anger but managed to choke out the last few statements. "Well, it appears it has been done. You are commanded to come home immediately and marry in his presence."

Dare looked over at Nivea and saw that all the color had drained from her face. He could imagine what she was thinking.

"No!" Turning back to the messenger, he restated, "No, I will not be marrying the Billingston chit."

The messenger looked at him, unsure what to do. Dare knew the feeling.

Then, in the blink of an eye, he came to a decision. "Sir, I will travel to my father's home. And I will be married. But not to someone of his choosing. I have found a woman to be my wife. I just pray that she will say yes."

Turning to Nivea he reached for her hand. He brought it up to his lips and placed a kiss on her fingers. His heart was thumping madly in his chest. This was the most difficult moment of his life. He'd never thought to make such a public declaration, but it must be done.

Taking a deep breath, he looked into Nivea's beautiful blue eyes—eyes that had seen the real man inside and shown him what life could be. And he said the words he'd never imagined he'd utter. "Nivea, I love you. I love your kindness, I love your honesty, and I love your faith in life...in me."

Her eyes begin to well up and her lip quivered and it gave him courage to continue. "I know I am not perfect, and I will, no doubt, make a very challenging husband, but I love you and I want to marry you. Will you do the honor of becoming my wife?"

Chapter 43

Nivea blinked at him, unable to comprehend what he was saying. She must have misheard him. Or she'd been kicked by a horse and was now stretched out on the stable floor, trapped in the arms of Morpheus. Yes, that must be it. If she could survive this long without air in her lungs, she was probably dreaming.

Then she looked around the room at all her friends. They were staring at Dare with varying degrees of amazement. Her brother's expression was the most amusing, with his mouth hanging open like an oversized haddock. That made her laugh and got her breathing again.

The past few weeks had been torture for her. While Dare had been remarkably cordial, he hadn't tried to get her alone. She had tried everything to entice him, but it appeared he'd conquered his desire for her and was satisfied remaining friends.

So, when this messenger issued his pronouncement, she knew Dare would marry the Billingston girl. Even though he hated his father, he could not refuse his dying wish. Since Nivea was not the type of woman Dare would marry, her most fervent dream evaporated. She'd lost him.

And then, he did the unthinkable. In front of all their friends and family, he asked her to marry him. He loved her! Was it really possible?

She turned back to gaze deeply into his ebony eyes, warm and sincere. For the first time, she allowed herself to hope. To believe. Because in his eyes, she saw love…love tinged with worry and a touch of fear.

Fear? Was he scared of her? Did he think she would say no? *Of all the crazy, insane, ridiculous things.* As if Nivea Horsham would refuse to accept Adair Landis.

Turning a dazzling smile on him, she threw her arms around him. "Yes, yes, of course I'll marry you!"

"Oh, thank God," he groaned into her hair. After returning her bone-crushing hug, he put her aside and turned toward her brother.

"William, I know this is a bit of a shock. But please believe me when I say I love your sister and will do everything I can to make her happy. Will you accept me as your brother-in-law?"

William turned ghostly pale. Then his cheeks brightened to a mottled puce, before flaring to an alarming shade of scarlet. He appeared to be trying to speak, but nothing emerged but a strange gurgling sound.

Betsy gave him a hearty pat on the back and took charge. "Lord Landis, I never expected this day to come, but it seems your declaration is heartfelt. If you are sincere in your attentions toward our Nivvy, we will welcome you into our family." Narrowing her eyes, she added, "But if we discover you are playing games with her affections, we will horsewhip you till you beg for mercy."

Nivea gasped. For her normally good-humored sister-in-law to have selected such a punishment was quite unsettling. But Dare didn't flinch at her proclamation. Quite the contrary, he looked pleased. "Madam, I would expect nothing less."

Then the messenger cleared his throat. "Yes, well...erm...this is all well and good, but I remind you your father has promised you to the Billingston girl. And you are expected at home, immediately."

Dare let out an exasperated sigh. Turning his back on the man, he captured her hands in his. "Nivea, I know it is highly irregular, but I ask that you accompany me to my father's estate. I would like to get this settled immediately and introduce him to the next Marchioness of Raynsforth."

Her heart caught in her throat. "Oh, no, I couldn't. The man terrifies me. You go and make peace with him. I will be here upon your return."

"I must insist. I wish for you to meet my family. They need to know that I will not be caving into my father's demands."

She pressed a hand to her stomach to still the sudden churning. She was not ready for this. How could she possibly face the man who had so little humanity, he would harm his own son? How could she stand up to his derision, knowing what he was capable of? She was not that strong.

Then she looked at Dare. Her love. Her life. And she saw the need in his eyes. Perhaps he was scared too. Was that possible? Did he need her to help ease his fear?

If so, then of course she would go.

"When would you like to leave?" His answering smile brought tears to her eyes. It was filled with relief and joy, and love. He loved her. She wanted to dance around the room.

Her brother was not so easily swayed. Finally finding his voice, he barked out, "Nivea, I cannot allow this. No!"

He shook off his wife's calming hand and pulled Nivea away from Dare. "You're not thinking clearly. Landis is an unrepentant rake. How many times have you heard him say he has no respect for marriage? He calls it a prison. Whether he means to or not, he will break your heart. He will!"

Nivea smiled at his protective declaration. He only had her best interests at heart. She appreciated that, but it would not deter her. "William, it is not like that. Dare loves me. I know it is hard to believe—it is hard for *me* to believe—but he does. I trust him. And I will marry him."

"*No!*"

Dare moved to stand in front of his dearest friend, and in the most humblest tones stated, "William, please. I swear to you, this is not a game. I intend to be a faithful husband to your sister. You know, for all my faults, I am a gentleman. I can be trusted."

William took a slow measure of his friend before turning his attention back to her, and sighed. "Niv, if this is what you truly want, you know I will not stand in your way."

Delighted, she threw her arms around him and hugged him until he gasped for breath.

Breaking free, he took her face in his hands, smiling into her eyes. Then his expression grew serious. In a quiet voice he said, "Regardless of your decision, I urge you not to go to Raynsforth. You don't know what you'll face there. His father…he's not like us. He's a vicious, heartless bastard, who will stop at nothing to get his way. I don't want you to get hurt."

Nivea couldn't hide her surprise. So, William wasn't so obtuse after all. He may not know the extent of Dare's torment, but he wasn't completely ignorant of the abuse. She was so touched, she pulled him into another hug. "Thank you, Wills. I appreciate your concern. But I will be with Dare, and I will be fine. I promise."

At that, Betsy spoke up, "Would you like us to accompany you? You need a chaperone, after all, and we could offer you support."

"No!" Dare snapped. Then softening his tone, he turned to Betsy. "Thank you, but that won't be necessary. My sisters will be in residence and will be vigilant in impeding any manner of happiness on my part. Nivea will be quite safe from me."

"Oh, Dare, how horrid your family sounds." Briar exclaimed.

He laughed without humor. "You have no idea, my dear. And that is why I must decline Betsy's kind offer. I will meet with my father, have my say, and will leave with as much haste as possible. With Nivea beside me, all parties will be made to understand that this ridiculous engagement to the Billingston chit is both unnecessary and unwarranted."

Nivea smiled at him. "Now that we've settled that, when would you like to leave?"

"Tomorrow morning, if that is amenable. With fair weather and a hard ride, we should be there by evening."

"All right, then. I will go home and prepare."

The bewildered messenger stirred from the corner where he had been hiding. "I will inform the marquess of your impending arrival." Then he flew through the door as though pursued by the hounds of hell.

As he left, the others also headed for the door. Nivea lingered, hoping for a final few words with Dare. Of the same mind, he grabbed her hand and pulled her into his study. She flung herself into his arms and kissed his beautiful, soft lips. He tasted like heaven. She couldn't believe she would be able to enjoy this delicious sensation for the rest of her life. His kiss turned hard and demanding, his hands gripping her waist, pressing her close. Heat radiated through his chest, warming her to her bones.

She moaned and he pulled away. His black eyes glowed. "I love you, Nivea. I need you to know that. I don't want you to think I proposed simply to thwart my father."

"Oh, Dare, I would never think that." When he raised his eyebrow, she giggled. "Oh, all right, I may have considered it at some point. You must admit that this forced proposal came as quite a shock to us both. You can't have been considering marriage for some time."

She had barely finished the sentence before Dare pulled away and strode across the room. Reaching into his desk, he pulled out a small object that glinted in the fading light. Closing the drawer, he crossed the room in two quick strides. Lifting her left hand, he placed a kiss on her knuckles, his dark eyes boring into hers.

"Nivea Horsham, in honor of our engagement, I would like to present you with the Raynsforth family ring. I retrieved it from my solicitor weeks ago. Although I wanted to ask for your hand soon after Joseph's party, I have spoken so disparagingly about marriage, I feared you would not consider my suit."

She laughed. Not consider his suit? The man was a lunatic.

"That is why I have been behaving as a perfect gentleman around you. I wanted to prove that there was more to me than just a lascivious rake."

He pulled her against him and buried his nose in her bodice. "You did not make it easy on me, you know. Every time you came near, I became desperate to touch you. Love you."

She shivered as he ran his tongue up her neck and nipped her earlobe. He slid his hand down her arm and raised her hand. Eyes locked with hers he said, "I want you and only you. I love you, and I ask, once again, if you will do me the honor of becoming my bride." He slid the ring on her finger.

The stone, a deep blue sapphire, almost black in its depth, was set in an ornate band of silver filigree. Nivea twisted her hand left and then right, catching the flashes of light from the waning sun. It was the most beautiful thing she had ever seen.

"Oh, Dare, I love it," she cried, crushing him into a hug. "Yes, I will marry you." She dashed away her tears and kissed him again.

At the sound of throat clearing coming from the doorway, they sprung apart.

"We were waiting to leave," Briar announced, a quiver of amusement in her voice. "Will you be joining us?"

Nivea flushed crimson. "Yes, I'm coming." She flashed a final beaming smile at Dare and dashed out the door.

* * * *

Dare arrived at the Horsham's house early the next morning and was ushered into the earl's study. When they emerged, Nivea was glad to see both men looked content.

"Nivea?" Her father beckoned to her. "I understand Lord Landis has requested your hand in marriage and that you have accepted. Is this true?"

"Yes, Popa. I love him and dearly wish to marry him."

"Are you certain?" His expression was earnest. "I know you have tendered an affection for the man for many years, but are you sure, that as a husband, he will make you happy? Marriage is not all about admiring glances and fancy balls and such."

Her heart squeezed at his concern. He was trying to protect her. And she understood his fears. But one look at Dare standing there, stoically awaiting her answer, and she laughed out her response. "Yes, Popa, he will make me happy. I have seen the joy a good marriage can bring, and I would not settle for anything less. I'm certain Dare and I can have that kind of marriage."

After one more probing inspection, he nodded. "All right then, I give you both my blessing."

"Thank you, Popa," and she hugged him joyously.

"Thank you, Lord Horsham." Dare bowed and the earl grunted.

"Now, I understand you will be traveling to Lord Landis's family home. Nivea, you will bring your maid, and I expect you to be properly chaperoned at all times. Upon your return, we will begin making arrangements for your wedding. Heaven knows, Amelia will be ecstatic to plan another one," he said with an indulgent smile.

"Yes, Popa. I will behave just as if I were under my own roof." She refused to look at Dare as she offered those wicked words.

But they satisfied the earl and he went off to tell Amelia the news. As expected, she came flying down the stairs to envelop Nivea in a hug. "I am so excited! You'll finally be married ...and to Lord Landis. I must say I'm shocked, but ever so happy." Following that outburst, she turned to Dare and her smile dimmed. "I am sorry to hear about your father. I hope things are not as dire as they appear."

When he shrugged, her fervor returned. "Everyone will be overjoyed at your news, Nivea. Please return quickly, so we can post the banns."

Nivea smiled indulgently at her. "Yes, Amelia, we will return home as soon as possible."

With that, Dare arranged for her luggage to be loaded into his carriage. Her maid, Emma, climbed in and took a seat across from Dare's valet. Nivea sat facing forward and Dare took the remaining seat across from her.

As promised, the ride was hard and fast. They stopped at noon for a brief meal, and then pressed through until late afternoon.

"This is the start of Raynsforth," Dare announced as they approached a stark village, consisting of a smattering of cottages, a church, and a few tattered shops. Used to the bustling town near Durham, Nivea was surprised to see it so austere. It was obvious the marquess was no more generous with his tenants than he was his family.

They crossed a number of fields and streams before coming upon a row of twisted chestnut trees hovering over a long drive. The mammoth trees blocked the sunlight and obscured the view of the sprawling castle ahead. Nivea felt a shiver of foreboding as they approached. Breaking through the trees, the ancient manor house loomed large. There was little activity, no sign of a welcome for the prodigal son.

Nivea didn't feel any urgency to follow Emma and Jackson as they descended. The small meal she had consumed was threatening to make a reappearance. *Was she ready to face this?* Could she be gracious to the man who had abused his own son so egregiously? Would she collapse from embarrassment if he railed at her? She had no way of knowing.

But one glance at Dare's face and she knew she'd have to try. His eyes were cloudy, his jaw clenched, and her heart went out to him. This trip was to be the culmination of all his misery.

She reached over to squeeze his hand, but he jerked at her touch. His despair was so apparent, it slashed pain through her heart. "He can't hurt you anymore. You will speak to him, explain why you can't marry the Billingston girl, and tomorrow we will return home."

He tried to put on an accommodating smile, but his expression remained bleak. Gazing up at the house a final time, he rose, helped her from the carriage, and together they entered the front door.

Chapter 44

Dare approached the bed, shocked by what he saw. His mother had tried to prepare him, but one could not appreciate the effect of the disease until witnessed firsthand. The marquess was propped up in bed, barely visible in the fading light of day. That was most likely a good thing.

Dare stared at his misshapen visage, the telltale lumps of advanced syphilis swelling his lips, his cheeks puffy. What was left of his hair was grayed and lank. His large frame filled the bed, unnaturally still.

His mother had proclaimed it fitting that the marquess would suffer so, after flaunting all those women in her face. Still, Dare couldn't help experiencing a moment of...not sorrow really...perhaps compassion, when he entered the room. It dissipated the instant he heard his father's voice.

"Who is it?" barked his father from the shadows.

Dare stiffened his spine and took a decisive step forward. "It is I, sir."

His father peered at him, unable to discern his features in the dark. Dare refused to give him satisfaction by leaning closer. *After all,* his father had always stressed the importance of an erect posture.

"Boy? Is that you?" the voice croaked once again.

"Yes, sir. It is Adair." He took a step forward and gave the slightest hint of a bow. "I understand you wished to see me."

"Bah! I wouldn't care if I never caught sight of you again. What I wished for was to have a son that I could be proud of. A son who appreciated a day's work and didn't go flitting around London like a bloody fripon." He'd sat up during the tirade, but now collapsed back into the pillows.

Taking a breath, he continued, "I ordered you here to finally bring you to heel. Now that I am about to cock toes up, you must marry. I know you have taken great joy in threatening to end our lineage, but that will not happen. I have arranged for you to marry the Billingston girl next door. She's pretty enough, which is more than you deserve. And the older girl has already proven to be a hearty breeder, bearing two sons in as many years. Slap a few brats to Marta's breast and then you can continue your life as you choose. Surely, even you can manage something that simple."

Again he sunk back into the bed.

Dare felt sick. That was the exact sentiment he had relayed to Nivea when describing marriage. Had he truly been that baseless? That heartless? Good God, it was lowering. Nivea was a noble soul, indeed, if she could overlook his abhorrent behavior.

He felt a pang of guilt, knowing she was currently at the mercy of his mother and sisters, no doubt fending off vicious taunts and slurs with all the grace she could muster. Eager to rescue her, Dare strode forward until he was inches from the bed. Seen at close range, his father's appearance was more horrifying. It was as though the ugliness of his soul was now visible for all to see.

Taking a deep breath, he announced, "Father, I will not be marrying the Billingston girl. So not to disappoint you entirely, I will tell you that I have, in fact, found a woman to marry. She is more than I could have ever hoped for and has graciously agreed to be my wife."

His father's eyes flashed. "A trollop? A whore? Will you be tainting the blood of my lineage with some bit o' muslin eager for a title? I won't have it!"

Dare's anger rose to meet his father's. "No sir. Nivea is no trollop. The daughter of the Earl of Cheltenham is a sweet and well-mannered lady. I expect she will provide me children of uncommon intellect and temperament."

He stared down at the figure lying in bed, waiting. The response was unexpected. The old man laughed sharply. "Do not presume I will believe that load of codswallop. You worthless pup, you could not get a lady to marry you for all the gold in Croesus. Enough games. You will marry Marta tomorrow, and that will be the end of it."

Lacing his fingers behind his back, Dare tried to tamp down his anger. It was galling to know his father still harbored such resentment.

But this time, he would have the last word. "I am sorry to disappoint you, Father, but Nivea does, in fact, exist. She is downstairs at this very moment. I hesitate to bring her up because I would prefer that she never learn of the depth of your perversion. But if it will help convince you of her existence, I will go fetch her."

The marquess waved his hand in dismissal. "No need. Play whatever game you like tonight. Tomorrow, you will marry. Now go. Tell Stevens to bring my dinner and light some more tapers in here. I'm not ready for eternal darkness yet, no matter how hard you all wish for it."

Eager to escape, Dare exited the room and headed downstairs. There, he paused to gulp in a few steadying breaths before opening the parlor doors.

Nivea was sitting on the settee where he'd left her. While her lips formed a polite smile, he could see her fingers gripped together in her lap, a stunned expression in her eyes. When she saw him in the doorway, a look of relief washed over her. "Dare—Lord Landis, how is your father?"

"He is the same as always." Walking over, he sat next to her and patted her hand. Before he could say more, his mother drew his attention. Still a handsome woman, with her aristocratic features and neatly coiffed hair, she couldn't conceal the hardness around her mouth and eyes.

"Did you have a pleasant visit upstairs?" she sneered.

"Certainly not, but I expected no less."

"Yes, well some things never change. I'm sure the marquess relayed how eager he is for you to marry."

He inclined his head, but offered no response. Instead he rubbed his thumb over Nivea's hand, marveling at its warmth.

"Do you think you can convince your father of your little charade?

He jerked his head up. "Charade? What do you mean?"

"Her." She waved a hand dismissively in Nivea's direction. "Surely, you could have picked someone a little more"—she let her eyes pass over Nivea—"believable."

His sisters snickered in response.

He didn't realize he had started forward until he felt Nivea place a restraining hand on his arm. "What do you mean, mother?" he growled between clenched teeth.

His oldest sister, Fiona, piped up, "Come now, Adair. I know it was short notice, but I would have expected you to have a number of more suitable looking women to choose from. Imaging trying to pass *her* off as an earl's daughter? Just because Father's dying, do not think he's a fool."

Nivea begin to quiver next to him. He did not dare to look at her, because if he saw the inevitable tears in her eyes, he would no doubt slaughter the entire room. Good God, too much time in their presence and Nivea might decide to back out. That he could not allow.

He drew in a breath to calm his fury, but before he could respond, a footman entered. "Tea is ready, Lady Raynsforth. Should we bring it in?"

"Of course you should bring it in," she snapped, "do you expect us to serve ourselves in the hallway?"

"No, my lady." The poor servant bowed in subjugation and retrieved the tray from the hallway table. Placing it on the table in front of Lady Raynsforth, his sleeve brushed against the plate of biscuits and caused one to slide from the plate.

"Get out, before you dump it all on the floor, " she shrieked, driving the poor man from the room.

While Lady Raynsforth poured the tea into the cups, Dare's youngest sister, Anne, grabbed for a biscuit. "I'd better get one before Adair's betrothed spots them. I'd wager there wouldn't be enough left for all of us."

They all tittered with amusement.

Except for Dare. He jumped to his feet and roared, "You will apologize now! Nivea will be the next Marchioness of Raynsforth, although why she would want such a distasteful title, I cannot guess. Regardless, I will be marrying her, and I demand you treat her with respect!"

Before they were able to form a sentence, he grabbed Nivea's hand and dragged her from the room.

Chapter 45

"Oh, Dare, they were so hateful!" Nivea cried as they raced up the stairs. "They teased each other in good humor, but the things they said about you were so cruel, so blatantly evil."

They were traveling at such a quick pace down a long hallway and up another set of stairs, she could hardly breathe. But there was no stopping Dare as he pulled her along, his face hardened granite, and his eyes black with rage. He said nothing until they reached the landing where he spotted a maid in the hallway.

"You there! Where has Miss Horsham been placed for the evening?"

The woman looked startled. "Milord?"

"Miss Horsham. My betrothed. Which room will she be using?"

"I believe she's in the west wing, milord. The Cherub Room."

Nivea was unprepared for the violence of his response. He stalked over to the young woman, face livid with anger and bellowed, "You put my future wife in the room my father bedded his whores? You will see to it that her things are moved immediately. I expect her to be settled into the walnut room within the quarter hour. Do you understand?"

Cowering with fear, the woman nodded before racing down the hallway as though chased by the devil himself. Even Nivea was shaken by the fury emanating from him. Knowing there was nothing she could say to make this better, she waited quietly until he had regained control.

"Come," he announced after a moment. He walked halfway down the hall and opened a door on the right. Nivea followed, entering a charming room of green and taupe. The walnut furniture was light and whorled, giving the room the appearance of a forest hideaway.

"I'm certain you will be comfortable here."

"Oh, this is lovely," Nivea gasped.

"Good. I'm glad you like it." He did his best to smile, but his face was strained. "I am sorry about the delay, but it shouldn't be long before you can get settled. Now, if you will please excuse me, I must take care of a few things. Be assured the rest of the visit will be more accommodating." He took her hand, kissed it gently, and left.

Dazed, Nivea collapsed on the bed.

This was bad. It was so much worse than she could have imagined. It was a wonder Dare was able to function at all growing up in this house. She had prepared herself for an uncomfortable few days, but this was horrific.

She sat there, trying to sort through the day's events. Every so often, she could hear snippets of Dare yelling downstairs.

"...the Cherub Room? How dare you...? If you ever act like that..."

Then she heard a door slam, his footsteps stomping in the hallway, and then silence.

She had started to drift off when her maid tapped on her door. "Milady, we have brought your things." Emma was followed in the room by two footmen carrying her bags. "Oh, this is much more suitable."

The other room must have been quite disturbing, judging by the scandalized look on her maid's face. "Don't worry, I will just need a moment to set your things out," she said, bustling about. "In the meantime, you can read this note. Lord Landis asked that I give it to you."

Nivea broke the seal and sat by the window to read it. The writing was so like Dare—bold and meticulous, with no unwarranted flourishes.

Miss Horsham,

It appears I spend most of my time apologizing to you. I hope you will forgive me once again. I should never have subjected you to my family. I offer you my deepest regrets for their behavior.

I have asked that a tray be sent to your room for supper this evening. There is no need for you to associate with those cretins any more than necessary.

I have left for the Billingston's to negate my father's agreement. As much as I would like to be with you, it would be best if we stay apart to reduce any hateful gossip my family may chose to spread.

I anticipate one final meal with them tomorrow and then we can return to London.

Once again, please forgive me.

Your devoted servant,

Dare

The poor man. She wished she could see him, comfort him, but he was right. Staying apart would be best for now. Eager to return home, she had Emma bring her supper without delay, and then climbed into bed, falling fast asleep.

* * * *

The next morning, Emma brought up another missive from Dare, along with her breakfast tray.

Miss Horsham,

I trust you had a pleasant sleep. Today we will be taking our mid-day meal with my family where we will bring this matter to a resolution. I assure you, there is no need to worry. By tomorrow, we will have put this behind us and returned you to your loving and supportive family.

Until then
All my love,
Dare

All my love. How delightful that sounded.

Nivea could sustain anything, knowing that Dare truly cared for her. It was almost worth facing his family again, just to see him, be with him.

She took special care getting dressed for lunch. Her heart was racing as she let Emma apply the final touches to her hair. Stepping into the hallway, her heart surged with joy.

Dare was standing there, waiting for her. Although he was as handsome as ever, his eyes were shadowed. He didn't touch her, but his voice betrayed his emotions roiling beneath the surface. "Did you sleep well?"

"Yes, thank you. I won't ask the same of you."

He grimaced. "No, I'm afraid it was an uncomfortable evening. But today will put it all to rest."

He took her hand to escort her downstairs and then stopped. "Where is your ring?"

Confused, she stared at him.

"Your engagement ring. Why aren't you wearing it?"

"I didn't think it proper. Not until everything is resolved." After the ugliness with his family yesterday, she had taken off the ring and tucked it into her reticule. Much as she loved it, she was afraid it might set off a firestorm if his sisters spotted a family heirloom on her hand.

Dare glared at her. "That issue has been thoroughly resolved. I asked for your hand, you gave it to me, and you will wear my ring. At all times."

Flustered but pleased, Nivea hurried into her room, placed the ring back on her finger, and dashed out. When she held up her hand for him to see, he brought it to his lips for a kiss and flashed her a smile so full of heat, her knees went weak.

"That's much better. Come, let us brave the lions together." Taking her arm, he guided her down to the dining room.

To say lunch was a strained affair would be exceedingly generous. Dare's father sat at the head of the table, slowly and painfully spooning broth into his mouth. He refused to acknowledge either of them as they entered.

Lady Landis sat at the foot of the table flanked by Dare's sisters. They were slender, poised, and dressed to the height of fashion. Nivea sighed, feeling awkward as usual. Dare gave her hand a comforting squeeze before taking his seat at the opposite end of the table.

The marquess wasted no time dominating the conversation. In between spoonfuls, he railed against everything from the cost of livestock to the weather. But his favorite topic was disparaging his son.

It was difficult to look at him; his disease had left him so disfigured. His face and hands were swollen with boils. His eyes, black and fierce, glared out from beneath untamed brows. His cravat was dotted with stains, as a lack of teeth permitted soup to spew forth with every pronouncement.

Fortunately, he did not expect a response, so Nivea followed the lead of the others and concentrated on her meal. Her nerves destroyed her appetite, so she toyed with her plate while listening to the ranting of a madman.

"I received a note from Billingston today. I see you defied me once again and forfeited your marriage contract. Made me a laughingstock, of course. He was quite eager to tie his daughter to a title such as ours. And no wonder. His other chit married a baron, if you can imagine." Agitated, he waved his spoon in the air, before taking another mouthful. "He expected better, but I guess everyone has children that disappoint them," muttered the marquess. "Damn shame. Good, sensible fellow, Billingston is."

Silence fell as he turned his attention back to his meal. It didn't take long before he was waving his spoon again. "I suppose I was too soft on you. Never was able to break that stubborn streak of yours."

Enraged at that proclamation, Nivea chanced a glance around the table. She noticed Dare's sisters smirking at each other. Dare sat there, seemingly unaffected, methodically cutting his food and placing it into his mouth. He never acknowledged he even heard his father.

But there was no stopping the man. "Don't expect an inheritance now, boy. I know you've been counting on it, no doubt frantically putting off creditors for years, waiting for me to put my spoon in the wall. You'll be in quite a corner now. You'll get the title, nothing I can do about that, but not a single groat if I can help it. I was willing to change things if you'd finally married, but you shot yourself in the foot with that one, didn't you? No Billingston girl, no inheritance. Maybe poverty will teach you a valuable lesson." He let out a wheezy sound that Nivea assumed was a laugh.

She was startled when Dare suddenly spoke up. "Father, have I ever asked you for a shilling?" His eyes were black and focused. When no response was forthcoming, he continued. "Truly, have I ever given you the slightest indication that I am in need of your money? Because, I assure you, I am not. I want nothing from you. You distribute your precious money as you see fit, and I can promise you, your death will bring me nothing but peace."

Hearing this, delivered in a tone so casual and calm as to be almost bored, turned the marquess apoplectic. He banged on the table with his fist, causing all the women to jump. "I will not be talked to in my house like that! Of course you need money, you frivolous fool. Billingston would have seen that you had a proper dowry, and then I would have kept you in my will. But now, I will be stripping you of all funds. You will be penniless. You will never find a woman to marry you once you're thrown into debtor's prison," the man crowed in victory.

Dare laid down his fork, dabbed his mouth with a napkin, and in a very controlled voice responded, "Sir, you are mistaken. As I have explained, Miss Horsham has agreed to be my wife. She is not interested in my title or my wealth, although I'm certain she will be relieved to hear that she will lack neither. The very thought of holding your title fills me with revulsion, but fortunately for her, nothing can be done of it."

Nivea couldn't help but smile in response. It never occurred to her that either would matter. She just wanted him. More so now than ever. Noting her response, he quirked a slight grin in her direction and turned his attention back to his father.

"I know you have no confidence in my abilities or intelligence, but I assure you, I am a shrewd investor and quite comfortable. Best of all, I managed to achieve my wealth without treating people like animals. So, you and your money can go straight to Hell."

Then he picked up his fork, speared a tender carrot, and popped it into his mouth.

The response was so explosive, Nivea's heart nearly jumped from her chest. The marquess flung an arm in her direction and bellowed, "Surely you don't mean to marry her. Look at her, boy—she's God awful. She's plain, obviously overly fond of biscuits, and timid as a church mouse. You think to make her the Marchioness of Raynsforth? You think she's worthy? I couldn't think of a less worthy prospect. If you are doing this simply to spite me, than I will get the last laugh. You will be stuck with her and I will be long gone. What a fool you'll be then."

Nivea went pale. What if he were correct? Maybe Dare had concocted this scheme as a way to irritate his father. That would explain why he'd asked her to marry him. Then she glanced down at the beautiful, sapphire ring, sparkling on her finger. He'd had it in his desk, waiting for her.

She raised her head and all doubts were erased. Dare was quivering with rage. He gave her a quick shake of his head, placed his napkin on the table, and rose from his seat. Standing to his full height, he locked eyes with his father. "Plain? You think Miss Horsham plain. And timid? Unworthy to be a Raynsforth? You, sir, are as blind as you are stupid. Of course she is pale here, where one's very life is squashed from their soul. But when she is with her family and friends…when she is happy, she is the most beautiful woman imaginable. Her eyes glitter like sapphires, her warm smile lights up a room. Yes, she can be quiet and respectful, but she is also strong in spirit, and has more love in her than anyone I know."

But that did not cow the old troll. "Bah," he mocked, "that just proves what I said. She is weak, soft. Trust me, you could not be making a worse choice."

"Soft? Nay, sir, her love is not soft. It is fierce and burning and has made me a man."

Nivea could not have been more proud of him. But he was not finished. He took a breath and hissed, "You are absolutely right about one thing, sir. You would have selected someone completely different. Nivea comes from a kind and loving family who could not fathom the type of horror we've experienced in this house. Frankly, if you feel she is a mistake, then marrying her will be the best decision I've ever made."

That was one of the most romantic declarations she'd ever heard. She wanted to leap across the table and kiss him senseless. Instead, she pressed her ring to her lips, and he winked at her in return.

Now that the yelling had stopped, the room had become deathly still. The women were all staring at the head of the table.

The marquess's mouth hung open, as though shocked into silence. Then he began flailing his arms and ripping at his throat as though being choked.

Dare didn't move. "Don't pretend to die. I shan't believe it."

But before he could return to his seat, his father collapsed in his chair, unconscious.

"Good God, you've killed him," screeched Fiona.

"Call the doctor," screamed Anne.

Two footmen rushed into the room. Lady Landis ordered them to carry her husband upstairs. Before she followed them out, she turned to Dare and said, "Don't look quite so guilty, darling. This has happened before, and he has always returned. Odds are the bastard will outlive us all." With a swish of her skirts, she left the room.

Nivea sat in her chair, dazed. Never could she have pictured a family such as this. How was Dare capable of even the slightest glimmer of humanity growing up as he did? She could not fathom the insults, the yelling, the sheer hatred, smothering all hope of kindness.

Dare stood there, rigid…broken even, and her heart clenched. Pushing back her chair, she circled the table. "Dare? Are you all right?"

Black unfocused eyes turned to her. It took a moment before he crooked a very shaky grin at her. "I have had better days. Although, to be honest, I've had worse as well." Grabbing her arm, he said, "Come, let's take a walk. I feel the need to clear my head."

She followed him outside, surprised to find the sun shining overhead. It was quite incongruous to the mood inside. She walked by his side without a word, letting him gather his thoughts. As they passed through the garden and into an orchard, the leaves rustled softly in the cool breeze.

Finally situated far enough from the house, Dare stopped and turned to her. "Darling, I know we'd hoped to leave today, but I can't go now. I must speak to the doctor. I promise you, tomorrow we will leave here, regardless of the outcome. Then we can marry, if you'll still have me."

His tone was so grim her heart almost broke. "Of course I still want to marry you. More now than ever." Squeezing his hand, she was shocked to find it cold and stiff. She cast a quick glance at the house, before pressing it to her lips—warming his skin as she soothed her soul. "You can join our family and never give yours a second thought."

"Truly? I…I thought for certain you would run from here and never look back."

She laughed. "Well, I will most assuredly be running, but not without you."

"You are not scared that I will become like them? That their misery will become ours?"

Oh, he looked so forlorn, she could hardly stand it. She threw her arms around him and pulled him close. "My darling Dare, just the fact that you worry about it, makes half the battle won. You have spent time with my family and know how life can be. Have no fear, with love comes happiness. We will be fine."

He turned his eyes to hers, and she saw the terror lurking within. But she held his gaze, willing him to understand. To believe. And the walls began to crumble. Hope appeared and his entire being relaxed. A smile began at the corners of his mouth and then echoed in his eyes as they crinkled in joy.

Suddenly she found herself twirling in the air. Dare was laughing and spinning and kissing her soundly on the lips. "Yes! My darling Nivea, I think you are right. I can put this behind me and become the man I should be. The man you deserve." He put her back on the ground but did not stop kissing her. He trailed his lips down her jawline to her neck and heat flared in her belly.

"I've missed you," he murmured. "I can't wait to make you mine. Forever."

How wonderful those words sounded. She reached her arms around his waist and pulled him close, craving his warmth, his scent. Him. When she looked into his handsome, precious face, she could see desire echoing in his obsidian eyes. Brazenly, she glanced around. Could they?

He laughed. "Not here, my love. Not now. Let us go back, finish with my father, and go home."

Oh, how she loved the sound of that. She would finally have a home of her own. With Dare.

Walking back toward the house, hand in hand, she marveled at the beauty of the day. Near the garden wall was a clump of flowers. "Oh look, forget-me-nots. How odd that they would bloom this late in the season." Reaching down, she plucked one and handed it to Dare. "Keep this with you. Perhaps it will give you serenity with your family."

He took it and solemnly placed it in his pocket.

"I love you," he said simply and escorted her back into the house.

Chapter 46

Nivea sat in her room, idly twirling her pen as drops of ink splattered the blank parchment. Although she had thought to compose a poem, no words emerged. Her emotions were too jumbled to formulate thoughts. She longed to be home again, to begin the next chapter in her life with Dare. But all she could do was wait.

Taking out a clean sheet of paper, she began writing her name like a silly schoolgirl. It was a name she had practiced long ago, and now, her dream would come true.

Nivea Landis, Marchioness of Raynsforth
Lady Landis
Adair and Nivea Landis

Was it even possible? She wriggled with joy. Hearing a tap at the door, she balled up the paper and stuffed it into the drawer. "Yes?"

Emma entered, carrying a tray. "I have brought you some tea and biscuits. Would you like me to place them on the table?"

"Yes, that would be wonderful. Thank you." She crossed over and selected a biscuit from the plate. Taking a nibble, she asked, "Is there any word on the marquess? Has he…?" She paused, unable to finish the question.

Emma poured the tea and handed her a cup. "Oh, no, the doctor said he'll not die today. I heard a footman say Satan don't want him yet. He is enjoying the show on earth far too much."

"Emma!"

"Beggin' your pardon, miss. That's just what I heard."

Nivea tried to hide her smile as she sipped the tea, but was certain she failed miserably. After all, she pretty much felt the same way.

"Will we be leaving soon? I don't care too much for this house," Emma whispered with a nervous glance, as though someone might be eavesdropping.

Nivea agreed, but thought it prudent to keep that to herself. "Yes, we should be leaving first thing tomorrow."

"Very good, miss. I'll begin the preparations." She gave a quick curtsey and closed the door behind her.

Nivea carried her cup over to the window and sat down to watch the fading sun. A carriage was proceeding down the driveway, presumably taking the doctor home. A few moments later, a figure on a horse went streaking from the stables and across the field.

Dare.

Bowing low over the neck of his horse, his hair blowing in the wind, he was the picture of unrestrained energy. Powerful, masterful, and utterly enticing. A surge of desire ran through her, and Nivea knew she could not spend another night apart. She needed to be with him, feel his skin against hers, revel in his kisses.

She giggled. Maybe, even discover another of his intriguing tricks.

She gulped down her tea and rang for Emma. Once she appeared, Nivea yawned loudly and announced, "Today was such an emotional day, I think I will retire early. Please prepare my things and then have the rest of the evening to yourself."

Her maid did not suspect a thing. She helped her into her night shift, gathered up her clothes and tray and, after bidding her good night, left the room.

Could she really do this? Could she be so wanton as to sneak into his room?

Yes.

Before she could change her mind, Nivea quickly donned a robe and scampered down the hall. Darting into his door, she smothered a scream.

"Oh! I—I—" She flushed to the roots of her hair.

His man, Jackson, was standing at the dresser, arranging Dare's cravats. Appearing startled for a second, he recovered, gave her a courtly bow and said, "Good evening Miss Horsham. I can see you wish to leave Lord Landis a note before retiring. I will not interfere."

She looked at him, confused, but he continued to assemble Dare's wardrobe. "You may compose your missive at his desk and he will find it upon his return. Please give me a moment while I prepare his bath and then I will adjourn for the evening."

He walked into the adjoining room, moving around for a few moments before whispering to her from the doorway, "Milord has been much improved since your appearance. I am quite grateful for the change. Have a good evening, miss." Then she heard a door click and he was gone.

Well, that was quite unexpected. Nivea sat on the bed, listening to her heart pound furiously in her chest. Would he be back? Should she stay?

Taking a deep breath to calm her nerves, she smelled…Dare. His delicious scent permeated the room. It was on his clothes, in his bed.

Yes, she would stay.

Unwrapping her robe, she began to climb into bed when she felt the sash slither down her leg. It was silky and smooth and gave her an idea. Feeling delightfully wicked, she pulled the ribbon from the robe and eyed the headboard. Oh, yes, there were handy little pigeonholes in the woodwork. She threaded the sash through, tied a loose knot at either end and slid her wrists through the openings.

Dare was in for quite a surprise.

* * * *

Nivea startled awake. She was lying in a strange bed, bathed in shadows. It took her a moment to remember where she was. In the next room, she heard Dare yell for Jackson. He must have finished his bath.

She squirmed in anticipation. Hopefully, he would not be mad finding her here.

"Jackson!" he bellowed again, but there was no answer. Accepting that his manservant was not coming, she heard him muttering obscenities as he toweled off. He stormed through the door, his face cloaked in anger. Until he saw her.

The look in his eyes was precious. She saw them change from anger to surprise to desire in a heartbeat. Wearing nothing but a robe, water glistening on his hair, he was a sight to behold. He stopped in the doorway and a smile curled up his face. He leaned against the doorframe and crossed his arms, as though lounging in a ballroom. "Well, this is a pleasant surprise," he purred.

Her skin tingled in anticipation and her heart stuttered. "You said some very nice things about me today. I thought you might deserve a reward."

His eyes widened. "A reward, you say? Just for being nice?" Then his expression turned wolfish. "Exactly how nice was I?"

She held up her arms, showing she was tethered to the headboard. Feeling absolutely decadent, she cast an alluring smile his way. "I would say, the way you defended me deserves a very, *very* big reward."

His eyes went dark. There was a brief moment when he paused, perhaps to consider the wisdom of his actions. And then desire overcame all reason. He was by her side in a flash and she felt the full weight of him covering her, warming her, and soothing her.

"Oh, Nivea, you cannot imagine how much I have ached for this." He nuzzled her neck, inhaling deeply. "I could bear anything as long as I knew I could lose myself in you once the day is over."

The feel of his warm skin against hers was intoxicating. She felt herself grow wet and he hadn't even touched her yet. Then he began to kiss her neck, run his tongue along her jawline.

She shivered. "Oh, Dare, I have missed you too."

He stroked her bare arms, stretched over her head. "I see that you are at my mercy. I wonder what I should do with you."

The seductive tone sent another shiver through her. She watched as he ran his gaze over her body, halting at her legs. Noting the predatory look in his eyes, she squirmed.

"Oh, my dear, I think it is time to introduce you to another one of my tricks."

She giggled nervously. "I was hoping you would say that."

He raised an eyebrow in surprise and then smirked. "I see I am going to enjoy having you as my wife, Miss Horsham."

He stood up and let the robe fall from his shoulders. She quivered at the sight of his lean, muscled body. The dark hair on his chest swirled around his nipples, growing faint around his stomach and then thicker between his legs, where his desire was evident. She barely had time to lick her lips before he lay down, covering her with his warmth. Starting at her finger tips, he proceeded to kiss his way down her wrists, forearm, and elbow. She giggled when he reached the inner part of her arm and twisted away, her wrist slipping from its restraint.

"Oh, you've escaped. That won't do at all." With a devilish grin, Dare captured her hand, stretched it over her head, and retied both her knots.

"That's better." he said, with a light tug. "Now, where was I?"

She shivered as he skimmed his hand down her arm, throat, and breast. Being wicked was delicious fun.

She strained up to increase the pressure of his hand, but he had other ideas. He slid down farther, kissing her stomach through the fabric of her shift. Lower still, until he was sitting at the bottom of the bed. Running his hands up from her feet, he nudged the virginal white fabric up her thighs, exposing her womanhood. The fiery look in his eyes wiped away the flare of embarrassment. But when he dipped his head toward her inner thigh, she almost changed her mind. Surely he wasn't going to…

"Oh!" she squeaked. He had flicked his tongue across a sensitive spot high on her thigh. She tried to squirm away.

"Now, now, my dearest, don't turn bashful." He ran a finger from her breastbone, down her stomach, through her navel, and stopped just between her legs. "You trust me, don't you? You know I will give you pleasure."

His ebony eyes burned through her. She licked her lips in nervous anticipation, but nodded.

"Good girl," he purred.

Edging his finger lower, he delicately rubbed the sensitive bud between her legs, and she arched her back with delight.

"That's right. You want me to touch you. Now I will give you a different sort of touch and you will crave it as much as I do."

He dipped his head and licked her wetness. The first time he kissed her, she was too surprised for the sensation to register. But after she felt him press and swirl his tongue around her most sensitive area, she flamed with desire.

"Oh, Dare, that is…wonderful," she panted, "do not stop."

He chuckled. "I won't, my dear," and returned to his work.

Nivea writhed with need. She tugged at her arms, wanting to touch him, run her fingers though his hair, hold his head in place to ensure he did—not—stop.

Pinned as she was, she could only arch her back and press more firmly into his mouth. He kept up the onslaught, sucking, licking, teasing her until she couldn't breathe.

He lessened the pressure, nuzzling against her thigh.

"Please." She thrust upward.

"Soon, darling. Very soon." Even his voice sent her pulse racing.

He shifted his weight and pressed her hips back onto the mattress. Once she was still, he slid his hand under her shift, up her ribs, and gently pinched at her swollen nipple.

Exquisite agony.

He licked her once more and then squeezed again.

Oh God, she was quivering like a new foal.

He palmed her breast, reverently kneading her skin and allowed her to catch her breath. "Are you enjoying this?"

She whimpered.

"You have been a very patient woman and I think you deserve a reward as well," he cooed. "Are you ready for your reward?"

She nodded so hard, the bed shook.

With a wolfish grin, he tweaked her nipple, sucked her swollen nub, and drove his finger into her center. And she exploded into blazing bits of light.

He continued to lick her through the spasms of pleasure until she could take no more. Keening softly, she pulled away from him. While her body was still sending aftershocks quivering through her, he reached above and untied her hands.

"I want you to touch me," he urged. "I want to feel your hands on me. Wrap your arms around me, my love, and heal me."

Tears pricked her eyes as she stroked his back, running her hands over his scars.

"I need you, now, my love." He nudged her legs apart and drove into her with one thrust. Her skin was so sensitive, the contact was almost painful in its pleasure. Giving her time to adjust, he buried into her neck, kissing and nipping at her skin. When she pressed against him, he raised up onto his palms and began to move. He loomed above her like a magnificent satyr. His hair, luxurious as black silk, fell down around his face. His jaw, firm and strong, was clenched in concentration. And his eyes, black, intense, penetrated her very soul. They were one.

She ran her fingers down his cheek in a tender caress. "I love you."

He smiled and kissed her finger. "I love you, too. Now and forever."

"Now and forever," she repeated.

He dropped down, covering her body with his heat, his delicious scent. She kneaded his muscles, slicked with sweat. Roiling and rubbing his manhood against her womanhood, she groaned with pleasure. The sound spurred him on and he increased the tempo, sending shivers through her body.

Pumping, pulsing, pounding into her, he brought her closer and closer. Almost there. Almost there...and then with a burst of pleasure, she cried out.

He covered her mouth with his to swallow her scream and then shuddered to completion.

They both laid there panting, their chests heaving from the overwhelming exertion. "Good God, woman," Dare finally choked out, "you are going to kill me."

In a voice heavy with sleep, she managed to mumble, "Hopefully not until we have tried out all your tricks."

He gave a strangled laugh and then drifted off to sleep in her arms.

Chapter 47

The next month was a whirlwind of activity. True to her word, Amelia took over the wedding plans, inviting the guests and dragging Nivea to endless dress fittings. "Darling, you must have a trousseau for your new husband. He will be a marquess someday. You must be attired appropriately."

Nivea loved her stepmother, and tried to be patient, but it was exhausting. "Surely, I have enough clothes now. We've been to every modiste in London."

"And they have designed some marvelous creations for you, don't you agree? You'll be the envy of the *ton*."

That was pushing it a little far. Yes, the clothes were nice, but they would still be worn by her. If she was to be envied, it was for the man she had somehow convinced to marry her. She still could not believe it.

In public, he played the cordial gentleman, as though scared to show his true feelings. But every so often he would catch her eye, and his lips would curl into a sultry smile. His eyes would darken, and heat would flare between them. It wouldn't be long before he would sneak up on her, tug her into a quiet corner, and kiss her senseless.

She'd told him they could do no more until they were married, and he seemed to take great pleasure in making her regret those words. She couldn't wait to become his wife. To make him hers.

And Amelia was right, she wanted to make him proud. So, she sat through numerous fittings, stops at the millenary, and embarrassing visits by the modiste charged with designing her nightclothes. In no time, the preparations were complete. There was nothing to do but wait for the day to arrive.

* * * *

It was a week before the wedding, when Dare received a letter from his mother. It was shockingly short and to the point.

Adair,

Your father has passed on. His burial will occur in two days. As you are no longer under an obligation to marry, we await your arrival.

Dowager Marchioness of Raynsforth

He put down the paper.

Blinked.

And read it again.

His exhale was so intense, the missive fluttered across the desk.

That was it. He was now the Marquess of Raynsforth. He could do as he pleased, no longer shackled by the demands or expectations of his father. He knew he should feel some sadness or remorse for his sire, but at the moment, there was only relief.

And then the words began to sink in. *No longer under an obligation to marry. We await your arrival?*

He shook his head in disbelief. Was his entire family delusional? Did they truly think he would abandon Nivea and return home? To live?

The idea was ludicrous.

His wedding was days away and nothing would stop him from starting a new life with the woman he loved. Then a sense of dread prickled down his spine. Could he marry just days after his father's death? Protocol dictated they wait at least six months.

Dammit to Hell! He slammed his palm on the desk. That would be completely unacceptable. He could hardly wait six days, little yet six months. He loved her. He *needed* her. He'd leashed in his rampant desire for as long as he could. They *must* marry.

But first he would have to inform her of the news. After all, the Horshams might have an opinion on the matter. He would just have to convince them to have the *correct* opinion.

Snatching the note off the desk, he stuffed it into his pocket and headed out.

Upon his arrival at the Horsham's London home, Nivea raced down the stairs to greet him. "Oh Dare, this is an unexpected surprise. Why are you here?"

He kissed her cheek, inhaling her magical, soothing scent. She was his lifeline. His love. Home. The thought helped steel his soul for the upcoming unpleasantness.

He stepped back, laced her fingers in his, and gazed into her eyes, unsure what to say.

"What's wrong?" Her cheeks went pale. "Has something happened?"

Not knowing how to start, he reached into his pocket and withdrew the note.

Her eyebrows pinched, eyes full of worry. Raising her hand to her throat, she sucked in a breath and reached for the paper.

It didn't take her long to read—it was appalling how brief it was.

She stiffened. Her mouth dropped open. And her eyes lifted to his, wide with fear. "I'm not certain what to say. What will you...?" And she trailed off, unable to voice her thoughts.

Oh God, she had assumed the worst. That he would withdraw his offer. Of all the ludicrous... As though he could live without her.

He opened his mouth and—

"Good day, Lord Landis. We didn't expect you today." The earl and his wife emerged from the study.

Damn, he'd gone about this all wrong. He should have addressed this with Nivea in private. Then, once he'd made his intentions known, they could have presented a united front to her parents.

There was nothing to be done about it now. He'd just have to press forward. He bowed at the couple. "Good morning, sir. Madam. I fear I just received a missive from my mother, and was just sharing it with Nivea. My father has passed on."

"Oh, Dare, I'm so sorry." Amelia crossed to him and pressed a comforting hand to his arm. "I know it wasn't unexpected, but that doesn't make it any less painful."

Painful? No, that was not one of the words that had come to mind. But he responded in the spirit it was offered. "Thank you, milady. I appreciate your concern."

"What will you do now?" At her question, all eyes turned to him. It was obvious she asked the question at the forefront of everyone's mind. Would he beg off?

Time to make this unequivocally clear. "No, madam, I haven't finalized any plans yet. But I imagine I will travel to Raynsforth sometime this week to see the bastard buried and return well in time for our wedding."

Nivea squeaked in surprise. "So, you still wish to marry me?"

With a hoot of delight, he pulled her into his arms. "Of course I do. By this time next week, you will be the Marchioness of Raynsforth. Does that please you?"

Before she could respond, the earl exclaimed, "Surely you are not thinking of marrying so soon. We must postpone the ceremony."

Dare turned, but did not release his betrothed, maintaining a possessive hand on her waist. "No. Surely, we must not."

"See here, Landis. I know you did not get along with your father, but you cannot expect to eschew the mourning period all together."

"Frankly, having me marry was his greatest wish," Dare stated. Quite pleased with himself, he nuzzled into Nivea's neck. "He cast a pallor over my life for far too long, and I think it very fitting to embrace my new wife along with my new title."

When he continued to protest, Dare plucked the note from Nivea's hand and passed it to the earl. As he read it, his expression hardened. Without a word, he handed it to his wife.

"Oh, how cold!" cried Amelia. "Was there no love at all in your family?"

No. None at all. But the words were too hard to say, so he just shook his head.

"But why?" He was touched by her plaintive question, her eyes full of concern.

He shrugged, having no response.

"Well, *I* have no intention of delaying this marriage," Nivea declared. "The *ton* may be shocked by it, but the sooner we invite Dare into our family, the better."

"Yes, we must." Amelia encircled her husband's arm and with a pretty pout, said, "Darling, it's for the best. Please say you agree."

The earl was no match for his wife. Chucking her under her chin, he sighed. "If that is what you wish, then we will just brace ourselves for the scandal and carry on."

Nivea rushed over and gave them both a swift hug. "Thank you, Popa!"

* * * *

Despite his nonchalant attitude at the Horsham's, Dare spent the next few hours puzzling over his upbringing. He had come to expect his father's cold behavior, but what had caused his mother to become so uncaring?

He'd never asked her for anything. He'd never harmed her in any way. And yet, once the marquess reappeared, her manner toward him alternated between apathy and irritation.

And now she demanded that he return home. For what purpose?

A visit from Petrick, his father's solicitor, cleared up some of the mystery. Dare had only met the man a few times, and was well aware he shared his father's disdain of him.

Sitting in a chair across from Dare's desk, Petrick removed a sheath of papers from his bag. With a pinched expression, he began, "It is my duty to inform you of your father's estate. As expected, you have inherited the title of Marquess of Raynsforth, with all its duties and responsibilities. I'm sure you are aware that the marquess had every intention of stripping you of all financial bequests. He did not feel you brought honor to the title, and he did not wish you to benefit in any way from his hard-fought financial gains.

Dare forced down a growl. The man had been a vicious slave owner. Whatever Dare had done could not begin to approach the degradation his father had embraced.

The solicitor, untroubled by the obvious hypocrisy, continued, "Once you declined to marry the Billingston girl, he was determined to divide the money between your sisters and leave all unentailed estates to your mother."

That was interesting. "But this did not occur?"

"Correct. The marquess was not able to complete the necessary documentation prior to his untimely demise."

"Are you saying that he did not actually change his will?"

"No. He did not."

"So, despite the marquess's best efforts, I am now the sole heir to my father's fortune?"

Petrick nodded.

"And my mother and sisters, do they know of this? Did they know they would be the beneficiaries if I did not marry?"

"Yes, I am fairly certain he informed them of his plans." His tone was grim.

"But since he didn't change the will, they get nothing?"

Petrick narrowed his eyes. He was not at all pleased with the outcome. "Correct."

"This will not sit well with them."

"No, milord," he replied, sounding miffed, "it will not sit at all well with them."

Tapping his fingers on his lips, Dare sat there absorbing that information. He supposed, living in that house all those years, it was inevitable the money would be at the root of all their misery. As it stood now, his mother was penniless. She was more trapped by circumstances than he ever was.

She simply wanted what she was owed, and if it came at the expense of her son, so be it. By convincing him to come back home, without a wife, she would be able to maintain her current lifestyle. Otherwise, she was destitute. As difficult as she had been, he couldn't allow that to happen. He would put this ugly chapter of his life behind him.

"I will take care of my family." Then he paused. "But only if they agree not to interfere with me in any way."

The man showed a flicker of emotion before resuming his haughty demeanor. "That will be entirely up to you, milord."

What a thrill to hear those words. His future was now in *his* hands. There were to be no more insults or reprisals. Without the shadowy specter of his father threatening him, he could now marry Nivea and together they could create a new life.

Dare stood up, eager to get started. "Thank you, Petrick. You have been very accommodating. I will come to your office in the morning and we can determine what sort of compensation my mother and sisters are due."

"Very good, milord." With a tight smile, the man took his leave.

Dare took a deep breath and exhaled with a loud sigh of relief. It was over. His secret was safe. He was a free man.

Returning to his desk, Dare pulled out a box tucked in the far recesses of his drawer. He had one more task to complete, and then he would be ready for his wedding day. Smiling, he set to work.

* * * *

The night before their wedding, Dare knocked on the Horsham's door and requested to meet with his betrothed. Hearing of his arrival, Nivea skipped down the stairs, and in no time, they were sequestered in the parlor, snuggled on the sofa.

"I have something for you," he said, his voice rumbling in his chest as she lay against it.

She chuckled. "I'm sure you do, Lord Landis, but I told you it would have to wait until we're married."

"Vixen, that's not what I meant." He gave her a squeeze, and then sat up to pull a small package from his jacket. "I—I wanted to give you a wedding present."

"Oh Dare, you are so sweet. You didn't have to. I didn't get you anything."

"Please, don't get too excited. 'Tis but a trifle. But first I want to tell you the meaning behind it."

How mysterious. He put his arm around her shoulders and she snuggled in close, eager to hear his tale.

"Remember the last day we were with my family and my father lost consciousness?"

"Certainly. It was a horrible moment."

"Yes, it was. I'm sure you will not be surprised to hear that I was afraid our heated conversation had led to his collapse."

She hummed. "I confess, I was a little worried about it myself."

"Yes, well, it came as quite a relief to hear from the doctor that it was simply a symptom of the disease."

"Thank goodness."

He gave her a squeeze. "Yes. As much as I despised the man, I did not wish to cause him harm. In fact, the doctor seemed to feel that after years of angst and anger, the contrary old troll probably enjoyed the fight."

Nivea grumbled in agreement.

Dare sat her upright and twisted in his seat so he was facing her. "I decided I couldn't leave without seeing him one last time. He was lying on his bed, only semi-conscious, and I wasn't certain what I hoped to accomplish or what I was going to say. Then, I sunk my hands into my pockets and discovered the flower you had given me. Remember?"

"Of course." She smiled. "The forget-me-not."

He kissed her cheek. "Yes. When I touched it, it was as though you were in the room with me. I knew you would want me to forgive him. So I started to talk to him. I told him I would bring honor to the title and not disgrace the family. I would not squander my inheritance. I also told him I would marry, and you would bear me as many sons as God would allow. I did not want him to worry—the Raynsforth name would live on. I don't know if he heard me, but I made my peace with him, and I felt relief."

Nivea's couldn't have been more proud. She loved him more with every passing moment.

"I'm so glad." She stroked his cheek, and he kissed her hand.

"I am, too. Your little flower gave me the strength and courage to clear the air before it was too late. I just wanted to thank you."

He pressed the box into her hand. She slowly untied the blue bow, lifted the lid, and paused. Nestled inside was a delicate, white handkerchief. Embroidered in the center were what appeared to be blue flowers. Curious and confused, she lifted it from the wrapping. Along the bottom, in uneven but legible stitching were the words: *Forget me not, my dearest. September 30.*

Their wedding date.

She looked up at him in wonder. "Did you make this? For me?"

He nodded, so nervous and uncertain he was unable to meet her eyes. "I told you once I had learned to embroider as a child. It seems I am a little rusty."

Eyes full of tears, she threw her arms around him and crushed him into the sofa. "Dare Landis, this is the sweetest, most romantic, most precious gift I have ever received. I love you so much!"

He wrapped his arms around her and held her as she laughed and cried and covered him in kisses. After a few moments, he cupped her face in his hands and with a wry grin asked, "So, can I assume you like it?"

She swiped away her tears. "Yes, my dearest man. I will cherish it forever."

He leaned in to kiss her. Once, with a soft press of his lips. Twice, with the tip of his tongue. The third time set her pulse pounding. And she pulled away.

"One more day, my love. After tomorrow you can spend all day kissing me, but tonight, you need to go home."

He growled, but obediently followed her to the door. Tomorrow was far too long.

Chapter 48

Their wedding was the event of the season.

Nivea was not surprised. After all, confirmed rake, Adair Landis, was getting married. And not only was he marrying an over-the-hill spinster, but it was to take place only days after the loss of his father. It was scandalous. No one in the *ton* would miss it.

Nivea didn't care. She could not have been happier. After all those years of waiting and dreaming, she was going to marry Dare.

The day dawned warm and clear. The church was overflowing with people. And Dare was at the altar waiting for her.

She practically skipped down the aisle, she was so eager to see him. There he stood, handsome as always, dressed in an elegant suit of deep indigo. The perfect foil for her frothy gown of blue. The color of forget-me-nots. She halted by his side, and the look he gave her was so hot and so sweet her knees almost buckled.

He loved her. Was it truly possible?

It wasn't until they'd said their vows and kissed before God and man, that she could finally believe it.

Giving her no time to absorb the moment, Dare dragged her up the aisle, dashed through the throng and headed straight for the carriage.

"Dare! We should stay a moment to accept congratulations." She laughed at his impatience.

"We can see them at the wedding feast," he growled. "Now get in."

He handed her inside the carriage and disappeared for a moment. She heard him say something to the coachman before climbing in next to her. Before she could protest, he pulled her into his arms and gave her a kiss. Unfortunately, she was smiling so wide, all he encountered were teeth.

"Happy?" he asked with a laugh.

"I'm so happy, I can hardly breathe. I am married. Married to the infamous Lord Landis." She sighed.

She reached over to hold his hand. "You know you broke the hearts of dozens of women today. Hundreds perhaps. I could feel them glaring at me, wondering what sorcery I invoked to ensnare you." Keeping her eyes focused on their hands she murmured, "I'm still wondering the same thing myself."

Shyly, she raised her eyes and gasped.

No ravenous wolf had ever looked at his prey with a more predatory expression than her husband had fixed on her. His dark hooded eyes raked her form as a smile curled up just enough to bare his teeth. Her heart began racing, knowing exactly what that look meant.

She froze as he raised his hand to her face, slowly gliding his fingertips over her cheek, down her throat and across her shoulder.

"I have no doubt," he said, his voice thick with emotion, "that every other gentleman in the church would know exactly how you ensnared me"— his finger nudged the small capped sleeve down her arm—"if they could just experience this." He tugged the second sleeve down, causing her bosom to spill out of her dress and into his hands.

"A man would do a great many things to experience this pleasure." He licked his lips, his eyes black with desire.

She trembled as he leaned closer. He placed a chaste kiss, first on her left breast, then her right.

"Too bad no other man will ever learn what they are missing." And he sucked her pink tip into his mouth.

"Oh, God," she screamed.

"Now dearest," he murmured, "I'm your husband. You can just call me Dare." Then he turned to suck her other tip, hardened and sensitive.

Her brain was so fuzzy with desire, she was barely able to understand his humor. It managed to break the spell, however, long enough for her to choke out, "Dare, we can't do this here…now. We are on the way to my family's house."

He raised his head, replacing his mouth with his hands, kneading the soft flesh. His eyes were smoldering obsidian. "You said we had to wait until we were married." He paused to nibble her earlobe. "We're married now. I will wait no longer."

He brought his lips down on her breast again and she bit her lip to keep from crying out. Struggling to stay rational, Nivea squeaked, "But we are only minutes away from my doorstep. Surely we can't—" The rest of the sentence was cut off as he pressed her into the cushion.

"You will come to learn that I am the Marquess of Raynsforth and can do anything I want," he boasted. "I told my driver if he took us to the most secluded corner of the park,"—his hand began to snake up her leg, caressing her knee—"and disappeared for thirty minutes,"—then rose higher up her thigh, and she gasped with delight—"I would double his wages."

His hand reached her center, and she lost the thread of his words as heat flashed through her.

"We should be completely alone in about forty-five seconds."

True to his word, Nivea felt the carriage bump over uneven ground before coming to a stop. It listed to the right as the driver climbed down, and they heard him whistling as he made a show of striding away.

"Have no fear. We will claim there was a mishap with the carriage and no one will be the wiser. It has happened before, you know."

Then he drove his fingers into her moist flesh and she screamed with pleasure. No more thoughts were possible. She gripped his head, lacing her fingers through his silky hair, pulling him down to her.

He reached between them to unfasten his breeches and pushed into her. "I love you, Nivea." His eyes burned into hers as he slowly moved his hips. "I don't know why this happened, or how I lived without you, but I love you. This is so much more than I ever dreamed possible."

Try as she might, she could not answer. The emotions were too great, the sensations too much. She threw back her head and let passion overtake her.

* * * *

Once they were able to breathe again, they tried to straighten their clothes. Despite their best effort, there was no helping the fact they looked like they'd just survived a shipwreck.

Dare ran his hands through her hair. "Perfect." He laughed.

She tugged his crumpled cravat. "No one will ever suspect." She chuckled. Reaching down to retrieve the handkerchief he'd made her, she tucked it back into the bodice of her gown. At his questioning look, she vowed, "I will keep this with me forever."

He tugged her to his side and gave her another searing kiss. Before it could evolve into more, they heard the sound of whistling as the driver reemerged from the park.

Sighing, Dare gave her a final nuzzle. "I know you like horses now, darling, but I fear I'm going to have to insist on frequent carriage rides."

She kissed him hard on the lips. "I couldn't agree more."

"Heaven"

Tiny bundle, napping in my lap,
my dearest husband, in miniature.
Black hair, eyes, and temper when crossed,
he sleeps content for now.

Cooing nearby,
his milder twin
is wrapping her fingers around her father's hand
and heart.

Patient, kind, and loving,
Lord Landis has buried his demons
and is now the finest sort of rake.
Reformed.

Lady Nivea Landis

Meet the Author

Alleigh Burrows loves romance novels. For years she tore through anything she could find—mainly regency romances, but would never pass up a hot Navy SEAL, an overbearing Scotsman, or shape shifting feline.

After reading a particularly intriguing series, she decided she, too, could write a romance novel. How hard could it be? She had worked in communications for years.

So, she started writing Dare to Love while working full-time and raising two teenagers. Not surprising, it was slow going.

Fast forward five years. The kids go off to college, and she was finally able to dedicate time to her husband, her cat, and her writing.

Dare to Love is Alleigh's first novel, but it won't be her last. Be sure to visit www.alleighburrows.com or @alleighburrows to see what her next project will be.

Acknowledgements

While I always considered writing to be a simple, solitary endeavor, I quickly discovered that writing a novel is very complex. I could never have made it to print without the advice and support from the Valley Forge Romance Writers, Written Remains, and the New Jersey Romance Writers' Put Your Heart in a Book conference.

I'm certain my editors at Lyrical Press would say that I should have solicited even more advice. To you, I offer my most sincere thanks for helping to bring Dare and Nivea to life, by correcting my appalling punctuation, adverb fixation, and filtering obsession.

And finally, I'd like to acknowledge my friends, family, bunco players, and coworkers, for continually asking, "How's your book coming?" Your unintentional pressure ensured I could never give up. Thank you all. I hope it lives up to your expectations.

CPSIA information can be obtained at www.ICGtesting.com
Printed in the USA
LVOW11s1725010615

440720LV00001B/169/P